**PRAISE F⟨...⟩
AND ⟨...⟩**

"Drawing inspiration from the likes of Mary Higgins Clark and Sue Grafton, Stiefel creates a tenacious but vulnerable heroine in Massachusetts homicide counselor Tally Whyte."

—*Publishers Weekly*

"An interesting read that concludes in an unexpected, dramatic fashion."

—*RT BOOKclub*

"Stiefel has the psychological thriller down so well you might think she invented it. An original, brilliant novel of the human experience worthy of anything James M. Cain could have done."

—*Crimestalker Casebook*

"Tally Whyte is full of warmth and wit—and she'll keep you turning pages through this engrossing mystery thriller."

—Jan Brogan, Author of *A Confidential Source*

AUTHOR'S NOTE

No Massachusetts Grief Assistance Program lives within Boston's Office of the Chief Medical Examiner, whereas Philadelphia's Grief Assistance Program continues to work out of the Philadelphia Medical Examiner's Office. There exist many grief assistance programs throughout the U.S., and they continue to do amazing work with the families of victims of violent death. I applaud them all. Please remember that Tally and her gang at MGAP exist in a world of fiction.

Winsworth, Maine, is also a part of Tally's fictional world. Winsworth and those who live in and about the town do not exist in any way, shape or form.

WAITING IN THE DARK

The night was ink black, moonless, the road near invisible. I got lost. As I drove narrow, serpentine roads to nowhere, my sense of frustration was fueled by my anxiety. My rearview mirror showed only blackness.

My eyes kept darting to the road, with its faint white line, then behind, where I hoped to see something. A car. Lights. Anything.

I turned left, hoping I'd found the road back to town. Just then a light flared from behind.

I peered into the mirror again. Blackness behind me still, but, wait. Wasn't that glow the tip of a burning cigarette? Was it a match or a lighter that I'd seen? Hell. Someone was tailing me—lights off—and he'd had the balls to light a butt. The hot ash pulsed in my mirror. I watched, hypnotized.

The killer had smoked as he'd viewed Laura's death throes, like some damned movie or something. And the car following me had to know these roads a hell of a lot better than I did to drive with the lights off. He drove very well, indeed.

Up ahead, a streetlamp. My foot itched to floor it, but I waited. I had to be patient. *Be calm*, I told myself. Calm. My hands on the wheel were greasy with sweat.

The spill of the streetlamp neared. I pumped it, just a little. There. And behind me… Nothing?

Then what had I seen? Or had I just imagined it?

But in my mind's eye, I pictured the pulse of the cigarette, saw it heat and dissipate, like the coals of a bellows fire. No, he was there. Hiding for now. But waiting for me.

THE DEAD STONE

VICKI STIEFEL

LEISURE BOOKS   NEW YORK CITY

To Bill, Blake, and Ben.
For years of boundless love and unstinting support.

A LEISURE BOOK®

March 2005

Published by

Dorchester Publishing Co., Inc.
200 Madison Avenue
New York, NY 10016

If you purchased this book without a cover you should be aware that this book is stolen property. It was reported as "unsold and destroyed" to the publisher and neither the author nor the publisher has received any payment for this "stripped book."

Copyright © 2005 by Vicki Stiefel

All rights reserved. No part of this book may be reproduced or transmitted in any form or by any electronic or mechanical means, including photocopying, recording or by any information storage and retrieval system, without the written permission of the publisher, except where permitted by law.

ISBN 0-8439-5520-1

The name "Leisure Books" and the stylized "L" with design are trademarks of Dorchester Publishing Co., Inc.

Printed in the United States of America.

Visit us on the web at www.dorchesterpub.com.

ACKNOWLEDGMENTS

Without the following people, I could never have written this book. Blame me for any errors, not them.

My dear friend, Donna Cautilli, whose spirit and homicide counseling experience continues to inspire me; Dr. Rick Cautilli, for his incomparable medical expertise; Massachusetts State Police Detective Lieutenant Richard D. Lauria, for his invaluable aid; the members of Massachusetts State Police Canine Corps, both human and canine, who enabled my Penny to continue her work in my books; the MEs, Crime Scene Services teams, support staffs, and Chief Medical Examiners of Maine and Massachusetts. Dave Badger of the Badger Funeral Home, who keeps me a truth-teller; Wanda Henry-Jenkins and Paul T. Clements, Ph.D. RN, whose work with Philadelphia's Grief Assistance Program is legend; Dr. Barbara Schildkrout, for her psychiatric expertise; Saundra Pool for her tenacity; Andrea Urban, my guide; Lee Sullivan, my compass.

To Kate Mattes of Kate's Mystery Books, Willard Williams of the Toadstool Bookshops, Debbie Tomes of The Paper Store, Maynard, and John Garp of Epilog Select Books: A profound thanks to you and your staff for your support and enthusiasm for my work.

To Mainers Sergeant Jackie Theriault, Maine State Police; the Ellsworth Police Department, Hancock County Sheriff's Office, Office of the Chief Medical Examiner, Augusta, Maine; Scott Hogg.

To Ellsworthians Susan and Dudley Gray, Nancy Patterson, Mary and Danny DeLong, Jane and Stephen Shea, Karen Dickes, Trish Worthen, Becky Sargent, Janet Owens, and the many other memorable friends and townspeople who made my life in Ellsworth both marvelous and indelible; radio's Joel Mann; Mark Osborne; David Brady; Jim Ferland.

To fabulous Hancockites Kim B., Nancy M., Cath and Fred C.H., Barbara Q., Peg and Tony B., Amy M., Pat F., Karen P., Nancy G., Kin and Annie; John and Deb, Polly, Bob and Karlene, Tony, Scott, Fiddleheads Sherry, Hancock Inn's Robert and Nancy and many more. The five wannabes—D, Pat, Suz, Carol and Linda.

To Dorothea Hamm and Barbara Fitzgerald, whose warmth and wit inspire me. My writer's group— Barbara Shapiro, Jan Brogan, Floyd Kemske, Judith Harper, Thomas Engels; my tireless critiquers— Bunny Frey, Tamar Hosansky, Pat Sparling, Barbara Shapiro; my trusted agent, Peter Rubie; my amazing editor, Don D'Auria; and Dorchester's wonderful public relations guru, Leah Hultenschmidt.

My beloved family: dear Mom, Mom R., and Mum T.; Melissa, Mike, and Sarah; Blake and Ben; Peter, Kathleen, and Summer.

And my adored husband, William G. Tapply, whose critiquing is priceless and whose love is above all price.

I thank each and every one of you for making this book a reality.

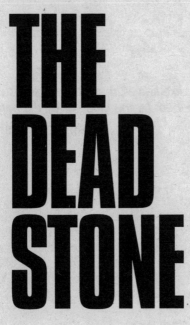

THE DEAD STONE

Mishaps are like knives, that either serve us or cut us, as we grasp them by the blade or by the handle.

—James Russell Lowell

Chapter One
Emma Who?

Eight-thirty A.M., and I was running late. My pumps clacked on the asphalt, as did Penny's nails. Even on three legs, she loped ahead of me, always on guard, ever vigilant. The door to Boston's medical examiner's office swung open easily, and I barreled into a wall of wet, hot air.

"Crap!" I said.

Penny stood poised, instantly alert.

"It's okay, girl." Not that it was. The Grief Shop's air conditioner in its "public" areas—the Massachusetts Grief Assistance Program's offices, Crime Scene Services offices, and the lobby—was on the fritz again. Backstage, where medical examiners slice corpses, and bodies wait patiently in refrigerated rooms, and techs prep the remains of loved ones—those AC units work beautifully. Since we had no AC in MGAP on this unseasonably broiling June day, I could only hope that my coworkers and counselees were in exceptionally tolerant moods.

Not likely.

I tossed my backpack on the sofa in my office, zipped open the top of my Dunkin' Donuts iced coffee, and took a sip. I had the medical examiner's daily meeting at nine, a group of homicide family survivors at ten, and, as MGAP's leader, a never-ending pile of paperwork.

"Hoy, Tal," hollered Gert from MGAP's central office. For all the years Gert and I had worked together, my chief assistant's Brooklyn accent had not grown one whit softer nor had her colorful vocabulary become one ounce less flavorful. I was glad.

"Who's been in to check the AC?" I asked.

"You kiddin' me?" She handed me a stack of phone slips. "Awl from yestaday aftanoon."

"Let's just burn them, huh? You see Kranak yet?"

She nodded, her platinum bangs bouncing. "Mr. Sergeant Grouch was in early. He's got his team workin' on some case that's got a rod up his butt. I'd avoid him."

"Will do. I'll soften him up later with a cheese pretzel." I checked my watch. "I'll be ready for the nines. No newbies at ten, right?"

"Not today."

I retreated to my office, where I sifted through the stack of pink phone slips. I sucked on my iced coffee as I read each one.

Harvester interview. Rip. *Talk show, Harvester.* Rip. *Harvester book.* With friggin' photos, no less. Rip.

The damned Harvester was still haunting me in more ways than I cared to think about. Months earlier, a killer had stalked Boston, taking body parts from exceptional women, and leaving broken homes and withered hearts. I'd helped stop the Harvester, and now the media were relentless.

They demanded interviews. They bugged me for talk

shows. They popped flashes in my face as they took photos of me and my loved ones. They wouldn't leave me alone in trying to ferret out the "real" story. My boyfriend had found it too much, and so now we were back to being just friends. I couldn't blame him. All because of the Harvester.

I winnowed down the stack of two dozen to the three *real* messages. One was from a gal I'd counseled two years earlier, her husband a homicide. The second was from a fundraising organization, hoping MGAP, an organization I'd founded to counsel the loved ones of homicide victims, would contribute time and energy. Of late, I had little time or energy for anything but homicide counseling.

There are fewer than forty of us in the United States. Homicide counseling has yet to make the top-ten list of professions. But I like it; it brings meaning to my life. And I'm proud to be a member of this small fraternity.

Penny clanked her dish. I refilled it with fresh water—she's fussy—and got myself a Poland Spring from the fridge. Damn, it was hot. For the millionth time, I wished my windows opened. There wasn't a breath of fresh air in the place.

I was tempted to check out an autopsy just for the chill.

I picked up the third phone message, read it, and sat down hard. The slip was addressed to an Emma Blake. Whew. Gert had scrawled a huge purple question mark. No wonder. There was a name I hadn't heard in years. In another life, before my nickname Tally had stuck, I *was* Emma. And Blake was my surname prior to a contentious marriage and an even more contentious divorce.

"Gert, did you take this?" I waved the slip as I walked into the central office.

"Yeah. Some guy. Low voice. Gruff. Breathless. He said to give it to Tally. 'She'll know,' he said. So do ya?"

"Do I what?"

3

"Do ya know?"

"I know the 'who,' but the 'what' is eluding me. He gave no hint of what he wanted?"

She blew a purple bubble and sucked it back in. "Didn't say. He definitely sounded not all there. I figured it was somethin' to do with the Harvester."

My heart raced, and I nodded, aiming for cool. Gert knew something was up. We'd been through a lot together. She blew another bubble and went back to her paperwork.

Emma Blake. I hadn't heard that name for almost twenty years. Who would be calling *her?* And why?

A week later. I went to court in support of a counselee whose parents had been slain in a drive-by and to dinner at my foster mothers' home, one of whom happened to be the chief medical examiner for Massachusetts. I counseled, flogged paperwork, and romped with Penny in the park.

What I didn't do was get a phone call from Mr. Breathless about Emma Blake.

When it came, I was unprepared for it.

I checked my watch for the tenth time. Crime Scene Services Sergeant Rob Kranak was supposed to call sixty minutes earlier with a forensic report on a headless torso found in the Charles River. So when the phone rang, I was a wee bit exasperated.

"Rob, how come—"

"Emmaaaaaaaaaaaaaa," the voice said, drawing out the final *a*.

"Who is this?"

"It's about your faaaather. He did not do what they say. You must come."

Geesh. This guy sounded like *Tales from the Crypt*. "What about my father? What are you talking about?"

"Things in Winsworth are being stirred up. Bad things. And your father did not do it. Come. Or worse will happen. You must come."

"Who is—"

Click.

I dialed star-69.

Your last incoming call cannot be reached in this manner. Please try again.

What the *hell* was going on?

Another week passed. I went to a gallery opening with Gert. I visited the Canine Corps in Stoneham with Penny, who romped with her old pals. I ended a ten-month group counseling session on a very good note. I did lots more stuff, too, but mostly I stewed about one thing: that phone call for Emma Blake.

The caller knew me as Tally *and* as Emma. I chewed and chewed and chewed on that message. I saw no reason to return to Winsworth.

Winsworth was nostalgia for me: sailing with Dad, climbing apple trees with my two gal pals, going to summer camp on the Winsworth River, earning gold stars in school, slushing down Union Street during a blizzard, pigging out on lobsters and steamers. A home unlike any other I'd had since, but one I left when I was twelve.

Everything Winsworth related to my dad, and he was murdered in Boston three years after we moved from Maine. I even had him buried in Winsworth, but he was long dead. What "worse things" could possibly happen?

Hell, I was a city girl, had lived in Boston for the past two decades. It was all I knew. The T, Newbury Street, Fenway. North End Italian festivals, Faneuil Hall, the Duck Boat tours. And the families of the dead. I knew those, too.

Okay—so I fished out west occasionally. Took trips. Went on hikes.

But that wasn't *living* somewhere.

"Right, Pens?" I said, stroking her neck. She lay sprawled on the couch in our apartment in the South End. "No point in going back. The call was from some nutcase or something. I have work here. Lots of it."

Hell, I hadn't been to Winsworth in twenty-some years. I missed it, sure, but the way you miss a dear old doll you had as a kid. It's not something you want to play with as an adult, just remember with fondness.

Right.

The second time, Mr. Breathless found me at home.

"They will dig up his grave. They will destroy—"

"Who *is* this and what are you talking about?"

"Emmmmaaaa. He is *suffering*. You must come. He will . . ."

He hung up.

"Dammit, Penny!"

They will dig up his grave. Geesh.

Mr. Breathless sure knew how to press my buttons. What false accusations could people be making about my dad? And the thought of someone suffering . . . Yeah, this guy was a real button-pusher.

I fixed myself a bourbon on ice and chose to put the call from my mind. There were plenty of disturbed people out there. Mr. Breathless was just one of many.

But the truth was, our house had burned. We *had* escaped town in a strange and hurried fashion in the middle of the night. Not that I remembered much of it. That was the first time we left "on the run," so to speak. I shuddered. It wasn't the last. Since Winsworth, or maybe because of it, things had soured for my dad. Life was never simple again.

Absurd to go back, really. Why complicate it more?

But with some things, you have no choice.

I phoned Gert to tell her I was taking a little time off. She was expecting my call and had everything in place.

So I put in for a month vacation, shocking all of Crime Scene Services, MGAP, and my foster mothers, I might add. I said I needed a rest after the Harvester, which wasn't exactly a lie. I wanted to recharge my batteries, which was also sort of true. I longed for the sea. Absolutely.

I told only Gert and Kranak the true motive behind my mission. They both agreed—I was nuts. I made sure I had complete and excellent coverage, and gave my keys to Gert.

"Cawl if you need me," she said. "I'll come help out. You're practically going into the wilderness."

I chuckled. "Not really, Gertie. It's just coastal Maine."

"Oh, yeah? That *is* the wilderness."

Kranak shoved his hands deep in his pockets and shook his head.

The following morning, Penny and I headed north for Winsworth, Maine.

Chapter Two
Who Goes There?

The movie let out around eleven. The night had thickened to a moist almost-rain. Typical for June in Maine, but too noir-ish by half, especially after Scorsese's dark drama. Too much time to think on the hour drive back to the cottage from Bangor to Winsworth.

I'd been in Winsworth, Maine, three days. In that time, I had rented a cottage on a bay in Surry and visited old haunts—restaurants, the library, the general store. Some places, like Mrs. Cavasos's hardware store, were gone. Others had new owners. I checked out some new places, too, like the post office and Jeb's Pub and Stop & Shop. Every place I went, I used "Tally Whyte." I hadn't lived there since I was twelve. No one would recognize me. I was comfortable in my anonymity. Yet I made a point of mentioning my dad's name. Each time, I was met with blank stares.

I scanned the microfiche in the library for events concerning my dad, but found only articles I'd read dozens of times over. I even Googled Dad, and, again, nothing.

I visited the cemetery. Dad's grave looked fine. No one had dug him up or written graffiti on his tombstone or ignited the tree shading the grave.

I admit, I wasn't ready to look up my old friends. I was hesitant. They hadn't heard from me in twenty-odd years. I doubted they'd greet me with open arms. Tomorrow was Monday. A good day to begin a journey down memory lane, one I expected would be a bumpy one.

I still had no idea who Mr. Breathless was.

One thing I *had* discovered was that weather in rural Maine could be violent and unpredictable. I hunkered in for the long ride home.

I turned onto the Bangor Road, headed east for Winsworth. Tried to find something cheerful on the radio. Twenty minutes later, rain cascaded across the windshield and my mood was the least of my worries. My tires squealed as I rounded a curve. I was doing sixty. I eased my foot up.

Wind slapped the trees, and water sheeted the road so that it glistened in my high beams, the only light except for the yellow glow spilling from the occasional house. It was a Stephen King kind of night.

My sweaty palms greased the steering wheel. I leaned forward, counted the beats of the windshield wipers.

A waterfall of mud splattered my windshield, the blare of a horn, then a minivan vroomed past me.

"Christmas!" I screeched. "Who the fu—"

I inhaled deep breaths. The van was still in the wrong lane, zooming forward. Suddenly, it swerved back into my lane—too fast—and did a 360. It was facing me—*oh, hell!*—

and began hydroplaning across the road right in front of me. *Sonofabitch!*

I yanked my wheel to the left, my 4-Runner fishtailing and me screaming "Shitshitshit" as I pounded the brakes.

I rested my head on the steering wheel, taking hard breaths, calming down. I was fine. In one piece. Everything was cool.

I lifted my head and peered through the driving rain. The minivan lay canted half on its side in a shallow ditch. *Damn*. I hoped the idiot had been wearing his seat belt.

I grabbed my flashlight and slipped my pepper spray into my jacket pocket before I left the truck. I wished Penny were with me.

"Hey?" I called as I ran toward the van.

My flashlight caught a man slithering from the van's window. I stopped short. He was waving his fist, mouthing words I couldn't hear as rivers of rain streamed off his bill cap.

He hit the road hard, hands first, then slowly uncurled—a tall, skinny guy with a bushy beard framing a mouth taut with anger.

He jabbed the air with his finger aimed right at me. "You stupid woman! It's all your friggin' fault!" He staggered toward me.

"You're okay and so am I," I said, using my most soothing psychologist tones.

"Li' hell I'm okay," he replied in a slurred voice. "If you hadn't been crawlin' along like a snail, none of this . . ."

"I'll call a tow truck." I backed toward my 4-Runner. The wind was screaming now, slapping our faces with rainwater. His eyes glinted with a feral light, and I was afraid.

"Th' hell you will!"

He lunged, grabbed my arm, twirled me around. I raised the pepper spray at his face. "Don't!"

He jerked away from me, but my threat had nothing to do with it. His body twitched, as if he were in the throes of some seizure. He raised his hands to cover his face.

I had no idea what was causing it, but I couldn't leave him there.

His hands slumped at his sides. "Where's my van?"

I paused a beat. He'd relaxed, his seizure done. "Over there."

"Oh. Oh, yeah." The rage, the rasping fury, had vanished, leaving a soft, tentative voice. "I need a lift."

The thought of sharing the cab of my truck with this stranger was not a comfortable one. "Let me call a tow truck. I'll wait with you."

The man trembled. "Take forever for them to get here."

"I'm sorry, but you just threatened me. I really can't give you a lift."

"I *need* a ride," he whispered, his hands balled into fists.

"I can't. I'm sorry." I reached for the door of my truck.

He exploded past me and jumped into my front seat.

"What the hell are . . . ?"

He floored it, door flapping, engine screeching.

"Oh, shit." I watched my 4-Runner's taillights vanish over the hill.

Minutes later, I was still berating myself for leaving my keys and cell phone in the truck when I heard the vroom of a car speeding down the highway.

I backpedaled off the road and watched in shock as my 4-Runner's lights crowned the hill, did a neat U-turn, and parked next to the broken van.

11

"Like I said, miss, I real . . . real . . . really need that lift." The stranger jumped down from my truck.

I took the keys dangling from his long, bony fingers. I was probably nuts myself, but . . . "You convinced me. Let's go."

Instead of climbing back in, he jogged over to his van and crawled up into the front seat. He finally stumbled back out with a huge dog draped across his arms. The dog was almost as long as the guy. Its bared teeth were long, too, as was its bandaged leg. I thought of Penny, at home, sleeping cozily on her bed.

My heart squeezed. "What happened?"

The guy didn't hear or wouldn't answer. Whatever. I pushed open the passenger door, cautious still, but terribly anxious about the dog. The stranger eased himself and his dog onto the seat. Blood oozed from the dog's damp bandages. The man let out a sob and buried his face in the dog's wiry wet fur.

I gunned it toward Winsworth.

The dank, coppery smell of blood and fear reminded me of the Grief Shop. Strange how much I missed the place and my friends.

The dog let out a pitiful howl. "I wish you'd told me you had a hurt pup."

"And if I ha'," he said, slurring his words. "You'd've give . . . given us a ride? Yeah, sure."

"Probably. Yes. I wouldn't have been so afraid."

He grinned, a perfect Crest smile. "I got my ride, didn't I?"

"That you did. What's your name?"

"Roy Orbison." He spat it out like a challenge.

I rolled my eyes. The guy seemed drunk, yet . . . "I'm Tally Whyte. You in the mood to tell me what happened?"

He stroked the dog's muzzle. "Leg-hold trap."

"Geesh. Any idea who set it?"

12

The man ignored me, and I listened to the dog's soft whimpers as we sped down the road.

The dog's bandage continued to seep blood, and though the heat was cranked up high, he constantly shivered. The stranger speared me with haunted, fearful eyes. "Go faster," he mouthed.

I pushed the 4-Runner to seventy. Easy to picture Penny draped across my lap, leeching blood and fading from life. I scratched the pup's ears. "I'm so sorry he's hurt."

"She's a girl dog, stupid!" He rubbed the bridge of his nose with his thumb and forefinger. "Sor . . . sorry."

The lights grew more frequent. The outskirts of Winsworth, thank God. The dog was either sleeping or passed out. Almost there. The bandage was soaked in blood.

"Where's my van?" asked the stranger. "Where is it?"

"Um, you left it on the Bangor Road. Remember?"

"Oh."

Slurred words, trembling, memory issues. Alcohol? PCP? Illness? Psychosis? No time to analyze him now.

I sped past the YMCA, bore left at the fork, and hit a red light at the corner of Main and Grand. Lights blazed all around us, and up ahead lay Grand Street's store upon store of outlets, fast-food joints, minimalls, and amusements. Beyond that the road led to Mt. Desert Island and Acadia National Park.

"Which way to the vet?"

"Take Grand. My vet's down the street."

We zoomed past Katahdin Mountain Sports, Beal's Realty, Union Trust Bank, Piper's Restaurant, a couple of strip malls, and an L.L. Bean outlet. Where the hell was the dammed vet?

"She was just lying there . . ." His voice was pitiful.

The light at the shopping center snagged me and I braked hard.

13

Fingertips covering his mouth, he shook his head like an animal ridding itself of a coat of rain. "She was on that big, flat stone. With that knife sticking into her stomach. And it pinned her to the rock. Pinned her. And there were claw marks and . . ."

"I thought she was in a leg-hold trap," I said.

"Not her!" he spat. "The woman, stupid. The woman on the rock with all the blood."

What the hell . . . ?

A car honked and I jumped. The light was green. I pressed the gas. Up ahead, just past the Jones Jeep/Chrysler fork in the road, a neon sign flashed the letters VET. Finally.

"The woman on the rock with all the blood," I said. "Was she dead, hurt? What happened to her?"

He didn't answer.

I careened into the vet's empty parking lot. "Are you sure she had a knife sticking out of her?"

"Yes! That woman never liked my dog. Never." He hefted himself and his dog out of the truck.

"Wait a minute!" I ran around the truck. "What about the hurt woman? *Where* did you see her?"

A tremor rippled his body. Then another. "Wha' woman?"

"The woman with the knife!"

"A woman had a knife?"

"Geesh! You just said you saw a woman with a knife in her. On a stone?"

A porch light flicked on.

His eyebrows shot up. "Are you crazy? I've gotta get my dog to the vet, lady. Go home. Get some rest. It looks like you could use it."

Twenty minutes later, I knelt beside Penny, my nose buried in her fur. I was glad she was safe. If the stranger's dog lost

14

its leg, it could be worse. Penny did just fine on three legs. I let her out for a trot, poured a finger of bourbon, then dialed the police.

"Winsworth Police," the dispatcher announced, pronouncing it "Winswuth."

I reported the van on the Bangor Road, paused, then . . . "I gave a lift to the guy in the van. Um, he told me a pretty weird story."

The dispatcher sighed. "Ayuh?"

I recounted the stranger's woman-on-the-rock-with-the-knife tale, realizing how lame I sounded. "Have there been any reported injuries like that? Or missing persons or. . . ."

"Ma'am, it's been a quiet night. What was the guy's name?"

I cleared my throat. "Roy Orbison. I know. I know. It wasn't real, but I let it pass."

He chuckled. "Sounds like you been shined on, ma'am."

"Yes, except I heard some truth in his voice. Are you sure no one's missing?"

"Shortie LeJeune went missing, oh, maybe three months ago now, but we suspect he's—"

"A woman. The stranger talked about a woman."

He inhaled. "Nope-suh. Not a one."

I reviewed the stranger's slurred words, his disconnect with reality. The injured woman could have been in a movie he'd seen or a book he'd read. "I don't know if it was real or not, but I thought I should call."

"Women shouldn't pick up men on the Bangor Road."

"True. Maybe you could have an officer give me a call."

"Yup-suh. I'll run it by Officer DeLong when he gets in."

DeLong never called, and I wasn't surprised. There are plenty of real crimes out there to keep cops busy, even in a small town like Winsworth. Nonetheless, I wrote down everything the stranger had said.

The following morning, as I reached for the phone to call the Winsworth vet to see how the pup was doing, it rang. On the other end was Rob Kranak, my buddy from OCME.

Talking to Kranak, a Crime Scene Services sergeant, took my mind off the injured dog, and suddenly it was noon.

The crunch of gravel signaled the cable guy's arrival. Kranak and I said our good-byes, and I left the cable man to hook up the cable and my new modem. The cottage's owner had scheduled the setup before I rented the place. I thought it was a great idea. Tough doing Internet research on Winsworth and my dad with a dial-up.

I went out onto the screened porch, which overlooked a postcard-pretty Maine cove. Time to call a couple of my old gal pals, start asking them some questions about my dad. One of them might know something about current doings that would implicate Dad, which would mean progress on why Mr. Breathless had called me.

But I was reluctant, mostly because I feared doors slammed in my face or, even worse, indifference from people I remembered with immense fondness. We had, after all, left town in the middle of the night.

Stalling, I jotted some notes for a paper I was presenting on homicide counseling, made more notes for my fall class at Northeastern. I finished up with work around one and dialed the Winsworth vet.

The recorded message said Dr. Dowling's hours were eight until one on Mondays. My watch read ten after. I was bummed.

I made some lunch and ate it out on the deck of the cottage—a "camp" in Maine parlance—in the Adirondack chair, Penny beside me. While I ate, I watched a little family of cormorants bob around the inlet.

I'd better keep it simple for a few more days, as well as distant as Tally Whyte. I could still learn stuff. A smart plan.

Or was I chickening out?

Reluctant to shrinky-dink myself, I turned my thoughts to last night's stranger.

He was troubled, obviously. Schizophrenia, degenerative dementia, bipolar disorder, an assortment of pharmaceuticals or booze, any of those things, and others, could precipitate the behavior he'd exhibited the previous evening. His stuttering could be from a variety of conditions, too. I shook my head. No point in pursuing it without more information.

I peered inside. The cable man was still struggling with the setup.

After last night's storm, the day was warm and clear. In a few hours, it would cool off enough for a test of my new 4-weight Sage rod in the pond across the street. I'd catch only sunfish and maybe a small bass or two, but I'd pretend they were wily trout.

Later, I located the owner of the cemetery where my father rested. The same guy owned the local funeral home, which made things convenient. He agreed to meet with me on Thursday. If someone had been snooping around my dad's grave, I wanted to know about it. Then I scheduled a meeting on Friday with a Bangor private detective. Maybe she could learn things that had so far eluded me.

Gert called from work, and I answered her rote questions about the paperwork with ease. When she finished, I asked her to hop on the Web and see if she found any missing persons from the previous evening in downeast Maine.

While I waited for Gert, I watched a kid carrying a bucket and a rake thread her way through the rocks to the beach, preparing to dig clams. I spied a small Maine Friendship sloop heeled in the wind near the mouth of the inlet.

The bell buoy clanged, swaying in the wake of a passing lobster boat at the cove's narrow entrance. Through the leafy screen of beech, oak, and birch, I watched a pair of seals pull themselves onto a large, flat rock, a fish flapping in one's mouth. The scene was so bucolic, it was almost scary. Gert would surely be horrified.

"Gert?" I said.

"Almost done."

I kept an ear cocked for the paperboy's bike on my gravel driveway. I'd started the biweekly paper. It might have something about a woman on a stone.

"Tal?" Gert said. "I'm not seeing anything. You into somethin' up there?"

"I hope not."

"You're supposed ta be lookin' around for ya father's stuff. Rememba?"

"Believe me, I remember. Thanks."

The paper thumped against the front door.

"Gotta go," I said. "I'll talk to you later."

I snapped open the *Winsworth Journal*. There had been a "fracas" last night at the Oyster Bar. Some teens had "borrowed" a car and crashed it into a fence, no serious injuries. The rain had caused a farmer to slip and break his leg in the mud. But no missing person, no woman with a knife in her, no nothing to get my antennae twitching.

"So, waddya think, Pen? Fishing?"

She perked her ears, wagged her tail. She knew what I was talking about. I fetched my rod, and Penny and I crossed the road, walked down a small wooded path, and arrived at a

18

sweet fishy pond. When I needed to clear my head, a good thing to do was go fishing.

I cast, let the fly float for a sec, then twitch, twitch, twitch, stripped it in. Cast again. Penny snored beside me in the late-afternoon June sun.

The rhythmic motion allowed me to focus, not on hurt dogs or disturbed men or women with knives in their bellies, but rather on why I was here in the first place. According to Mr. Breathless, "things" had been stirred up. Someone was trashing my dad's name. People could get hurt.

My dad had been my world for many, many years. I owed him.

It was time.

Emotionally risky or not, I had to contact my old friends. Now.

Chapter Three
Old Friends

Back at the camp, I looked up Carmen Cavasos's name in the phone book and found her address. She either hadn't married or kept her own name. A cool breeze blew off the water, so I shrugged into a sweater, loaded Penny into the truck, and headed for town.

I drove over the Winsworth River bridge, turned left up State and then right onto Gray Street. Number seventy-four had a minivan in the drive and a pink bike on the lawn.

I parked out front, tapped the steering wheel with my fingertips. I sighed. "Whaddya think, Pens?"

She didn't answer. Typical. But she lapped my face. I hugged her. "Yeah, I'm a chicken. Got to do it. She was my best bud."

I stepped from the truck and in seconds was knocking at the door.

A thirtysomething woman opened it and smiled. She was blond, like me, but with straight hair. I was shocked Carmen had bleached her Titian hair. Or maybe it had just darkened, and . . .

"Hi," I said. "Um, Carmen?"

The woman uttered a girlish, high-pitched giggle. "You're looking for Carmen? She doesn't live here anymore."

Thank heavens. I couldn't handle that giggle. "Can you tell me where she's moved to?"

She shrugged. "Don't know. Somewhere quiet after the fracas she got in."

"Fracas?"

She giggled again. "Sorry. That's all I know." She gently shut the door.

Well, now what?

I could go home and Google her. But I was starving and had yet to visit our favorite restaurant, Piper's. It was still in working order. I wondered if it was still great.

I walked through the front door and grinned. Nothing had changed. Nope-suh.

Still paneled in mellow pine, its walls were hung with fishing nets and giant lobster claws and sailing prints. The air smelled of boiled lobster, fried clams, pancakes, and the strawberry/rhubarb pie that was a Piper's specialty. Piper's was noisy from tables jammed with tourists and locals.

A vivid memory of Dad and me seated at a booth, Dad telling me about this great place he dreamed of, Trenton-by-the-Sea. How it would make our fortune. How he'd get me a horse and . . .

"Please follow me."

The hostess seated me at another booth, and I ordered the boiled lobster dinner with all the fixings. A tall, beehived waitress sprinted from table to table, and I ate slowly, savoring each rich bite of lobster and corn on the cob and johnnycake and homemade slaw. I dipped the last bit of lobster into the drawn butter and signaled the waitress for the check.

"Here you go," said DeeDee the waitress.

"Thanks. Top off my Diet Coke, would you?"

"You're gonna OD on caffeine." She grinned as she went to fetch it.

The hostess notched her head DeeDee's way and detoured over to an elderly woman leaning on a walker. The hostess slid the woman's suitcase beneath the booth next to mine.

"You sit right here, ma'am," DeeDee said, patting the seat.

The woman's parchment face pleated into a smile. "Thank you, Dee."

A wisp of recognition tickled me.

"You're off to England, right, Mrs. Lakeland?" DeeDee said as she scribbled the woman's order.

"That I am."

Mrs. Lakeland . . . A warm, cozy feeling rippled from my heart outward. Same sharp chin. Same short hairdo crowned by a widow's peak. Same voice. Except now dewlaps hung from her chin, her hair was pure white, and her voice quivered with age.

She'd been hard and fair and loving. An outstanding teacher and a friend.

Snapping brown eyes peered up from her novel and caught me staring. I pretended to fiddle with a speck on the table.

DeeDee topped off my soda, then delivered Mrs. Lakeland's scrambled eggs. I watched her dig in.

What if she didn't remember me? I'd feel like an idiot. Oh, what the hell. "Mrs. Lakeland?" I tried to smile as I stood beside her booth. I was so damned nervous.

Her fork hovered midair. "Yes?"

"Mind if I join you for a sec? I had you in school."

She beamed as she pointed to the seat across from her. "How nice."

I slid into the booth. "My name's Tally Whyte. I haven't lived here for a long time, but I had you in fifth grade."

Her smile drooped. "I'm afraid I . . ."

I smiled. "Of course you don't. It was twenty-two years ago. Tally's a nickname. Whyte's my ex-husband's name. You knew me as Emma. Emma Blake."

"Oh. . . . Yes . . . yes, of course. Emma."

I beamed. It felt great to reconnect.

Except Mrs. Lakeland wasn't smiling. In fact, she'd cut her eyes from mine and was dabbing her lips with her napkin.

"It was such a long time ago," I said, plunging on, eager for her smile to return. "But you introduced me to *Anne Frank*. I loved it. Carmen sure hated it, didn't she? And remember how it made Annie cry? How are they? Carmen and Annie? What are they . . ."

Mrs. Lakeland carefully laid her napkin on the table and raised her eyes. They were as cold and hard as black ice. Ignoring me, she waved a hand. "I'll take the check now, Dee."

"But . . ." I said.

She tucked her book into her purse and lifted herself to her feet.

"Mrs. Lakeland, I . . ."

She turned from me and smiled at the hostess, who was helping her on with her coat. She examined the bill, then placed a ten on the table. "No change."

I lifted my hand to her elbow, intending to help her, wondering why she'd turned from sweetness to acid.

She held up her hand. "Don't, Emma. Just don't."

23

"Mrs. Lakeland, what—"

"You *don't* want to know about *him*. What he did to us all. You really do not."

She moved her walker forward, toward the door.

I stumbled backward, propelled by the revulsion I saw in her eyes.

The drive home was fast and contemplative, with Penny's heavy head resting on my thigh. The *him* had to be my dad. Had to. Her feelings made no sense—Mrs. Lakeland hadn't known my dad—yet they had to be connected with Mr. Breathless's phone call. What had Mrs. Lakeland said? *You don't want to know about him. What he did to us all.*

What had Dad done? And why had the lovable and loving Mrs. Lakeland turned into a messenger of hatred?

The following morning, I awakened with the same thought: What could my dad have done that would have kept Mrs. Lakeland's hatred alive for more than twenty years? The vitriol she'd spat was fresh and intense, so intense I wasn't about to look up Carmen. Not until I knew what was going on.

As Mr. Breathless had implied, something must be taking place in the now to nourish that anger. That something had prompted Mr. Breathless to call me in Boston. He was warning me. About *what*, exactly?

I fed Penny, showered, and again surfed the Web for my dad's name. Nothing appeared. Nothing.

I did the same for Mrs. Lakeland, but all I found were articles relating to her teaching. I scanned the titles, but none seemed to apply.

The crunch of pea gravel on my driveway jerked me from the computer. I walked outside just as a blue boat of a Pontiac pulled up. Trouble had driven into my dooryard.

THE DEAD STONE

It was a cop. I'd lay money on it.

The guy inside the Pontiac wore a brown Stetson. Since it wasn't the Marlboro Man, I figured he was from the county sheriff's department. He unfolded himself from the car and walked over.

Penny sat beside me, ears perked forward, not hostile, just alert. I was curious. Cops I could handle, even those who hid their eyes behind silvered aviator glasses.

"Ma'am." The officer nodded as he reached me.

I'm five-ten, but I was forced to look up a good six inches to the officer's lushly mustached lips. Crap. He reminded me a little of my former boyfriend. Sigh. Talk about baggage.

"Okay if I give her a pet?" He looked at Penny.

"Sure."

He scooched down and stroked Penny between her ears. He scratched her stump, and she let him. Interesting. I'd swear I heard her purr.

"Nice dog." He stood. "Three legs. A shepherd, huh. Belgian? With the K-9 Corps?"

"Czech. And she was with the Corps before someone blew her back leg off. How can I help you, Officer . . . ?"

"Cunningham. Sheriff Hank Cunningham."

Whoa. I removed *my* sunglasses to get a better peek. It was little Henry Cunningham, all right. Not that he looked much like the love-struck pest who'd pursued me in grades five through seven, the carrot-top with the squeaky voice.

Little Henry had evolved into a beefy six-four, auburn-haired, deep-voiced man wearing a cloak of authority tinged with weariness. He had a slight Buddha belly, and his bushy mustache almost qualified as handlebar style.

I never would have recognized him. And thank God he hadn't recognized me, either, given Mrs. Lakeland's glacial

25

greeting. I would know why Mrs. Lakeland had reacted in such a toxic way before I said "yo" to my old friends.

"I presume you're not here to sell me tickets to the policeman's ball," I said.

His lips twitched. "Couple nights ago, you called our police dispatcher, Ms. Whyte. Correct?"

"Guilty as charged, Sheriff."

He nodded. "Thought it was you."

"Pardon?"

"I took your two-day seminar, oh, about four years ago at Northeastern. The one on working with homicide victims' families."

Geesh. It was like old-home week. "I hope you found it worthwhile."

"That I did. So tell me about this fella you picked up on the Bangor Road."

I shifted gears. "Have you found a . . ."

"Dead woman?" he said. "No, thank God. But I'd like to hear your story nonetheless."

I notched my head. "C'mon. I'll fix you some iced tea and tell you the tale."

Hank took a seat at the scarred kitchen table while I refilled Penny's water bowl and made the iced tea. He removed his sunglasses. The navy eyes were as I remembered, except they were old, too old for a man of thirty-four. I couldn't help wondering why.

We sipped tea as I told Hank Cunningham about events on the Bangor Road and driving the stranger and his dog to the vet's. He took notes in a little flip pad and asked quite a few pointed questions, including ones about the dog's injury.

"You're a psychologist as well as a homicide counselor."

I nodded.

"How would you assess the guy?"

"That's a tough one, since he's not a patient. I never like making snap judgments."

He leaned forward. "Just give me your impressions, then."

"Hallucinations? Maybe. Drug induced? Maybe that, too. He'd segue in and out of connecting with the present, with reality. He got hostile, threatening. He took my truck. Nervy. Schizophrenic? I'd say no. Bipolar? Possibly. Although I sensed something else at work there, too. He had a pronounced stutter at times. And then he'd lose it. What you really want to know is if the woman with the knife in her was real."

"Yes."

"At first I believed she was. His disjointed ramblings *felt* real. But on reflection, the answer's not so simple. He could have seen that scene in a movie, on TV, read it in a book."

He exhaled, and I realized he'd been holding his breath.

"You know him, don't you?" I said.

He grinned. "Roy Orbison? He's dead."

And at that moment I knew that Hank Cunningham had a whole second agenda about the stranger on the Bangor Road. Hank *did* know him. And Hank was afraid, not of him, but *for* him.

"Thanks, Ms. Whyte, for the info and the tea." Hank stood. He ran his paw through his long crew cut, and it looked like so much rust-colored wheat tossed by a storm. "I'll be in touch."

Funny, but I knew he would be.

The following morning, I finally got ahold of the vet.

"Dowling's Vet Clinic. How can I help you?" The voice was female, chipper, and crisply British.

"I'd like to check on a dog brought in around midnight

Sunday. She was hurt quite badly, and I want to make sure she's okay."

"Not your dog, I take it."

"No. I gave the owner a lift to the vet's."

"The owner's name is . . . ?"

"Um, I don't have it."

"Really? Do you have the dog's name? I can search that way."

"No, I don't. But I can describe her. She was immense. Square-jawed. Bony, even. She was wet, but her coat was long and wiry. Maybe you'd check the time? I mean, how many dogs could have had emergencies Sunday night?"

"Not too many, I suspect. Let me try." Computer keys clicking, then . . . "Here she is. Dr. Dowling saw her at 12:40 Monday morning."

"Will she be okay?" I asked.

"Yes. So it seems. From Dr. Dowling's notes, she had a pretty nasty leg break and some blood loss. The doctor set her leg and gave her some meds, including antibiotics."

"Does it give her name or that of the man who brought her in?"

"Hold a second. Hmm. Not that I can see. Quite unusual. Dr. Dowling is very thorough. All it says is that the man paid in cash. The animal couldn't be a regular, or Dr. Dowling would have pulled up the dog's record to add this latest visit. Ah, but here we go. Dr. Dowling does describe the dog." She chuckled. "Yes, of course. An Irish wolfhound. A pure-bred, by all appearances. Interesting."

"Sure. I've seen pictures of them. And they are huge."

"And sweet as can be. The only one I've ever heard of hereabouts belongs to Sheriff Cunningham."

Chapter Four
The Fat Bird of Inevitability

Penny and I went for a sail around the cove in the little Blue Jay that came with the cottage. I needed to think. I was ticked off at Hank Cunningham. I suspected he knew not only the type of dog I'd driven to the vet, but the dog's owner as well.

Winsworth always was a closed, sometimes claustrophobic kind of town. That was its strength and its bane. Hank knew the man with the dog, and he was protecting him for whatever reason he deemed necessary. That reason made for some interesting mind-surfing.

While we sailed, I downed a tuna sandwich with a Diet Coke. Penny paddled around the cove for a bit. For an hour, no more, I would leave all problems on shore. The wind was soft against the sails. I tossed some bread to our cormorant family. I read. And I dozed. It was that kind of day.

When I looked up, a tall figure in a brown Stetson was staring at me from the pebbly beach.

I came about and sailed for shore.

* * *

His bushy mustache was pulled down in a frown. Hands on hips, he stood watching as I clipped the boat to its mooring. I waded ashore. Penny beat me and made a fuss over the sheriff.

"Why didn't you tell me you owned an Irish wolfhound, Sheriff?" I said. "One like the dog I brought into town the other night."

He hitched his thumbs around his belt. "Because my Charm's dead, is why."

"I'm sorry."

"Me, too. Got a minute?"

"Why do I sense you'll need more than that?"

" 'Cause you're smart." He shifted his stance and removed his sunglasses.

Dread climbed from my gut to my throat, choking me. "You found the woman."

He nodded, his eyes straight ahead, focused not on me but inward on some personal horizon.

"I'm taking a break from homicide counseling, Sheriff. That's what you want, isn't it?"

"Yes."

We walked toward the cottage.

"I don't think . . ." I said. "I need to mentally give it a rest, if you know what I mean. How about I give you some names. Good people down in Boston."

"I did some research. I know about the Harvester who killed those women in Boston . . . and about you."

I held the porch door for him and slammed it behind me. "See, horrible as that was, it's not why I'm up here."

"Didn't think it was, actually."

"Forget it. This isn't about me, but some poor family who's just lost a daughter or sister or wife."

30

He laid a hand on my shoulder. "These people need you."

His hand was warm and heavy and sparked a jumble of feelings I chose to ignore. I shoved my hands into my back pockets. "I don't think my counseling them is for the best, Sheriff."

His lips thinned to a white line. "They're good folks, Ms. Whyte. Things like this don't happen much in Winsworth."

Now he was ticking me off. How long had this elected official been playing sheriff? "Murder happens all the time."

"That it does. But not some bastard ripping Ms. Beal's gut open with some kind of combat knife."

I hitched my hip against the sink, steadied myself, pretended I was getting some water, anything, as if I didn't feel blind with fear. Plenty of Beals lived in Hancock County. Tons of them, in fact. But . . .

I shouldn't do it, not even if the victim was an old friend.

I left him standing in my kitchen staring after me, as I walked out onto the deck.

The breeze was cool and gentle, like a lover's hesitant caress. I spied two seagulls dive-bombing some clams. Zoom—down the clams would plummet from the seagulls' mouths, smashing onto the rocks. Then the gulls would swoop down and pluck the meat from inside the broken shells.

Zoom. Zoom.

"You've done this for a long time, right?" His voice was soft in my ear.

"Long before it was considered a profession."

"So you're an old pro at it."

"Old pros need R&R, too."

"The family's not coping so well. They just found out late last night, and . . . It would be a good thing to help them."

31

Of course it would.

"Simply put," he continued. "I can't see you refusing."

Neither could I.

As I changed my clothes, I figuratively climbed into my professional garb. Up here in Maine, it wasn't a perfect fit, but it was the only outfit of its kind I owned.

We took Hank's boat of a car; unlike other cop cars I'd ridden in, it was pin neat. He drove toward town—lumbered might be a better word—at a pace that would rival a blind eighty-year-old's.

"I'd like to know the particulars about how you found the victim," I said. "The *modus operandi*, how the family learned of the death, their reactions, how the ID went. I'll meet them and assess how they're doing. That's all I'll agree to."

Hank nodded. Then: "So what happened Sunday night on the Bangor Road?"

His voice was calm, conversational. But I heard the weight of the real question behind all that calmness. I paused. He waited. I knew I'd lose the game, so I didn't bother playing.

I told him again about picking up the stranger and his injured dog.

"So who was the guy with the dog?" I asked as we finally reached the outskirts of Winsworth.

Hank chewed the end of his mustache and said nothing.

"You know him, don't you?" I said.

"Maybe. Fella named Andrew Jones has a wolfie. Can't recall the dog's name, though."

Damn, but he was lying to me. I wanted to call him on it, but I was more interested in the *reason* behind the lie. I played it out. "Is this Jones a friend of yours?"

"In a sense."

"He was pretty specific about the knife and all. He could be involved."

"Doubt it. But I'll check it out. Thanks for the info."

He'd just circled the wagons, and I sure as heck wasn't inside. Who was this Andrew Jones he was shielding? Three nights earlier I'd met a stranger, and he'd been right about a horrific homicide. What didn't the sheriff want me to know about Jones and his involvement in the woman's death?

"When did you find her?" I asked.

"Late last night."

"Didn't anyone miss her? Work? Her family? Her boyfriend?"

"People at work thought she was down at a conference in Boston. She's single, lives alone, and speaks with her family every few days or so. No boyfriend, or so they say."

"I need to know the particulars of her death." That knowledge—paper cuts to my soul—was essential to my counseling the family.

We crossed the bridge over the swiftly flowing Winsworth River. As Hank turned right onto River Street, he gave me as much as he claimed to know.

Two men, out to the Penasquam quarry to haul stones, had found her late yesterday. The quarry wasn't used much anymore, according to Hank, so he wasn't surprised that the body went undiscovered for so long. Ms. Beal hadn't been seen for two nights, not since she'd left her radio station around 7 P.M. Sunday night.

I'd picked up Jones a little after eleven that night.

"Even with the rain," Hank said, "there was still plenty of blood at the scene because the body was sheltered under a big, old oak tree. Most, if not all of the blood, was the victim's—she'd bled out from multiple stab wounds."

Multiple stab wounds. Just like my dad. The years dissolved, and I was again chilled by that image, an almost-friend I knew far too well.

"Ms. Whyte?" said Hank.

"Oh, um, sorry." We were climbing Elm Street, away from the river. Hank turned left onto Grand, and—geesh. I knew exactly where we were going, and it was bad. "Please continue," I said.

"The ME's got sometime Sunday night as the time of death."

Again it meshed with Jones's commentary about the woman on the rock. "Was a knife protruding from her belly?"

"No sign of the murder weapon."

That didn't fit, but . . . "Shit."

"Pardon, ma'am?" Hank said.

"Uh, nothing, Sheriff." Hank had turned off Grand Street onto Beals Avenue, where Annie Beal had lived twenty-some years ago.

Beal is a common name in Winsworth. I really didn't want to imagine that the murdered Ms. Beal was my childhood pal, Annie, the sweetest and gentlest of my childhood friends.

At this point, I was afraid to ask Hank the victim's first name, and he sure hadn't offered it. The victim *couldn't* be Annie.

We pulled into the dooryard of the gray Cape Cod I'd visited hundreds of times.

Of course, it was Annie Beal's house.

Chapter Five
Cha . . . Cha . . . Cha . . . Changes

Noah Beal peered out the mudroom door, a pipe jammed in his mouth, just like always. Annie's dad now wore a shock of white hair above those same intimidating black brows that beetled as Hank and I walked the flagstone path to the side door.

The verdant lawns, the duck pond, the grove of apple trees—they were all the same. Of course, the trees were bigger, the house smaller, the lawn narrower. The tree nearest the pond had been our favorite climbing tree.

I could still feel the bark's nubby texture beneath my palm.

God, I wanted to bolt.

Hank must have sensed it, because he rested his hand on my elbow and practically shoved me toward the door.

"Who've you got there, Hank?" Noah barked.

"Tally Whyte. I told you I was bringing her by."

Noah scowled. "You're welcome, Hank, but we don't need some grief counselor here. Nope-suh."

"Can't hurt," Hank said.

Noah blocked the doorway. "Don't want it."

Hank's face tightened. "Noah, you're being—"

"Sheriff, wait." I slipped in front of Hank, studied Noah's slate-gray eyes, let him see into mine. "I found my dad in a pool of blood, Mr. Beal. He'd been repeatedly stabbed, right on our door stoop. I wanted to kill the man who'd done it. If he'd been there when I found my dad, I would have picked up the knife and . . . I know what you're feeling. I can help you. Please let me."

Noah gave me his profile, the granite one I'd once likened to New Hampshire's Old Man on the Mountain, before he'd fallen off. "Appreciate the effort, but we don't want to talk to a stranger."

"But I'm not one. Not really. We share a bond. May I come in?"

"Nope-suh, I can't do it. Folks down to Boston do things different. Again, appreciate the thought."

Should I tell Noah who I really was? Would that make a difference?

He shut the door in our face.

Hank's anger filled the inside of the car.

"Now what?" I said.

He sat for a minute, his hands tight on the steering wheel, knuckles white. "Noah's so damned pigheaded, I could shoot him."

"Bad plan. Look, his reaction is not unusual for grief after violence."

"His daughter's death has hit him hard. But it was a waste of time."

"No, it wasn't. I've been there, done that plenty. He may come around."

Hank backed out the driveway and drove toward downtown.

I finally had time to think, to feel. Annie was dead. *Dead.*

I peered out the window, the trees blurring from my tears. But I had to keep it tight. Tight. Couldn't have Hank see me blubbering all over his car. Then he'd start asking questions. *"What's wrong?"* he'd harp. And I wouldn't tell him. Couldn't. Not until I knew why my old teacher had spat poison at me. Maybe Hank would curse me, too. I definitely wasn't up for that.

He stopped at the end of the maple-lined street. I blew my nose. "Allergies," I said, and got it together.

"That true about your father?" he asked.

"Yes."

To our left, a small valley cradled downtown Winsworth and, beyond that, across the Winsworth River bridge, Long Hill rose in a steep incline to where my old house stood, a speck of white perched near the crest of the hill. Someone had rebuilt after the fire.

I had to see Annie's body. Had to.

Static sputtered from Hank's scanner, then a voice staccatoed some numbers and a locale.

"Do you have to answer that?" I said.

"Nope. Freddy'll be on it. I'll take you home."

"If you're going over to the ME's to view the post, I thought I might ride along. It's in Augusta, right?"

"Why the hell do you want to do that?"

"I'd like to see her." Why *anyone* would hurt Annie . . .

Hank hooked a left onto Upper Main. "There's no point."

"I know my job. You should let me do it. You sound like Noah."

He choked out a laugh. "There's a first, comparing me to Noah Beal."

"This is my business. Believe me, I know what I'm doing."

"She's left Augusta. About an hour ago, they brought her down here to Vandermere's Funeral Home."

I took that in, nodded. "Drop me at Vandermere's, then."

"She's not *ready* to be seen." His mouth clamped tight, his jaw muscles bulging. He turned left onto the Surry Road and toward my rented cottage.

He'd taken my class, knew I worked out of the ME's office and had seen plenty of "not ready" bodies. So why was he stonewalling me again?

Hank could have been her lover. Or maybe his friend, this Jones guy, had been.

After Hank dropped me off at the cottage, I waited twenty minutes, piled Penny into the truck, and headed back to town.

Vandermere's Funeral Home sat on a good piece of acreage on a shaded downtown side street. The Colonial-style building stood proudly behind a tall screen of evergreen hedges, and I followed the curving drive, bypassed the main entrance beneath the porte cochere, and bore right, down a split in the drive that hooked around back.

It was Vandermere who owned the cemetery where my dad rested.

I parked beside a gleaming hearse, got out bearing the spray of flowers I'd bought on my way over, and climbed the delivery-entrance steps. When I opened the back door, I peeked my head around, then crept inside. I reluctantly squeezed the door closed behind me.

Irrational as it might be, I hated funeral homes.

I stood in an alcove surrounded by closed doors. I took a

breath. Nothing like that antiseptic mortuary smell to perk one right up. So far, so good.

I started opening doors. The one to my right led to the bathroom. The one on the left, to a cleaning closet. The second on the left revealed . . . a face?

I jumped. So did he. Fortunately for him, he hung on to the railing and so didn't fly backward down the stairs accompanied by his arsenal of cleaning supplies.

After calming him down, I learned his name was Mo Testa. "I'm Chip's go-to guy," he said, puffing his chest.

I flashed him a smile, along with my Massachusetts Grief Assistance Program credentials, while I whipped up a doublespeak story.

"Sure. Follow me." He led me down stairs that creaked and through a low-ceilinged room containing closed caskets and cremation urns, flipping on lights as he went.

A chill rippled through me.

For all the corpses I'd seen at OCME, funeral parlors still gave me the creeps. Ridiculous, eh? Maybe it was the music or the smell or the wax effigies that once had souls. For whatever reason, I disliked them intensely.

We approached a closed door, and the strains of some rapper, like Fat Daddy somebody, grew louder.

"In here, ma'am." Testa switched on a light.

She lay encased in white plastic on a metal gurney. They hadn't started working on her yet.

I inhaled strong chemicals and twitched at the blare of the boom box that masked the whoosh of the air blowers. I laid the flowers I carried on an empty chair.

"Would you mind turning down the music?" I said.

"Yeah. Oh, sure." Testa punched it off, then waved me over to her. He put his fingers on the zipper. "You ready?"

No, I wanted to say. *I'll never be ready to see Annie dead.* "Thanks, but I'll do it." I brushed his fingers aside and unzipped the bag to her breastbone.

I gasped.

"You're not gonna faint, are you?" Testa said.

"No," I whispered.

If I erased the pallor of death, it was Annie as I'd imagined her grown up. Same cascade of raven hair, same tilted eyes, same voluptuous lips, which in death were ghost gray. My God, it hurt. Except . . .

What was that pronounced Cindy Crawford mole beside her upper lip? Annie never had . . .

I grabbed the clipboard from the gurney.

Bold, typed letters spelled out LAURA BEAL. *Laura* . . .

I shook with relief. Then felt guilty as hell.

Laura. Annie's younger sister by six years. A gnat we'd hardly noticed back when we were kids. In my mind, Laura was still a chubby six-year-old. In reality, she was grown. And dead.

Earlier, at Noah's house, Annie must have been inside. Devastated. Later. I'd work on helping Annie later.

I brushed my hand across Laura's lovely hair, then added her to my snapshot album of the dead. I closed my eyes.

I'm sorry, Laura. So sorry.

I opened my eyes and examined Laura Beal.

Whichever ME had opened her up was a neat and tidy person. I looked beyond the careful autopsy stitches.

The left side of Laura's face and shoulder was black with lividity.

"Seen enough, ma'am?" Testa asked. "Mr. Vandermere's gonna start working on her any minute."

More than enough, but . . . "I'd like to see all of her."

Testa rolled his eyes, then snapped on a pair of latex gloves.

He unzipped the rest of Laura Beal's body bag to reveal her full breasts and tiny waist, both seemingly free of actual wounds. But jagged slashes and stabs, dozens of them, marred her abdomen. Her shins and the tops of her feet were abraded and marked by small cuts. Ones not from a knife, but rather the kind of scrapes you'd get climbing a tree or. . . .

"Her feet, please," I said.

He opened the plastic further. The lividity ran down her left side to her red-painted toes.

"A bad one," Testa said, glancing nervously at the door.

I should have worn gloves, but . . . I lifted her hands. The palms were also abraded. I laid them carefully beside her again.

How long had Laura survived with those terrible abdominal wounds? Were Noah or Annie aware of her suffering? I prayed not.

Sadly, I'd learned a lot about Laura Beal's death. Now I needed to understand her life.

"Turn her, please. I'd like to see her posterior."

As Testa tugged Laura on her side, a voice boomed from the staircase.

"We gotta vamoose," Testa said.

"Wait."

"Man, we gotta go."

There was a circular bruising on the small of her back. "Did the ME say—"

"Oh, shit," Testa said just as the heavy door swung open.

Before me stood a red-faced, blue-suited man about my age with hands on hips, glaring at us. "What is going on, Mr. Testa?"

"Hi." I grinned, hand thrust forward. "I'm with the ME's office in Boston. A psychologist and homicide counselor. You must be Mr. Vandermere."

I guess Boston was the magic word, because Vandermere took my hand and pumped it like mad, while his eyes annoyingly dropped to my breasts.

He ordered Testa to return to his duties, then escorted me from the room and upstairs to his office. He gestured me to the burgundy leather wing chair while he sat behind his immense desk. Already I knew Vandermere was an ass. I just hoped not a nasty one.

"I've never met a homicide counselor before." He brushed a speck of something off his immaculate white shirt. "Perhaps you'll clarify, Ms. Whyte—"

"Tally."

"Tally. Why is that name familiar?"

I shrugged, not wanting to remind him about our appointment regarding my dad's grave.

He pursed his lips, folded his hands on his desk. "If you don't mind my asking, and considering you were trespassing, why *were* you inspecting Ms. Beal's remains? Rather ghoulish of you."

"I try to always examine the body before I counsel the family."

"That's horrible. I haven't even embalmed her yet."

Was he kidding? "I try to understand what the family has seen and how they're feeling."

"Ahhhh," he said, nodding. "That makes sense."

"Please don't get angry at Mr. Testa because of this, eh?"

Vandermere rolled a gold Cross pen between his fingers. "He breached protocol."

"Not really. I showed him my credentials. I had to see Laura Beal. Period."

"You could've waited until I'd made her beautiful." He bit his lip, his eyes shifting away from me.

42

"What are you worried about, Mr. Vandermere?"

"Call me Chip, please. And you see, it's just . . ."

The door flew open and in walked Hank.

"Gee, Sheriff," I said. "Twice in one day."

He frowned, then turned his chilly gaze on Vandermere. "*This* the dangerous felon you had me leave the scene of an accident for?"

Chip puffed up. "I thought Ms. Whyte was a thief."

"Body snatching common around here, Sheriff?" I said.

"I'll escort the perpetrator out." Hank reached for me.

Vandermere sprang to his feet. "No! I mean, uh, it's obvious Ms. Whyte is really not a thief or felon."

Hank clasped my elbow. "It's out of your hands, Chip."

"But it was a mistake," Vandermere said.

I yanked my elbow from Hank's grasp. "This is ridiculous."

"Is it, Ms. Whyte?" Hank said. "I'll be in touch, Chip."

Over Chip's protests, Hank steered me down a narrow hall filled with gaping-eyed mourners attending a viewing, and out to his Pontiac parked beneath the porte cochere.

Mouth tight, jaw clenched, Hank gestured me into his car. At least it was the front seat. He walked around and slid behind the wheel.

"Look, Sheriff, I . . ."

He rested his forehead on the steering wheel. His body trembled.

"Geesh, Sheriff, it wasn't such a—"

Hank's laughter boomed.

"You think this is funny?"

"Damned right I do." He swiped a forearm across his eyes. "God, that was rich. Chip Vandermere is the biggest jerk in town."

"It's not *that* funny," I said. "I mean, I should be pissed.

43

Hauling me out in front of that guy." I shook my head. "You had me going."

"Well deserved. You shouldn't have been there."

"Yes, I should have."

"Truce?" he said. "Lemme buy you a cup of coffee."

No doubt about it. The little Henry Cunningham I remembered had definitely changed.

Chapter Six
The Dead Stone

Hank pulled up to a green-and-white refurbished diner on Main Street. Colorful begonias and geraniums bloomed on the small piece of land and in window boxes. The place looked well-loved and inviting. You just knew the food would be great.

I'd loaded Penny into his car before we'd taken off. I gave her some of the water that I carried for her and told her I'd be back.

"Town Farm Restaurant," I said as we entered. "Looks yummy."

"Good stuff." He threaded his way down the narrow aisle and took a booth upholstered in red vinyl and shiny with wear. "Organic."

Hank removed his hat, revealing a flattop crushed to hat-head status. He scraped a hand through it, making it worse. Now he reminded me of Kranak. I missed his curmudgeonly ways and generous heart.

"Feel like a late lunch?" he asked.

"Just iced tea."

We talked inconsequentials until the waitress delivered my tea and Hank's bean burger and fries.

"Why didn't you want me seeing Laura Beal's body?"

His scowl bowed his mustache. "Didn't think it was appropriate. Simple as that."

"Is it? Because you and Laura Beal were friends?"

He gave me major teeth. "I'm friends with lots of people. Hey, you shrinkin' me, or what?"

I smiled. "Even cops need to talk out their grief. Especially cops."

"Let it lie, Ms. Whyte." He carefully rearranged his bean burger—rebuilding the onion, lettuce, and tomato with precision—added ketchup, then took a bite. A deliberate man. A thoughtful man.

I stirred my iced tea. "Are you still ticked at me?"

"Never was. Learn anything from what you saw?"

"Perhaps. Laura's attack was savage. The guy was furious at something. Laura Beal? Could be, but he could just as well have transferred his anger *to* her."

He nodded.

"Judging from the abrasions on her shins, palms, and tops of her feet, I picture her folding her knees up, like in a fetal position. I see it as defensive. Anything to get away from that knife. Then she crawled."

Another bite of burger, then: "You're right about that. We found traces of her blood along a twenty-foot path. Don't know how she did it. Then again, Ms. Beal had a will of iron."

"Twenty feet! My God. How long do you estimate she survived after the attack?"

"Half hour, maybe."

I saw Laura crawling, in immense pain. Or maybe not. Maybe by then the adrenaline rush and shock had trumped the pain, her enormous will urging her to escape, to move any way she could to get away from the killer.

"The bruising on the small of her back," I said. "I see someone with a gun, maybe. Prodding her in the back, hard, making her walk to where she didn't want to go, then pulling the knife."

"You see a lot," Hank said.

Too much. "Strange that she had no defensive wounds on her hands. It wouldn't have mattered, though, would it? The killer was in a rage. But can you see how afterward he cooled down? After his kill, he moved her onto the stone. And posed her on her back. That's calculated. Calm, even. Anything spooky about this? Local lore? Ritual?"

"Not to my knowledge." I felt a deep sorrow coming from him.

"This reminds me of the kid in Boston who stabbed his best friend's mother nearly a hundred times."

"Maybe." Hank swiped his napkin across his mustache and lips. "Profiling's an art, not a science."

"Absolutely. And I'm not a profiler. I just try to see inside." Our waitress topped off my tea and Hank's coffee. "So who could have done this? And why?"

"You think I haven't been asking myself that maybe a million times?" he said. "I've no idea. Not yet. You sure you don't want something to eat? Dessert, maybe?"

"Not right now. Thanks."

"We found her Jeep over to the radio station. Because of the quarry's hardpacked stone road and this odd June we been having with hardly a lick of rain, we hoped to find some foot or tire prints. But that mean storm the night Ms. Beal disappeared washed away anything useful. You're new to town, but believe me, this kind of thing isn't typical of Winsworth."

"How much have you told the family about the way she died?" I said.

"Not much. Haven't talked to Annie, her sister. I told Noah that the killer used a knife, is all. I didn't see any reason to—"

"I agree," I said. "What about the Jones fellow?"

"Like I said, I'll tell you after I've spoken with him."

Maybe. But I doubted it. I would learn things only in trade for what Hank Cunningham needed from me. "Why do you call her Ms. Beal and not Laura?"

He flushed. "It keeps her distant, which is dumb. I'm seeing that."

"I'd like to know about her."

"She owns WWTH, one of the local radio stations, and is one of the two flaming Democrats in the county."

"You the other one?"

Hank's look of horror gave way to a chuckle. "Not hardly. Laura is—was—an opinionated and strong young woman. A town mover and shaker. Controversial as hell. Always raising a ruckus. Noah ordered her not to buy the station, so she bought it. When he ran for selectman, she campaigned against him. Of course, he won anyway. Naturally."

"The family's local, right?" I said.

"Practically founded the place. The Beals go back hundreds of years. Cranberry Islanders originally, fishermen who relocated to the mainland. Noah owns a real-estate office just up from here, on Grand Street. Successful place. His other daughter, Annie, works for him, and a nicer, more bighearted girl you'll never meet."

I leaned forward in the booth. "Laura sounds like a major rebel. How come?"

"Annie was just about grown, but Laura was only thirteen when her mom lit out for California with Joe Tarbuck. He was a dentist in town, and not a very good one. Noah remarried, but it didn't take." He sipped his coffee. "Laura might have been Noah's black sheep, but he stuck by her. I can't see him killing his own child. And I sure don't see Annie involved. Some nut must have gotten Laura. Makes sense, given her taste, or lack of it, in men. She was forever picking up strangers in bars."

"You said she didn't have a boyfriend."

His long fingers scratched his auburn mustache. "Not in the regular sense. But enough so it's a problem. State cops have focused on Gary Pinkham. He's a lobsterman out to the Island, but has family in Winsworth. Not a giant intellect, mind you, but the kind of big, powerful body Laura liked best. Pinkham has done a disappearing act."

"From your tone, you don't seem to think he did it."

He shrugged, his eyes unfocused and distant. "You can't know about this stuff. About people. Not really, unless you're living in their shorts. But the man's a wet noodle. Has less spine than a sea cucumber. You see someone like that taking a knife and carving up Laura Beal?"

"I've seen lots of disturbed minds hide beneath mousy exteriors. Know what I mean?"

"Damned if I know squat anymore." Our waitress appeared with two plates of strawberry/rhubarb pie. She plunked one in front of each of us.

"Didn't order it, Pru," Hank said.

"Know it. Carm said to bring it ovah, so I brung it."

"Well, thanks."

I poked my fork around the steaming wedge of pie and tried to look casual. "Carm?"

"Carmen Cavasos. She owns this place."

49

Carmen? *Christmas*. I pictured Carm . . . I didn't know . . . but doing something wild and mouthy, not running a granola eatery. I looked around but didn't see her. Then again, would I recognize her? Cripes. I almost asked Hank what fracas she'd gotten in, but caught myself in time. "You said Pinkham has taken off?"

"North of Baxter, to the big woods, I expect. Plenty of places to hide. Pinkham knows it well. Like I said, he's no Nobel laureate, but I thought he had enough brains to guess fingers would be pointing at him and not to hightail it out of here."

"Maybe Pinkham isn't in any condition to come forward," I said.

"I thought about that, too."

Back at the funeral home, we found my truck blocked by a delivery van.

"Crap," I said, just as Hank's radio bleeped. "Now I've got to go back inside and see Vandermere."

He held a whispered conversation with the dispatcher, then took off down the driveway.

"What the hell are you doing?" I asked.

"Someone's prowling around the quarry where they found Laura. Everyone else is miles away. We're it."

"*We* are it?"

He grinned. "Sure. You and Penny'll be useful."

Nice. Useful. "Dare I ask how?"

"Penny can find them and you can block the road with the cruiser when I get out."

"Oh, those are *swell* ideas."

He chuckled. "Look, you see things other people don't."

"Now you're being downright silly."

50

"Remember, I took your class. I've read an article or two you've written. You understand victims. And killers. You've got a past, Ms. Whyte. And you *feel* things."

I shook my head.

"We're halfway there," he said. "So you're stuck. It's probably just kids anyway."

"I get it. You're emotionally engaged in this. You want me for some kind of buffer, right?"

"You in?" he said. "Or am I dropping you and the dog on the pavement?"

I didn't much like the role, but . . . "Yeah, I'm in."

We drove up State Street past the YMCA building and Winsworth Lumber, in the direction of Bangor. Even with a sense of urgency, Hank drove like an old fogy.

I hoped it was just kids messing around at the quarry rather than someone more malignant connected with Laura Beal's death.

Each of us hid our eyes behind sunglasses, our thoughts locked up tight. I propped my sneakered feet on the dash, rested my chin on my knees. Every crime scene I'd gone to with Kranak made me tingle with anticipation. I knew I'd learn about a killer, and that always frightened me. There was an intimacy I dreaded, yet desired. I always wanted it over with, that first, fresh knowledge.

Hank's slo-mo style of driving wasn't helping matters.

"There." I pointed. "That's where the stranger's truck crashed and I picked him and his dog up."

"Ayuh."

"Did I mention the leg-hold trap?"

"Yup-suh. Mentioned it."

Hank Cunningham had switched on his downeast drawl,

something he could turn on and off like a circuit breaker. Apparently, the "on" position meant zip's worth of conversation, so I shut up.

We turned onto Penasquam Lake Road, which meanders around the lake in a half-circle and ends up heading for Jonesport. On the left were undulating fields and the occasional house set far back from the road. On the right, houses and camps overlooked the large lake, which today reflected the cloudy sky.

"Can't you drive any faster?" I said.

"Nope. Can't."

Christmas.

Soon, fields gave way to steeper wooded hills, and behind them hid Emerald Lake, a fabulous body of water deep as sin and cold as death.

Just beyond a double-wide trailer surrounded by daffodils, we hooked a sharp left onto a dirt road that rose upward. Dust swirled as the Pontiac jounced over bumps and into ruts until Hank halted at the crest of the hill blanketed with pine and spruce and poplar trees. A locked gate barred the way.

Hank left the cruiser and snapped on some gloves. He examined the lock.

"Jimmied," he hollered to me, then swung the gate wide for the car to enter. We parked on the lip of a precipice. The quarry gaped before us, and just beyond it, clouds scudded high above the black waters of Emerald Lake.

"Popular necking spot," Hank said. "Coulda been kids who broke in." He'd already bagged the lock. "No tire tracks."

We walked around what I presumed were the foreman's small trailer and several giant machines meant for extracting stone from the quarry. Penny trotted alongside, her nose to the dirt, ever busy sniffing.

The terrain grew rougher, and I could smell the crisp freshness of the lake. Soon I was swatting June-in-Maine's bane: blackflies.

"You got any . . ."

Hank handed me some Ben's insect repellant, and I spritzed hundred-percent Deet on my exposed flesh and clothes.

Even so, bugs the size of pinheads formed black clouds around our heads as we walked downward on what turned out to be a small path to the bottom of the excavation.

"You see anything?" Hank asked. "Kids. Whatever."

"No. Penny hasn't reacted to anything in particular, either."

"Smell anything?"

"Just the lake and the dust. If I inhale too deeply, I'll get blackflies up my nose."

He nodded, and we kept scanning the quarry.

The bottom was a moonscape of jutting stones and sharp granite pebbles, broken only by two birch saplings and a lone oak that had somehow found purchase in the inhospitable soil. The feel of the place reminded me of Dante and lost souls. I lifted my digicam and snapped off a few shots.

Crime-scene tape surrounded a fifty-foot area where the oak grew. Following Hank's lead, I ducked beneath the tape and into the cool shade of the tree.

A flat ovoid hunk of stone the size of a kitchen table nestled close to the tree's trunk. Hank didn't need to say that's where Laura Beal was laid out. I *knew*.

Penny circled the stone, whining. She knew, too.

I walked closer. The stone—dark and porous and cruel-looking—was unlike others in the quarry. It was an angry stone, a dead stone, with sharp, splintery edges and what looked like grease stains across the top. Not grease, of course, but blood.

I photographed it, and as I did so, I saw Laura's supine form through the viewfinder. I saw her arms wrap around her knees, her belly leaking blood, her mouth parted in a scream.

Help me!

Chapter Seven
If Stones Could Talk

I stumbled backward.

"You all right?" Hank asked.

"Sure. Sure." I rubbed my temples, trying to squeeze the vision of a pleading Laura Beal out of my mind. "Just a little headache."

"You want to go?"

"No . . . No, I'm fine."

"Give me your impressions," Hank said.

I walked around the stone. "Disturbing. Ritual-like. A perfect sacrificial altar. I collect stones, rocks. This one is angry. Are you sure there aren't cult rumblings around here?"

"Naw. Most Mainers don't buy into that crap."

Maybe this killer did. "I assume the blood on the stone was Laura's, yes?"

Hank chewed his mustache. "Yeah. Just hers. I'm gonna do a circuit. Why don't you take Penny and go the other way? We can spiral toward the center."

"Gotcha." Penny and I knew the drill. She'd done it many more times than I, in her role as a K-9 Corps dog. I opened myself up to the site. Tried to see without preconceptions.

"*Revir,*" I said to Penny, indicating a "blind search." "*Revir.*" I followed Penny, panning left and right as we worked our way toward the center of the spiral. Others had done this, but it never hurt to do it again. And they didn't have Penny, who was particularly intuitive. The late-afternoon sun made me sticky with sweat, a feast for the blackflies. I pulled my shirttail from my jeans and wiped my face. Occasionally, I'd glance over at Hank. His back was soaked with sweat.

Penny stopped maybe ten feet from the dead stone. She sniffed the air, her head weaving back and forth. She sensed something. What?

She barked twice, then lowered herself almost to the ground and moved forward, directly in line with the trail of Laura's blood. She turned toward her right, and I followed. A large boulder lay in front of us.

I almost called Hank, but would wait and see what she'd found.

Someone's eyes, on my back. I turned, looking for some kids or evildoers or even sightseers. I shaded my eyes with my hand. I saw no one.

I was spooked, that was all. The place would creep anybody out.

Penny stood in front of the boulder. I smoothed my hand over it. She whined and circled, then began to dig at the base. "*Nech to!* Leave it!" She instantly stopped.

"Hey, Hank!" I called.

He moved swiftly across the circle. "What'd she find?"

"Something here." He helped me move a smaller rock. "Look."

We exposed three white-filtered, half-smoked cigarettes.

"Nice," Hank said.

"*Hodny*," I said as I scratched Penny's muzzle. "Good girl. *Hodny*."

I took some pictures, then Hank bagged the butts.

"These'll help," he said. "Our boy might have DNA or fingerprints on file. If Pinkham does, these could rule him out. I wish the idiot hadn't run."

I leaned against the rock. "This is bad, Hank."

He nodded.

"We've got three butts. Our killer smoked three cigarettes as he watched Laura Beal bleed to death. He felt he had all the time in the world. He watched her crawl, listened to her moan. He let her lie there long enough, dead, for her blood to pool onto her side. Only once he was sure she was dead did he move her to the stone. He arranged her. Fixed her clothes."

Hank nodded, looked away. "That's a hard picture."

"I know. He's a frightening person, this killer. He could have put Laura out of her misery at any time, but he took pleasure in her struggles, reveled in her pain. If anyone gets in his way over this, he'll kill again without hesitation."

"I'm not gonna sleep too well tonight," he said.

I wouldn't, either.

I took some mental jabs at Laura's relationship with the killer, while Hank climbed the far slope, looking for what he called "new perspective."

I heard "Shit!" and snapped around.

A shower of rocks and stones tumbled around Hank. He flipped to the left, dangling off the cliff by one hand.

I ran toward him. "Hold on!"

Stones bounced around him, then a large rock smashed right on his hand. I ran faster. "Hank!"

He shuddered, tried to hold on, fingers slipping, then

butt-surfed down the hill, cradling his bloodied hand to his chest.

He landed hard and sat there, his back to the quarry wall, big chest bellowing in and out.

I knelt beside him. His eyes were closed, his nostrils flaring. Blood smeared his face, the front of his shirt. His blood-covered hand was unnaturally bent.

I touched his cheek. "Are you okay? Hank? *Hank?*"

Through gritted teeth, he said, "Gimme a sec."

I flipped open my cell phone to call for help.

"Don't," he growled. "Help me up."

"Dumb idea." But I maneuvered him to his feet. He swayed, his pallor a sickly gray.

"Don't you dare faint on me," I said.

He rasped out a chuckle. "What a shrew. Come on, let's get out of here."

Somehow we got up the cliff and into the cruiser. By the time I loaded up Penny and ran around to the driver's seat, he'd passed out.

I turned on the car, cranked up the AC, then reached for his police radio.

His good hand shot out and stopped me. "No calling. Just get me back to Winsworth."

"But . . ."

"Drive."

Little Henry Cunningham never had been a great listener.

"I thought you were out of it," I said.

"I am," he said. "Thanks to that sonofabitch who started that rock slide."

"You saying someone was up there?"

"Yes. No. I don't know, dammit." He held up his bloody

hand. "But I need to be pissed at somebody, since I most likely started the thing myself."

Hank sat on an emergency-room bed at Winsworth Memorial while we waited for a doctor. He refused to lie down. I kept replaying his fall. I tried to picture whether another person was on the cliff. No image came to mind. I worried. He looked horrible, white-faced, bloodied, and broken.

"I'll take you to see the Beals again tomorrow," he said.

"Okay, sure."

His forehead furrowed. "You *are* going to help them?"

I shouldn't get more involved, but . . . I whooshed out a breath. "I said I would. Yes."

"Didn't doubt it for a minute."

The way he said it . . . I turned. He wore a funny look not all that different from the time he kissed me as the Frog Prince in the fourth-grade play. Or perhaps it was pain that softened his expression.

A doctor poked her head in. "Be right with you, Hank. How you hanging?"

"Just fine, Lexie," he said, grinning.

"Like your pals on *NYPD Blue*?" The drapes fell closed.

"What was that about?" I said.

"A really bad joke."

When we returned to the cottage, Penny took a run down the beach and I checked for messages. Debbie Tomes, a pal from Philadelphia's GAP, the model for MGAP, had called about a referral I'd made. I returned the call, and we scheduled a conference call with the client in two hours. Veda had phoned, too. After our gabfest, I was finally able to take a breather and start organizing my thoughts and feelings about Laura Beal's killing.

I made a folder for Laura on my computer and typed some notes about today's events—Noah's reaction to being counseled, Laura's body, the murder site, the cigarette butts, Hank's accident. I wrote about how I'd felt seeing Laura. That took time. Then I added Noah, the death site, Chip Vandermere—just the way I did it at MGAP. The routine felt comfortable, familiar.

A serial killer? Revenge? Jealousy? What had caused the killer to repeatedly plunge a knife into Laura Beal's flesh? Why had he watched and smoked while she slowly died?

I took a break and called the hospital. Hank hadn't been admitted. I didn't have his home number, but I assumed he was okay or they would have admitted him.

I lit three candles, dimmed the lights. I had another hour before the conference call.

I held my courage stone, carved by my dad. I needed the stone's wisdom.

I can't say any came, other than an urgent desire to see Annie Beal. One thing—Laura's homicide had sure put the quest for answers about my dad and Mrs. Lakeland's cruel behavior on my back burner.

At 8:30 the next morning, I parked in a small strip mall on Grand Street that housed a True Value hardware, Kim's Sophisticated Nails, and Beals Realty.

I intended to catch Annie Beal alone.

I sipped Starbucks high-test, needing the java jolt, while I watched cars pull into the mall. I'd already been to the post office, hoping a woman named Joy was on duty. I'd met her a couple times picking up my mail and hunting for info about my dad. She loved to chat.

THE DEAD STONE

I wanted to find out more about Annie and Laura and their father. All I'd learned was that Annie was single, then a bunch of customers had streamed through the doors. That was that.

Laura's murder and Hank's accident had translated into a lousy night's sleep. Or was Hank's fall an accident? We'd never caught a glimpse of the intruder who'd sent us out to the quarry in the first place. Maybe he'd started that rock slide.

I cracked the window and horns blared and tires screeched and epithets got yelled, courtesy of the bazillion tourists driving down Grand Street on their way to Mt. Desert Island and Bar Harbor even at that early hour. I chuckled. I'd forgotten about the noise and craziness of Winsworth's summer season. Although I wanted fresh air, I closed the window and opted for the AC while I waited.

At 8:55 Annie and Noah pulled up to their parking spot in a newish Jeep Cherokee. Knowing stoic Noah, I wasn't surprised they opened the real-estate office just days after Laura's death. I wondered about the funeral. I'd heard nothing.

I continued to wait. Noah always used to open the office, then meet his cronies for coffee down at Piper's. At 9:30 sharp, Noah returned to his Jeep and headed "up street," as they say in Maine. I raised my cup to rituals that didn't change, then left the truck.

My hand shook a bit turning the doorknob. A lot of years had passed. I'd been so close to Annie. I didn't think she'd recognize me, but . . .

The room was empty, the smell of Noah's applewood pipe tobacco taking me back some twenty years. I started to call "Hello," stopped myself. I walked to the large oak desk, an island of chaos amid the room's studied Maine ambience.

A muffled voice filtered though the inner office door as I examined the cluster of photographs on the desk. Annie's desk.

And there was Laura, pulsing with life. What a stunner, with mischief twinkling from her jade eyes. Lots of pictures of people I vaguely remembered but couldn't identify. But one picture . . . I picked up a framed five-by-seven of a couple. High school, obviously. Annie's arm was wrapped around the waist of a blond boy—tall and handsome and wearing an All-American grin. I thought I remembered the boy but wasn't sure. Some BMOC, apparently. Annie peered up at him as if he owned the world.

According to Joy at the post office, Annie had never married. Obviously, this boy still meant a great deal to her. Where was . . .

"Can I help you?"

The photo clattered from my fingers. "Uh, sure, yes. Sorry. I'm a photo hound." I righted the picture and turned to Annie.

My smile faded.

Laura had looked just as I'd imagined Annie would, twenty-odd years later. Annie? She looked dreadful.

Same black fall of hair parted in the middle. Same periwinkle-colored eyes. Same pointed chin. But she was pale and thin, and plum half-moons pouched beneath eyes empty of joy.

What had happened to her? The Annie I'd known had been a sweet lark of a girl. This woman carried some great sorrow, even beyond that of mourning a sister's recent death. She was a blurred shadow of the friend who'd invented lame jokes and twirled a baton and sang in our quartet's short-lived rock band.

I ached for her.

Annie showed no hint of the recognition I'd secretly hoped for. I almost told her who I was. But Mrs. Lakeland's cut hadn't hurt half of what Annie's would if she rejected me.

"Please, have a seat." Annie led me to the alcove of captain's chairs. She frowned. "You're crying."

"It's these darned allergies." I chuckled, exploring my purse for a wad of Kleenex.

"How can I help you?"

"I'm a friend of Hank Cunningham's. Tally Whyte."

"Oh! You're the woman who rented the old Brady cottage."

Ah, those Winsworth tom-toms—effective as ever. "Yes."

"Daddy said you're from Boston."

"That I am."

A smile. A small one, but it flooded her eyes with warmth. "So how do you like it here?"

"I like it a lot. It's a beautiful place."

"Are you looking to move here, perhaps? Buy a house on the water? In town?"

"Not exactly. Hank suggested I see you. I, um, I'm a psychologist . . . and I counsel the families of homicide victims."

"Really? How interesting. I've never heard of that."

"No, most people haven't. That's why I'm here. Sheriff Cunningham thought I might be of help."

Her brow wrinkled. "You mean in Winsworth?"

My heart squeezed. Annie was in denial. It wasn't uncommon, but it was terribly difficult.

"Is there anything you'd like to talk about with me?" I said.

She took a handkerchief from her pocket and started folding it on her lap. "Not that I can think of, other than acquainting you more with Winsworth if you're thinking of moving her permanently."

I wrapped my sturdy hand around her delicate one. "I know it's hard and that you're in pain and—"

"I feel fine." She looked at me as if I'd sprouted a second head.

Slicing through the denial was an option, but not a great one. Yet it would be worse if someone called with condolences and she was unprepared. "How about we talk about your sister Laura, Ms. Beal?"

Annie's eyes widened, then a peal of laughter burst from her mouth. "Forgive me. People from away sometimes have the oddest sense of humor. And call me Annie."

"Why would I make a joke about Laura, Annie?"

"Because the minute she goes off on one of her crazy escapades, everyone in town starts flapping their big, fat mouths."

"Annie, Laura isn't off on an escapade."

"Well, of course she is. Daddy's mad as heck."

"So your father said Laura has gone somewhere."

"Not exactly." She straightened her spine. "It's not really your business, Ms. Whyte."

Swell.

The door flew open and in came a big-boned, flame-haired woman in overalls and Birkenstocks. Good God, it had to be Carmen, my childhood best friend who now owned the Town Farm Restaurant. She didn't spare me a glance, but rushed over to Annie and enfolded her in a hug.

"I'm so sorry, sweetie," said Carm. "Old Noah wouldn't let me near you yesterday."

Annie pushed herself away. "What are you talking about, Carm? What's everybody talking about?"

The door slammed against the back wall. "What's going on here!" shouted Noah. Chaos ensued, with Noah bellowing for Carmen and me to get out, Carm screaming Spanish epithets, Annie getting bug-eyed, and someone's cell phone bleeping away.

I began steering Annie toward a quiet corner.

Noah latched onto her arm, his eyes frantic. "Don't you go with that woman."

Confusion crossed Annie's face. "Daddy, what is going on?"

"Nothing. Everything." Noah smoothed his hair with shaking hands. He stared straight ahead. "Your sister Laura has gotten herself killed."

Silence, stretching forever, all eyes on Annie.

"Killed?" Annie finally whispered. "No, it's not possible."

Noah's tanned face hardened. "It's true."

"Laura can't be dead!"

"Well, she is," Noah said, finally looking her in the eye. Then he crushed Annie to him. "I didn't know how to tell you."

Chapter Eight
Trick or Treat

Annie swayed. I sat her in a chair while a cursing Noah pushed Carmen out the door. Then he kneeled beside Annie, patting her limp hand.

"Come on," I said. "Let's get Annie home."

Annie's doctor arrived soon after, but all Annie would do was stare at the pink canopy above her four-poster bed. I wanted to help, but while Annie was shut off from the world, I was helpless. Dr. Cambal-Hayward, an imposing woman with a head of steel-gray hair, a Roman nose, and a no-nonsense manner, assured me of Annie's resilience. I felt Annie was in good hands as I led a strangely passive Noah downstairs.

We sat at the round table in Noah's homey kitchen. Over and over his shaking hands smoothed his mane of silver hair. "I meant to tell her. Planned it all out."

Furious as I was at his not telling Annie, I couldn't help but feel sorry for him. I understood how difficult the "telling" was. "Perhaps a part of you didn't believe Laura was dead."

His eyes squeezed tight. "Oh, I believed. Saw her myself down to Vandermere's."

"That must have been terribly hard."

"Hard?" Noah started to laugh. "Hard?"

Dr. Cambal-Hayward strode into the kitchen. "I've given Annie a heavy sedative. Noah, you're an old fool."

Noah nodded. "Been told that before, Cath."

The doctor pecked him on the cheek. "Don't be so tough on yourself. And on Laura." She slapped some pills down on the table. "Now, take one of these and save the other two for Annie. I mean it. Take 'em, or else."

"Or else what, you old harridan?"

"Or I'll spread the rumor that you cheat at poker."

"You wouldn't dare."

"Bet on it."

She left via the mudroom, her sensible shoes sounding like squeegees on the flagstone floor.

"Best poker player in town." A smile flitted across Noah's face, then he covered his face with his hands. "The night Laura died, Daniel and I were up until five A.M. getting massacred by that woman in Texas Hold 'Em. And Laura, she was already dead, for God's sake, and I didn't even know."

"How could you have, Noah?"

"We don't need any damned pills." He went to throw them. I grasped his hand. "You might. Keep them. Just in case."

He lowered his arm, then plucked a handkerchief from his pocket and wiped his eyes. "It was that god-awful Pinkham. If I could escort him to hell, I would."

"Why are you so sure it was Gary Pinkham?"

"Excuse my language, but he's a no-account sonofabitch.

Taking advantage of her, using her. Now he's lit out. What more do you want? I'll fix you some tea."

I let him fix. "Talk to me about Laura. Tell me what you're feeling."

"That I'd like to kill Pinkham."

"I wanted to do the same thing to the man who killed my dad."

He nodded, but after a couple of heartbeats he shook his head. "Beautiful girl, Laura. Her mother ruined her."

Sounds from the mudroom, then the door opened. Noah stiffened. A blond man stood in the doorway, arms crossed.

"Get out of my house," Noah hissed.

"I'm here to see Annie."

"I don't care if you're here to see Christ himself. Get. Or I'll toss this straight at your face." Noah shook the kettle, sending scalding droplets onto the table.

"Noah, don't," I said.

"You, too, woman. I don't need any fancy counselor. And neither does my daughter."

"Screw you." The man started to cross the room.

Noah's face mottled crimson as he wagged the kettle at him again.

I hooked my arm through the blond man's. "Not now," I whispered, dragging him from the kitchen.

A crash followed the slam of the mudroom door.

"Who are you to drag me out of Noah's?"

"A friend of Annie's."

The man expelled a long, slow breath. "Me, too."

"So I assumed. But not one of Noah's, surely."

Mischief lit his blue eyes. "Ayuh. Could say that."

"You might have given him a seizure."

He grinned. "Hold that thought."

"Annie's sedated, so she couldn't have talked with—"

"I could have sat with her."

"She wouldn't want to awaken to find her father hospitalized."

He pushed out his lower lip. "We're all pretty beat up about Laura. Not acting normal. Are you some relative or something?"

I explained. "And you are . . . ?"

"Sorry." He wiped his hands down his jeans, held one out. "Steve Sargent."

"About Annie," I said. "Why don't you wait a bit. Noah needs time."

"And Annie needs me."

"Maybe. But her family is her father now. For all his unfriendly ways, I doubt she'd thank you for hurting him."

"Hurt him? The old bastard just threw a scalding teakettle at us!" He jammed his hands into his jeans pockets. "You're right, though, about Annie not wanting to see him in the hospital."

"Once they find Pinkham, we'll know more about Laura's death," I said.

Sargent rolled his eyes. "Pinkham? See ya." He headed down the path toward a Sargent Construction pickup parked in front of the house.

"Hold on." I fast-walked after him. "You can't just walk away after that eye roll."

Lips pursed, he nodded. "Sure I can." He reached for the truck door.

"You obviously don't think Pinkham killed Laura."

"He's a sap. And a sandwich short of a picnic. They're all focused on him because no one wants to look at the guy who *really* hated Laura Beal."

"Who is . . . ?"

He leapt into his truck. "Try our esteemed former congressman, Drew Jones." He winked, then backed down the driveway. Just as he was about to pull away, he leaned out the window.

"And watch out for Noah. His bite's worse than his bark!"

Drew Jones. *Drew Jones.* An*drew* Jones. That was the name Hank had used for the guy I'd given a lift to on the Bangor Road, the one with the wolfhound, who'd seen the knife in Laura Beal's body. A town this small, they had to be the same man. If so, I'd bet Jones was the BMOC, the hotshot, the boy in the photo on Annie's desk. And a congressman, to boot. I hadn't known that. Yet there was another memory, one that persisted in playing hide-and-seek.

Why would Sargent accuse Drew Jones of killing Laura Beal?

"He hated Laura." Joy Sacco stood behind the postal counter, arms crossed. She was more than happy to fill me in.

"I didn't blame him, either," Joy said. "*I* voted for Drew."

"But . . ."

She leaned forward across the counter. "See, two years ago, Miss Left-Wing-Laura messed up his second bid for the U.S. Congress."

"Really."

"If someone did that to your career dreams, wouldn't you be pissed? I thought they hated each other. Funny thing, though. They were in here, maybe a month ago. It was like they were old buddies. So go figure."

I called Hank on my cell and was told he was somewhere "out to Hancock."

Right from the beginning, I'd tried to find out more about

Drew Jones. Hank had stonewalled me, but Steve Sargent had handed him to me on a platter. Jones was a man who inspired passions, I suspected.

Joy loaned me a local phone book, and I quickly found Drew Jones's address.

I crossed town and drove down to Lake Street. Leopold Lake lay on my left, along with snippets of land where grasses and maple and oak and wildflowers grew. On the right, most of the homes sat high on the hill. I watched for number 197.

What had transformed Congressman Jones into the wreck of the man I'd met? Booze? Drugs? Guilt? He could have been bipolar for years, without that illness being recognized. There could be a million causes.

Mini-whitecaps roiled across Leopold Lake, where Carmen's uncle had died landing his seaplane. At Noah's realty office, Carm hadn't recognized me, either. Funny how it made me sad. I mean, why should she?

I spotted Drew Jones's red mailbox—number 197—and turned into the driveway. I slammed on the brakes. That hide-and-seek memory. There it was.

I'm a ballerina, at least today—Halloween—and I'm feeling very grown up, 'cause I'll be eight in one and a half months. It's just starting to get dark, and I'm on Winsworth's big street, sitting on a chilly stoop outside Martinez Music Store. Daddy is inside doing something I don't understand.

I don't care, because I'm all prickly inside, so excited about the parade I'll be marching in down Main Street in a little while, with moms and dads and kids carrying lanterns and dressed like ghosts and Batmans and witches and . . . ballerinas!

It had been warm today, and so I don't need my coat. I jiggle my leg as I eat from the fat bag of candy I've gathered from Mrs. Corkle and Jimmy's dad and all the other houses we've visited.

I rest my chin on my knees, wishing Daddy would let me trick-or-treat after dark, like the big kids.

Except for an old man going into LaVerdier's Drugstore, no one's on the street, and then I see four boys, lots older than me, coming my way wearing scary masks. I grin. They look cool, especially the wolfman. They see me and point fingers and wave, and I straighten my ballerina skirt to make it look pretty.

They're coming nearer, and I get all embarrassed, and duck my head and watch their untied sneakers as they walk by me. And then a big, nail-chewed hand reaches down and, so fast, grabs my bag of candy. It's gone. All gone.

"Noooo!"

The boys are laughing, skipping down the street, Wolfman holding my precious sack of candy. The pushing starts behind my eyes, just before the tears come so hard I can't stop them.

Another shout. A big blond boy is racing across the street, his face mad, hair wild as he runs. He stops right in front of the bad boys and says something to Wolfman. But the bad boys are laughing, until the blond boy grabs Wolfman's shirt and shakes him, and then he holds out his other hand.

Wolfman gives the blond boy my candy bag!

Then the bad boys run off. But the blond boy walks slowly toward me. He gets bigger and bigger as he comes closer, until he blocks out the sun. I can't see his face.

He squats down right in front of me and I see he's very handsome, with bright teeth and comfy eyes. His smile gets big. So big it closes his eyes almost shut tight.

"Here you go, honey," he says, holding out the sack.

I'm afraid to take it. What if he's really mean, like the other boys, and when I lift my hand he'll snatch back my candy bag and laugh?

"Don't be scared," he says, setting the sack in my lap. He sits down next to me and I feel how warm his body is. "My name's Drew. I'm twelve. How old are you?"

"I'm Emma. I'm al . . . almost eight." I sniffle. I can't help it.

Drew takes out a red bandanna and brushes it over my face. His hands smell like a boy's hands, with dirt on them. A good smell.

"You're a very pretty ballerina," Drew says. "Please don't be sad."

My face gets hot, and I think I smile. I widen the neck of my candy sack. "Want some?"

"Sure. But just a few. And then I've gotta run."

I like the Reese's best, but Drew's favorite is the Snickers.

Drew stays with me on the stoop of the music store, and we're eating candy the whole time, until my dad comes out.

Oh, my. I could almost taste Drew Jones's kindness. I shook my head, trying to loosen the intensity of the memory. But I couldn't, and I felt an overwhelming affection for the man I'd met again on the Bangor Road in the blinding rain.

It proved how much I'd missed in the years I'd been gone from Winsworth. Unfortunately, I hadn't missed Laura Beal's murder. Sometimes my timing sucked.

I put the 4-Runner in gear and gunned it up the steep driveway.

When I landed at the top, all I could do was stare. What had Drew been thinking? Stupid question. He obviously hadn't been.

Chapter Nine
Small Talk

Drew's house was Tara North and worth no small change. It was also garish as hell. Marble steps led to massive pillars, which rose two stories high. All it needed was one of those hideous jockey statues. I walked over to the black Jeep Cherokee parked in the drive. It was covered in sap, and the tires were going flat.

Dandelions grew between the flagstones and the hedges needed trimming. I climbed marble steps and rang the bell. Chimes bonged sonorously. No one answered.

I walked along the verandah and peered into a front window.

Charred furniture lay stacked in a heap in what I supposed was the living room. Shaking off the shivers, I did a circuit of the house, going from window to window. Some rooms stood empty, others were piled with more broken furniture. The kitchen was a mass of smashed crockery and tossed pots. Oddly, the library sat in pristine splendor, its furniture, Persian rug, and oil paintings all in order.

It started to drizzle. I skedaddled back to the truck half expecting some skeleton to grab my shoulder.

Drew sure wasn't living here. I could pump Joy, but I'd gone to that well once already that day. I needed to find out where Drew lived, to talk to him, to understand the sweet boy who'd rescued my Halloween candy. I headed down the steep driveway. Of course. Carm would know. Carmen always knew everything.

I needed gas, and so headed east on Grand toward the Island. At the Route 1 fork light, I could have borne left toward Hancock and Sullivan, stayed straight down the Bar Harbor Road, or taken a U-turn, which was my plan.

It took forever for the light to turn green. I tapped my foot to the Beach Boys' "Surfin' USA." Straight ahead, on the asphalt island, was the Jones Jeep/Chrysler dealership, with its rows and rows of shiny new cars and trucks.

Of course. I chuckled. Crossways from the dealership was the emergency vet, the one I'd driven Drew Jones to last Sunday. All he'd had to do for a ride home was walk across the street to his family's car dealership.

The light turned, and I almost steered for the dealership. I could confront Drew about Laura Beal's death. Instead, I made a U-turn. Tackling Drew wasn't a wise move, not yet. I needed more context and to understand more about Laura.

A man named Toddy Brown owned the local gas station. The few times I'd been to the station, I'd made a point of chatting him up. He apparently knew nothing about my dad, but he was a cheerful fellow. He always wore impeccably clean overalls and a smile planted on his round, ruddy face.

Toddy gave me his usual hand wave, swiped my Master-Card, and began to fill the 4-Runner.

"Hey, Toddy."

"Hey, Tally." He whistled a few bars.

"Figaro?" I said.

"Yikes, you're bad. Puccini. *Madame Butterfly*. First act." Toddy whistled while the pump glugged. When he replaced the pump, his eyes slid to mine. He pulled on the bill of his cap. "Heard you been askin' Hank 'bout Laura Beal."

The Winsworth tom-toms were hard at work. "That's true. You knew her?"

"A course I knew her." Toddy swiped a hand across his face. "One a the worst things ever to happen 'round here."

"So what's your take? Was it Pinkham?"

"That pretty boy?" Toddy wagged his head. "Wasn't him, and I tell you why. That boy was Laura Beal's puppy. But it wasn't love, not on neither of their parts, least to hear Joy down the post office tell it."

"What else did Joy say?"

"She's got the right of it. Laura was having a good time, and so was Pinkham. But that's all it was. Even if you've got a bee up your butt, you don't kill a person unless you're all tangled up with them."

"So who could've killed Laura?"

Toddy shrugged. "That's the problem. Laura Beal was an expert at pissin' people off. But not enough so anyone'd take a knife to her."

"I heard she sabotaged Drew Jones's last campaign."

"Whoever told you that don't know diddly. Oh, she made a mess of things, all right, but . . ." Toddy's eyes slid to the car dealership. "Enough other things worked against Drew to . . . No, Laura stepped where she shouldn't, but I can't lay that at her door. Nope-suh."

Toddy slapped the roof of my truck and went to unhook me from the gas nozzle.

"So what made you gift me with this info, Toddy?"

He turned back to me, winked, and began whistling some aria as he walked away.

I sat at the Town Farm Restaurant's speckled Formica counter, which was smooth and shiny from wear, and watched the cook's head bob as she worked. I could see it wasn't Carmen. An overalled waitress, high school age and wearing a sassy grin, passed me with some fabulous-smelling blueberry pie. Impossible to resist, so I ordered a slice. When the waitress delivered it, I casually asked her about Carmen.

"In back," the girl said with a hitch of her head.

I looked around. The place was bustling, a success. Made me feel good for Carm. I poked with the fork at the thick blue syrup of the pie, licked the tines. Yum. I was stalling.

I left money on the counter and walked down the diner's narrow aisle toward the back. Movie and art posters hung on the walls, along with a bulletin board plastered with notices.

Two men and two women sat eating pie and playing cards at one of the booths. A man wearing a blue beret was bent over a protractor as his pencil glided across a piece of paper. His coffee looked cold. Town Farm must be a hangout of sorts. A bald guy, head bobbing over bacon and eggs, shoveled food into his mouth with an odd desperation. The guy looked beaten down, as if he hadn't had a meal for days.

Bald. Like Gary Pinkham. Was Pinkham clever enough to "hide" right in the heart of Winsworth?

I leaned toward the bulletin board, pretending to look at a

camp-for-sale notice. The bald man didn't look up but continued forking food as if he were starved.

"Excuse me," I said.

He held up a finger, scooped up the rest of his eggs, then his head bobbed up. "Help you?"

He wore a neatly cropped beard and black-rimmed half-glasses and had ten years on Pinkham. His eyes were . . .

"Sorry. I thought I recognized you."

He stared at me, then beyond me, down the narrow aisle. His fingers gripped tight to the table, his thin chest heaving, his face crumpled into a mask of fear.

"Sir?" I looked behind me, saw nothing.

"Carm!" he wailed at the top of his lungs. "Carm!"

"Coming!"

An overalled whirlwind materialized behind the counter. "Hush. Hush. It's okay." She ducked beneath the counter, stood before me, hands thrust onto ample hips, one Birkenstocked foot beating a tattoo.

"Someone scared him," I said, digging for calm. I refused to be intimidated by Carmen's snapping black eyes like in the old days.

"Who, if not you?" Carmen said, glowering.

"Somebody who came in, I'm guessing. My back was to the door."

Carmen ran a hand across the bald man's cheek. "It's okay now. Okay. I'll take care of this." She lifted his empty plate and slid it on the counter.

I folded my hands. "I'm not sure he'll be all right." I stared into rheumy eyes busy with fear.

She flapped a hand. "He'll be fine. He's a regular. He'll settle down."

Something *had* scared him. I wondered what. "Fine" was all I said. "I'd like to talk to you."

"Yeah?" Carmen peered over the rims of her granny glasses. "Do I know you?"

"We met at Beals Realty this morning."

"So we did. Come on. I don't have much time for small talk."

"Small talk" had nothing to do with what I had to say.

Chapter Ten
Auld Lang Syne

I stood in an office no bigger than a bathroom, surrounded by black cats, only one of which was the breathing kind—an immense tom with a spot of white on its chin who sprawled on Carmen's computer keyboard. The other cats were made of ceramic and wood and fabric and covered the desk and walls.

The smells and hustle-bustle of the restaurant permeated the room. Carmen shut the door, then pointed to a cat-themed armchair seriously in need of springs. I sat.

"The man out front who became so distressed," I said. "I thought he might be Gary Pinkham."

"Not hardly," Carm said.

"So what scared him?"

A faint smile twitched her lips. "We never know with Herbie. So what's your poison? Coffee, pop, tea, water?"

"Diet Coke?"

"Sure. I feel others should be free to kill themselves with that crap."

"This is all yours?"

Carmen's slow, infectious smile grew from her eyes and traveled downward to her lips. "With a little help from my friends." Carmen reached into a small refrigerator. She handed me a Diet Coke and opened a Winsworth Chai with a Town Farm label for herself.

A framed newspaper hung on the rear wall: "Restaurant Beats Selectmen," "Cavasos Opens Doors Tomorrow."

Carmen must be proud. "When did you open Town Farm?"

"Three years ago."

"That recently, huh."

As she sipped from the bottle—her eyes curious, studying me—I tried to reconcile my childhood best friend Carmen with the woman sitting behind the desk. We'd once made quite a pair.

As kids, my curly mouse-colored hair had contrasted with Carmen's poker-straight Titian red. My eyes were a leafy green, hers an impenetrable sable. Her body had curves long before mine even thought about it. Mine *still* didn't have all that many, whereas Carmen's—much like her personality— were overly round and full of zest. Her Latino looks had come into focus with time. She had great beauty.

Had we met in Mongolia after all this time, I would have known Carmen.

So why wasn't there a hint of recognition in her eyes?

I was dying to tell her I was Emma. But would her eyes then turn dry-ice cold as Mrs. Lakeland's had? Would she pulse with hate? Turn away from me?

Or was she playing some game and knew exactly who I was?

Either way, I wasn't about to open up like some interviewee in a Barbara Walters special. I reached across the desk and shook Carmen's outstretched hand. "I'd like to help Annie and Noah Beal."

"You're from Boston," she said. "Winsworth's different."

"Not in that way. Murder's murder. By the way, Noah threw me out of the house."

"No surprise there, the old *pedo*. He's a stiff-spined *cabrón*. He was far crazier about Laura than Annie. Believe me, it wasn't for Annie's sake that he didn't tell her about her sister. Probably . . . God knows why."

"Tell me about Laura."

"She was dynamite in a lot of ways. If she touched something, it became a success. Gorgeous. A way with men, did she ever. She always got what she asked for, whether it was a new car, a radio station, or even Mr. Standoffish himself, Hank Cunningham."

"The sheriff?"

"Ayuh." Carmen shook her head. "But this last time, it looks like she asked for the wrong thing. God knows what it was."

"Some people think Gary Pinkham might've killed her."

Carmen snorted.

"Others have accused Drew Jones."

Carmen smiled. "Steve Sargent, right? He's a good man, but he's got a bug up his ass because of Annie."

"How did you know it was Sargent?"

"Nobody else would say such a dumb thing about Drew."

"I went to his house. Jones's."

She smirked. "Snooping."

I shrugged. "I wanted to talk to him."

"I thought you were a therapist, not a busybody." Carmen always relished pressing buttons.

"Finding Laura's killer would help heal Annie Beal's pain," I said. "I thought Mr. Jones might have some insight."

"Well, Drew didn't murder Laura, I assure you."

"So you know him well."

"He helped me get this restaurant past some of our good-ol'-boy selectmen. One of our selectmen planned to buy this piece of property for a parking lot."

Carmen owed a debt to Drew, something the girl I'd once known would take very seriously. "His house . . . It appears abandoned."

"Problems," she said. "They're a dime a dozen. You must have a few, escaping up here out to the old Brady place."

"I haven't been—"

"Sure you have. Grapevine's been yakking for the past week. About you and that killer down to Boston. I suspect you keep to yourself."

"Just like plenty of Mainers."

"But you're not one of us, are you?"

"Neither are you, Madame Cornhusker!"

Carmen jerked and glared.

"It doesn't feel so hot, does it, Ms. Cavasos? Having your guts opened up."

Her bosom swelled, then deflated as she barked out a laugh. "No doubt about it, you're as sharp as some are saying."

Just like the old days, I couldn't stop my smile. "I guess that's a compliment."

"How'd you know I was born in Nebraska?" she asked.

"I'm almost as good at research as I am at counseling. So if it wasn't Pinkham or Jones, who do you think killed Laura Beal in such a savage manner?"

"A stranger."

"Doesn't that make you afraid?"

Carmen smirked. "Hell no. It comforts me. I can't stand

thinking somebody in this town did those awful things to Laura."

The box on Carmen's desk squawked. "What's up?"

"The Farmer's Market guy's here."

"In a sec." Carmen pushed herself to her feet.

I smiled. I wanted to reach out and touch Carmen's hand again. But I didn't. "Thanks for the time. I know you're busy. I'd still like to see Drew Jones."

Carmen's warm eyes faded to opaque. "I'll tell him you're looking for him."

"What's the big deal? I just want to ask him some questions."

"Uh-huh. Why not turn your talents to some good use by looking up Joy Sacco."

"You mean the gal who works in the post office?"

"Uh-huh. She's hurting. First off, Gary Pinkham is her stepson-in-law, though he's only got two years on her. Gary was married to Tish, Will Sacco's daughter, until Tish died, oh, about three, four years ago. Will is Joy's husband."

Talk about convoluted. "Tish died how?"

"AIDS."

"Sad," I said. "You said first off. Is there a second off?"

"Joy and Laura Beal were like sisters."

In my conversations with Joy Sacco after Laura Beal's death, she'd never hinted at their close friendship. I was curious to know why. On my way over to the post office, I detoured down a side street. From the phone book, I knew Carmen's mom no longer ran the hardware store, but I hadn't seen it with my own eyes. The building once occupied by Mrs. Cavasos's hardware store now housed a bead shop and a florist. A terrible sadness blanketed me. I wanted to yank time, make everything right.

I'd written Mrs. Lakeland about the source of her anger, but had yet to hear back. She might still be in England. I should just say something to Carmen. But what I could bear with Mrs. Lakeland, I couldn't handle with Carmen. The thought of seeing hatred on Carm's face sickened me.

Enough.

I drove back to Main toward the new post office and Joy Sacco.

Joy stood behind the counter chatting with a customer. I got in line.

Postal workers often know everyone and everything, particularly in small towns. My postmistress friend Pat surely does.

A little over a week ago, when I first walked into Winsworth's post office to retrieve my forwarded mail, I figured the petite brunette might have some knowledge of my dad. But although Joy had never heard of John Blake, she did joke about our shared Medusa-like hair.

Today, Joy had leashed her wild hair into a scrunchie and her uniform was a bit disheveled. Her usually animated face had taken on a serious cast. Instead of a smile, I got a one-fingered wave.

In her late twenties, Joy must have been in the same grade in school as Laura. They'd most likely grown up together. Along with family, dear friends suffered badly when a loved one was murdered. All too often, they were squeezed out of the counseling loop.

The teenaged boy juggling a load of packages finished up, and I moved to the counter.

"I'd like a sheet of the breast cancer stamps, Joy."

"Sure, Tally. How's it going?"

"Swell. You?"

"Great." She winked, grinned. She rubbed a finger across the flowers on her silver belt buckle. "Like it?"

"I do."

She nodded. "Art nouveau. Here are your stamps."

No one was behind me in line. "You have the time to talk for a sec?"

"Time . . ." She sighed. "It gets away from us, doesn't it?"

"It does. You're hurting, aren't you."

Joy's smile wobbled. "Oh. Um, you know, don't you."

"About you and Laura? Yes. And I'm very sorry."

"Me, too."

"I think I mentioned I counsel people for a living. If I can help . . ."

"Thanks, but I'd feel funny talking to you about it. You didn't even know Laura."

"That's true. But we still could talk."

She shook her head. "Naw. I'm okay. Y'know, you're the first to ask me about Laura. Everybody knew we were close, but no one's said diddly."

"And Gary? He's your stepson, right? I'd heard he was dating her. He must be terribly upset."

She shrugged. "Yeah, I guess. I haven't seen him. But you know what they're saying? That he killed her."

"Was he capable of that, do you think?"

She cut her eyes to the counter. "I don't want to say. In a way, it was my fault."

A song I heard time and again from the grieving. "How so?"

"Well, Will and I were supposed to meet Gary and Laura at the Giddyup." She sighed. "Our son, Scooter, had an ear infection and we were out of medicine, and I didn't want a sitter, even though Will said it wasn't a big deal, and so . . ." She rubbed her forehead, back and forth hard. "So after

Will came back from getting Scooter's medicine, we stayed home. Don't you see? I blew off my best friend, and she . . ."

"And if you had met them, you believe she'd be alive."

She laced her fingers together until the knuckles whitened. "It would've been different for Laura. I *know* it would've."

I reached for her hands. "What you're feeling, Joy, is normal. First of all, I'm betting Scooter needed you that night. Second, whoever killed Laura planned it all out. I doubt it would have made a difference. I really do."

She punched her chin forward. "But it might've."

"Joy, try to . . ."

Someone queued up behind me. I handed Joy my card. "Look, if you'd like to talk some more, call me. My cell's on it. Nothing formal, understand?"

She fought off the tears pooling in her blue eyes, squared her shoulders, and pushed the card back toward me. "Thanks, Tally, but I've got it under control."

As I moved from the counter, my heart felt the familiar twinge of knowing I could help stanch the pain and not being allowed to do so.

I slid behind the wheel and found myself looking at a neon green Post-it note flapping on the windshield. I got out and pulled it off.

Missing you. UL. Missing me? UL?

I racked my brain but couldn't come up with any UL, missing me or not.

All of the other parked cars had Post-its, too.

I checked them out. The other Post-its were unsigned and said things like "Wash me!" or "Save the Whales!"

Mine was personal. Maybe my Mr. Breathless from Boston?

I didn't need any more damned weirdness in my life.

I drove off totally pissed. And curious. *UL?* Life in Winsworth was definitely strange.

I pressed the brakes just after I crossed the Winsworth River bridge and pulled into the dooryard of the old Victorian that housed a karate studio.

Ever since giving a lift to Drew Jones and his dog, I'd shunted aside the real reason for my return to Winsworth: my dad.

Dad had felt connected here. He'd always talk about Winsworth, said how he wanted to rest in the only place he'd ever called home. And so I'd buried him here.

Damn, but even after twenty years, I missed him.

I headed back the way I'd come, bound for the Winsworth cemetery.

I parked on a narrow dirt road beside the small cemetery. A stone wall laid without mortar two centuries earlier outlined its boundaries. Headstones marched up the steeply rolling slope, where tufts of browned-out grass mixed with green lawn. I walked toward the stone-arched entrance where two ancient lilac bushes stood sentinel. The air was warm, fragrant with their blossoms. I raked a hand through my hair. My scalp was moist with sweat.

I slipped on my sunglasses and walked beneath the cemetery's stone arch.

I wound between diminutive markers and grand monuments, cherubs and angels, tilted headstones and soldier-straight ones. It seemed as if here was where all of Winsworth had come to rest.

Through my work, I'd been to countless graveyards over

the years. This one . . . It made me breathe with a little catch in my throat.

I nodded to Arnie Thornton, a kid I'd gone to grammar school with. There was Mrs. Ostermeyer, my classmate's mom. And over there was Martha Kelton, the elderly lady I'd read to once a week. How could they be here when they lived so vividly in my memory?

Suddenly, I was desperate for my dad.

I raced across rows, breathing hard, until I came to a spot high up on the hill, hunkered close to a corner of the wall and shaded by a twisted old red maple.

I sat beside the brass marker and ran my fingers over his name—John Blake.

Funny what we think of. Right after we'd met, Veda had said I was "such a Tally," whatever that meant. She never explained, but the nickname stuck. So I was Tally Blake, until I married and became Tally Whyte.

I found it hard even to remember that girl, that Emma Blake.

I hooked my arms around my bent knees. The sky was so blue it hurt. I plucked a dandelion blossom and twirled the stem beneath my fingers until the flower blurred into . . .

Red and orange flames lick the black night, blotting out the stars. My nightie tangles about my legs as Daddy drags me from the house, through our field out back, then into the woods, Daddy pulling me faster and faster as he lugs that silly suitcase. I trip going down the steep slope to the river, but by then Daddy is running funny, like he has a stitch in his side, so he can't even help me up. When we make it to the dock, he lifts me into our tied-up motorboat, then climbs in himself, landing hard and coughing. Through the screen of trees, I see the flames shooting from our house high on the hill.

Daddy curses as he pulls the motor's cord once, twice, three times. Finally, it sputters to life, and with a fat moon bobbing just above the trees lining the shore, we putt down the empty river toward the sea.

"We made it, Emma," he says. "Everything will be fine now."

"But you're hurt." The right side of his shirt is black and he puts his hand to it.

He scowls as he steers our small boat. "Not so bad."

"But . . . What's going on, Daddy?"

He presses a finger to my lips. "Listen. I, uh . . . Things weren't going so well, sweetie."

"But what about all the houses you were building? You said Trenton-by-the-Sea would be the greatest thing in the world."

"Well, it was going to be," he snaps back. He sighs. "And now the fire. We've lost the house, baby. I'd remortgaged it and there was no insurance except the bank's and, and . . . Oh, never mind. But we're starting over, Emma. Fresh. Just like newborns."

I start to cry. "I don't understand."

"Someday you will."

The night wind snakes inside my gown and I shiver. Daddy reaches behind him and puts his old peacoat over my shoulders.

I can't stop crying. "But, Daddy, I don't want to leave."

"You'll see. This'll work out just fine."

Moonlight shines off the tears coming from Daddy's eyes.

We'd ended up in Boston, in a high-rise beside a Laundromat named Crystal's Duds 'n Suds. On another night, that one rainy with a September squall, we drove in Daddy's clunker to East Lexington, a blue-collar neighborhood long gone from that now-upscale town.

In all that time, all the craziness of Daddy's grand schemes and bizarre getaways, all the making of friends and parting from them, all the plunging into new schools and leaving them, I never minded it much. Daddy's smile and funny jokes and tall tales turned everything into an adventure.

True, his adventures had begun to seriously sag, almost as badly as the floor of our apartment. By then I realized my bighearted dad was a dreamer whose grandiose plans inevitably collapsed like a house of toothpicks under the weight of reality.

I loved him anyway, so finding him barely breathing on our front stoop, stabbed repeatedly by a petty thief who probably got no more than twenty bucks and Daddy's lucky money clip, put me into a dark place.

Dr. Veda Barrow had rescued me. She comforted me and counseled me and held me when my dam of grief finally broke. She and her sister Bertha became the mother and father I no longer possessed.

She parented me and introduced me to the counseling business. But I was the one who chose to "minor" in homicide counseling.

The fire . . . I'd forgotten much about it. Now, for the first time in forever, I actually *saw* the memory of it. At least a part of it. I shook, angered and saddened.

It made sense that the fire and Mrs. Lakeland's hatred were connected. But how? Was that the connecting thread? I had to know.

Chapter Eleven
The Simple Life

I was about to step from the cooling shade of the maple into the blazing sun when I spotted a man at the graveyard entrance. At least, I thought it was a man. The day was hot for Winsworth in June—in the eighties—yet he wore a long, dark duster, the kind Australian cowboys used when herding sheep. His hand was raised to the bill of his blue baseball cap as he glided beneath the arch. I was fascinated.

The brush of something familiar. I searched for people I'd known as a child, but failed to find the man in the lineup. He made me faintly apprehensive.

The man serpentined up and down the rows of graves, every so often swiveling his head to the right, then to the left. Checking for something. Or someone.

The guy was on a mission. With each step, my nerves jangled a bit more. I chewed my lip.

I slid deeper beneath the maple's sheltering branches and scooched down, watching. If he was unwell, I sensed he'd either bolt or get aggressive. He methodically worked his way from the right side of the cemetery to the left, closer and closer to where I crouched. Occasionally, he'd sniff the air, like one of the Night Riders from *Lord of the Rings*. Disturbing.

My breathing was shallow. I consciously deepened it.

I could see him better now. He wasn't big—maybe five-seven—and his extremely long neck and small head contributed to his unnatural appearance. The flapping coat sure didn't help, either.

He was almost below me, at the bottom of the hill, and ascending the last row of headstones toward me. As he climbed, he bent at the waist to examine each headstone, then he moved on. He grew near. My breathing quickened. My anxiety increased. Yet experience had taught me that it was the ones who *didn't* make me anxious who were most dangerous.

Cemetery Man ducked out of sight.

Shit. I rubbed my goosebumped arms. Absurd. Yet . . .

I inched forward, keeping to the shade, and peered over the small rise. There he was, hunkered beside a headstone. He was talking emphatically, spittle spraying from his mouth, a fist punching the air. Like Drew Jones.

But, no, this guy was too thin, too short, and too strange-looking to be Jones.

I'd swear he was speaking to an old enemy. Settling old scores, maybe? He could be delusional. Hearing voices? Perhaps.

I was acting foolish, hiding beneath the tree. I should talk to him. Maybe I could help. I started to stride down the hill when a boom shook the air. Cemetery Man lay sprawled on the ground. Yet it was just the backfire of a car.

Cemetery Man lay quivering in fear.

I started to trot toward him. A chattering couple holding

red carnations entered the cemetery. Cemetery Man's head slithered to follow their progress. Not his body, but just his head. Geesh, he was creepy.

As the couple walked across the graveyard, Cemetery Man leapt up, sped down the hill and over the wall. He ran to a beige sedan and climbed inside.

I shaded my eyes, waiting for him to peel out. Instead, he let the car idle for a minute—I swear his eyes were on me—then drove off steady and slow.

I walked to the headstone with whom Cemetery Man had been conversing.

The stone read "Jeremiah Blake, Born in Joy, 1905, Died in Sorrow, 1942." My grandfather? I didn't think so. I'd never heard of the guy.

J. Blake. Like my dad.

A breeze ruffled the downy hairs on the back of my neck and raised a chill up my spine.

Still prickly with fear, I turned my thoughts away from my dad and back to Laura's murder. I wondered if there was any new information or if forensics had produced anything worthwhile. Hank should know, so I drove to the courthouse and headed for his office.

"Hold on theyah," said the dispatcher. "You can't . . ."

"Sheriff said it was cool." I flashed my MGAP credentials and smiled as I swung open Hank's door. "Hank?"

The office was neat, tidy, and stuffed with books and a collection of Eeyores. A framed roach-clip display hung on the wall and a well-worn *The Tao of Pooh* lay on the desk.

Eeyore himself sat slumped in his chair, eyes closed. Face gray and haggard. Baggy pouched eyes. A mean bruise on his forehead. He looked lousy, all played out. His fingers jutted from the dirty cast covering his left hand. I suspected Percocet was in the meds bottle on his desk.

"What the *hell* are you doing?" Hank barked.

"Visiting. That stuff's supposed to make you mellow."

"I'm mellow enough," he said, not bothering to open his eyes.

"How did you know it was me?"

"Smelled ya," he said. "Whaddya need?"

I sat in the chair opposite the desk. "I thought you might have something new on Laura's murder."

He cranked open a bloodshot eye. "Not much. The lab's all over the cigarette butts. The state boys think they've cornered Pinkham at his camp near Baxter State Park. Some bright guy, our Gary, hiding out at his own place." His lids drooped shut and he sighed.

I crept out of the chair and eased the door open, trying not to wake him.

"Hold on," he said. "Wanna get some pizza."

"Pizza?"

"You know, that *I*-talian stuff with red sauce on it."

"Cut the hick Maine act, Sheriff."

"Got me figured out, have you?"

"No way."

"So, you want to grab some pizza or not?"

It sounded sort of nice, but . . . "Sorry, no. I've got to get home."

Back home, Penny's jubilant greeting made up for the emptiness I felt in refusing Hank's invitation. I hadn't accepted because . . . Silly thing, really, not to accept. But I wasn't sure I was up for a romance, even a short-term one.

I ruffled Penny's coat and relished the lap of her tongue on my face. I felt loved.

I took her for a quick "business" walk. A brisk wind came from the east, off the water, ruffling her fur and spicing the air. Back inside, I opened Laura's folder and began entering data on my Mac.

Noah and Annie, Carmen, Hank, Joy, Gary Pinkham, Steve Sargent, Drew . . . I underlined Drew's name. Tough to mesh the memory of the kind boy from Halloween with the disturbed man I'd met the night Laura Beal had died.

I'd felt this before—a tornado of small events and moments that swirled around a homicide. Murder could be simple, impetuous, fueled by anger or lust. But another kind involved layers and layers of emotions that led up to deliberate and hideous butchery.

The pulse of Laura Beal's homicide was most assuredly the latter.

I took a break, leaning back in my chair, soaking up the calm. A heartbeat, then another, then I again saw the fire, my father's desperate desire to flee Winsworth. Tendrils of icy fog inside my mind, squeezing tight, squeezing out more, worse memories.

I opened my eyes, shook my head, banishing memory. I dialed Veda. She was an expert at bringing me back to today's reality.

I got her machine and left a message.

The night was cool and clear and comforting. Moonlight washed the surface of the cove. A soft westerly breeze and the moon lured me outside. I tied on my running shoes, then walked onto the porch with Penny for an evening run. That would de-cobweb my head.

Penny bulleted toward my truck parked in the dooryard.

"What the hell . . . ! Penny!" Some rabbit, maybe. I trotted over. Round and round and round the truck she went. Penny was circling as if . . . Oh, no. Penny smelled dead, human dead. "Shit."

I cautiously opened the driver-side door, smelled nothing. Penny whined, then urinated beside the truck. She froze.

"Double shit." I lifted the seats, looked under them. This was ridiculous.

"Where, Pens?"

She leapt onto the driver's seat, sat, and pawed the glove box door.

Oh, my. I'd left today's mail in the glove box.

Penny's legendary status as a former Canine Corps dog had been proven time and time again. I hoped this time she was wrong. I gingerly opened the glove box. All flat letters . . . and one slightly puffy envelope that I was suddenly very reluctant to open.

Had to do it.

I retrieved a pair of kitchen tongs and a new manila envelope from the house. I tonged all the mail into the envelope, then brought the pile inside, Penny glued to my side, whining.

I distributed the pile on clean, unread newspaper.

Should I call Hank or just open the thing? I reached for the phone, then went for the scissors instead. I would open the lumpy package first, assuming it was the culprit in setting off Penny. After cutting, I pried apart the yellow envelope. Inside was some sports wrap, the kind that athletes use to cool sprains and such. I unrolled it.

"Oh, geesh."

The wrap encased a finger. Not just any finger, but a small child's forefinger.

Dear God. What sicko . . . "I got it, Pens . . ." I searched for the Czech words. "*Nech to*," I said, which means "leave it." "*Nech to!*" I repeated. She finally relaxed. "*Hodny*, Penny. *Hodny*. Good girl!"

I sighed. A child's finger. I worked in the ME's office for enough years to know the finger was an old one—dried and aged and . . . from whom? From where? And why? What kind of horrid message was this? Or was it a gift? Whoooeee.

Suddenly, I was back with the Harvester, fighting, bleeding, sliding in that chamber of horrors, seeing an arm, a leg, eyeballs, a torso. . . . I sat down, hard.

The Harvester, fodder for the tabloids, had taken body parts. And here was a child's finger. The sender had studied me. Had to have. Knew about my life in Boston. Knew . . .

I was being sent a message, a nasty one.

I rewrapped the child's delicate digit in the original covering, carefully placed the entire package in a clean Tupperware, then put it in the fridge. I tried not to be grossed out. A finger was sitting next to my leftover egg salad sandwich. Cripes. I tossed the sandwich.

I called Hank and ended up leaving a voice mail.

Maybe I should contact the Winsworth police, as opposed to Hank at the sheriff's office. But I trusted Hank. I'd wait.

I washed up, then slid into bed. I felt better, more normal, if that was the right word. That "gift" sure was a capper to my day. No note. No warning. Just a grim "present." I tried to crawl inside the head of the person who'd sent it. If the finger wasn't a reflection of my past, intended to frighten me, then what was it? A plea. A warning. A cry for help. Any of the above. Or all. Thank heavens the finger wasn't fresh. At least I didn't have *that* to contend with.

THE DEAD STONE

I tossed and turned for an hour. What was I doing here in Winsworth?

Being back in Maine was surreal, especially since I'd gotten involved in a homicide. I found I actually was liking the country—its silence, its earthiness, its intimacy. But Laura's murder, tied so to my childhood memories, was beginning to haunt me. I was obsessing on it. I should be missing MGAP more. Gert, Veda, Kranak. I missed them, yes. But felt an unaccustomed rightness in where I was. Even more odd, I had a crush on a bristly sheriff with a Buddha belly, all the while trying to unravel the accusations against my dad, and yet again probing a horrific death.

I'd find all that funny if it weren't so appalling.

Obviously, the simple life was eluding me.

Chapter Twelve
Single Digits

Friday morning, the phone awakened me at the unheavenly hour of six.

"Yeah?" I croaked into the receiver.

"What the hell's going on there?" Hank said.

"Damned if I know." I pushed up on my elbow, the better to pretend I was awake. I told him about the finger, how Penny had found it, and what I'd done with it.

"I gotta make a call. I'll get back to you." Slam.

"Okay," I said to no one in particular. Penny tilted her head, always the avid listener. She was grinning, tongue lolling from her mouth, like, *Gee, cool, Mom's up at six!*

I was not "up," but figured I might as well be. I fed The Madame and let her out, then put on some much-needed java.

My plan for the day had been to spend some time with Annie Beal, helping her with Laura's death. Annie was hurting. I knew she was. I also knew that dragon of a dad was making life even harder for her.

But conversation with Annie would have to wait until I heard back from Hank, aka Mr. Terse.

I shrugged into some sweats and took the coffee and my laptop out onto the porch. Penny was romping around in the frigid surf. "Crazy dog!"

She'd forgotten all about that finger. I could not. The thought of a body part in my fridge hit way too close to home for comfort. I shivered.

Just then, Penny grinned up at me. Then her beautiful black and tan body loped down the beach.

While I waited for Hank's call, I hopped onto the Web. I Googled Laura Beal, then went to Winsworth's site. Ditto for the *Winsworth Journal*'s. I gathered pages of info and took my stack of printouts and coffee onto the deck. A sharp wind snapped off the water, and I was glad I'd worn my sweats. Penny didn't mind the chill in the least. As I read, I'd toss her rope throw, she'd retrieve it, and then we'd repeat the game. Per usual, my arm got tired way before Penny's enthusiasm waned.

According to the *Journal*, Gary Pinkham had been arrested, then released after a fight at the Oyster House bar. Several small pieces detailed Annie's work with the Winsworth Coast Memorial Hospital Auxiliary. Noah's name appeared often, in conjunction with either real-estate matters or the Winsworth Rotary. No surprise that most mentions of Steve Sargent dealt with his construction firm, although he was in the Rotary, too, as was Hank, who also showed up in articles on the Sheriff's Department.

Joy had exhibited some art at a Hand Auditorium show. Carmen's continuing hassles with the town over her restaurant were interesting, but they offered no surprises.

I found a gem about Laura, one that gave me a snapshot of the public Laura Beal. She had engaged in a roller-coaster ride with her radio station. The town had almost shut her down when she'd brought Howard Stern's New York show aboard. Apparently, even Laura's dogged will shriveled under Winsworth's virulent reaction to Stern's obscenities, and she jettisoned him two months later. Ironically, the station's numbers were way up for the period.

Drew Jones starred in numerous articles about the car dealership and his last run for Congress.

Penny nudged me, and I tossed the rope. With pleasure, I watched her three-legged dash down to the beach. She loved the country. Maybe I was starting to love it, too.

Well, lookee-here. Drew's campaign had been cruising along until Laura put up some speed bumps about what she called Drew's "antihuman" policies, whatever those were. Her accusations were always vague and vitriolic. But the surprise came in an article from last October. I'd assumed Drew had lost the race because of Laura's interference. He hadn't. In fact, he was way ahead in the polls.

At the crescendo of her "Don't go with Jones" campaign, Drew had resigned from the race. Follow-up articles pointed fingers at Laura, and a scathing *Journal* editorial roasted her over the coals. Yet the only real explanation for Drew's leaving the race quoted him as saying, "I find I need to move in new directions."

Hello? Maybe I'd missed something, but nothing in the *Journal* indicated Drew running anything but a fierce and committed race. So how come he quit?

Maybe his estrangement from his wife. I laid down one article and dug out the other on his marriage. He was married to someone named Leticia Lee. She owned a shop in town named Perceptions. The name was familiar. Oh, sure. Patsy Lee. She'd been a year ahead of me in school.

Funny, I just couldn't see it. I'd known her from the seventh-grade twirling team. Dear God, what a memory. She was quiet, mousy even. What had vibrant Drew seen in her that he didn't see in Annie?

From the photo on Annie's desk, he still meant a great deal to her.

If I gave Patsy a visit, maybe she could help me locate Drew, since nobody else seemed to be volunteering.

The phone bleeped, and I raced inside to pick it up.

"Ach, *liebchen*, how are you?"

"Veda! Oh, I'm swell. I miss you."

"I miss you, too. Very much. And you are . . . ?"

I deliberated for a split second. "Fine. I'm just fine. Where are you?"

"On my way to a conference in Albuquerque. Feel like a break from Maine?"

"No. I'm learning things."

"Don't learn too much, eh? We need you back home. Ah, my plane. Love you."

"Love you, too. So much."

I was smiling as I hung up. Yes, I needed to be back home, as Veda said.

Home. Boston. Except I was starting to feel almost at home in Winsworth, and it was unnerving.

I stacked up the pages I'd printed out from the Web. One slipped to the floor, and I bent to pick it up. Huh. The *Journal*'s social page. Hank and Laura had been an item for more than a year. Here was a snippet on their attending a big "do" with Noel Paul Stookey playing guitar.

Hank's vibes said he'd cared for Laura, but I hadn't realized the depth of their involvement. It sure read like a romance to me. I didn't like that much. Not at all. Nor did I like the fact that he hadn't told me about it.

Well, dammit if I was waiting around for him.

The day remained cool. I packed up the Tupperwared finger in a Styrofoam container filled with ice, which I placed in my truck. No fun driving around with a child's amputated digit, so I'd just try and not think about it.

"Penny, where the hell are you?!"

She bounded out of the water, the rope throw between her teeth. Naturally, she was grinning. I loaded my soaking dog into the truck, and we were off.

I drove to town at a record pace, windows open, Penny's fur ruffling in the breeze. God, maybe that would clear out my cobwebbed brain. Why couldn't I find Drew Jones? Who had killed Laura Beal? Why send me a finger? Who the hell knew? I could do at least one thing.

I stopped by the sheriff's office and handed the dispatcher the cooler.

"Tell Hank this is from me, okay? It's important evidence"—*of something*, I thought to myself. "If he needs me, have him call my cell." I swooped out, like some furious Valkyrie, annoyed for no logical reason that Hank Cunningham had once had the hots for Laura Beal.

As I cruised down Beals Avenue, I spotted Noah's Jeep hunkered down in his driveway. Crap. Was he never going to leave Annie alone? The last thing Annie needed was a confrontation between me and Noah. I worried for Annie. I wondered if she was still locked away in her mind, a prisoner of fear and pain.

No call from Hank, so I drove to Patsy Lee's store. I

pulled into the Katahdin Mountain Mall, an upscale strip mall just down the street from Piper's and diagonally across from Beals Realty.

The "mall" was housed in a converted nineteenth-century warehouse, a leftover from Winsworth's glory shipbuilding days, the cavernous Katahdin Mountain Sports, Ltd., a gourmet food shop, and Perceptions. The shop window revealed artistic clothing, jewelry, and ceramics. Gorgeous stuff. And pricy.

As I reached for the door, an elderly man with spaniel eyes and a cane shoved open the door and plowed into me. We exchanged "excuse me"s as I stepped onto the foot-deep carpet, the depth of which saved my life.

Okay, I exaggerate. But the stiletto shoe moving at Mach speed in my direction only grazed my cheek instead of spiking me in the face.

"Shit," I said.

"Oh, my word!" said the woman holding aloft the stiletto's mate. The blonde lowered her arm. "I am so sorry."

Had to be Patsy Lee, although she sounded much like Scarlett O'Hara. Her porcelain complexion was flushed, her platinum French twist askew, her eyes darkened from runny mascara. True, her lavender cashmere dress hung beautifully, but it's tough to mess up good cashmere.

No more the mouse, Patsy Lee was one gorgeous woman.

"I assume this is yours, Ms. Jones." I held up her thrown shoe, figuring it couldn't hurt to have my own weapon.

"Oh. Oh. Oh, my word." Patsy held out her hand to embrace mine, except that was the hand holding the pointy-toed stiletto. "I am so very, very sorry. And it's Lee, not Jones. I'm Patsy to my friends."

"Those bad sales can be a bitch." I gingerly handed her the shoe.

She slipped on the shoes, dabbed at her eyes, and re-arranged her coif, managing to look perfectly put together, a task I consistently failed at.

"Bad sale?" she said. "Hardly. A bad in-law, is what!"

So Patsy's wrath had been directed at the man with spaniel eyes at the door—Drew's father, the former governor of Maine, and the owner of Jones Jeep/Chrysler. Obviously, everything wasn't copacetic in the Jones family.

Patsy started to laugh. "I must've looked like a lunatic. I apologize. Daniel and I get hot with each other from time to time. He's really a sweet old man. Come on. Let me show you around the shop."

"Not necessary. I'm happy to look around myself."

Pasty hooked her arm though mine. "Oh, come on, Ms. . . ."

"Call me Tally."

"Well, then, come on, Tally. I'll give you the tour, plus a twenty percent discount for the tossed shoe."

Who can resist a discount?

A half hour later, I was about to be the proud owner of a lime sueded-silk blouse and a black leather miniskirt. It was an outfit to die for, even though it nearly equaled a car payment *after* the discount.

I sipped the iced cappuccino Patsy gave me while she ran my MasterCard through the machine.

"Your store is terrific, Patsy."

"Didn't I tell you?" she said, smiling. Her smile widened when my MasterCard went through.

My cell phone bleeped. I walked to the front of the store and answered it.

"Thanks for giving me the finger, Ms. Whyte."

"Pardon." Could this be the guy who . . . It was Hank,

putting on some dumb accent. "Oh, you are one funny man. Not! Where the hell are you and why didn't you call?"

"Planned to. I'm at the hospital. In the lab."

"I'm on my way."

"Thought you would be. Ask for Dr. Cambal-Hayward."

He disconnected, and I turned to see Patsy peering over my shoulder, having silently inched forward.

"As you may have heard, I've got to go."

She smiled and batted her eyelashes. What the hell was *that*? It was now or never. "Look, Ms. Lee, Patsy, my reason for coming here today was twofold. The shopping, of course, but I'm also looking for your husband."

Patsy's smile tightened. "Really?" she said in a controlled whisper.

Geesh. She thought I was hot for Drew Jones. "His dog was hurt, and I was hoping to see how she was doing."

Patsy laughed, then wiggled her perfectly waxed eyebrows. "I thought it was for *other* reasons. Peanut's fine, although she's limping around in that awful cast. Poor baby, not that I'd ever have the animal in *my* house, you understand, but I do care for her. So you're the woman who gave Drew the ride in the rain. I was also coming in from Bangor that night, and when I saw Drew's van, I wondered who picked them up."

"Guilty as charged. So you were on the road that night, too."

"We went to a movie in Bangor."

We? "I was hoping to visit Drew and Peanut."

"Keep hoping, my dear." She smoothed her French twist. "Drew doesn't want visitors. He doesn't even want *me*."

Hard to comprehend. Not. "He left something in my truck. I'd like to return it."

She held out a hand. "I'd be happy to."

"It's no bother, Patsy. I'd prefer to do it myself. I tried at the house in town."

"That shambles. Drew never liked it anyway." She bent over her desk, rifling through papers, as though I was dismissed.

"So he's staying at . . ." I said.

"Oh, I can't give it out to a stranger."

What happened to Tally and Patsy? "Then how about a phone number?"

She wagged a finger, her eyes dancing with laughter. "I don't think so."

"Carmen Cavasos gave me the same runaround."

Patsy's face grew Botox tight. "Does this have to do with Laura Beal? Are you really a reporter?

"No, I'm not a—"

"Mitch said some strange woman was poking around."

"Mitch?"

"Just you never mind, my dear."

"Look, Patsy, all I want is to contact Drew. I'm not getting what the big deal is here."

"You won't get it, either. Drew's in hell. You wouldn't much like visiting him there."

Chapter Thirteen
Body Part

When I entered the lab, I found Hank and Dr. Cambal-Hayward hunkered over a table with, I assumed, the finger between them.

I hovered in the background, straining to hear their muffled voices. Hank's arm shot out and pulled me forward.

"It's a fake, Tal." Hank pointed to the small digit centered in an enameled tray.

I shook my head. "Impossible. Penny's uncanny. I've never seen her scent anything fake."

"The thing is clever," Cambal-Hayward said. "It's made of some polymer or plastic, shaped and hardened to resemble bones and flesh and skin. It's quite artful."

"Quite," I said, my voice martini dry.

Cambal-Hayward barked out a laugh. "Forgive me. I understand it was intended to upset you. If it wasn't for such a nasty purpose, I could admire it. I suspect whoever did this injected and applied some form of human scent, which is why your K-9 dog reacted. In truth, it's quite like the reverse of hunters who disguise their human scent when hunting. I expect the finger has been bathed in human urine or feces or blood. I'll analyze it to learn what was used."

"Thanks, Cath," Hank said.

"Yes, thank you," I said. "It's good to see you again, since Annie's. I didn't mean to snap at you. The body part thing . . . it's hard for me."

She nodded. "I'm sure it is. You're somewhat of a celebrity because of that killer."

Lucky me. Not. "Have you seen Annie again, Doctor? I haven't been able to get near her. Noah's been, well, rather uncooperative."

"Typical Noah," she said. "With the girls, it was always what he didn't understand, he'd forbid. I haven't seen Annie since that day myself."

I peered down at what appeared to be a small, child's finger. It looked perfect in every way. Somehow, knowing it was fake didn't help matters. "Along with the living, I see you also do forensic pathology, Dr. Cambal-Hayward."

"Call me Cathy. It's easier. And I wear two hats. Odd, yes, but we're a small town. When I learn more specifics, I'll call about this bit of nastiness." She gave a two-fingered salute and returned to the tray.

"I don't like it," Hank said as we exited the hospital. "That finger was an ugly thing to do to you. Someone who knew your past. The Harvester situation."

"Situation?" I said. "That's one way to put it."

He grabbed my shoulders and turned me toward him. "This isn't good, Tally. You've been sent a message. Not a nice one, either."

I shrugged myself loose and pushed open the door to the parking lot. "Believe me, I know that. I'm not one to dance to the beat of someone else's voodoo. I *will* see Annie Beal. I *will* meet Drew Jones. And I *will* figure out who killed Laura. So either help me or leave me alone."

Once again I cruised Beals Avenue.

I was fuming with Hank. But he was right in a sense. Laura Beal's murder swirled with undercurrents. Hers was no straightforward homicide, but a killing with passion, one that had murky depths and dark crevices filled with a potent hate. What had Laura Beal done to so inspire such passion?

I pulled in front of Annie's house. Noah was still home. Crap. Had the man planted himself there?

I switched to plan C, crossed town, drove up State Street, and turned into the WWTH radio parking lot. My, my. The radio station, a stately Victorian in the historical district, was a striking shade of purple. Laura Beal had yet again thumbed her nose at convention. Or perhaps her father. Ditto for the large gnome lawn ornament beside the gold-lettered WWTH sign.

I gave Penny a trot in the bushes and more water, then walked up the path over purple footprints painted on concrete. I smiled. I couldn't quite decide if I would have liked or been infuriated by Laura Beal. I had a feeling that both would have been true.

I tapped the brass door knocker, entered, and tumbled into *The Hobbit*. At least it felt that way, since someone had painted a trompe l'oeil rendition of Bilbo's world on every available inch of wall space. Far beyond whimsy, this was art, beautifully rendered. It was also busy as hell, and was making me slightly dizzy.

A "vined" mahogany staircase led upward, but I was glued to the mural of Bilbo's hobbit hole, complete with tea set.

"Hey."

The Valley Girl accent tugged me from my happy recollections of Bilbo's adventures. A twentyish blonde in braids sat at a desk tucked into the hall's far corner.

"Hi," I said, walking over. The desk plaque was hand-painted, too. "Ms. Gropner?"

"Yeah. Ethel Gropner. And let's not make any cute comments about my name. Okay? Just call me Eth."

"Gotcha, Eth. I'm Tally. The art's amazing."

"Yup." Ethel nodded. "Laura painted it."

"Wow." My concept of Laura Beal turned yet again.

"It'll all be gone next week." Ethel sighed.

"No. You're kidding. Why?"

"Old man Beal," she said. "It's, like, his big idea. Totally, radically crappy."

"So Mr. Beal's cleaning house." Noah sure worked fast.

She flicked a braid. "He's such a prick. He's repainting all Laura's art. Like, I mean, can you imagine? This is her legacy. What a dumb move. He's gonna sell the place. Radio station, building, everything. I can't believe it. Like, what am I gonna do in this burg now?"

"Um, maybe the new owner will keep you on."

"Yeah, sure." She frowned. "I liked it here with Laura."

"I can understand why." The paintings showed the workings of Laura Beal's head and heart. "Would you mind if I took some photos of the art?"

She grinned. "Nope. You're the first one to ask. They're all over the joint."

"Thanks." I pulled my little digicam from my purse.

"Excuse me?"

A whippet of a man glided down the stairs and stood before me, arms dangling, fingers tapping his blue-jeaned legs. His fine-boned, angular face wore a petulant sneer. His hair was slicked back and stiff. I'd somehow pissed him off.

"What did you say you were going to do?" He jittered with annoyance.

"Get a life, Foster," Ethel said. "She's just gonna take some snaps of Laura's stuff."

He sucked on his lower lip. "Are you with the *Journal*?"

"No, I'm—"

"Mr. Beal?"

"Not at all. I'm—"

"The cops?"

Ethel poked a finger. "Will you let her get a word in, for Christ's sake!"

Foster's nostrils flared. "Well?"

"I'm a psychologist and homicide counselor. I'm trying to learn more about Laura. I'm hoping to counsel her sister, Annie."

"Annie's a saint, but Laura . . ." Foster collapsed onto the stairs, head in hands. "I miss her so much."

"I'm sorry." I scooched down. "You were . . ."

"Friends. Just friends." He sobbed. "And everyone's being so harsh."

"In what way?"

He clasped my hand. "They're saying she was involved with all these men. And that she got what she deserved. And that she was . . ." He shuddered. "Loose. Well, it's just not true. She loved one man. Only one. With all her heart."

"I hadn't heard that. Who was it?"

He released my hand and straightened his shoulders. "I don't know. And I wouldn't tell you if I *did* know. He was Laura's secret soul mate and she wouldn't tell anyone." He waved a hand. "I mean, if she had told anyone, it would have been me. We were close." He held up intertwined fingers, then looked away.

Ethel handed him a Kleenex. Foster wiped his eyes and blew his nose. Ethel's eyes rolled heavenward.

"Foster's our station manager," she said. "He's gay."

Foster puffed out his chest. "Just because I'm out doesn't mean you have to announce it to any stranger, Eth."

"But it's so cool," said Ethel.

Foster's face grew serious. "Only to you, my dear. Only to you."

Foster acted as escort while I photographed Laura's art. As we walked around the station, he introduced me to the DJ on duty and his producer, as well as the newsman. Each one had something kind to say about Laura Beal. Apparently, she'd been a terrific employer.

Except for the smudges of fingerprint powder left by the police, Laura's third-floor office was large and tidy and painted with magnificent scenes from *Lord of the Rings*. These were of Lothlorien, the golden realm, and far more impressionistic than the literal representations downstairs.

Frodo's face was mirrored in Galadriel's pool, and Samwise climbed the stairs of a giant mallorn tree. Aragorn spoke with Celeborn and, in another scene, with his love, Arwen Evenstar. Directly across from Laura's desk, the dark-haired Arwen laid herself to rest amid the abandoned mallorns. I loved *Lord of the Rings*, too, long before the movies had ever been released, and I remembered Arwen's death from the novels' appendix. I photographed it all.

"Do you mind, Foster?" I asked, pointing toward Arwen's death scene.

He sighed. "Not in the least. They're so painfully beautiful."

I walked closer. The mural was poignant and timeless, just like the scene where Arwen gave herself up to death, faded mallorn leaves falling like jewels to the ground. Tears pricked my eyes. How strange of Laura to paint this particular scene, and in a spot where she must look at it each day. I felt a well of sadness for Laura.

How sad that her death was in such violent contrast to Arwen's.

"The police scrambled around in here," Foster said. "I had to let them in, but I haven't been in here myself since . . . You know."

"She was quite a romantic."

"Oh, yes."

I brushed my fingers across Arwen's face. I should say Laura's, for she'd given Arwen her own features. And perhaps something else. I angled the desk lamp toward the painting. Camouflaged within the folds and design of Arwen's red and gold gown was a baby nestled in her belly. The infant, curled in a fetal position, sucked its thumb. Everyone could see it in plain sight. Yet if you didn't look at the proper angle, up close, the child was invisible. I crossed back to the desk, closed my eyes, opened them again.

The infant had vanished.

Arwen hadn't been pregnant at the time of her death. But I suspected Laura was.

If more of Laura's secrets were hidden in her office, I wouldn't discover them then. Foster hovered like a bee in search of nectar. Minutes later, he escorted me to the top of the stairs, we said our good-byes, and I went looking for Ethel. She wasn't at her desk. I rechecked the *Hobbit* murals but could find nothing hidden in any of them.

The phone rang. "Shit!" Ethel flew in and lunged for it. "WWTH."

I waited until she switched the caller. "What do you think happened to Ms. Beal, Ethel?"

She flicked the end of a braid. "One of the nutcases got her."

"Nutcases?"

"Yeah. I'd show you, but I gave 'em all to the state cops. All the notes, I mean. People were forever writing letters. About the music. The Howard Stern thing. For Laura to get off Congressman Jones's case. Even crap like commercials we played bugged some of 'em. She got death threats, ya know?"

"I didn't."

"They weren't a big deal, according to her. Whackos and winos, she called them." She grinned. "Some were really far out. One night, she and me got really drunk over at her place. That's when we read them all together."

"You were friends."

The wide grin faded. "Yeah. I really miss her, too."

"Could she have been pregnant, Ethel?"

"Maybe. Or maybe she just really wanted to be." She shrugged. "Laura was sometimes hard to understand. It doesn't matter now."

I waved good-bye as she picked up the ringing phone.

I called the sheriff's office from my cell, hoping Hank had the results of Laura's autopsy. Except Hank was out to Otis again. I left a message for him to call me, then swung over to Moody's Market on Grand Street.

The market, once a small mom-and-pop grocery, now sported all the trappings of a farmstand–cum–gourmet food emporium. Outrageously expensive, it offered lushly succulent fruits and vegetables.

It happened when I left the market toting a bag of strawberries, yogurt, and kiwi-strawberry juice.

THE DEAD STONE

The late-afternoon sun bounced off the mirror of a car, blinding me for a minute. I pushed on my sunglasses, blinked, and saw the man from the cemetery.

Minus his duster, he stood in the parking lot, his small head swiveling back and forth on his long neck. His back was bowed, either from a deformity or poor posture, and his leathery complexion matched the brown shirt and pants he wore. Tufts of hair the color of nicotine sprouted from the sides and back of his bill cap. I couldn't see his eyes.

I literally rippled with fear and jerked back into the market's entrance alcove. I rested my hand against the wall, catching my breath. Maybe Cemetery Man had left the fake finger. Absurd. A teen on his way in asked if I was okay. "Fine, fine. Thanks."

I wasn't fine.

My reaction had to be because of the Harvester. I'd never been this jumpy. Never. Hell, I knew creepier people as clients. The wall was reassuringly firm. I chuckled. So why the magnetic fear, the kind that furs the hair just before lightning strikes?

I pressed my back tight to the alcove wall and inched my head forward to peer across the parking lot.

Cemetery Man was smack in my face! I swallowed a breath. "I . . ."

He brushed past me into the market carrying a sack of empty cans.

I made it to my truck on Gumby legs only to find a neon yellow Post-it flapping on the windshield.

See you soon. UL.

Cute. I tossed it inside, then sat in the truck, eating lunch and fuming at myself. I should have followed Cemetery Man into Moody's.

117

Six months ago, that's what I would have done. Then, while he was busy with his cans, I would have casually said to the checkout guy that I'd forgotten something and, by the way, who was that guy, hadn't I seen him around town? And I might've found out something useful.

The man hadn't even glanced at me when he'd walked by. And the stupid Post-it note thing was making me paranoid.

I sighed. I was letting bogeymen frighten me when Laura's homicide was far more real and scary.

I opened my yogurt and juice, sat the bottle in the drink holder, and took a spoonful of peach yogurt. I gave the lid to Penny to lick.

Drew Jones, Laura with a knife in her belly, the only witness. Could Drew Jones be next?

I tried to picture what Drew had seen that night. If Laura's death had to do with her unborn baby, if there was a baby, had the killer given Laura his personal version of an abortion? I'd seen a similar case years ago. I tapped the spoon to my lips. Say Laura *was* pregnant, then by whom?

There was Gary Pinkham. But that was awfully easy. Her "secret lover," if he existed? Even the pregnancy might be too easy an explanation. She wasn't showing, and not one person had mentioned it. Perhaps it wasn't relevant to her death at all.

I needed answers, not more questions.

I tossed my lunch trash and peeked inside Moody's. No Cemetery Man. It bugged me that I felt relieved.

I flowed into the traffic on Grand Street and headed for Beals Avenue. Maybe Noah had finally taken himself off to somewhere so I could see Annie.

Chapter Fourteen
A Potholed Memory Lane

Noah's Wagoneer wasn't around, but a green Sargent Construction pickup was parked in Noah and Annie's driveway. I pulled up beside it.

The wind had come up and the copper weather vane twirled and moaned. I walked down the flagstones to the mudroom door, knocked, and the door swung in. Huh.

I leaned into the red-tiled mudroom. "Hello?" I crossed the mudroom, opened the kitchen door. I was greeted by yeasty smells. A bunch of black-eyed Susans sat on the round kitchen table and bread rose from pans on the counter.

My second "hello" died in my throat. Voices raised in anger came from another room.

I walked through the kitchen and the dining room and into a narrow hall. The voices were louder, more shrill. I still couldn't tell what they were saying.

"Annie?" I said. "Hello?"

A man stormed down the hall, Annie running after him. I recognized Steve Sargent, the guy Noah had thrown out of the house along with me.

He whirled on Annie. "You're being used."

"That's not true." Annie saw me and her eyes widened.

"Isn't it?" Steve asked. "You've always been used. By your father, by Laura, by—"

"Don't say that!" Annie eyes welled with tears.

Steve jammed a hand into his pocket. "I'm sorry, hon. I shouldn't have. I . . . You can't do this. Please."

I wanted to reach out to Annie, but I moved backward, away from the fray.

Annie sighed. "We have a guest, Steven. Let's talk about it later."

"Later, huh?" He grabbed Annie's shoulders and pulled her close. She relaxed in his arms, tucking her face into his chest. She sighed.

"Will there be a later?" he asked.

Annie pushed herself away. "I can't."

"Fine. Shove me away." Steve balled his hands into fists. "But I don't want you going out there again."

"I have a responsibility," Annie said.

"Like hell you do. Annie, I—"

"Don't say it."

Steve's face purpled, and he reached for Annie.

"Steve!" I blurted out.

Annie and Steve turned in unison, their expressions ones of shock, as if awaking from a nightmare sleep.

"My apologies," Steve said. "My mamma taught me better." He kissed Annie's cheek. "I'll be here for you tomorrow. You know I will." He included me in his good-bye wave.

Annie followed him out and closed the outer and mud-room doors behind him. "Steven never closes doors. I'm sorry you walked in on that. He's, um, he's usually very sweet. I mean . . ."

"No problem."

Annie slumped at the kitchen table, clearly exhausted. "Daddy would die if he'd been here."

"May I join you?" I pointed to a kitchen chair.

"Where are my manners? Please."

I sat. "Annie, do you remember me from—"

"Of course I do. You were trying to be kind that day, and I was thinking you were a crazy person."

"You were kind, given the situation. It's good to have someone close, like Steve, to help you through your sister's death."

She reached for a paper napkin and her fingers trembled as she started folding it. "I guess. We were close, but . . . Um, are. I don't know. Today was my fault."

"It didn't look that way."

"No, it was. I can't seem to let some things go."

I hooked her eyes with mine. "You needn't let go of Laura yet."

"That's not . . ." She shook her head. Great tears splashed down her cheeks.

I wondered what she'd been about to say, but now wasn't the time. "You don't have to say good-bye to Laura. She was your sister."

Annie bowed her head, nodded. "One of the reasons Steven got mad was because I was watching videos again."

"And that's bad because . . . ?"

"That's all I've done since . . ." Eager eyes cut to mine. "Would you like to see some?"

"I'd love to."

I went and got Penny, at Annie's suggestion. I followed Annie into a small den, one that had been our fort, our castle, and the site of countless sleepovers with Annie and Carmen and me. Now it was just a den with a couch, an armchair, and a TV/VCR combo.

"Please," said Annie. "Have a seat."

We each curled up at an end of the sofa and Annie clicked on the TV and VCR.

"Daddy had all our old Super-8 movies put onto videotape. I'm so glad."

I hadn't thought, not far enough ahead at least, because I was unprepared to watch snippets of my old life unreel before me.

There was infant Laura, cradled in Annie's childish arms. My God, Annie was about six and we all were already fast friends when Laura arrived. In the next sequence, Laura toddled around the apple orchard with Annie.

My heart beat faster. It was as if *my* life was unreeling before me.

"Laura was three here," Annie said. "I'd started to babysit her by then. I was nine."

The camera jiggled wildly. It was a birthday party, Annie's eleventh, and the day after Carmen broke her arm. And there was Annie, blowing out the candles. And Carmen holding out her new cast.

And there was *me*, and we all started singing "Happy Birthday", and I wrapped my arm around Annie's waist.

I pressed a hand to my lips, filled with bubbling emotions desperate to erupt.

"These were my buddies." Annie pointed at the screen. "That's Carmen, who still lives in town. And that's Emma. She left town when we were twelve. I cried for a month. Dumb, huh?"

I cleared my throat. "Not so dumb. I'm Emma."

Annie's look said I had a screw loose. "You really aren't well, are you?"

"I didn't mean to blurt it out like that, Annie, but I really *am* your friend Emma. Look."

She looked, and her eyes gradually widened in recognition. "Emma?"

It was a whisper, so soft I could barely hear it. But music, of a sort. "Yes. I came back for, um, for vacation. And then your sister died, and I wanted to help."

"You mean you're not a homicide counselor?"

I smiled. "Oh, I am, all right. Down in Boston. Twelve years of it. I work out of the medical examiner's office there."

"Oh. Oh! Emma."

She hugged me hard, and I hugged her, and it felt grand.

When we settled, she said, smiling, "Is it really Tally?"

I smiled back. "Yes. A nickname, that's more me than 'Emma' now."

She frowned. "I'm different."

"It's okay. So am I."

"No, I mean really different. I'm glad you're home. I'm so glad your dad and the money didn't keep you away."

Oh, dear. "Um, see, Annie, I'm not sure I understand what you're talking about. I came back because of my dad and a disturbing phone call I received down in Boston. And after I arrived, I ran into our old teacher, Mrs. Lakeland. Well, she looked at me with hate in her eyes. And now you're saying—"

"You don't know, do you?"

"Whatever 'knowing' is, I don't. I very much want to."

Annie fiddled with the tissue in her hands. "Is your dad alive?"

I shook my head. "He died years ago. Murdered."

"I'm sorry. I'm afraid others won't be. Mrs. Lakeland hated him because he stole from her. She put her savings, her pension, into that scheme of his—Trenton-by-the-Sea. And he stole everyone's money. All of it."

"He couldn't have. We had nothing, Annie. My dad died poor."

"It's just . . . He took money from Dr. Spence and Dr. Lee, too. He cost Mary Cavasos her hardware store."

"Carmen's mom lost her store?"

Annie nodded. "She went to work at the Bucksport mill. She didn't do well after that. My dad helped, but it wasn't enough."

I leaned closer, desperate for her to understand. "But, Annie, we left because when our house burned, we had no money to fix it. We had no insurance. All this money went into Trenton-by-the-Sea. That's what dad said."

She wouldn't look at me. "Everyone in town believed that your dad *set* that fire. That's how Walter Cunningham, Hank's dad, died."

"No" tumbled out of my mouth. "God, I'm . . . I'm sorry. But that can't be right. It can't be. They must hate me. Carmen, Hank."

A sob. She sat back on the couch. Remembering Laura.

"Sweetie, I'm sorry. That isn't important now." I massaged her hands. They were cold and frail and reminded me of what death does to the living.

Minutes later, Annie flicked the VCR back on. "Oh, look, there's Laura. Wasn't she cute?"

"That she was."

We watched videos for another hour as Laura matured into a stunning young woman. Laura and Annie could have been clones all through Annie's high school years. But by the time Laura's high school graduation came around, Annie had already started to change. She'd lost weight and her hair had lost its luster.

I felt how much she wanted to tell me, about her life, her sister, Winsworth. But I felt her hesitation, too. I might be the enemy, the one whose father bilked a town.

Instead, Annie laughed and cried and gave me commentary about her and Laura's life after I'd left. That all felt normal and healthy to the grieving process, and though she wouldn't believe it if I told her, her wounds at losing her sister would slowly heal until they were bearable. Dealing with the *method* of Laura's death was another story.

Annie clicked off the tape and sighed. "I miss her. Every day. From now until forever. It's so unfair. I get, um, angry."

"Anger is incredibly normal, Annie. It's part of the process."

"I need to know *why* she died."

"Yes," I said. "That's a part of it, too."

A door opened somewhere in the house, then Noah banged in. He snapped me a frown, growled Annie a hello, and stormed out.

"He's suffering, too," she said. "Why would someone kill her, Emma, er, Tally?"

I wish I knew. "Laura sounds like a pretty assertive lady. Some people around town found her a bit, well, prickly."

Annie waved a hand. "Oh, I know that. But Laura did a lot of good stuff, too. Like her work at the hospital. She practically started the patient outreach program with Elyse Baxter, and Laura was forever supporting indigent artists in shows at the Hand Auditorium. She helped Carmen start her restaurant, too. Have you seen Carmen?"

"Yeah," I said. "She didn't recognize me."

"And that hurt, didn't it? You should tell her."

"Soon." After I dealt with her mother losing her store.

Because of my dad. "For now, let's keep it between us, okay?"

"Sure. The thing with Carmen's restaurant, that was pretty controversial. Something Laura loved. I never understood that part of my sister. That makes me sad, too."

"Unfinished business?" I said. "That's also part of it. But the understanding's there, Annie. It's just hiding right now. Tell me about Laura's relationships. Foster mentioned something at the radio station."

Annie folded her hands. "Poor Foster. He always kept insinuating himself into Laura's life. It mattered to him. And she was kind to him. He's sort of an outsider here."

"Because he's gay?"

"No, not really. It's more because he's such a city boy. He thinks he's hip and cutting edge. That puts some people off. He's really sweet. But Laura and boyfriends? I knew everyone she was seeing. She made a point of telling me. It was something we shared. No. There was no one special."

I hated slamming her, but . . . "Could she have been pregnant?"

Annie frowned. "She did want a baby, but . . . I don't think so."

The mural in Laura's office implied she was. A wish, perhaps? "I need to find Drew Jones. He's got answers."

Annie's eyes widened. "Drew? He's living out to his camp. On Emerald Lake. He's not well. He's been reclusive of late. Please don't hurt him."

It ached that she even imagined I could. "No. I won't."

She handed me an address and phone. "He's away for a couple of days. I'm not sure when he's getting back."

"Thanks, Annie. Laura was just a kid when I left. She seems to have grown into an interesting woman."

Annie dipped her head. "Unique," she whispered more to

herself than to me. "Laura was unique." The eyes she lifted to mine were hard and hot and brimmed with tears. "I will know, Tally. I can't stop thinking about it. I keep picturing . . . I *will know* who killed my sister, and why."

"We'll find out, Annie. I promise."

Chapter Fifteen
Company!!!

I pulled into my dooryard Friday night around six after leaving Annie's. I took the turn way too fast and crunched to a stop on the dirt and gravel. The breeze soothed my hot cheeks. I rubbed them against Penny's cool nose. She lapped my ear, and I laughed. Like always.

I brushed my hand across the glove box. That damned finger. Creepy. My body shivered reflexively. Just synthetic, but . . .

I flipped open the middle compartment and pulled out Dad's wallet, the one he'd last carried. I pressed it to my nose, smelled the musky leather, felt its remembered softness beneath my fingers. Pretended I could still feel *him*.

I'd always secretly wondered if he'd set fire to our house. We had no money. His land investment was doing so well, then it began to fail. Creditors were pounding the door and ringing the phone. Yet he seemed so positive—until the night we fled. He'd never brought it up about the house, and I'd never mustered the courage to ask.

I slipped the wallet back into the middle compartment and slammed down the flap.

Dad didn't bilk those people. No way. But something about that land deal had resurfaced. That *had* to be what the mystery call was all about.

Penny took off down the beach as I walked to the cottage. I laid the strawberry box on the kitchen island, then reached for the clicker, wondering about news of the world.

A shadow flickered. High up. A two-legged one. In my sleeping loft.

Penny was out romping. Dammit. Of all times. I had to get to my purse on the counter. I started tiptoeing over. Had to get that pepper spray.

The shadow moved, then a man thundered down the stairs holding a gun. Crap.

I spun, grabbed for the doorknob.

"Don't!" he barked as he vaulted the stairs into the light. Overalls and a bill cap, unshaven, filthy, feral.

I dived behind the kitchen's island, inched to where I could see spooky shadows, but no man. My hand crawled toward my purse.

"I said don't!" he yelled.

I didn't, mostly because he was in my face waving, not a .45mm Magnum, but a purple Popsicle from what I suspected was my stash.

"What do you want?" I stood and reached for the door, about to call Penny.

He wagged the Popsicle. "Don't you dare call that monster dog of yours." His bloodshot eyes narrowed. He reeked of body odor and something else I didn't wish to think about.

Calm. It was important that I remained calm. "Who are you?"

His forehead wrinkled like a shar-pei's. "Damned if I know anymore. Name's Gary Pinkham, and I'm scared as shit and need your help."

Gary Pinkham and I sat across from each other. His eyes never left mine, yet he kept sucking the Popsicle. He'd acquired a purple stain on his dirty white T-shirt. As I caught my breath, I glimpsed beneath the grime and sleepless nights a man who was Russell Crowe handsome.

I lifted the phone from its cradle.

"You're not gonna call someone, are ya?"

"Not if I don't have to."

"You won't have to. I'm not a killer."

I'd heard that song many times. "How did you get here, Gary?"

"Hitched. I don't dare use my Bronco."

"What makes you think I can help you?"

"Joy. You know her from the post office. She said you were a cool lady. Told me you were lookin' into Laura's death."

"Joy told you to come here?"

"Nah. Said I should call. Well, that won't do. Not at all." He tapped his hands on his knees, fast, nervous.

"I'm not sure how I can help." I was talking a lot cooler than I felt.

His eyes darted around the room. "Well, if you can't, who can? Tell me that now, who can? Huh? Huh?"

"Gary, take some deep breaths. Come on. Try it."

He pressed his fists to his eyes, inhaled. "I'm going nuts

here, see? Plain nuts. I'm being hunted by those state maniacs in their big hats, and I didn't kill Laura. Hell, why would I kill a woman who gave me such great sex?"

"Maybe because she was pregnant?"

He flushed. "I . . . I, um . . ."

"Gary? I'm thinking Laura was pregnant."

He folded his hands, looked down. "Well, it wasn't me. I can't have any kids. I was in the Army for two years. I had an accident and . . . Nobody around here knows, not even Joy, and don't you go telling nobody, either. You hear me?"

"I won't, I promise. And I'm sorry."

He gulped a breath, and then another, and another. Too fast. His face pinkened, his eyeballs protruded. He fumbled inside the bib of his overalls. He gasped for breath.

I started to press 911, but he squeaked out a "Don't!" and pulled out an inhaler. He shook as he held it to his mouth, pumped it, inhaled once, then did it again. By the third puff he was breathing easier. His shoulders relaxed and his arms fell to his sides. His head lolled back.

I leaned forward. "Gary?"

"I'm okay. Okay."

I got him a glass of ice water and a cool, damp towel, which I laid on his forehead.

"Thanks," he mumbled. "I'm near out of my medicine. Had the asthma since I was a kid. It scares me."

"It would me, too." I waited until he was sitting up and his eyes were able to focus. "You know Sheriff Cunningham. Call him. He'll help."

"No way. He'll put me in jail. And I didn't do *nothin'*."

Our conversation had taken on a certain circularity. What a mess. Stray dogs were my specialty, and I fought the urge to shelter him.

"Will you tell me about the night Laura died?"

He wiped some spittle off his lip, then scraped his hand across his overalls. "Thank you for asking, ma'am. People haven't been bothering with that. Sure. Me and Laura was out to the Giddyup. It's right outta town, just before the lumber yard."

"I know the spot."

"It was early, around six. We went for ribs and the dancing. If truth be told, we wasn't gettin' along so great that night. Part of it was my fault. After we ate, Laura kept wanting to dance. See, I was pooped. I'd spent the last four days hauling pots."

"What time was this, Gary?"

"Maybe nine o'clock. She wasn't very horny, either, which was pretty odd. Laura usually had her hands all over me. We really dug each other, ya know?"

I pictured Hank . . . Hank! Dammit. "Go on."

"So I said we should go back to her place and . . . you know."

"Right."

"She wasn't in the mood." He tucked his hands under his armpits. "I . . . um. We had words."

"Bad ones, it sounds like. Tell me, Gary."

"Why should I?"

"Maybe because I'm the only one who'll listen."

My words hung on the air, Gary staring at me, angry. Oh, I could feel the anger.

"Okay, so I called her a bitch. And she slapped me. Right in front of everybody. Then I hauled her ass outta there."

"You mean you forced her?"

He rocked and looked every which way but at me. "Gary?"

"I did. And I'm not proud of it. I'd never done anything like that before. Not to a woman, at least."

"What happened then?"

"She kneed me in the balls." His loopy grin was infectious. "Hurt like hell, but that's what I liked about her. She had gumption. No man was gonna get on her case, no way."

"And . . . ?"

He shrugged. "I told her to screw herself, and I left her there and went out to Joy and Will's place for the night."

He was lying, but I couldn't tell exactly about what. "You're sure? I mean, maybe, after this many days, your memory's a bit fuzzy. You know? Why don't you go back to that night, make sure that's exactly how it happened."

Pinkham smiled, and again I saw the devilishly handsome man hiding beneath the coating of filth.

"You got me this time," he said. "Laura and me was . . ."

Gravel crunched just outside the open window.

Pinkham sprang to his feet. A ten-inch hunting knife flashed in his right hand. "Fuck. Who'd you tell?"

"Tell? You've been with me the whole time."

He blinked rapidly, then let out a whine like a hurt dog while he waved the knife back and forth. Its serrated blade glinted in the lamplight.

"Put that away," I said, standing. "I'll see who it is. I won't let them in."

Gary's left hand flashed out and he grabbed my wrist. He drew the blade across an inch of skin. I watched, fascinated, as small beads of blood oozed to the surface.

"I'm not kidding around here," he said.

"No, I can see you're not."

He dragged me to the mudroom, peeked out the window, then pushed me to the ground. I landed hard on my fanny. "Ouch! Gary, wait!"

He hesitated by the sliders. "I can't. He'll lock me up. I'll be in touch."

He slipped out the slider and ran across the deck, then disappeared just as the mudroom door slammed open.

In rushed Hank, gripping his 9mm.

"Pinkham," I said. "Out toward the beach."

Hank flew after him.

I sat on the sofa, sucking my cut. Minutes later, Hank and Penny walked back in through the sliders. Both were winded, and I suspected that Penny had joined the apparently unsuccessful chase for Pinkham. Hank holstered his gun, then pulled the slider shut behind him.

"I didn't even spot the stupid shit," he said, foraging in my refrigerator. He pulled out two V-8s and plunked one down in front of me. "Penny flew after the guy, but he vanished. Poof. You okay?"

"I've had better nights," I said.

"Haven't we all?"

"What prompted your to-the-rescue arrival?"

He flopped onto the sofa, cradling his cast hand. "Rescue, nothing. You left me a message this afternoon, remember?"

That I had. "Perfect timing. Just perfect." I recounted the scene with Pinkham.

"Goddammit." Hank slammed his juice down. "I would have listened to the kid. Doesn't he know that?"

"Apparently not," I said, hugging Penny.

"It was a rhetorical question, Tally."

"Oops. My brain-meter's off a tad."

"How much of what you heard was truth?"

"Well . . ." I thought for a minute. "I'm sure he lied about parts of it, especially when he said he left the Giddyup and went to Joy Sacco's place. He was about to say more when you arrived."

"Damn lucky I did."

"Maybe." The cut had stopped oozing. "His cutting me was strange. He didn't really hurt me, but—"

"He might'uv." His eyes flashed anger.

"Perhaps."

Hank stretched an arm across the back of the sofa. "Perhaps? What, are you nuts? He's dangerous, Tally. And don't you think he's not. What did he say about the finger in your car?"

"Hell! I forgot to ask. I know, incredibly dumb, but . . . It was all in the moment with Pinkham, know what I mean?"

"I do." Hank stretched his legs out on the coffee table. "You think he killed Laura?"

"I don't know. No. Maybe. The thing with the knife. I saw pleasure in his eyes when he cut me. But it was oddly childish. No, I doubt he killed her."

Hank nodded. "I've got another reason."

"Go. I don't want to think too hard. I'm pooped."

Hank grinned. "You're cute, is what you are."

I got tingly, which apparently kick-started my brain cells. The inhaler sitting on my coffee table didn't hurt, either. "Of course. He's an asthmatic. The cigarette butts. I doubt Gary's even capable of smoking."

"Right you are." Hank slid the inhaler into a plastic bag. "Which means he probably didn't smoke those cigarette butts out at the quarry. Wish we'd gotten some DNA off of them. Won't hurt to test this, though. Have it as a record."

I started to blurt out Gary's claims of sterility but recalled my promise. "Maybe Gary's asthma angle will convince the state boys to cast a wider net."

He swiped a hand across his face. "Maybe. Depends. They're overworked."

"And you're not?"

"It's different for me."

"In what way?"

He shrugged. "Just . . . different."

For a brief moment I saw a man raw with pain. How much had he loved Laura Beal? I told him about my visit with Annie, minus the identity stuff. He was already hurting. How much more would he hurt with the knowledge that his dad's alleged killer was my father?

"That's why I called," I said. "To find out if you had the autopsy report back, to see if the ME or the lab learned . . ." I sighed. ". . . if Laura was pregnant."

Hank grew intensely still.

He moved to the sliders, opened them, let in the night breeze. He leaned against the door frame. "Same stars everywhere in the Northern Hemisphere. Same nighttime sky. You look up and see what a person in New York's seeing. Florida, too. Chicago. Poor, rich, sick, hungry, happy. Doesn't matter. There it is, that beautiful blanket of stars. Long time now, I've had a telescope. Got a new one last year, in fact. Keeps me from going crazy with some of the stuff I've got inside me. It's not helping much now, though."

I walked up behind him and rested a hand on his shoulder. "Hank?"

He rubbed his forehead. "It hurt when Laura died. I don't see why learning she might have been pregnant makes me feel so much worse."

"Because you loved her?"

When he turned, his eyes were infinitely sad. "Because I didn't love her enough. Or maybe Laura's a symbol for all the dead women I've seen, mutilated, maimed, some with babies inside them."

"Oh, Hank."

His lips twitched upward, just a little, but his eyes stayed sad. "I've been having a little game with you, Tally. A dumb one, I guess. But you're a big hotshot from Boston, looking at me like I'm some hick."

"But I don't."

He retrieved his juice from the table. "Sure you do."

I couldn't hold his gaze, because maybe he was right. Maybe I saw myself as superior to all my old friends in Winsworth. Maybe I did think I was better than them. Maybe I'd been just condescending enough to alert someone like Hank. God, I didn't feel that way, but . . .

I forced a smile. "Let's hold the point/counterpoint for tomorrow, okay? I'm beat." I walked to the mudroom door and held it open.

He snugged on his hat. "So you don't want to hear, huh? Can't deal with your own fallibility? Or you think you're so damned savvy, you've got my number? Which is it, Tally?"

I started to say I was sorry, but instead . . . "I am sick and tired of this shit. Of whining and whimpering when men like you play me like a frigging puppet. I've had a crappy five months, and I came ba . . . to Winsworth to do anything but homicide counseling. And here you've involved me in just that. You're also playing footsie with me about Drew Jones, and you're now accusing me of an egregious insensitivity, which, dammit, I do not feel! So crap on you, Hank Cunningham, we'll talk tomorrow."

His big paw of a hand grabbed me and pulled me close, and then he kissed the dickens out of me.

Chapter Sixteen
Home Is Where the Heart Is

I awakened Saturday morning hot and bothered by dreams of Hank and me romping in the outdoor shower, which certainly hadn't happened the previous evening. Hell, he hadn't even kissed me a second time, but merely waved good-bye, and I'd watched as he lumbered his boat of a Pontiac out the dooryard.

How could a man who'd so set me on fire leave so quickly and drive so slowly?

Mysteries were everywhere in Winsworth, including the unexplained game Hank had been playing with me.

Or maybe he was all smoke and mirrors. I leaned back against the pillows. Maybe . . . maybe he loved Laura Beal all along, maybe she carried his child, and maybe he'd been involved in her death.

Loving Laura I could imagine. Killing her? I couldn't picture that one, but . . . I checked my schedule. I had no conference call with Gert and clients today, so I dialed Drew

Jones's number at his camp. Annie had said he was away for a few days, but it couldn't hurt to try. As I listened to the bleep-bleep of the ring, I downloaded the photos I'd taken of Laura's office onto my computer. I hung up when Jones's answering machine clicked on. I called Annie. Penny nudged me, and I let her out just as Annie picked up.

"How about I stop by?" I said.

"Thanks, but no. I'm okay."

"Annie, it's not a bad thing to talk out your feelings about Laura."

"I know. It's Daddy. When he came in and saw us together, it upset him. I don't want to upset him more. Um, we're having Laura's service down at the Congregational church tomorrow, then the interment. We're having people over here afterwards. Will you come? Please?"

"Of course I will."

"There's one thing. Um . . ."

"Annie?"

"I would swear I was followed yesterday. It was the strangest sensation. I got all prickly. Maybe . . . I dunno. Maybe because of Laura I'm being hypersensitive. But I didn't like it. Am I crazy, Tally? What's going on?"

I paused, breathing deep to suppress my fear. "No, you're not crazy. Someone could be following you, perhaps to watch out for you. Or, well, just be careful until Laura's death is more clear. No point in taking unnecessary risks. Okay?"

"Yes."

"Have you told your dad?"

She sighed. "He's got enough worries right now."

"Tell him, Annie. Don't carry this alone."

"But I've got you, Emma . . . er, Tally. Right?"

"That you do."

* * *

And she did. I chewed on Annie's words as Penny and I drove toward Winsworth through dense morning fog. I didn't like them. Not one bit.

Hard to believe that nearly a week ago, I'd picked up the stranger and his dog. Laura Beal would be dead a week tomorrow night. And in a little over two weeks, I'd be back in Boston.

I scratched Penny's muzzle and got a lick in return. "What to do, Pens?"

I pulled into the Pine Tree Convenience and Bait Shop. Although I craved Piper's pancakes, I opted for a granola bar and tomato juice. Back in the car, I let my fingers do the walking and found Laura Beal's home address. I didn't even need my map.

The CC road lies less than a mile east of town. It was built in the late 1930s by Roosevelt's Civilian Conservation Corps—hence the name CC.

I wondered what happened to the third C.

I crossed the Winsworth River bridge, then turned right onto River Road and drove past the Chevy dealership and the boat launch, from where Daddy and I had made our escape that night so long ago. I soon passed a bucolic landscape of farms, an occasional antique shop, and trees that played peek-a-boo with the river that paralleled the road.

Today, the river was pewter, colored by the layer of clouds overhead. Reminders of the morning's dense fog ghosted across the road. I drove slowly, mulling over my plan to enter Laura Beal's home. I thought about who would track Annie, and if the family was involved in something a desperate person would want to end. Minutes later, I came to Bryer's farm and turned left onto the CC road.

I drove up the gently undulating hill past a former farm

turned MacMansion subdivision, then into the stands of towering pine, where I turned right at Laura's teal-blue mailbox. I headed down a long dirt road that spilled me out onto an acre of meadow dotted with pink, yellow, and purple wildflowers. Beside an outcropping of rounded ledge sat Laura's small home.

It was painted white, with lavender trim, and had a peaked roof and a farmer's porch and a white-painted deck that wrapped around two sides. Flower beds, which were tucked into nooks beside the ledge and lined the front path, had yet to show their tender's absence, while wicker rockers invited guests to relax and chat.

For all of the house's charm, a desolate air clung to it and its grounds, as if it knew its mistress would never return.

Penny and I walked up the wooden steps. I knocked and, as expected, got no answer. I circled the house, searching for an open window.

I really didn't want to break in, but I knew I had to see Laura's home. A sense of urgency and fear for Annie made me feel both reckless and desperate.

I pictured Joy, and her friendship with Laura. What if the killer had plans for Joy Sacco, too?

A clump of meadow grass parted and out slunk an orange cat. It gave me the once-over, then titled its head toward Penny, who leaned down and nuzzled it.

I checked the cat's collar and gave him a chin scratch. "Tigger, huh? So you're Laura's poor kitty. How about I bring you home with me. Deal?"

"Wurrrp." Penny received another affectionate head butt.

Inside the house the phone rang, then a woman's message, then a man saying words I wished I could hear.

I got out my AmEx, aiming to open Laura's front door with the credit card, something I'd never even tried before.

I felt absurd.

"Are you going to charge the door open?" A peal of feminine laughter shooed Tigger off.

"You scared the cat," I hollered with an indignation that masked my feelings of guilt.

A person emerged from behind a large pine, someone with swinging braids and overalls and granny glasses. Carmen.

"Greetings, Ms. Cavasos," I said. "This is Penny."

Carmen walked toward me. "You've been watching too many Sherlock Holmes reruns."

"Inspector Morse, please."

She joined me on the deck. "At least you have some taste."

"Have you been following me?"

She rolled her eyes upward. "Right. I live just up the road. There's a path through the meadow. I came to get Tigger. I haven't been able to catch him, so I've been feeding him out on the deck. Maybe you can help me capture him after you're done snooping."

"Snooping?"

Eyes narrowed, Carmen studied me. "I doubt you were bent on robbery."

I bit back the riposte. I wanted us to be friends, not sparring partners. "Honestly? Yes. Snooping. I'm trying to understand Laura and find out who killed her and why. I don't mean any harm to her, or those close to her."

She reached into her bag and pulled out a cell phone. "I'll just call Sheriff Cunningham. If it's okay by him, we'll—"

"Don't! He's a pain in the ass. He'll just interfere."

"So the wind blows that way, does it? We'll bag Hank for now." Carmen pursed her lips. "I'll make a deal with you. I've got a key, which will unlock the door. You can go inside, as long as you do it with me and tell Hank when we're through."

I'd be damned if I'd report to Hank. Crap. "All right, fine. But you're ticking me off."

Carmen smirked as she turned the knob and pushed the door open. She grinned at me over her shoulder. "Laura never kept the damned thing locked anyway."

I owed Carmen one. But good.

Laura Beal kept surprising me. The Middle-Earth look that pervaded her office was absent. Instead, her home was light and airy, decorated with a postmodern seaside feel found in Pottery Barn catalogs. In search of her answering machine, I walked through the white kitchen, with its state-of-the-art appliances and scarred pine table, into the living room.

She'd done it up in limes and turquoise and painted it with murals of the Caribbean. But the place was a mess. Books and papers and magazines cluttered every horizontal surface. A pair of cowboy boots sat on a club chair, a Miller beer bottle beside them.

"Is this mess from forensics?" I said.

"You mean the CSI guys?" said Carmen. "Naw. It's quintessential Laura. Not much for housekeeping, but she sure has some great books." Carmen plucked a large art book from one of the white shelves lining the living room walls. "And great taste."

I found the answering machine sitting on the hall table, a framed Far Side cartoon hanging crooked above it. I pulled on a latex glove I'd brought, then pressed play. Laura's voice, eerily like Annie's, asked for a message. A man selling insurance left one, then hung up.

I turned to Carmen, who was peering at me over the rims of her granny glasses. "A rubber glove? You kiddin' me?"

"How did Annie's boyfriend, Steve Sargent, feel about Laura?" I asked.

"You're really shoveling all the dirt up, aren't you?"

"Just sorting through relationships."

She slid the book she'd been holding back into its spot. "Steve liked her . . . up to a point. Couple of years ago, she came on to him. It gave him a sour taste because of Annie. Annie forgave her sister. I don't know if Steve ever did. I sure didn't."

"Why go after her sister's boyfriend?"

"First off, the boyfriend thing is unofficial. Second, Laura and Annie had the usual sib rivalry, exacerbated by their mother's leaving. Third, Laura saw Steve as her soul mate, at least for a while."

Her secret soul mate? That's what Foster had said. "Steve Sargent doesn't seem the soul mate type."

"You wouldn't think it," Carmen said. "But Steve's one exceptional artist. He paints, just like she does—did—and Laura had a romantic streak a mile wide."

That part wasn't a surprise. "What about her relationship with Hank Cunningham?"

She smirked. "It was disgusting how crazy about her he was. And vice versa. She thought *he* was her soul mate for a while, too."

"So what happened?"

"I don't know."

Right. "When did they break up?"

"Maybe six months ago. It bothers you, doesn't it?"

"Why should it?" I said reflexively. Boy, she was good at getting under the skin. "You missed your calling."

Carmen laughed. "Go on."

"What about you and Laura?"

Carmen nibbled a nail. "It's funny. Laura and I were friends. She helped me get the restaurant off the ground. But honestly? I never liked her much. Mostly because she connived things to go her way. She's the one who turned Annie, a sweet, fun kid, into Saint Annie of the Martyrdom."

"How?"

"Too long a story for here and now."

"I've got plenty of time."

Carmen shook her head.

"What about Drew Jones? Laura must have made him furious."

She brushed her hands along the sides of her overalls. "Dusty. Time's a-wasting. Snoop away. I'm going to collect Tigger's food and his toys."

There it was again, the silence when it came to Drew Jones.

My annoyance dissipated as I checked out Laura's books. She'd collected works on everything from historical art to trashy romances to genetics to computers. One section was devoted to Southwest American Indians, another to New Age stuff. Eclectic, to say the least.

The cellar held little more than trunks of old clothes, tools, and about a gazillion jars of veggies she'd apparently pickled. I went back upstairs, then kept going to the second floor.

The two bedrooms and bath were pristine, telling me only that Laura didn't use them other than as guest accommodations.

On the main floor again, I followed the short hall, peeked into the bathroom. More mess, with deodorant, toothpaste, and hairbrush sitting on the counter and a roll of toilet paper on the floor beside the john. Laura appeared to have been in a rush that morning, which was probably typical. Funny how the half-squished toothpaste tube brought tears to my eyes.

I could picture her so clearly, her long hair flying as she raced around the house getting ready for work. Would she have done it differently, had she known?

The garbage was empty, no doubt cleaned out by the police, and after I peered into the medicine cabinet and under the sink, I headed for the bedroom.

Laura had decorated her bedroom with white wicker and transformed an adjoining bedroom into a studio. I breathed in the paint and turpentine, enjoying the smell. Laura's easel stood by one of the windows. Sun splashed onto an impressionistic oil of two girls, teenagers in big hats and pretty peasant dresses, arms entwined. Laura and Annie.

They wore matching belts, identical to the art nouveau one I'd seen on Joy. Laura could be generous, and it wouldn't surprise me if she'd given her belt to her best friend. Or maybe each girl owned one, just like our gaggle of girl pals used to own identical stuff. I missed that closeness.

The painting was lovely, done up in Monet pastel colors and more abstract than Laura's murals down at the station. Such talent—erased.

Forensics had left their black fingerprint dust on an old jelly jar that held a few soaking brushes. Another brush, a green-handled one stiffened with paint, lay beside the easel.

Food for thought while I perused the studio's bookshelf. Not a note or diagram fell out as I opened and closed dozens of books on radio and tarot, human health and Maine history. I played with dust bunnies under the bed, sifted through her drawers, searched her art materials and jewelry box.

I shuffled through the pile of bills mounded on her desk and burrowed in her closet for clothing other than hers.

So where was the lurid letter from her secret lover? The kinky sex toys? The note exposing an elected official's perfidy?

"Well?" Carmen said when I reentered the kitchen.

"Complex woman."

"That's for sure." Carmen smiled as she hoisted Tigger's large bag of cat food into her arms.

"It didn't seem to fit, the hardened paintbrush lying beside the easel rather than in the turp jar. Maybe the killer surprised her while she was painting."

She shifted the bag of cat food. "I guess it's possible. But you can see from the mess how scattered Laura was."

"Annie was familiar with her sister's habits. She'll know."

"Leave her alone. The cops have been at her. Even Hank. She's got enough on her plate."

"Boy, you're just raring for a fight, aren't you? Annie very much needs to know what happened to her sister. Rather than hurt, it'll help her."

Carmen turned away, but I caught how she flipped me the bird. She was one pissed woman. No point in going at it right now.

"Do you know if the police have her laptop?" I asked.

"How do you know she had one?" Carmen said.

"With the station and all, I'm sure she did."

"You'll have to ask Hank. And, yeah, she carried one everywhere. You dredged enough dirt yet?"

I bit back an X-rated retort and reached for the ceramic bowl with "Tigger" painted on it.

"Let's go, huh?" Carmen popped kitty toys into a pocket of her overalls.

"I thought we might get some coffee. Talk things over."

She smiled pleasantly, her eyebrows raised, her hand poised on the outer doorknob. "Can't. I'm needed at the restaurant."

I scooped Tigger up from the back deck and passed him over to Carmen.

"I'll stop by at the restaurant again," I said.

"You do that."

Funny, her words sounded the very opposite of an invitation.

Chapter Seventeen
Anyone Have a Light?

For sure, things had deteriorated with my old best buddy Carmen. When I took stock of my Winsworth mission, the word *grim* came to mind. A brutal killer was loose. I had found out little about my dad and the night of the fire. I hadn't learned squat about the mysterious phone caller. And I suspected Hank was keeping Laura's autopsy results secret. What else was he hiding? That question, in particular, bugged me.

I took a mug of coffee and the portable phone out to the deck. I crossed my legs on the rail. If only I could relax. I rolled my shoulders, wishing away the kinks.

Boy, was it gorgeous here. Winsworth was like a sly addiction that would be tough to shake. It was pretty cool knowing the guy at the gas station and the gal at the post office and feeling as if I might be a part of a small town. Maybe I should call it Small Fish, Small Pond syndrome, and present it at the next New England Psychology Forum. Or maybe that's what had gotten Laura killed, that level of comfort and safety.

Now Boston, she was busy and chaotic and distant at the same time. Not so hard to remain anonymous, for sure. I continued to miss my town, and I missed Kranak and Gert and Veda. I missed work, the daily pulse.

I wasn't sure I knew *how* to take a vacation, even a working one.

I tapped out Crime Scene Services's number at Boston's OCME, then did the same for Kranak's extension.

"Kranak."

"Hey!" I said "I didn't expect you to answer."

"What do ya need me for, Tal?"

"Nice. We haven't talked in days, and you're grouching on me."

"Yup. Seems to me you forgot who your friends are."

"My ass. There's been a murder up here. Wish you were here with me."

Kranak snorted. "So whaddya need?"

"Didn't you go to college with some guy who's at the ME's office in Maine?"

"How do you remember crap like that?"

"Because I love you. I need an autopsy report on a Laura Beal. She was killed almost a week ago. I know they've worked it up, because her body's back in Winsworth for burial."

"Just for once, stay outta it."

"No can do. The homicide victim is the sister of an old friend."

Kranak snorted. "Wouldn't ya know. How's it going with the stuff about your dad?"

How the hell . . . "My dad? What are you talking—"

"C'mon, Tal. How would I *not* know?"

"Nothing is sacred or secret in that place. It's not going well." I sighed. "I've actually had to be incognito as myself—"

"What the fuck! You are going to get your ass kicked *again*. How the hell can you forget your last undercover job?"

"This is different, Rob. Look, I'm doing what I have to do. That's all. I've got to know the truth of what happened with my dad twenty years ago. If that means not admitting I grew up in this place, then so be it. And I don't want any more crap from you. How've you been feeling, by the way? The diabetes?"

"Not bad. Good, I guess. I've got it under control. Look, Tal, you should have someone watching your back."

"Yup. Thanks. Get me that report ASAP, deal?"

Big sigh. "Deal."

While I waited for Kranak's e-mail, I took a shower out-doors, a nice hot one, then lingered for a few minutes out-side while the breeze played a tune on my body. Oh, Laura, what were you all about?

Inside, I shrugged into my baggy jeans and a fresh top, then brushed my Medusa locks. Snarl city.

Kranak's e-mail arrived a short while later. First thing I read was how he couldn't get Laura's results until Monday. Damn. Penny scratched at the door to go out. I told her to stay around—not chasing stuff—then went back to the e-mail.

My heart skipped. I'd imagined Hank was hiding stuff, but the reality stunk. He'd had the results of Laura's autopsy since yesterday morning. And he hadn't shared.

I sat down hard. What the hell was going on with this town? With me? I was romanticizing it to death, and that could be literal if I didn't watch out.

I kept coming back to Drew Jones having killed Laura Beal, and that one and all were hiding him, protecting him. Even his awful estranged wife was in on it. Which made no sense whatsoever.

No one seemed desperate to catch Laura Beal's killer. The town and state cops were convinced Gary Pinkham had murdered her. They were confident, in fact. So Drew was off the hook.

Maybe I should let it and my dad's situation go. It could be time for me to leave. Maybe. But first . . .

"Hey, Penny! *Ke mne!* Come!" I piled her into the car and off we went.

I simmered down a little as I drove into town. Well, enough so that I didn't wig out on Hank, although I was pissed, for damned sure.

At the courthouse, I spotted Hank's car. I opened the windows for Penny, left her with a chilled bowl of water, and went in search of him.

As I was climbing the granite steps, he was coming out the double doors. I waved and moved toward him. I'd swear I saw a frown when he spotted me.

"Hey," I said, going for casual. Had he forgotten that kiss?

He towered over me, a growl coming from his chest. "What the hell were you thinking at Laura Beal's? It's a fucking crime scene."

"Hope you're having a swell day, too. I can't believe Carmen really called you."

"What? One of my guys saw you exiting Laura's driveway and took your plate number."

Okay, Carmen was cool. But that autopsy report was making me crazy. *Be calm, be composed*, I told myself. "Question—why would Laura, a thoughtful artist, leave an expensive sable brush out of the turp?"

Hank straightened. He slipped on his sunglasses and sighed. "You ask the damnedest things. What the hell is turp?"

"Turpentine."

"Who knows why she left the brush out?"

"What about her laptop?"

"The state police have it. You're really winding me up, Tal."

"A shame," I said. "I'd like a peek at it."

He laughed, but it was grim, as if I'd gone over some line. "You *are* doing good drugs. Not a prayer. They're sending me a report on it tomorrow or the next day. I'll share."

"Share? Really? Hard to believe. So tell me, Hank, was Laura pregnant or not?"

A pause so long I thought he might just turn and walk away. I felt his eyes, hot on me behind those glasses. I sensed his anger, and his hurt. I'd be damned if I backed down.

"Sheriff Cunningham?"

"She was," he said. "Two to three months. She had an ectopic pregnancy."

Oh, boy. A pregnancy is ectopic when the fertilized egg is implanted outside of the womb. Ectopics, especially untreated ones, can cause pain, fainting, internal bleeding, and even death. They do not result in a live fetus.

"Did she know?" I asked.

"I don't know. And that's the truth. She also had gonorrhea. The ME said a relatively new case, less than a year."

His voice was sad, his lips tight.

"The father?" I said.

"No idea."

"Do Annie or Noah know about any of this?"

153

He hitched his hands through his belt. "I don't know. I'm going to have to talk to them about it at some point after the funeral. You should attend it, by the way. It'll be tough on them. Noah, especially."

And you, tough on you, Hank Cunningham. I took a deep breath and modulated my voice to soft and gentle. "How come you didn't tell me, Hank? You knew yesterday."

Another pause. "You ask the hard questions, Tally. Always. You ever figure that sometimes people don't know the answers?"

"I'm sorry about you, about Laura, about your relationship." I waited a beat, then: "You think it was Gary?"

"I do."

"I plan on going to the funeral tomorrow. But after that . . ."

A brief nod and he trotted down the courthouse steps.

This time, he didn't even bother with a good-bye.

I gave Penny a brief walk on the grass, then I crossed State Street to WWTH. I walked through the radio station door and gasped. "Ohmygod."

Bilbo's world was gone, replaced by industrial green walls. The hobbit hole, Bilbo himself, the table with its steaming tea set, the hats hanging from . . .

"Miss Tally," said a voice to my right.

Foster stood, arms akimbo, at the top of the stairs.

"Foster. I'm here to—"

"Oh, I know, I know." He walked down the staircase. "You were going to take pictures of the hobbits and such, I don't doubt."

Actually, I'd hoped to spy out Laura's paperwork along with the photos, but . . . "Yes, that's what I planned. The murals upstairs?"

He rubbed his forehead. "Gone. All gone. Mr. Beal has painted over *everything*. Apparently, he's found a buyer for the station. I don't know. I just don't know."

"I'm so sorry. I can't believe her art is gone, poof. How sad. I'd still like to look around."

"I'm afraid it just won't do."

"Won't *do?* And just why won't it do?"

"Because Laura has been *raped*. Not only by her killer, but—"

"Laura wasn't raped, Foster."

"That's not what I mean. Her things have been invaded by everyone from the state police to Sheriff Cunningham to her own father. They found *nothing*. Neither would you."

I sighed. Here was another who adored Laura yet was hiding much. "I'm trying to help, Foster. Although everyone's shielding Laura, no one seems to be helping to find her killer. *Why?*"

Foster waved a hand at the wall. "Look what he's done to her art. Desecration."

"C'mon, Foster, talk to me."

He climbed the stairs. "Never."

Blind with frustration, I hopped into my car and headed for Drew Jones's camp. What the hell, I figured. Nothing was going right. At least I could see if the mystery man was home.

The night was ink black, moonless, the road nearly invisible. I got lost. As I drove narrow, serpentine roads to nowhere, my sense of frustration was fueled by my anxiety. What was I doing, a Boston girl, driving around countryside I didn't know on a mission that had to lead to more aggravation? My rearview mirror showed only blackness.

Penny, sensing my unease, butted my face with her cold nose.

I turned right, then left, expecting to be one place but landing another. Was I still even in Winsworth?

My eyes kept darting to the road, with its faint white line, then behind, where I hoped to see something. A car. Lights. A convenience store. Anything. My rearview mirror, with its LED compass, said I was going north, which wasn't what I wanted to do. East, dammit, I wanted east. I rubbed my eyes, annoyed at my own ineptitude.

I turned left, hoping I'd found the road back to town. Just then a light flared from behind.

I peered into the mirror again. Blackness behind me still—but wait. Wasn't that glow the tip of a burning cigarette? Was it a match or a lighter that I'd seen? Hell. Someone was tailing me—lights off—and he'd had the balls to light a butt. The hot ash pulsed in my mirror. I watched, hypnotized.

The killer had smoked as he'd viewed Laura's death throes, like some damned movie or something. And the car following me had to know these roads a hell of a lot better than I did to drive with the lights off. He drove very well, indeed.

Up ahead, a streetlamp. I *had* made the right turn. My foot itched to floor it, but I waited. I had to be patient. *Be calm*, I told myself. Calm. Penny whined. I wasn't frightened. I had Penny with me, right? My hands on the wheel were greasy with sweat.

Oh, yes. The spill of the streetlamp neared. I pumped it, just a little. There. And behind me . . . Nothing?

I slowed to a crawl.

No car, nothing, was on my heels.

Then what had I seen? Or had I imagined it?

But in my mind's eye, I pictured the pulse of the cigarette, saw it heat and dissipate, like the coals of a bellows fire. No, he was there. Hiding for now. But waiting for me. I sensed his patience and deplored it.

I returned to the cottage, no closer to finding Drew Jones than ever.

Tomorrow is Laura's funeral, I thought, from the comfort of my bed that night. Not a happy prospect, but one I knew oh, so well.

An intimacy with death is not an appealing trait. Sometimes I wished I could leave death behind. But that would mean having amnesia about my dad's homicide. No way to extract the horror of that death.

Had Laura known she was pregnant? I tried to climb inside her and see from her eyes, feel with her heart.

She had known. And she had reveled in it.

The ocean breeze drifted through the window. Fishy smells and anticipated treats brought back my dad. We'd had fun sailing our Blue Jay around the bays and inlets. He always had stories to tell, ones that fascinated me. Winsworth had been such a welcoming place when we'd lived here. Dad had made it colorful, each day vivid and bright.

He'd also brought darkness and chaos, like shards of glass sprinkling the landscape.

Dad was an imperfect soul. I loved him madly.

I was coming to despise my current masquerade. Emma Blake had lost her way in all this.

So much about my dad's alleged con made no sense. If the town believed he'd set the fire that burned our home and killed Hank's dad, then where were the newspaper reports? The indictments? The accusations? And why had the stranger who'd called me in Boston, who'd insisted I return here, failed to contact me? Questions were clouding the sky like a spinner fall on a river. A clearing wind needed to blow through my mind.

I turned out the light, slid onto my belly, and closed my eyes. The wuffle of Penny's breathing added a comfort I needed. I hiked the comforter up to my chin. The night was chilly.

Tomorrow is Laura Beal's funeral.

I suspected a killer would attend.

Chapter Eighteen
Another One

Laura's funeral began on the dot of nine—a melancholy affair, made worse by the mockery of the blue sky and relentless sun that sparkled off the granite headstones at the Winsworth cemetery.

I watched everyone, sure I could spot her killer and knowing, realistically, that killers often look like you or I. They do not wear signs, or carve tattoos into their foreheads, or grin with evil intent. But, my, how I wished they did.

Not far from my dad, Laura and her babe-to-never-be rested together, both stilled by the butcher's knife. Had the killer known about the fetus? I suspected the baby was an issue in her death.

How sadly ironic that the pregnancy was an ectopic one. Would Laura be alive if she and the killer had known that fact? I couldn't stop churning scenarios, yet none seemed a perfect fit. Even in a traditional town like Winsworth, out-of-wedlock births were not uncommon. If the killer was the baby's father, why not abortion or adoption? If Laura refused, and the man was crazed with anger or fear, then why not an efficient bullet to her head? Why the planning? The fury? The *watching*?

That disturbed me more than just about anything—that he watched her crawl and suffer before the life finally bled out of her.

Oh, I was having a dark morning.

I brushed my dad's headstone with my hand and left.

Back at the Beals' home after the interment, I hovered by Annie until Carmen was able to lure her upstairs for a much-needed rest.

The house smelled of roses and potpourri and lilacs, a combo that made me sneeze. I recalled tales of bodies on ice in parlors, and perhaps that might be a better way to go about things than our sanitized farewells.

Platters of food steamed on the dining room table while the soft strains of Pachelbel played in the background. The rooms grew hot, and someone threw open the doors and windows. If I hadn't known better, I'd swear I was at a party for Winsworth muckety-mucks. In a way, I guessed, I was.

I tried to speak to Noah, his charcoal suit and shock of white hair making him a tragically handsome figure as he worked the crowd. Each time I moved in close, he'd drift away. I gave up and hunted for Hank, all the while receiving covert looks from Drew Jones's former wife, Patsy. Gary Pinkham was nowhere to be seen, but a wan-looking Joy Sacco introduced me to her fifty-something husband, Will. I towered over both of them. I remembered that Will Sacco was Gary Pinkham's father-in-law, and Joy and Will's twenty-odd-year age difference was visually startling.

"Good to meet you, Will," I said. "Joy's terrific. I love chatting with her."

He nodded, tugging on his wisp of goatee. "That she is."

"I was wondering, have you seen Gary Pinkham lately?"

"Nope. Haven't." He took a covered platter from Joy's hands. "I'd betta get your brownies ovah to the table, hon."

I hadn't expected much of an answer, and that's exactly what I'd gotten. "How are you doing, Joy?"

She brushed a hand across her forehead. "If you only knew. Scooter chose today to make a fuss when we dropped him at Will's sister's."

"I'm sorry."

"He sensed it. This thing today with Laura. Poor baby loved her." Joy smoothed her hands down the green silk skirt. "Does my outfit look okay?"

"Perfect. It's a great suit, Joy."

"It's Laura's. I had to take six inches off the hem, but . . . You don't think she'd mind, do you?"

"No. Did Annie give it to you?"

She flushed, shook her head so that her mane of curly hair trembled. "Annie's giving all of Laura's clothes to Goodwill. This was at the cleaners. I wanted something to wear as a tribute."

I understood. Best friends are often relegated to off stage when it comes to grief and grief counseling. "You wear it well."

Chip the funeral director joined us, eager to talk about Laura's embalmed beauty. I spotted Dr. Cambal-Hayward and off I went. When I reached her, she'd been joined by the older man who'd bumped into me outside Patsy's store the other day.

"Tally," Dr. Cambal-Hayward said. "I'd like you to meet Governor Daniel Jones."

Daniel Jones cleared his throat. "Oh, pish-tosh, Cath. Forget 'governor,' my dear. And it's a pleasure to meet *you*. I know all about your work in Boston. Well done!"

"Oh, well. . . . thank you." I never knew what to say in those instances.

Jones raised an eyebrow. "I wanted to apologize for plowing into you the other day, m'dear." His folksy voice and smile belied the sadness in his spaniel eyes. I'd seen eyes like those before. They belonged to someone with an unshared burden.

"No apology necessary, Governor Jones."

"I'm plain Daniel now." He glanced at Patsy Lee Jones, her hand tucked into the crook of a tall, blond man's arm. "Why can't that woman leave our family alone? That's my younger son, Mitch. Patsy's latest conquest. I'd introduce you, but . . ." He sighed as he turned back to the doctor.

Patsy clung to Mitch like a limpet. Dear God, she was a piece of work.

The room suddenly hushed, and I turned. Oh, boy. Annie and Steve Sargent descended the stairs together while Noah made a beeline for them.

I sensed fireworks from Noah and moved to head him off at the pass.

I felt a hand on my shoulder.

"Hold a minute, Tally," Daniel said.

"Noah's going to—"

"—do nothing," Daniel said. "He's foolish but not stupid. He won't make a fuss with Annie and Steve. Not today."

"I don't know."

He had a smoker's chuckle. "I do. Noah's a good man, although his crustiness sometimes gets in the way."

I wasn't sure I agreed. "Annie's fragile right now."

"Perhaps. Tell me, m'dear, do you really think finding Laura's killer will put Annie's demons to rest?"

The heat from Daniel's watery blue eyes hinted at the power that once was. "It will help. Yes. The person I've wanted to talk with, for days now, is your son, Drew."

That bushy eyebrow shot up. "Really."

"Absolutely. Do you know when he's getting back?"

"Getting back? Why, m'dear, he's right over there."

My eyes cut to the tall man talking to Carmen over by the refreshment table. He wore a dapper suit and tortoiseshell glasses, and his close-cropped beard had been neatly trimmed. Yet his back was bowed, and he appeared to lean against a wall for strength.

Whoa. I'd seen him at Carmen's restaurant the other day, the guy using the protractor and wearing a beret. He looked nothing like the disheveled man with the hurt dog I'd picked up on the Bangor Road. Funny, I'd already talked to Drew Jones and hadn't even known it.

Carmen knew, of course. I was sure she'd found it quite amusing.

Drew's hand shook as he lifted a punch cup. Just as it had on the rainy night. His long, bushy beard might be gone, along with the sunglasses that hid his eyes and the bill cap that covered his bald head, but I now saw his likeness to the stranger in my car.

As Drew brought the cup to his lips, our eyes met.

His one-fingered wave, almost a salute, held a hint of irony. He knew I'd been looking for him and that the chase was now over.

"Excuse me," I said to Daniel and the doctor.

As I wove through the crowd of mourners, I dropped back into my past to the boy who'd rescued my Halloween candy

163

and soothed my hurt and sat on a stoop keeping me company until my father returned. A handsome boy, grown handsomer as time passed, according to myriad photographs of Congressman Drew Jones. But he'd morphed again, and now his cheekbones cut like blades in a face lined and hollowed.

As I neared, Drew walked to meet me.

His eyes twinkled as he held out his hand. "Ms. Tally Whyte. I heard you've been looking for me. Me and Peanut, that is."

"That I have, Mr. Jones. It's good to finally, um, meet you."

His soft chuckle was disarming. "Yes. Well, forgive my rude behavior that night. I haven't been well lately and feel uncomfortable around st . . . st . . . strangers."

The Congressman Jones I'd heard on tape hadn't slurred his words. Or stuttered. I searched his face. He could be on drugs, or drink, although I didn't smell any liquor on him. "I'm sorry you've been ill."

"And I'm sorry to have played cat and mouse with you. Carmen says I've been acting like a jerk." His grin produced two gorgeous dimples in his cheeks. Then a tremor erupted, rippling his body, erasing the smile.

"Mr. Jones, I—"

"Wha' did you say your name was?"

Oh, dear. "I'm Tally, Tally Whyte."

He gently traced his trembling hand across my face. "You remind me of someone. A long, long time ago, I think, but these days time is bent. I . . . Thank you for saving Peanut."

"I'm glad she's okay. Could we talk? Maybe outside?"

"Not here." He shook his head, like a dog ridding itself of a coating of rain. He pulled a notepad from his breast pocket, a pen from its spiraled spine, wrote, then ripped off

164

the page. "Directions to my camp. Come see me tomorrow, or the next day, or the day after that."

"Does the time matter?"

His laugh was filled with sadness. "Not since leaving Capitol Hill. What did you say your name was again?"

I slid the pad and pen from his hand and wrote my name and phone number. "There you go."

"I forget sometimes."

"Me, too." I tucked the pad back into his breast pocket. "We all do the . . ."

Drew wandered off in the middle of my sentence.

"He's not well."

I turned. Dr. Cambal-Hayward's concerned eyes followed Drew's progress.

"What's wrong with him?" I asked.

Her eyes stayed with Drew until he took a seat beside Annie on the couch. "It's not my place to be telling my patient's business."

"Forensics, Annie Beal, now Drew Jones. You're one busy woman."

"That I am," she said, clasping her hands behind her back. "Again, please call me Cathy, won't you? We're pretty informal up here. Come with me."

She took my hand and led me from the room. We squeezed through the crowd and entered the mudroom, refreshingly barren of people. Cathy gestured me to the pine bench.

"Whew," she said, joining me. She pulled a handkerchief from her sleeve and wiped her brow. "Winsworth funerals. Sometimes they're too much. As you may have noticed, the whole town turns out."

I hadn't attended my dad's interment. I was sick, hospitalized with grief. It must have been a lonely affair. "You knew Laura well, yes?"

"Since she was a baby," she said. "A gifted child, damaged by her mother, who almost destroyed her sister. That's why I brought you out here. Had to get you away from my Daniel."

"Your Daniel?"

She blushed, then pushed back a wing of her glorious white hair. "Noah'll do fine, but I think you can help Annie. Heard you've been talking to her, helping her with Laura's death. Your reputation says you're pretty darned good at counseling. I've been trying to knock some sense into that girl. I can tell you, I've gotten nowhere. She's got to stop living in the past. That's part of Laura's legacy. It'll kill Annie if she marries him."

I thought Steve Sargent might be good for Annie, but . . . "Because of his hot temper?"

"Hot temper? Why, there was never a boy with a more controlled personality."

"Cathy, I saw them arguing, and Steve was the opposite of controlled."

The kitchen door opened and in burst Chip. He took one look at us and jerked to a stop. "Uh, Tally, Cathy. Um, hi."

Talk about mood spoilers.

Cathy leaned close. "I wasn't talking about Steve. Heck, it's Drew's obsession to marry Annie that's got me worried."

Annie and Drew? "But I thought—"

Chip walked toward us, obviously bursting with *something*.

Cathy slapped her thighs. "I'd best get back to Daniel. See you folks later."

"Wait!" Chip flapped his hands. "I just got a call on my cellular. There's been another one."

"Another what?" I said.

"Murder! I've got to go get my assistant and the hearse. A couple of summer people found Gary Pinkham. He's dead."

Oh, no. "Where?"

"Out to the Penasquam quarry. On some big, black stone."

Chapter Nineteen
A Dark and Stormy Day

I sped to the quarry where Gary Pinkham lay. The day had darkened. Leaden clouds scudded overhead, the wind had turned nasty, and the smell of angry rain hung in the air. I felt a terrible sense of urgency—why, I didn't know. Gary was dead, after all. Yet my pulse raced and my throat tightened. I wished Penny were with me.

I parked near a bunch of cars scattered around the dirt lot. No hearse, so Chip hadn't arrived. I peered over the quarry lip. People moved around the site with an air of purpose. A uniformed trooper stood before that horrible stone, so I couldn't see Gary's body. The heavy air dampened sound, and I heard nothing but the keening of the wind.

I slipped my digicam into my pocket, left my black pumps in the truck, and descended the quarry path. Sweat stained my sleeveless linen dress before I was halfway down. When I reached the quarry floor, I sat on a rock and massaged my bruised feet. Hank spotted me and started walking over. I finally saw Gary. He lay supine on the Dead Stone beneath the large oak, which thrashed in the wind. I felt bad for him. He'd been a frightened man when we'd met. *When we meet later, I'll have things to tell you.* Or so he'd said. Maybe he'd simply been looking for sanctuary. And absolution.

What looked like a couple of plainclothes police officers stood off to the side, one talking on her cellular. A man in a gray business suit was packing his black doctor's bag.

"Nice outfit," Hank said when he reached me.

"Thanks. I always dress for the occasion."

He glanced over his shoulder. "How did you know?"

"Chip spilled the beans at Laura's wake. To me, at least. What happened?"

"You shouldn't be here."

"It's a *fait accompli*, Hank."

The woman detective headed in our direction.

"Not a problem," hollered Hank, pointing to me. "She's okay."

The woman nodded, and rejoined the other officer.

"She's a state cop, homicide," said Hank. "I don't know the other one. The man in the suit's one of the local sworn medical examiners."

"And . . . ?"

"There's no sign of foul play. It appears Gary was a suicide. Only so many burdens a man can take."

Suicide didn't fit the Gary I'd met. "What about the autopsy?"

"They're still chewing on that. There's not a thing out of order, Tal."

"As a suicide, he would be routinely autopsied in Massachusetts."

Hank chuckled and shook his head as if I didn't get it. "You haven't noticed this isn't Mass., Tally Whyte?"

"I've noticed." I assumed in Maine, as in Mass., any unattended death would be autopsied. "Who found him?"

Hank rubbed the back of his neck. "Hikers. Around eight."

"So if it's suicide, how'd he do it?"

"Induced his own asthma attack."

"Cripes. How come they're so sure?"

"I admit, Dottie had reservations . . . at first. But there's nothing out of place. It's clean. Straightforward. No sign of any foul play."

"I'd like to see Gary. You mind?"

Hank walked me over to the state police officers, introduced me, and sketched my professional life in Boston. The sergeant gave me the okay.

I walked up to Gary Pinkham, closed my eyes, and put him in my photo album of the dead. *I'm sorry, Gary. You were so afraid.*

I opened my eyes. Unlike the night I met him, he was shaved and clean, exposing his cleft chin and rounded, almost-baby face. The blue tinting his lips and the grayness of his skin were the only signs he'd died a death that gave nightmares to most asthmatics.

Sad. He looked like a *Men in Black* wannabe, down to the Ray-Bans pushed to the crown of his head. His eyes were half open, his right arm lay outthrust across the stone, his left arm dangled down the side. Only his fingers appeared stiffened with rigor mortis, which made sense. Rigor typically commenced two to six hours after death.

Something threaded through the fingers of his right hand, and I bent closer. It was some kind of medal on a black chain. Runes and the head of a beast, its mouth agape, marked the medal's face.

"You know anything about this medal, Hank?"

He shook his head.

The wind momentarily hushed, and I inhaled the stench of death. So distinctive. So indescribable.

Stones clattered behind me. Chip and his assistant, Mo Testa, skidded down the path, landing hard on the quarry floor. Chip trotted toward Hank and the sergeant, while Chip's assistant walked toward me holding the body bag.

"Ma'am," Testa said as he unfolded the bag on the ground. "I hope I didn't get you into hot water the other day."

"Naw. Mr. Vander . . . Holy shit." He crossed himself.

"What is it?" I asked.

"That medal's bad stuff." He finished laying out the bag and backed off. "Real bad."

"Explain, please."

"No, ma'am. No way." Testa walked back to Chip, and I returned to Gary. Voodoo stuff, maybe. Santeria. Satanism. Hard to know.

He looked younger than I remembered. Too young. And scared. So scared. I could feel the fear in the air, as if Gary Pinkham's horror had yet to dissipate.

So easy to picture Gary in his overalls, eating that Popsicle, wearing that loopy grin. But he'd changed to feral when he'd cut me. I could picture that, too.

What wasn't I seeing?

"Tally?" said Hank.

"Was there anything else?" I asked.

He led me about a dozen feet from the Dead Stone and pointed toward a small rock. Gary's inhaler lay behind it.

"Gary must've stretched out on the stone," Hank said. "Thrown the inhaler, then induced the attack."

"That's a huge stretch, Hank."

"We all thought that at first, until the hikers admitted Gary was alive when they found him."

"Alive?"

"He was on the stone, suffocating, when they spotted him," Hank said. "They gave him their version of mouth-to-mouth, even did the pounding-on-the-chest thing, like you see on *ER*. They didn't know about the inhaler, and Gary couldn't talk by that point. I suspect they didn't know diddly about what they were doing."

"Didn't he point to it?" I said. "Try to get up? Do *something?*"

"He lost consciousness almost immediately after they arrived. Or so they said. They were pretty freaked by the whole thing. Nobody else around. Back-to-nature types without a cell phone. We checked 'em out. They're a young married couple from Vermont, just bought a camp a little ways down the lake. Big on hiking and stuff."

"His clothes are awfully neat for a guy who died from suffocation."

Hank shook his head. "The girl tidied him up. She thought he needed it."

So much for the unattended death. I pulled my digital camera from my pocket and began to shoot pictures.

I took some wide-angles of the scene, narrowed to a few shots of Gary's body, then zoomed close to his face. As the shutter clicked, Gary's face became an old friend's, one who'd been murdered. I lowered the camera.

"You done?" said Chip.

"I . . . I'm all set."

Chip and his assistant began bagging the body. When they pulled the zipper, I déjà vued on that sound, too.

Hank and I leaned against a large rock, watching Chip and Mo Testa manually carry Gary Pinkham's bagged remains up the quarry path, which was too steep and rocky for a stretcher. Chip's assistant was doing most of the hoisting.

"Gary left us a note." Hank handed me a piece of paper. His eyes followed Gary's remains as he was hoisted over the crest of the hill. "This is a copy I made."

One week ago I killed Laura. I'm going to Satan because he told me to kill her and our baby and I did. Now I'm killing me. I made it painful for me, like I did for her. Please, God, forgive me?

"Gary signed it," Hank said. "Some papers sitting in his truck were a match. So was his driver's license."

"Satan, huh?" I couldn't keep the sarcasm out of my voice. "He spells it all out. How nice."

Hank scratched his mustache with his cast hand. "Dottie was skeptical at first. Me, too. Especially with Satan telling him to kill Laura. But we got the kids as witnesses to the death, the match on the signature, and the Tish thing."

"Gary's dead wife. Will Sacco's daughter, yes?"

"Yup. Tish was a sweetie. Everybody loved her. She worked at the hospital, and, well, word has it she wasn't as careful as she should've been. She got AIDS. Big deal in town, as you might imagine. Got a bunch of people scared and upset."

"Do you know how rare it is to get AIDS that way?" I said.

"Yup. But that's how Will and Gary both told it. No way to know the real truth. Not now. But Gary didn't have the disease. Got tested and all, and he made a point of sharing the results with just about everybody. Will took Tish's death hard. Gary even harder. They'd been childhood sweethearts. Grief bends people in strange ways."

Didn't I know it. I pictured Gary choking, suffocating, changing his mind, but unable to reach the thrown inhaler. Then passing out. What I couldn't picture was him murdering Laura. "I'm still having trouble with it, Hank. Look, Gary could have been murdered to cover up Laura's murder."

"There wasn't a mark on him, Tal. His Bronco's parked down the road. Once we found the note . . . See, murder's just too much of a stretch. Someone would've had to lure him here, take his inhaler, induce the attack, have the suicide note ready, not to mention the medal. And what about the hikers? They could've interfered."

My feelings clicked into place. "But don't you see, it's perfect, Hank."

"Huh?"

"It's just like Laura's murder."

Hank rolled his eyes. "It's nothing like Laura's murder."

"The killer was clever and organized, yet obsessed."

"Obsessed with what?"

I gnawed my knuckle. "Well, I don't know. Yet. But by murdering Gary, it gets us off the killer's back. There are plenty of places to hide so those hikers wouldn't see him. I bet he watched Gary suffocate, just like he watched Laura bleed to death."

He rested a hand on my shoulder. "You read that in some crime novel?"

I shook off his hand. "I *wish*. I've lived it. Well, something like it. I've got pretty good radar, and I don't care if it sounds wacky. Gary Pinkham was murdered. My gut says it and so do my bones. Don't you smirk, dammit."

"Me? I never smirk." Hank was quiet for a minute. "I'll give you a maybe. I'll tell the detectives what you've said, too. That's it."

Better than nothing. The nape of my neck itched from sweat. My feet ached. Blackflies swarmed around my face. I batted them away. And remembered something I'd completely blanked on. "Gary told me he couldn't have kids. Look at the note. It refers to 'our baby.' There's no way."

"What the hell are you talking about?"

"That's what Gary said, the night he paid me a visit. That he was incapable of having children."

"Why didn't you tell me then?"

"Because I promised I wouldn't. He said no one knew."

"Convenient, huh." A grunt. "No one knew because Gary was lying to you."

"Can't you check? If he was autopsied . . ."

He crossed his arms. "I don't know. Let me see what I can find out."

"Gary said it happened when he was in the military."

"That was six, seven years ago. He was in the Army, I think."

"Could there be something to the Satanism angle?"

"I'm going to look into it, but the only whisper I've heard was two years ago. Found a bunch of kids drawing pentagrams in some clubhouse. They stole Ernie Nestof's prize rooster and hacked off its head. Not nice, but not *Rosemary's Baby*, either."

I tried on Laura and the cult angle. "Laura had books on tarot in her library."

"Laura had the world in her library."

Hank had an answer for everything. He was humoring me. I'd been humored before and it felt lousy.

A drop of rain splashed my cheek. The sky had turned the color of night.

I thought of meeting Drew Jones earlier that day. The fact that Hank had lied about Drew. "Hank, we need to talk about—"

Thunder cracked.

"Come on. We'd better go." He stood, offered me his un-injured hand. Lightning stabbed just above our heads.

I tucked my digicam back into my pocket and took his hand.

"Now, come on," he said.

As I crossed the quarry floor, the wind tore my hair and slapped my arms and legs. Black clouds churned one next to another, blanketing the sky. Techs pitched a tent above the Dead Stone and the area surrounding it. More droplets fell. Hank hollered to the detectives that he'd call them.

"Will and Joy don't know yet," Hank shouted over the wind as we climbed the path. "I've got to get over there fast."

"Of course," I said.

Lightning zapped a stand of pine to my left. The reek of cordite and burnt wood stung my nose. Swell. I scrabbled faster up the slope. The air smelled of ozone and rain, and then a sheet of water blinded me. The path became a mud-died ski slope. I climbed, but my stockings made it even more slick. I started slipping backward, felt a hand on my butt, another on my back. That's how we made it to the top. Then I lay half on the crest and literally pulled myself over the lip.

So much for my favorite linen dress.

I pushed myself to my feet, and Hank took my hand as we raced to his car.

Hank cranked up the heat. Around us, the detectives and doctor were firing up their cars and leaving the scene. Chip's hearse was long gone. I pushed a hunk of sopping hair from my eyes. Mr. Boy Scout Prepared handed me a towel, his soaking face wreathed in a grin.

"Don't say it," I grumbled.

"Wouldn't think of it, ma'am."

"Right." I corralled my hair into a scrunchie. "It would be good if you were there when I talk to Joy and her husband."

"What?"

"I've met them, and I know Joy a bit, but you know them much better than I. It'll be good to have a comforting face when I talk to them about Gary's death. In Boston, we always have a detective in the room during the initial interview."

"So you've gone from not wanting to talk to Annie Beal to being everybody's favorite counselor?" He flicked up the car's defroster.

"What's with the sarcasm?" I toweled off the fogged window.

"Nothing. Is it because Gary's a suicide?"

I blew out a breath, trying to exhale my exasperation. "I just got through explaining why I think it's murder. Didn't you tell me Gary was a wimp?"

His eyes narrowed. "Wimps kill, just like you said."

"Obviously, but—"

"You're talking down to me again."

I swiveled so I was facing him. "No, I'm not."

"Bullshit. You're thinking that I'm some hick cop who hasn't seen much, been anywhere. Some rube who doesn't know about guts and feelings and hasn't encountered many homicides, so I wouldn't know what to look for in the first place."

"Where the hell did that come from?"

"Look inside yourself, lady."

I fumed. "Did it ever occur to you that wimps are a lot more chicken when it comes to taking their own lives?"

Hank's face was grim. "The wise counselor speaks."

"Dammit, Hank. Why are you doing this? Acting this

way? Just because I want to talk with the Saccos? I believe I can help them."

Hank cut his eyes to me, and his scowl deepened. Just as little Henry Cunningham had when I'd refused to go to the junior high prom with him. "How about you tend your own garden, Ms. Tally."

He was right. I was in Winsworth to find out about my dad, not be a homicide counselor. I hadn't learned nearly enough about Dad's dealings in town. Instead, I was embroiled in a murder investigation that I believed had become two homicides.

"My own garden?" I said. "That is me. That *is* my garden." I shoved the door open and ran for my truck.

Hank gunned his car backward, did a three-point turn, then blasted through the open quarry gate. The Pontiac flew into the air, thudded hard. Where the hell was Mr. Slowpoke?

I tore after him in my 4-Runner.

When I reached the Bangor Road, Hank's car sat idling beside the stop sign. Fat raindrops bounced off the hood. The passenger window was half down.

I pulled beside him and lowered my window. "Hank, I—"

"Okay, ma'am, I concede," he yelled over the downpour. "You can come with me to the Saccos. Tell 'em their Gary just offed himself."

"Nice, Hank," I hollered. "Nice way to put it. And he didn't 'off himself.' He was a homicide."

"My ass. Tell me again why you're so damned sure he wasn't a suicide?"

"Maybe I'm skeptical because I *have* seen more facets of human nature than you have, living up here. You said it yourself."

"Did I, now?" Hank started to laugh, yet through the curtain of rain I saw his face turn serious. "You haven't figured it out. I'm surprised, a clever woman like you. I was a homicide cop in New York City for ten fucking years, so don't give me any more of that 'what you've seen' crap, okay? Meet you at Noah's. Joy and Will should still be there."

He burned rubber as he peeled out.

Chapter Twenty
Cemetery Man

I sat in the truck on the corner of Penasquam and the Bangor Road and slammed the steering wheel. *Damn him*. Hank Cunningham had played me for a fool. Of course, maybe I was a fool. I sure as heck hadn't told him I was Emma Blake.

Screw it. I felt like a total jerk. He had nerve not telling me he'd been an NYPD cop. Grrrr. If I still smoked, I'd light up. Ohhh, he liked that game he was playing. Liked it a lot.

Well, crap on Hank Cunningham.

All the way into town I looked for something half decent on the radio. You think I could find it? No! When I arrived at Noah's, I shucked my sopping dress and torn stockings and tugged on the spare pair of jeans, denim shirt, and sneakers I always carried in the truck. I re-scrunched my hair, but it was a lost cause.

Hank had changed his muddied pants. Even so, eyebrows were raised when we entered Noah's home and shepherded Joy and Will to one of the empty bedrooms.

When we told them about Gary, Joy sobbed, tears streaming unchecked down her cheeks. Will Sacco's face tightened and he made little choking sounds, but he was one of those men who wouldn't allow the tears out. Instead, he folded a stick of Juicy Fruit into his mouth and furiously chewed. Will insisted on driving himself and Joy over to see his son-in-law, so we caravanned to the Vandermere Funeral Home. Once there, Will made more choking sounds and chewed faster.

Sitting in the mourners' salon, Will talked about his daughter Tish in a voice familiar with longing.

"She was my angel, y'know. My angel. Gone three years now, and I miss her. I do."

"Yes," I said. "That sadness dulls but never passes. My dad was a homicide victim. I understand. I'm so sorry for the loss of your daughter and, now, Gary."

Like bobble dolls, their heads wagged up and down. "So you know what it feels like," Will said.

"I do, and I'm so sad that you both have to experience it." They now belonged to that exclusive club.

"Wish that Tish and Gar had kids," Will said. "I do."

"I understand," I said. "A part of them would remain. But you're here, and you remember."

"And Scooter," Joy said. "He's part of Tish, at least."

"The remembering's good," Will said. "Sometimes. Poor Gar. He was a son to me. A son."

Joy hugged her husband. "We both loved him, even though he most likely killed . . . you know. How did he die?"

I looked at Joy, at Will. "It's not clear."

"The cause of death isn't certain right now," Hank said. "We'll be sure to tell you more when we know."

Their faces crumpled and more tears fell. I worried about both of them, especially Joy. She'd gotten a double whammy with Laura and Gary. She asked me to visit her tomorrow out at her place, and I agreed.

When the Saccos drove away, my anger at Hank bubbled anew. I stared at him out of the corner of my eye. Tall. Auburn hair. Broad shoulders. Buddha belly. Laid-back air. Eyes that told tales. I'd seen the depths in those startling green eyes, the knowledge, yet I hadn't thought he'd ever left Winsworth. Who was I kidding? The anger was for me, not Hank. I should have realized there was more to the man. But I'd gone only for the surface details, reveling in the memory of little Henry, instead of plumbing the depths of the man before me.

I sighed and bit back half a dozen words I longed to fling at him. I had no right. I *knew* I had no right, yet I couldn't let it go. I remained angry and embarrassed and chagrined. I turned away, unwilling to let him see the flush on my face. I felt like a fool. His kiss seemed a million years ago. I didn't bother to say good-bye.

Out the rearview mirror, I watched rain stream off Hank's Stetson as he stood in the funeral home parking lot, hands on hips, staring at me as I drove off.

I sped toward home, splashing though puddles. The rain drizzled to a finale halfway to the cottage. By then, exhaustion had crept into every molecule of my body. Maybe that's why it took me several minutes to notice the car behind me flashing its lights and riding my ass. Odd, since I was going a good five miles above the speed limit.

I slowed, pulled to the right shoulder so he could pass me. The sedan aped my 4-Runner's movements. *Not* what I needed now.

The sun hit the car just right, and I saw . . .

Cemetery Man. Oh, swell. More chaos. Just perfect after

today. I pulled out my pepper spray. I was far down the Surry Road. Not a store, hardly a car. Nothing.

Gert would say that's what I got for living the bucolic life.

I picked up speed again.

I flashed on Boston's shops and T-line and skyscrapers and bustle. The noise, the smells, she sheer vibrance of the place.

I took some deep breaths, talked to myself. There was no solid reason why the guy should creep me out so. But he did. And he was still following me.

I was a mile from home, but I could drive on to Blue Hill. Something would be open there.

I didn't want to drive to Blue Hill.

Penny was home, but inside. Maybe the guy was pissed off at something I'd done or said.

I was far more cautious in Boston. Here . . .

The few shining house lights cast a cozy glow. The storm had cleared and the twilight sun was warm and rosy and comforting.

Okay, so was I going to let this guy spook me or was I going to deal with it?

My driveway appeared. I cut a hard left and barreled down it.

Cemetery Man followed.

I flew from the car, flung open the cottage door, and released Penny.

"*Pozor!*" I said to her in Czech. "Guard!" I repeated, and boy, did she ever. She paced back and forth in front of me as the sedan jerked to a halt.

I held my pepper spray at the ready, but what if he had a gun and shot Penny?

This was stupid.

His door creaked open and he unfolded himself from the

car. Same long neck, small head, and humped back. Nicotine-colored tufts sprouted from beneath his Ace Hardware ball cap and gray bristles covered his leathery face. His long duster rippled over dark clothes. He wasn't smiling.

Neither was I.

"Hello," I said, using my best professional voice.

He lifted a hand, then walked closer in that same hunched-forward glide. It was dusk. The world seemed a little surreal. Was one of the Ring Wraiths from *Lord of the Rings* coming to get me?

Penny growled, teeth bared, fur bristled.

He froze three feet away. "That's some dog you got there."

"Can I help you?" I asked.

He peered at me through flat, sliver eyes. Waiting eyes. Eyes that spoke of possible mental illness in some form or other.

"Sir, I asked if I could help you."

He frowned, paused, then: "You don't remember me."

"I've seen you before. At the cemetery, Moody's Market." Maybe last night, following me.

"Not those places," he said, his voice dark and agitated. Hands on hips, chin thrust forward, he leaned closer. I caught a whiff of car oil and fish. "From before."

"Before." Penny stood directly in front of me, growling, muscles tense, ready to spring. "I wouldn't come any closer, by the way."

"You gone dumb or something, Emma? I'm Lewis. Lewis R. Draper."

Lewis Draper? I tunneled back though time. "You were one of my dad's friends. A banker. Sure, I remember. You always wore a pin-striped suit, wingtips, and a snowy white shirt." He gave me the heebie-jeebies back then, too, especially when he greeted me by pinching my cheek. I'd rarely spoken to the man. "It's been a long time, Mr. Draper."

"Call me Uncle Lewis, like before."

I never called him that. "It's good to see you. What can I do for you?"

He thrust out his lower lip. "You have any coffee?"

"Sure, yeah. Why don't you go sit on the deck and I'll bring some out."

He grinned or grimaced, hard to tell which, and it exposed a missing front tooth.

I brought a plate of cookies out to Draper while the coffee brewed. I'd been tempted to call Hank when inside, but restrained myself.

Draper could have antisocial personality disorder or he could be bipolar. His presentation could relate to half a dozen other illnesses. His behavior could also be induced or heightened by drugs. Or he might simply be putting on an act for me. Whatever the cause, I needed to take great care with the man.

He had some agenda, and I needed to find out what.

Penny Velcroed herself to my thigh.

"Here you go." I placed the tray on the deck table. I'd been jostling a memory, a sound, and I was now pretty sure that Draper was the man who'd called me in Boston about my dad. Similar intonation, same cadence, and it was also obvious he liked good drama. So why get me up here and wait until now to contact me?

Draper took a deep inhale on his cigarette, an inch-long ash dangling from the end. He was jiggling his foot, so his leg bobbed up and down.

"I'll get you an ashtray."

"No need." He flicked the ash off the deck.

At the kill site, Laura's murderer had smoked while watching her die.

"How'd your father die?" Draper asked.

I sat opposite him, Penny at my feet, ever vigilant. I told him the tale of my dad's death in clipped phrases. It never got easier.

Draper doused the cigarette between his callused fingers, then placed the butt in his pocket. "Sorry. John was a better man than most."

"He was," I said.

He lifted his feet, shod in black Converse high-tops, onto the deck rail. "I was hoping you'd remember me."

"I'm sorry. It's been a very long time."

He narrowed his eyes to slits. "You remember Annie Beal, don'tcha? And Noah and that Carmen girl? And I see you've been toolin' around with little Henry Cunningham."

How often had Draper spied on me? I fought the urge to rub my hands up and down my arms. "I need to get a sweater. Our coffee should be ready, too."

He nodded as he bent his head to light another cigarette.

Was he what my dad would have become had he lived?

Time to call Hank. I plucked the phone from its cradle.

"Don't bother," Draper said. He leaned against the door frame, the cigarette dangling from his lower lip.

"I've got to make a call. Do you have a problem with that?"

He snorted. "Just put it down."

I did. He watched while I retrieved my sweater off the sofa and fixed the coffee tray. I pictured Draper stabbing Laura. Not a comforting thought.

Outside, he lifted the tray from my hands and set it on the

table. He took a steaming mug and brought it to his lips. "Didn't want anyone interfering with our reunion."

Some reunion. "Um, Mr. Draper, I'm going to—"

"Uncle Lewis."

"Uncle Lewis, then. You called me in Boston, didn't you?"

"Mebbe."

"Why wait so long to contact me?"

"Wasn't sure it was you, Emma." He chewed a cookie, stared at me, grinning, his eyes crinkling so lines fanned across his cheeks. "When you appeared, I took an interest. Saw you tooting around town. Thought it might be you. Pretty sure, in fact. See, I've got your picture—one of those little grammar school ones—tacked up on my wall. Yesterday, I was going into Town Farm when Annie Beal was coming out. Saw you driving up Main Street. I said to Annie who you were, and she said I wasn't to tell a soul. And I haven't. Anyway, I wanted you alone."

Swell. "Why?"

"Now, here's the deal. Why I called and all. Trenton-by-the-Sea. I've got the plans pasted to the wall of my camp right next to your picture. I went down with your daddy. Down so deep, I've never got back up again. My Rubicon."

"I . . ."

He waved a hand. "You hearing me, Emma? This is taking too many words. I'm not used to it. Simple. I may look like a down-and-outer, but I've got a brain still. And eyes. And ears." He pointed a finger to his head and eyes and ears. "Thought you should know. That fire years ago at your house, it wasn't any accident."

Just like Annie had said. But . . . "The fire destroyed us. Daddy. Why would he set it? We had no money. No replacement insurance."

"Now you're getting it. You go out there, out to Trenton-by-the-Sea. You'll get it some more. Things are stirrin' up in town again. You watch out."

He moved his face close to mine, so I caught a whiff of alcohol and decay. He pressed his brown, callused hand to my cheek, then pinched it. "You go look."

Then he vaulted the deck rail and ran.

I hesitated for a heartbeat. Then I ran after him.

When I rounded the corner of the cottage, he was backing his sedan out of my dooryard.

After Lewis Draper's vanishing act, which was unfortunately reminiscent of a patient I'd had years earlier, I poured myself some bourbon, neat, and lifted the phone to call Hank. I figured he could fill me in on Draper. Except I really didn't want to talk to him. Not then, not that way, as if unkind words hadn't been spoken. I checked the number and called Carmen instead. Striking out at the restaurant, I tried her at home.

"It's Tally," I said when she answered. "I just had an unusual encounter, and I thought you might know the guy."

"You mean I attract 'em at my restaurant. Yeah, yeah. Go ahead."

"Lewis Draper."

"Lewis? You mean he actually talked to you?"

"Yes, he did. Does he eat at Town Farm much?"

Carmen chuckled. "Mostly on Fridays when we serve fish chowder. He's got a camp in the woods down to Trenton. More like a shack."

"He's not well, is he?"

"I'm not so sure I'd agree with that. The kids call him Loony Louie, but that's because he skulks around town rifling through garbage cans, leaving Post-it notes on cars, haunting the cemetery. Stuff like that. He scares them."

Mr. Post-it note. UL. Uncle Lewis. "What does he live on?"

"He digs clams in the summer, so I've heard. He hunts raccoon, too. He used to be a banker. Married once. Why? What made him talk to you?"

I was ready to tell Carmen the truth. About Lewis. About *me*. But not on the phone. "I don't know. He liked my truck or something."

"Did he, now?"

Carmen wasn't buying it. "Carmen, I—"

"It wasn't really the truck, was it? He hit you up for money, correct?"

"I'd rather not—"

"Don't start giving him money. Lewis is a bottomless pit. Annie, Dud Shea, Suki Moores, others. A lot of soft-hearts have contributed to his 'fund,' as he calls it. Still are, as far as I know. He latched on to Laura about three months ago. So be careful."

"Careful . . ." Lewis and Laura? "Yes, I will. Thank you."

"What did Hank say to you about going into Laura's house?"

"He wasn't pleased. Thanks for not calling."

"Who says I didn't?"

"Hank. Said some deputy saw me leaving the property."

"Bad about Gary Pinkham," Carmen said. "I guess I was wrong."

"Wrong . . . ?"

"I didn't believe he could have killed Laura."

"I'm not sure he did."

"It's looking that way." She sighed. "It's the image, you

189

know? I see him as an overgrown school kid wearing overalls, a purple stain on his shirt. Hard to believe that he murdered her . . . except I do."

"Do you? I don't hear it in your voice. Maybe you just want to believe, because it's easier. Because then your other friends are off the hook."

She snorted. "My husband's calling. Gotta run."

The dial tone hummed in my ear.

An hour later, I was decompressing in the claw-footed tub. Penny, curled on the rug, watched me sip my freshened bourbon.

"Want some?"

Penny squeezed her eyes shut, opened them.

I took it for a no. "So, what do you think, Pens? Hell of a day. I was too abrupt with Carmen. I've got to be more careful."

"Wuffle."

"I couldn't agree more."

Over the sound of the running tub, I heard the phone ring. Again. I let the machine pick it up. Again.

Steam rose around me, my muscles relaxed, my lids drooped.

And I saw a vision of Gary Pinkham, alive, grinning, tucking his hands into his overall pockets, licking that silly . . .

Whoa.

I set my drink on the shelf and swiped a towel across my face. Carmen had said she'd seen Gary with a purple stain on his shirt. He'd gotten the stain here, eating that Popsicle.

Which meant she saw him *after* he'd left my cottage.

A pounding at the mudroom door levitated me to the ceiling. Figuratively speaking, of course, although enough water splashed Penny to make her beat a hasty retreat.

I donned my robe and tromped to the door, leaving a wet trail behind me.

I doubted "Uncle Lewis" would pay me another visit so soon. Then again . . .

I peeked through the mudroom window, simmering with annoyance and a healthy dollop of fear.

My simmer bubbled to a boil. It was Hank.

He gave major teeth. I smiled back.

His nostrils flared. "Open up, Tally. Now."

Now, my ass. Who did he think he was? "Bite me, Hank."

"You'd better open that door or . . ."

I flattened my palms against my ears. "I'll talk to you tomorrow."

Hank got madder, shouting something that might have been "goddammed woman," although I wasn't sure.

I was in no mood to contend with this. I waved him a good-bye, then emptied the tub, dried off, and tromped upstairs to bed.

Chapter Twenty-one
Spilt Milk

The following morning, Monday, I phoned the radio station, hoping to get Ethel, the receptionist. Foster answered instead, so I chucked my plans for Laura's office in favor of a visit to what would have been my dad's Trenton-by-the-Sea. On the thirty-minute drive out, I conceded that I'd been an ass the previous night with Hank.

I powered down the windows and let the warm air fan my face. Why was I acting like such a jerk with that man? If I never saw Hank again, I could ignore the question. That made me feel worse. Whoever said ignorance is bliss was an idiot.

I began watching for landmarks so I didn't drive by what would have been my dad's development.

I was well beyond Laura's road, about twenty minutes from town, and was nearing the elbow where the Hancock River widened into Western Bay. Oak Point was at the tip, and it once had a superb lobster pound overlooking the water. As a kid, I'd done this drive with Dad dozens of times, but not since I'd been back. No reason to.

Apparently, Lewis Draper thought there was.

I passed an antiques shop on my right, then more houses, a farm stand. The river had vanished behind acres of trees.

As I curled around the elbow, the tang of the sea filled the truck's cab. Oh, I loved that smell. Then the land rose, and down below, the bay shimmered, and beyond it floated the emerald isle of Mt. Desert. I slowed down.

A split-level, a farmhouse, pastured cows, and then . . .

I slammed on my brakes, my eyes narrowing on the sign. The sign wasn't large, but was tastefully done. Carved out of granite, and with a date, one that coincided with the year my dad and I had left Winsworth.

Trenton Shores? Trenton *Shores!*

I turned right, drove through the pillared entrance that included mature pine and pretty plantings of mugo pine and coneflowers and ornamental grasses. I followed a sparsely treed road beside acres of low blueberry bushes and granite ledge and wildflowers that meandered down to the sea. My hands tightened on the steering wheel. I couldn't believe it. Town houses facing the bay perched on the exact spot where my dad had planned Trenton-by-the-Sea's homes. I'd have to check, but I'd swear they were my dad's design, too.

Someone had made a big, fat buck on my dad's misfortune. "This is too much, Pen."

Her eyes tracked to a man leading a Scottie down his azalea-bordered path and onto the road. I waved and met him as his dog lifted its leg on a bush.

"Hi, there," I said.

He nodded, his eyes sliding to his dog, who was busy with another project.

"Can you tell me who built this development?"

"I dunno. Like these Mainers are constantly harping, I'm from away." He pointed back up the hill. "Maybe he can tell you."

I looked behind me. "Thanks," I said to the man.

I walked to meet Hank.

Hank sat on a rock, part of an outcropping of ledge that flowed like frozen lava across a small field of unripened blueberry bushes. He was out of uniform, in jeans, and chewing a blade of grass.

"This seat taken?" I pointed to the rock beside him.

"Saved it for you."

"Thanks." I sat. "Sorry about last night."

"You should be. Christ, Tally, I practically banged my hand raw after you walked off like that."

"You were using your cast hand."

"I was worried about you."

"That's sweet. But I'm used to taking care of myself." I surveyed the town houses, then focused on the glittering sea. I should look at him, but I couldn't. "This was my dad's."

"I know," he said softly.

I cut my eyes to his. "When?"

"Last night. When you put your hands over your ears and had that mulish expression." He chuckled. "Damn if I didn't see Emma Blake standing right the hell in front of me. I nearly jumped out of my skin. Speaking of games . . ."

"I know." A gull cawed above our heads. "It wasn't intended as such." I told him about Lewis Draper's phone call and my reluctance to return. "I wanted to find out about my dad before I reconnected with people like Carmen and Annie. But it didn't work out that way. I ran into our former teacher, Mrs. Lakeland." As I explained what she'd said, I cringed.

"She lives in the past, Tal."

"Her words felt like acid. They burned. After that, I just couldn't tell people who I was."

He fanned his fingers across the back of my head, drew me close, kissed me long and hard and sweet. He kissed me again, and my hands slid up the side of his face and to the back of his neck, and I held him tight, cherished him, and felt his big heart encompass me.

Eons later, I opened my eyes. I studied his stern, kind face, found passion and understanding in his eyes.

He hadn't made the connection yet.

"Your dad, Hank . . ." I sighed. "I'm so sorry about your dad. Annie told me how he died fighting our house fire. I never knew."

Hank narrowed his eyes. "And that's why you didn't tell me who you were, because my dad died in your house fire?"

"I thought you'd resent me, hate me. Our fire took your father away. Mrs. Lakeland despises me. Annie doesn't. But she has a gentle heart. And her father didn't die. People believe my dad set that fire."

Two fingers pointed to his eyes. "You lookin' at me?"

Geesh, the DeNiro voice was back. "Hank, this isn't funny."

"No, it's fucked up. My dad died fighting a fire, all right. A warehouse fire on the Bangor Road."

"*What?* Oh, come on. How could Annie get it so wrong?"

"Because the warehouse burned right after your house. He went from one fire to the other. The paper messed it up, and there was no point correcting it."

I was dizzy with relief. Giddy with it. Except . . . "It must have been a terrible time for you. What about Mrs. Cavasos's hardware store? Did she lose it because she invested in my dad's development?"

"Yeah. I'm afraid she did."

"Oh."

"Carmen won't blame you, Tal. Come on. Start thinking straight."

Maybe it was time I did.

A beige sedan parked in front of my truck. "Damn!"

"Loony Louie." Hank stood and the sedan took off. He placed his hands on my shoulders. "I don't trust him. Be careful."

He leaned down and obliterated all thought with his lips.

Late that night, Hank leaned against the headboard of my bed while I traced the scar on his shoulder. Somehow we'd driven back to my place, doffed our clothes, made it to the loft.

"Who gave you that treasure?" I asked.

"A PCP-head with a knife."

I kissed it, then licked his belly button with my tongue.

"That itches. Stop, or you'll get in deep trouble."

I smiled. "Golly, Sheriff, I sure hope so."

He was as good as his word.

The following morning, while I fixed us some coffee, Penny slobbered all over Hank.

"She likes you already." Damn. That implied . . . Damn.

Hank wrapped his long arms around my waist, kissed the nape of my neck. "Might be nice if she gets the chance to know me even better."

I flipped around, faced him. "Don't assume."

"I didn't. All I said was it might be nice."

"Fine."

"And don't you get pissy on me because some guy messed with your head."

"Who says some guy messed with my head?"

"It's obvious." He brushed a hunk of curls back from my face. "Come on, Tal. I'm not the enemy."

I handed him a mug of coffee. "I know that. Sometimes I overreact."

He chuckled. "A gross understatement."

Speaking of . . . "Who built Trenton Shores?"

He chewed the end of his mustache. "This for some vendetta or something?"

I hadn't thought of it that way, but . . . "Maybe. I don't know. But they used my dad's layout. Ditto for the town house designs. He'd had it soil-tested, and it perced, and the wells and the road put in and the septic designed. If it hadn't been for the fire at our house . . . Don't you see? A part of me always believed that my dad had set the fire because he was going down with Trenton-by-the-Sea. But maybe it was the other way around. Maybe someone set our house on fire to get the land."

Hank took a pull of his coffee. "Someone tell you that?"

"Lewis Draper implied it."

"Christ, Tal. Loony Louie's been out of it for twenty years."

"Which doesn't mean he's wrong about this. Who built it, Hank?"

He whooshed out a breath. "Noah. The first of many he's built since."

"That bastard. That's unbelievable." But it made sense, at least in terms of him developing the land. Setting the fire? That seemed absurd. I poured some OJ for myself and Hank.

"It was a long time ago, Tally."

"To you. And it's small change compared to Gary and

Laura's deaths. But I won't let it go until I have some answers. Enough for now. Have you heard anything on Gary's alleged sterility?"

"I talked to a captain I know down at Fort Dix, where Gary was stationed for a while. He's digging around in the medical records for me."

I let Penny out for a run. "Laura's murder. I keep coming back to the emotions. The passionate, yet orderly method. The watching. It feels sexual, at least partly so."

"And . . . ?"

I pulled on my jeans, buttoned my white shirt, and returned downstairs. "What about the hard drive on Laura's laptop? Have they recovered anything?"

"Nope. Someone wiped it, and they did a very thorough job."

"Again, a high level of organization."

"Unless Laura did it herself," Hank said.

"What makes you think that?"

"We found it in her Jeep parked at the station."

"So, what would she need to hide so badly? Erasing your hard drive is like erasing your life." I sighed, thought about Laura's books, her home, the chaos, the stuff. "No, I believe it was most likely the killer. Was Gary a computer geek?"

Hank scratched his mustache. "He look like one to you?"

"Not hardly, but that doesn't mean anything." I headed for the bathroom. "I've got to wash up."

"I'm still not buying your theory that Pinkham was murdered," he hollered from the living room. "Not without something concrete."

"I completely agree." I scraped a brush through my hair.

"You *agree*?" he shouted. "What the . . ."

I turned on my electric toothbrush and went at it. A minute later, I sensed eyes on me. I turned. Hank leaned against the door frame, and my heart matched the speed of the brush.

His chest was bare, and he wore low-slung boxers, and his hair was spiked all crazy. But it was the hint of a Buddha belly that made me melt. And the smile that twitched his lips. And the freckles. *Hell.* I was having idiotic feelings about a man I hardly knew . . . even though we just had superb sex . . . and had shared junior-high kisses and . . .

"This is a clue," he said.

I rinsed toothpaste from my mouth. "What's a clue?"

"You're getting dolled up."

"I'm off to see Joy and Will."

His eyes narrowed. "You're relentless, aren't you?"

Echoes of my former squeeze. His distaste for my work had become a wedge between us. "Joy asked. It's what I do. You sucked me into this. When I'm involved, I don't half-ass it."

He scratched his mustache, kept staring.

"Go ahead. Feel free to say that what I do is grim, and how could anyone stand it for all these years. But it's me. It's who I am and what I do."

He grinned, then kissed me. "You haven't changed, Emma. Not a damned bit."

"I have," I said, unable to stop being so prickly. "And it's Tally to you."

"Don't get puffy. I'll go with you. Tally."

I was tempted. "No. I need to be alone, especially with Joy. I get the feeling she knew Gary better than almost anyone. I want to learn about Gary and Laura from her."

"Dinner, then?"

"Um . . ." I plucked my keys from the rack. "Maybe. I intend to pay Drew Jones a visit, too."

He crossed his arms. "Don't."

"Don't what? He invited me. He's the one who described a knife sticking into Laura's belly. A knife that's missing. Why aren't you pursuing this, Hank? Why are the state cops only seeing Gary as Laura's killer? Because Drew's a former congressman?"

Hank's eyes narrowed. "I'll let that pass. I know you're good at what you do, so I'll say this only once. Be careful with him or . . ."

"Or you'll shoot me? What, Hank? What's the big secret?"

Muscles bunched in his jaw and biceps. "Drew's got problems. It's not my business to tell you about them. Just tread lightly."

I smoothed a hand over his belly, got on tiptoe, and lightly kissed his unresponsive lips. "I won't hurt him."

I waited, but he didn't answer. I slung my bag over my shoulder and left.

My map of Winsworth said the Saccos lived out by Penasquam and Emerald Lake on Wilumet Road. It wasn't far from the quarry and fit only too well with the Gary-as-killer scenario, since he'd been staying with Joy and Will the night Laura died.

On my way, I called Joy, who said to come on along. I decided against calling Drew. I preferred to catch the former congressman in spontaneous mode.

I passed the barn that Joy had used as a signpost and pulled into the Saccos' place on the dot of one. Joy said I'd see an old black Imperial LeBaron in the yard. There it was, surrounded by a hedge of unmown grass.

That brought me back. We'd owned a car just like it. Sad how this one had gone to rot—rusted metal, tires deflated, a window smashed.

My pals in Boston would laugh if they knew I'd become nostalgia central. I parked beneath a shade tree and left Penny in the truck, with her portable water and the windows down. If she found the truck too hot, she could jump out and lie on the grass.

A kid's Big Wheel lay upside down beside a Chevy pickup in the dooryard of a good-sized yellow ranch house. As I crossed the lawn and skirted a large oak, goldfinches perched on the feeders scattered. Bluegrass twanged from the house. I climbed the steps; the music stopped and the front door opened.

"Hi, Tally." Joy wore a tucked-in baggy white dress shirt and tight jeans. Her curly mane swayed as she closed the door behind me.

The decor was retro fifties, fun and fanciful, except for the computer in one corner and an overflowing toy chest in the other. Nautical watercolors dotted the walls and the scrupulously clean room smelled of Lysol.

"Is Will home?"

She shook her head.

"How's he doing?"

"Okay."

"You?" I said.

Her lips wobbled and her eyes welled, but she hung tough. "I'm doing okay, too."

"It's okay to not be okay." I smiled. "You must be devastated to lose both Gary and Laura. You remind me of her. At least from the pictures I've seen."

Her lips turned up at the corners. "We used to kid about it. Especially since she was six inches taller than me. I'd have traded anything for her straight hair instead of this frizzy mop."

I could relate. "I bet she wished she had your curls."

Her smile widened. "She did." She rubbed the shirt collar against her cheek. "This shirt was hers. I miss her. Hey, have a seat. Sorry for the mess."

I sat on the sofa while she scooped up textbooks, a typewriter, and papers and piled them on the floor. "I'm taking a course in Orono on Web design."

I smiled. "Sounds interesting."

"It is. I'd like to combine it with my graphic work and do it full-time, instead of the post office. I need to stay home with Scooter. Will doesn't see it, but . . ."

I waited, then broke the awkward silence. "So you're a Mac addict, like me." I nodded toward the computer.

"Graphically, it's the only way to go."

"Did Gary play with it much?"

"Are you kidding? I swear to God, he was scared of the thing. Will and Gary went in on this new Mac for me last Christmas. Laura helped them pick it out. I love it. Boy, does it blaze." The spark in her eyes faded. She sighed as she sank into the recliner across from me.

"Mama!" howled a child's voice from the intercom on the end table.

Joy popped up. "He was napping. Poor baby was overtired. And that's how you catch a cold."

When she returned, a blue-eyed, blond-haired boy, maybe three years old, rode on her hip. "This is Scooter."

"Scooter wants to go potty, Mama. Potty."

Joy did a U-turn. "Good fella. Good boy." She returned minutes later bearing Diet Cokes and wearing a proud smile. "He loves going potty. I give him some books and he sits there forever. He's way ahead of the other kids in preschool. He's going to go to Harvard, I just know it."

"That would be a grand future," I said.

We sat across from each other sipping soda, and I waited.

Joy blinked rapidly, her hand death-gripping the soda can. "Scooter's going to miss his uncle. He is . . . was . . . crazy about him."

"You're all going to miss him, I'm betting."

"Yeah." She looked down, fiddled with the soda tab. "I, um, I went over to the quarry this morning. I wanted to see . . ."

"Where Gary died?"

She nodded. "I did the same thing with Laura. Isn't that weird?"

"It's not unusual at all. Seeing where a person died can be a sort of closure."

"I didn't tell Will. I felt crazy going there."

"You shouldn't."

Her head bobbed up. "Thanks."

"Do you believe Gary killed Laura?"

She ran the soda can across her forehead. "I don't know what to believe. It doesn't seem like Gary."

"In what way?"

"Oh, he was a happy-go-lucky type, you know? Not full of problems or worries." She put her ear to the intercom. "Scooter's fine. I hear him humming. No, Gary was doing pretty good. Lobstering, I mean. Laura got him to buy a new truck, had him put money down on a condo at Emerald Shores, even got him to buy that hunting camp he'd always been wanting up near Baxter."

"I see what you mean by doing well."

She sat back down. "You can make a lot of money lobstering. Gary was such a funny guy. A real tightfisted Mainer. Laura opened him up."

"Was she the love of his life?"

"No, that was Tish. But he was pretty nuts about Laura, even though he'd never admit it." She shook her head. "He

203

was two years older than Laura and me, but he felt like my little brother. He'd play dumb pranks. They would drive Will crazy, but I loved them. He'd bring me flowers after we had a fight."

"Did you fight much?"

She chewed her lip. "Gary's temper sometimes . . . He wasn't the brightest kid. He'd get frustrated. That's why I knew he and Laura would never make it. She was so smart."

"Did you know she was pregnant?"

"I knew. It was our big secret. Laura wanted kids more than anything. She was, um, a little envious of Scooter even. He called her Auntie. She was nuts about him."

"Huh. I'm surprised. Gary told me he couldn't have children."

She grinned. "Cripes, what a pile of bull. Typical Gary, though, making up stories. Probably because Laura was after him to have a kid. Laura thought she and Hank Cunningham might marry, make babies. But after she and Hank split . . . Well, I hate to say this, but I think she got desperate and wanted Gary for a stud. She must have maneuvered him into it."

"But why would Gary tell me that?"

"I'd guess so you wouldn't think he killed Laura." She listened at the intercom again for Scooter. "Tish got pregnant, but she miscarried because of the AIDS. That was before we knew she had that horrid disease."

"Maybe Gary got angry with Laura because she became pregnant?"

"I don't know. Maybe. What does it matter? Now they're both dead. And it's so sad." She started to cry, and I handed her some tissues. She balled the tissues in her fist. "Dammit."

"It's healthy getting it out. I worry about those who don't."

"Thanks."

"Joy, the night Laura died, did Gary leave any time after he got here?"

"Leave here? Gary was never here in the first place. Oh, damn!"

Chapter Twenty-two
Awakenings

I sat on the coffee table to get closer to Joy. I fought the urge to shake her. Ever since she'd said "Oh, damn," she'd been eyeballing the floor.

"Joy?" I masked the frustration in my voice and placed my hands around her shoulders. "Please look at me, Joy."

Her head slowly came up and her eyes met mine.

"Gary said he came here after he and Laura fought at the Giddyup. That he stayed here for the rest of the night. If that were true, he couldn't have killed Laura."

She played with a thread on the arm of the chair.

"A few nights after Laura's murder," I said, "Gary paid me a visit. He was about to tell me what really happened the night Laura died when Hank Cunningham arrived."

Her head bobbed up. "He was, huh?"

"It sounded like it. Yes."

"I shouldn't have said what I said. It makes Gary look bad."

It doesn't get any worse than dead. I sighed. "Joy, Gary's gone. It can't hurt to tell me now, can it?"

"Maybe."

"You know where Gary was that night, don't you?"

"Um, I think so."

"The truth matters, Joy."

"Does it?" she said. "I mean, it's all in the past now."

"Not for Annie or Noah. Or you or Will. Why would Gary lie about that night?"

"Like most folks in town, he was protective."

"Of?"

Her eyes filled with tears. "Of Drew. Drew Jones. Gary spent the night at Drew's place. They were hunting buddies. Had been for years."

The lobsterman and the congressman. Not such a stretch in Maine terms. Had Drew seen Gary kill Laura? Or was it the other way around?

"Please tell me about that night?" I said.

Joy plucked a tissue, blew her nose. "It was a bad one. Scooter was sick. Drew's dog got caught in a leg-hold trap. I don't like ratting on a friend."

"And you and Drew are friends."

"Sort of. I mean, well, it's nice. Drew acts like just any-body, even though he was a big-deal congressman."

"So you became friends through Gary."

"Just the opposite. About four years ago, I got onto the YMCA board with Drew. It was great, the way we *made* that building happen."

"So how did Gary meet him?"

"Drew was dropping off some Y papers. He spotted that dumpy LeBaron. Gary was here, and somehow Drew thought it was Gary's, so he asked him if he could buy it. As a present for his dad, who collects old Chryslers. Gary thought it was a great idea. Not Will. My stubborn old hubby wouldn't sell. Planned to fix it up. Hah. Strange as it seems, Will and Drew became pretty good friends, too. The guy hunting thing. Anyway, that's how Gary met Drew."

"Drew . . . He seems unwell."

Joy listened at the intercom, left the room, and returned in a few minutes. "My baby fell asleep looking at picture books. I put him in his crib."

"Is Drew sick, Joy? People act like it's a big secret."

She rubbed her hands up and down her arms, like she was cold. "I've heard stuff. That Drew's a drunk or popping pills. That he might have cancer or even AIDS. But no way would I ask. It's private, although I've seen his memory go haywire and the way he slurs his words. It scares people."

"What does Will say?"

"Nothing. And I don't ask. Ever since Tish's AIDS, well, people with illnesses weird him out. He hasn't seen Drew for ages, except like at the funeral, and then he gave him a wide berth."

"What about you? Have you talked to Drew at all?"

"No. He's like a hermit now. And Will would have fits if he saw me talking to him. Laura's death must've hit Drew hard. Someone told me Laura was like a little sister to him."

"Really? Who said that?"

"Either Annie or Hank. I can't remember which."

People often fought with their little sisters. "You think Drew might have gotten Gary into Satanism?"

"Gary wasn't into that stuff!"

I stayed silent and waited.

"I'm sorry for snapping at you," Joy said. "See, it wasn't really Gary's thing. It was one of Laura's . . . You know. In-terests. She was always getting into religions and dancing and art and medicine. That's why I loved her. She was such an explorer." She rubbed the collar of her shirt—Laura's shirt.

"Mama!" came a holler from another room.

Joy fetched Scooter, who walked over to me.

"Hi, Scooter." I ran a finger down his butter-soft cheek. When I offered him my keys, he laughed so his eyes squeezed tight, just like another child I'd known. Then he wrapped his fingers around the keys and started "unlocking" the coffee table.

"He's a package, isn't he?" Joy grinned.

"An adorable one."

Her face turned serious. "You have kind eyes. Anyone ever tell you that, Tally?"

"Not in so many words."

"Well, you do. Will said so, too."

"He seemed hit pretty hard yesterday," I said. "Do you really think he's doing all right?"

"Will's unique. He'll have a big blow, then he works it off out to his vegetable patch. That's where he is now."

"I didn't see him out back."

"You can't. The garden's way up beyond the house, over the hill."

"Gardening is food for the soul," I said. "I've got a small patch at home in Boston."

She shook her head. "Not like this one, you don't. Will grows monster pumpkins for the fairs. I swear, the bigger he grows them, the better he feels about life. Makes no sense to me, but that's my Will."

"I'd still like to see him."

"I don't expect him back for a while. Sometimes he surprises me, though."

I checked my watch. I'd been at Joy's for more than two

hours. She looked worn out. I could go search for Will out back, but I suspected he'd find more solace alone in his garden. "I'd better go."

Scooter wailed when Joy returned my keys. I fished around in my purse, then lifted him onto my lap. "I've got a present, Scooter."

"Present?"

The door opened and in walked Will.

"Hey, Ms. Whyte," he said, smiling.

"Hello, Will," I said. "This is one cute boy. Here's your present." I wiggled the plastic Big Bird puppet I'd put on my finger. Scooter's eyes widened. I wiggled it again. He giggled. So did I.

The jockey-sized Will gave Joy a peck on the cheek, then pumped my hand. "Nice of you to come out, ma'am. Nice of you."

"I'm happy to. And it's Tally, please." I slipped the puppet onto Scooter's finger.

Will swung Scooter up into his arms, then seated himself and Scooter on the recliner. "Joy, wash this off, hon," he said, handing her the puppet.

"Big Bird!" howled Scooter.

Joy returned it in a flash, rolled her eyes so Will couldn't see, and kissed her giggling son on his cheek.

"Hey, Miss Tally," Will said. "How about some rhubarb pie? Made it myself. Milk? Anything?"

"It sounds delicious, and I hate saying it, but I'm pretty full."

"Hey, Joy," he said. "Fix Miss Tally some pie to go."

"Yum. Sounds great." I was a bit surprised by his demeanor. Yesterday's weeping man was replaced by a cheerful fellow, his weathered face creased in a smile. Not unusual, but I hadn't expected it. "So, Will. How are you feeling today?"

He pulled a stick of Juicy Fruit from his pocket and folded it into his mouth. "You mean Gary, I'm guessing. Better. Much better. I prayed last night and accepted."

"And that helped."

He rested his chin on Scooter's head. "It did, Miss Tally. You know, when my daughter died of the AIDS, it put me though a hell I'd never known. I finally surrendered to nature and found peace. I know peace with Gary, too."

"That's a comfort, I'm sure."

"That it is. And this little fella." Will hummed Pete Seeger's "If I Had a Hammer" as he jiggled Scooter with his knee.

Joy handed me a paper plate of wrapped pie and Will a soda. He took a long pull. "Joy tell you about my vegetables?"

"That she did," I said.

Joy stood behind Will with her arms wound around his neck. Will patted her hand. "Gonna win big this year, right, hon? Yup-suh. Gonna win out to the Blue Hill Fair."

"Sounds wonderful." I stood. "If you ever want to talk . . ."

"I thank you for that," Will said.

Joy and Will followed me outside, Scooter riding on his father's shoulders.

"Solid machine." Will pointed to my truck.

"I like it a lot."

I shook his outstretched hand, then gave Joy a hug. Scooter slapped my palm in a high five.

"You'll call if you need me? The next couple of days will be hard, especially with all the arrangements for Gary's interment."

"Arrangements?" said Will. "I'm afraid we won't be doing any of that. After what he did to Laura, Gary's roasting in hell. I'll have no more truck with him."

Will's shocking words stayed with me as I drove back to the Penasquam road, then turned left in search of Drew Jones's camp road. I hugged Penny, who greeted me with licks and love.

I'd heard worse words, yet I was disturbed by Will Sacco's spurning of his son-in-law. How easily he believed Gary to be the killer. His unwillingness to bury his kin bothered me, too. Even with the knowledge of killing, most families buried their dead.

So Gary had spent the night with Drew. Surprising. Then why hadn't he helped Drew drive his dog to the vet? Maybe he'd arrived after Drew had left for the vet. Most people in Winsworth didn't lock their doors. If Gary and Drew were friends, then Gary could have just walked in and made himself comfortable.

Drew Jones appeared to touch each life involved in Laura Beal's death. He almost felt like the locus. Yet if others were to be believed, his role was both tangential and circumstantial.

A half a mile farther on my left, I spotted the sign for Drew's camp road. Just beyond it, another sign, a much larger one, proclaimed: EMERALD SHORES—A BEAL PROPERTY.

I shook my head. Noah Beal was still at it. I shot past Drew's road, then hooked a left. I wanted to see Noah's latest project, part of a many-branched money tree that had started with my father's seed.

I pulled to a stop and let Penny out to do her business. A cloud of blackflies engulfed me as I walked over to a huge billboard with an artist's rendering of condos. Tennis courts, a recreation hall, pool, even a croquet course—the place had it all, plus it overlooked Emerald Lake.

Trouble was, art didn't imitate reality. Instead, clear-cut acres of dried mud and stumps and scrawny trees surrounded me. A bulldozer stood idle beside a crude bench that faced the water, and I pictured Noah, some sucker beside him, declaiming on the beauties to come. From the condition of the pine-needle-draped dozer, the beauties to come were a long way off.

I inhaled the sweet breeze off the lake that had momentarily banished the blackflies.

Annie had to be involved, and I worried about her. I had difficulty weeping for Noah.

"*Ke mne*, Penny! Come!" She bulleted into the truck, and I could only wonder how fast she'd been with all four legs.

As I turned to leave, I spotted a Sargent Construction sign flattened on the ground. Huh.

I drove back down the rutted road. Emerald Shores offered more questions than answers, particularly why Laura would push Gary Pinkham to purchase a condominium in limbo.

I was about to pull out onto the main road, when I spotted a beige sedan idling across the way at the head of a camp road. I crept back into the shadows. The car sure looked like Lewis Draper's sedan.

"Pen, this is getting tiresome." I didn't feel threatened, exactly. *Invaded* would be a better word for it. I waited a few minutes for him to leave, which never happened. "Oh, screw it."

I pulled out, intending to confront him, and zoomed across the road. The sedan, tires spewing dirt and gravel and in a cloud of dust, took off northward. I floored it, too, hard on his tail.

It took less than a minute to realize how stupid I was be-having. I did a U-turn and headed for Drew Jones's place.

Minutes later, I rounded an elbow on a well-maintained camp road, passed a small brook and a monster rock painted with a smiley face, and went into the dooryard of Drew's camp.

What a contrast to Emerald Shores. It was a pretty place, on lower ground than Emerald Shores, but still well above the lake. To the left of the driveway, a field thick with wild-flowers rose gently upward toward the peak of the hill. Be-low the drive sat the red-painted camp, alongside a path that wandered downward to the lake and the camp's dock.

The cabin looked fairly new, yet old enough for a small lawn to have taken root and established lilac bushes to hug the house.

This time, I took Penny with me. I had no idea what I'd find and wasn't up for nasty surprises. I trotted down the steps. A two-person swing hung on the porch, tempting me to glide. Two crocks of colorful impatiens flanked the door, and someone had left on the porch light.

The screen door was closed, but the inner door yawned wide.

I cupped my hands around my mouth. "Hello?

A monster bark answered. Peanut. Penny responded with a bark of her own. But no one came to the door.

I peeked in the window, saw the U-shaped kitchen but lit-tle beyond the divider. I opened the screen door, poked my head inside. "Hello?"

A giant tongue attacked me. "Peanut!"

Peanut flopped her paws onto my shoulders, nearly knocking me down. The cast on her rear leg didn't hinder her one bit. Penny, apparently sensing Peanut's benign soul, allowed the larger dog's tongue assault with great patience and only mild jealousy.

"Okay, girl." I lifted her paws off me. "Some watchdog. Now, where's your dad?"

Both dogs followed me to the kitchen counter, where I wrote a note to Drew.

A sigh broke the silence.

Peanut vanished around the corner. I followed into a cathedraled living room and loft, much like my rental, but larger.

Drew was asleep on the couch, piled under quilts so only his nose poked out.

I peered down at him. Shadows darkened his thin face, and his eyes had sunk deep into his skull. He was bald, like Gary Pinkham, but paler.

It was as if I were seeing a wraith of someone I'd once known.

Peanut lapped his face, and his eyes slowly opened.

"Welcome to my pleasure palace, Ms. Whyte." His voice was reedy with exhaustion. "Have a seat."

He threw off the quilts and staggered to the kitchen. Bourbons all around, he said. He moved with great hesitation, then his fingers grew frantic as he searched his cabinets until he found the liquor and poured us drinks.

"It's a pretty spot," I said, accepting my drink from Drew.

"Sure is."

"All yours?" I asked, thinking of Patsy.

"Right out to the Penasquam Road. But you're not here to talk about the beauties of nature. You're here about Gary, right?"

"And Laura. And the rainy night with Peanut." I scratched her head. "She's looking good."

215

He smiled, but his eyes, so like his dad's, held such grief. "She's better." He nodded. "Much better. I'm sorry about that night. I . . . To be frank, I don't remember a lot about it."

"No problem. I'm just glad she's healing well." I took a sip of bourbon. "What about me was so frightening at the restaurant?"

"Restaurant?"

"The day you were drawing with a compass. At Town Farm. Carmen's place."

He signed. "I don't remember that, either."

"Not to worry. It wasn't memorable."

He held up his glass. "I'm going to freshen this. You?"

"No, thanks."

He returned with the bottle and set it beside a framed eight-by-ten of himself and Annie, both younger, both intensely attractive.

"Easier this way," he said, refreshing his drink. "So you didn't recognize me, huh. Lately, I let things go. Annie stormed out here last week, trimmed my beard, made me shower, cleaned up the place."

Hard to imagine Annie storming anywhere, but . . . "I know you, Drew. And not just from giving you a ride the other night."

His eyes widened with fear. "But how? I don't remember. I don't. I . . . I . . ."

I took his hand, thin, dry, near skeletal. "No. No. You wouldn't remember. It was years ago." As the fear passed, his face slackened. I told him I was Emma Blake, and I described that memorable Halloween.

A smile, a hint of his former self, eyes warm, glowing. "Yes. *Yes*. The little ballerina. My . . . I haven't thought of that in years. Those were good days."

"I expect it wasn't a big deal to you."

He laughed. "I'm afraid most of what I remember involves getting the best of Chris Delahanty, the kid who stole the candy. So tell me what you've been doing all these years?"

I sketched the outline of my life.

An ironic smile lifted his lips. "It's always complicated coming home, isn't it?"

"Boy, is it ever. Do you miss Washington? The excitement? The action?"

"Sometimes. Yeah, sure I do. But I've always loved Winsworth. Hank tells me you're quite a sleuth."

"So you knew about me," I said.

"Nope. Just the investigating part."

"Hank's the one who got me involved in Laura's death. Once I began counseling Annie, well, it's been hard. Her father's hostile, and she's feeling a terrible lack of resolution."

He rested his head in his hands for a moment, then looked up. "Emma, what's your name again? I mean now?"

"Tally. Tally Whyte."

"Oh, right. Sa . . . sad to say, I forget stuff."

"I'm sorry." His eyes were clouded, with fear, mostly, and I believed his confusion genuine. But I couldn't help but wonder if my radar was off because I felt a great sympathy for this man. "Um, would you mind if we talked about the night Laura died?"

"Wa..wa . . . would it ma' a diff'rence?" He smiled. "Sure, go for it. I'll do my bes'."

"Do you remember telling me about the knife you saw sticking from Laura's belly?"

"Did I really put it that way?" He ran a bony hand across his face. "Christ. I remember, and it was . . . hideous. I was out looking for Peanut. Sometimes she roams."

"Was Gary Pinkham with you?"

His hands tremored. "No. Not at firs'. I . . . I found Laura. Then spotted him up on the quarry lip."

He was lying. Why? "So you didn't see Gary kill her?"

Heavier tremors shook his body, like that night on the road. This was real. "Drew, what can I get you?"

He hugged his knees, rocked. Then he held up a finger and mouthed, *Water*.

I sprinted for a glass of water, and by the time I returned, he sat quietly, head lolling, eyes closed, like he'd passed out.

I pressed the glass to his lips. He drank slowly, swallowed hard, sighed.

He slowly opened his eyes, took the glass from my hand, and finished it.

"Better?" I said.

"Sure. I'm not well, and . . . Yeah. I'm better. Now, what were you asking?"

"If you saw Gary kill Laura?"

Eyes narrowed, he straightened his spine. Power reached out from him, expanded, embraced the room. He took command, and for the first time I saw him addressing Congress, scrutinizing a bill, arguing for an amendment.

"You're into the whole truth and nothing but, aren't you?" he said.

"Aren't *you?*"

"Remember, I've been to Congress." Drew's smile faded. "Did I see Gary kill Laura? Yeah, maybe I did."

Chapter Twenty-three
Bathing Beauties

I took a sip of bourbon. "Can you explain what you mean by 'maybe' you saw Gary kill Laura?"

Drew clasped his hands together. "Honestly? He was standing by the stone, not on the lip of the quarry. I saw him pull the knife from her belly. He was crying. When I walked over to him, he begged me to believe he hadn't killed her."

"And did you? Believe him, I mean?"

"I did. Yeah. Gary was a simple guy. I said he could spend the night. On our way back here, we found Peanut in the trap. I lost it. There have never been traps around here. *Never*. Days later, Hank and I dug up five more scattered around my property."

"Geesh. And Gary?"

"Oh, yeah . . . yeah. That night he helped me get Peanut out, then promised he'd be here when I got back from the vet. But he was gone when I did."

"Why didn't you tell Hank?" I asked.

"I . . . a . . . um. I think I forgot. All about it. Seeing Laura's body. Gary. Everything. I only remembered after they found her body."

"And the knife?"

"I'm pretty sure Gary left it there, but I don't know. Everything fades in and out. Don't tell Hank, huh? About Gary, I mean."

"C'mon, Drew. How can I not?"

"I know. I just was hoping . . . God, he can be straitlaced about stuff. He's not going to like it."

"Do you still believe Gary?"

He paused, then: "Yes. Yes, I do."

The drift of a cloud and the afternoon sun streaked light into the room. Drew moved to close the drapes.

"If Gary didn't kill Laura," I said, "then someone else did. That same person would've killed Gary and made it look like a suicide."

Peanut rested her immense head on his knee. He stroked her wiry fur. "I've thought about that. But I haven't spoken up because of what comes to mind. . . . You see, it would hurt Annie. She's been hurt enough."

I sipped my bourbon, peered over the rim at Drew. He looked more angry than anxious. "Could you be thinking Noah? He told me once he'd like to kill the person who murdered Laura."

"Noah talks big. Always. But he'd never get his hands dirty. Not literally. Not his style. Speaking of style brings me to Steve Sargent."

Talk about a leveler. "Why?"

"Money. Laura screwed him out of some serious dollars."

"Steve pointed a finger at you." I tried to make a joke of it. "Sounds like you guys have a thing going."

He laughed. "Maybe. Yeah, sure we have. Hey, I couldn't kill Laura. Steve probably told you I was angry at her, correct?"

"Correct."

He shook his head. "Typical. Oh, she was my gadfly, all right. But in private, we'd kid about it." He leaned forward. "Sargent doesn't know shit about me. See, I'd use a gun. On Laura. On Gary, too, except I'd shove it right in his mouth. Make sure it looked like a *real* suicide."

"What do you mean, a real suicide?"

He slapped his hands on his knees. "Christ, asthma attacks scared the hell out of Gary Pinkham. He had nightmares about them. Think he'd kill himself with one?"

"No, actually, I don't."

"Gary was quick, like me. I've hunted with him plenty of times. Neither of us could stand to see an animal suffer. Not for a minute. Neither of us would have killed Laura that way. Never."

"Interesting perspective," I said.

"What I don't understand is, why kill Gary? He didn't know squat."

"Perhaps it was because of what he learned later: the name of Laura's killer."

"But . . ." He squeezed his eyes tight. "Thinking about it makes me sick. Gives me a headache. Where's Peanut?"

"She's here, Drew."

His eyes sprang open. They were filled with panic. He pressed his cheek to Peanut's wiry muzzle, rocking, rocking.

I smoothed my hand over Drew's bald head, trying to give comfort any way I could. What had happened to his thick golden hair? What terrible thing destroyed the man who once was? "Drew?"

Drew kept rocking, rocking. Something about his behavior, his lightning changes, his shaking . . . I'd seen its twin. But where?

The screen door squealed open and Hank came barging in.

"What the fuck have you done to Drew?"

He stormed across the room, teeth bared, eyes blazing.

"Hank, I . . ."

He brushed past me, bent over Drew, shook his head.

"Hank," I said. "Drew was—"

"Don't." He eased Drew lengthwise on the couch, then covered him with the quilt.

I sat there, my fingernails dug into the arms of the chair. Hank's silence as he watched Drew disturbed me far more than his fury.

Drew wuffled out a snore. Then another one.

I blew out a breath. "Hank, now that Drew's asleep, can we please . . ."

Without a word, Hank stormed out of the house.

Right. I got up and bent over Drew. His sleep appeared natural. I brushed a hand across his cheek and went after Hank.

I walked around the camp, didn't see him. He wasn't in his car, either, but when I turned back to the camp, I saw movement down by the lake.

Penny followed me down the serpentine path to a small break in the screen of trees. Hank stood at the end of the wooden dock, his hands laced on top of his head.

As I approached, I spotted two loons surfing the wake of a lazy sailboat. Beautiful. I bent my face toward the sun, let the late-afternoon breeze comb through my hair. I wasn't going to take much of Hank's crap. "Hank."

He faced me, jaw muscles bulging. "I've been madder. Tough to remember when, though."

"I learned a lot from Drew."

"I warned you to take it easy," he said through clenched teeth.

"Why aren't we talking about Gary or Laura or Steve? Drew said Laura screwed Steve out of big money."

"Drew's interpretation."

"Then there *was* a money issue between Steve and Laura."

"So what? Steve's got plenty of the stuff. He'd never kill over it."

"But Drew was with—"

"Is this what you did? Argue with him to set him off?"

"I didn't *do* anything to Drew."

"No? You could've hurt him. Bad. You don't listen, dammit."

"I took it easy. Sadly, he kept slipping in and out of fugue states. What's wrong with Drew Jones, Hank?"

"I told you, it's not for me to say."

"Are you kidding? Two people are dead. Murdered. And you're—"

"Don't you tell me my job!"

"I'm not! But it doesn't take much to know murder eclipses Drew's addiction to whatever."

He wrapped his hands around my shoulders. Very calmly. Too calmly. "Now, you listen."

"Get your hands off me."

"You listen," he said, his voice low and raw. "Drew isn't addicted to booze or drugs or anything."

"I've counseled people for a lot of years. Has it occurred to you that maybe I can help him? But I need to understand, Hank. What's Drew's problem? What?"

223

Suddenly, Hank pushed me onto the dock, hard, landing on top of me. I couldn't breathe, felt I was suffocating.

A growl from Penny. A boom, then splinters flying, nicking my cheek.

Oh, hell. We were being shot at.

Another boom. More splinters. Hank gripped my shoulders and we rolled, and then the dock vanished beneath me. I yelled *"Skoc!"* and heard Penny's splash before cold water knifed my body. I went under.

I kicked my legs, swimming between the dock's pilings, feeling my way, and when my lungs begged for air, I inched my head above the surface. I saw Penny dog-paddling toward shore, a bunch of trees, the splash of sky, and acres of pewter water.

Where was Hank?

I clung to the board above my head as I searched for a foothold on a rock. Water lapped at my neck.

Hank surfaced, spitting water. "You okay?"

"Just peachy. Actually, I'm freezing."

"It's June in Maine. What do you expect?" He swiped a hand across his face. "Stay here. I'll go see if I can't get a bead on the shooter."

"Penny may follow. She can find him."

Hank nodded, then ducked underwater.

I paddled around between the pier's pilings, never staying long in one spot, popping my head up, trying to see something, anything. I expected to hear *ka-blam* any minute. Or feel it. Cripes.

A glint. Up on the hill near the camp. Or maybe I'd imagined it.

A noise from behind. I squawked, submerged, groped for another piling, inched up.

It was a bird. A loon.

Geesh.

Where the hell were Hank and Penny?

An explosion just beyond the dock. I slipped, went under, scrambled for a support beam, felt a . . . body! I shoved, hard, but he grabbed my leg, then my shirt, and I fought as he lifted me to the surface.

"Quiet," hissed Hank.

"You could have warned me!"

"What? Using scuba signals? Whoever was taking pot-shots at us is gone."

"How can you be sure?"

"Later."

"Welcome to Cryptography 101." I swam ashore, and a gust of chilly wind inspired me to run like hell up the steps to the camp.

"I need a bathroom," I said to Hank as I dripped puddles onto the floor.

"Are you sure you're okay?"

"Terrif." So was Penny, who at the moment was being lapped by Peanut.

Hank pointed to a door. "Towels are under the sink."

I closed the door, leaned against it, slid down so my butt rested on the cold tile.

A bullet fires. Flesh explodes. Blood spurts. The terrible stillness of death.

Laura disemboweled. Gary smothered. A man's head exploding.

I squeezed my eyes tight, took a deep breath, exhaled. Again. Again.

The man was then, an old case; Laura and Gary were now. Fear tastes like crap. Don't let anybody tell you different.

"You okay in there?"

"No," I breathed.

"What?"

"I said, I'll be right out."

I pulled a towel from beneath the sink, wiped my face, wrapped it around my hair. I stripped and used another towel to dry myself off, then wrung as much water as I could from my clothes. I put the slimy things on again and opened the door.

Hank was by the couch, bending over Drew.

I crossed the room. "How's he doing?"

"What do you think?" he said as he walked off.

Drew's flannel shirt was soaked with sweat. So were his face and hands. I unwound the towel from my head and dried his face, then his hands.

"Excuse me." Hank unbuttoned Drew's shirt, removed it, and replaced it with another one.

Crunching sounds from outside. A car had pulled into the dooryard.

"That's Mabel," Hank said. "She takes care of Drew sometimes. You might as well go."

Dismissed. Made sense. Hank knew that I'd seen Drew's arms, and he didn't feel like talking about it.

"I'll call you later," I said.

"Fine."

I gave Drew a last look, Peanut a scratch behind the ears, then left.

On my way up the path, I passed an elderly woman carrying a plastic sack of groceries. We exchanged smiles.

Mine was fake.

I barely found the energy to start the truck, turn it around, point it toward home. "I'm glad you were there, girl." I scratched Penny's muzzle.

Drew. The golden boy. I'd seen the ugly red needle tracks dotting the soft flesh of both inner elbow joints. And the scabs on his arms, like those I'd seen on heroin addicts and AIDS patients with Kaposi's sarcoma.

I wondered which one it was.

Chapter Twenty-four
Time After Time

Sick at heart, I called Carmen. Got her on the first try. Lucky me.

"Carmen, it's Tally. Mind if I come over?"

"Where are you? You sound awful."

"I feel worse. I'm on the Bangor Road, headed for town."

"I'll come out to your place. I'm on my way."

I pulled in front of my camp in a flurry of dust, just like in the movies. All I wanted to do was sleep. Why had I called Carmen?

On my way inside, I scooped up the FedEx package of Gert's reports from MGAP for the past week, then peeled off my clothes in the mudroom. I shivered through a quick outdoor shower and donned some dry yoga clothes. Even so, I was still freezing. I put on some coffee.

For all I knew, Carmen drank only tea.

What did I really know about the grown-up Carmen

Cavasos? Not much. I hated that. The need to tell her who I was burned me from the inside out.

A car thundered into the driveway.

Time to pay up. Carmen was going to be ticked. But good.

"Hey." I opened the mudroom door wide and tried to smile.

Carmen brushed by me without looking, and I simmered with anxiety.

"You got any coffee?" she asked.

"On the way." I pointed her to the couch and fetched us mugs.

She did a 360 twirl of the room. "I haven't been out here for years. Sure looks different from when the Bradys lived here."

"Does it?"

Carmen eyeballed me over the rims of her granny glasses. "You tell me, Ms. Tally Whyte."

She knew . . . she had to know . . . didn't she?

I sat beside her on the couch. "I'm Emma, Carmen. Emma Blake."

She wagged her arms like a gospel preacher. "Well, hal-lelujah. I be-lieve! Ye-ah. She is finally fessin' up."

"You knew."

Her lips pursed. "Of course I knew. Christ, Emma. Tally. Whatever. We picked out training bras together. How could I not know you?"

"But I look nothing like Emma. Straight teeth, blond hair, tall and skinny and—"

"You were always skinny."

"Well, I've got boobs now."

"You could've fooled me."

"Cute, Carmen. Real cute."

"You deserve it." She stabbed a finger at me. "You hurt my feelings, damn you. My best friend. Doesn't even tell me she's back in town. Oh, no, she decides to play cloak and dagger with *me*. How could you—"

"But, Carmen, I . . . Your mom, the store, her working at the mill. You must hate me for that."

She rolled her eyes. "*Tú idiota!*"

"I'm not an idiot. I know you, Carmen Cavasos. You hold grudges for years. *Decades.*"

She shrugged. "Okay. Okay. Maybe *one* decade I was super-pissed at you. But I got over it."

"I don't believe you."

"All right. A decade and a half. Mom finally got through to me, just before she died."

"Oh, geesh. I'm sorry."

"She loved you, you know."

"I loved her, too." I fought the tears. "But then what are you so angry abou—"

"Angry?" Carmen's ample bosom heaved. "I'm not angry, I'm fuckin' livid. You arrive back in town, not that I knew, because you don't go see anybody. So then you plop yourself in my restaurant, and you pretend you're not *you*. And then, every time I see you, you act the same damned way, and each time I'm getting madder and madder while I wait for Madam Mystery to reveal herself, since you must think I've had a lobotomy and won't recognize you. You should be shot!"

"I almost was."

Carmen's coffee hung mid-hoist. "Huh?"

I told her about my swim in Emerald Lake.

"You haven't changed. You still find trouble any which way you can."

"That isn't true."

"Ha!"

"Don't start again."

"Why not?"

I froze my face to serious. "Because I'm an eminent psychologist. And modest. And humble, too. In fact, I'm the most humble person you'll ever meet."

Laughter bellowed up from her gut. "Damn you! You always made me laugh better than anyone in the world. Why, you . . . Dammit! I will not be bought off with your smart mouth. No way. Not a word. Not one single word did I hear in all these years. Why?"

I grew serious. "Things happened. Bad stuff with Dad, with me, I . . ." I held it together . . . together . . . then the dam burst and the tears flowed and I hollered, "Oh, crap! Just forgive me, Carmen Cavasos."

Her face scrunched to a scowling prune. "Oh, what the hell." And she opened her arms, wide, and hugged me near suffocation. Just like always. Only better than I remembered.

Carmen held out her coffee mug, now doused with bourbon. Neat. Just like mine. It might have been our second. Or third. Or . . .

"Told Bob I wouldn't be home tonight."

She enunciated each word as if it were a pearl. No, a diamond. Maybe a ruby. "You think a ruby?"

"Huh?"

"Nothing," I said. "I've missed you, Carm. All these years."

"Me, too. More. Never found anybody with your warped sense of humor."

"Good thing. Hey, I've got a photo I want to show you." I stood, and the room whirled. I steadied myself, then gathered my dignity. "I think we'd better lighten up on the bourbon."

I opened the door to the room I was using as an office. "Holy shit."

"Ditto," Carmen said.

The room was trashed. A wreck. Stuff everywhere. I gently closed the door. A too-familiar chill skidded up my back, and then came the anger that burned it away.

Hank hovered while a forensics man dusted. A B-and-E in Winsworth was not a small deal.

The creep who'd invaded me had smashed windows and lights, ripped my appointment book, thrown something heavy, denting the walls. I was sure the camp's owner would be *thrilled*.

They'd left feces on the carpet, too, which made me rethink the anger behind the aggression. My gut said chaos was some sort of misdirection. That the move was one of gross calculation, rather than impassioned fury. Not that I ruled the fury out completely. No—rather, it felt more like a variation on a theme, like the plastic finger.

MGAP files lay everywhere, and when Penny raced in from her romp, she paced the room over and over, teeth bared, a constant growl deep in her chest.

If Penny had been here, she would have cornered the intruder. The intruder had to know she wouldn't be here. How?

Hard to know whether the destruction was tied to Laura Beal's murder or had to do with my dad's alleged perfidy. Someone bent on revenge could have found out my true identity.

As I watched Penny circle the room, I felt as if I were going in circles, too.

Hank sat in a chair, Carmen at the kitchen table talking to her husband, while I hunkered in on the couch. I scratched Penny's muzzle as I mulled over the evening's events, not the least of which was the gunplay out at Drew's camp.

"Interesting doings, huh, Hank?"

"You should be a damned sight more worried."

"Is that tip number seven, or what?"

"Sometimes you're a pain in the ass, Tal."

"And sometimes humor can mask anxiety, Hank. You think this was the same guy who shot at us on the dock?"

Hank cut his eyes to Carmen, who had her back to us. "I'm pretty sure that was Drew."

"Drew? No. I can't believe—"

"Yes, you can. You just don't want to." He rubbed the back of his neck. "You saw how he'd been sweating, how confused he gets. I expect he thought we were intruders down on his dock."

Drew's fugue states would make that possible. "Anything concrete?"

"His gun had been fired. I smelled powder on the barrel."

I peered out the window into the dark, cold night. "Drew and Gary were together the night Laura died."

"I know," Hank said softly. "All of it, which is a good part of the reason I believe Gary's suicide note. Drew told me when we were out digging up those traps on his property."

"He said he hadn't told you."

His face gave little away. "I'm not surprised. He's told me about Gary twice already. He keeps forgetting. I don't doubt that I'll hear it again."

"The bottom line is whether Drew killed Laura and simply doesn't remember his actions. It's out of character for the man you knew, but now . . . It's possible, Hank, whether you want to believe it or not."

He paced. "Well, I don't. He hasn't a motive in the world. Yeah, I'm sure he shot at us. But he doesn't have it together enough to wreck your place like this. What if this had nothing to do with Laura and everything to do with your father?" He held my shoulders.

I slipped from his grasp. "Twenty-some years is a long time for a grudge. But, sure, I admit I've thought of it."

He snugged his hands into his back pockets. "We were all your friends, Annie, Carm, me. Lots of people weren't. Lots were badly hurt. Some lost everything, every damned cent, because of your dad's schemes."

"But Trenton-by-the-Sea. We saw it, Hank. It's gorgeous. Successful."

"Noah's bailout, after your dad skipped town."

Oh, Dad, did you really do what they said you did? I left the house, trotted down to the beach, Penny by my side. Waves hissed against the rocky shore. *You stole from them.* But he hadn't. Couldn't. Not the dad I knew.

I saw us again sailing our little Blue Jay around the cove in Trenton, Dad laughing, telling marvelous tales, doing everything a mom should have done, would have done. But no mom was there, and so he'd made a life for us, until . . .

But he was always on the con. Always trying for the easy money.

No. Not always.

Would I ever find the truth of it?

People in pain could do almost anything. I knew the truth of *that.* Someone horribly hurt, breaking into my rental home, out for revenge, reacting to *their* pain. People's hearts can cling to the darkness for a very long time.

I ached for Boston. The Grief Shop was a jumbled world, but it was my world. It was straightforward. I knew where I stood. My past was unimportant. My todays were what mattered. I missed the comfort of that reality.

Hands on my shoulders.

"Don't pull away this time," Hank said.

His kiss probed my pain and filled me with warmth. I relaxed against him and acknowledged the kiss with my own. My hands tightened on his waist. The sea's tang filled my senses while his tall frame sheltered me from the sharp wind.

He would protect me, this man, from life's buffets and bruises.

I squeezed his waist and pushed away, not completely this time, but simply to look into his face. I could only see its outline in the light of the moon. His gentleness I didn't need to see. "You are a delicious man. A kind man. Thank you."

"A selfish man, when it comes to you."

So easy, but . . . "The comfort has to come from inside me, Hank. But I thank you from my heart."

We walked back to the camp hand in hand, and I released him as I slipped through the screen door.

An officer poked his head in from the office. "Almost done in here, Hank. Susan's finishin' up her pictures."

"Thanks, Charlie. I'm gonna hang around here awhile. Phone me if Sue gets any hits on those prints."

"Will do."

Later that night, I pushed Hank out the door, telling him to go home, get some sleep, and call me in the morning. It had become a small joke with us.

Carmen and I walked on the beach. We talked forever about our history since we'd parted. Life hadn't been gentle on either of us, and that made our bond even tighter. Having a history with someone is a good thing.

We crashed around two. Not much later, I sat up and wrapped my arms around my knees. I'd had a dream about Drew and myself as kids, once again my candy stolen by bullies, once again saved by Drew. And he was beautiful, so beautiful. But then he'd morphed into the "today" Drew—the distant and confused and shaking man. The skeletal Drew.

What *was* it about his condition that triggered a familiarity?

I tiptoed out of bed and into the trashed office. I blew out a breath. Damned if I let it spook me. I checked my computer again. Trashed. Totally. I sat on the pullout couch and wrote longhand about the night I'd picked up The Stranger and what I'd seen of Drew Jones at the camp. I made my notes as detailed as possible, then reviewed them.

I called my pal Kranak in Boston.

"This better be good," he mumbled, his mouth full of marbles. "And you'd better get your ass back here damned quick. We need you. Fuck Maine. Fuck it."

Hard to tell if he'd been drinking or asleep. I'd guess the former. He'd done a lot of that since his love had been murdered. "Thanks for picking up, Rob. I miss you."

"That's what all the girls say. Hang on. I'm gonna get some tea, so I'm more civilized."

"We know that's not going to happen." I chuckled.

While I was holding, I tried to recall a case we'd shared. I'd counseled, he'd done the forensics. I could see it so clearly. Yet . . .

"All right, what's up?" he said.

"About five years ago, a woman you brought in, elderly. I was counseling her after her husband's suicide. She was maybe eighty. Turned out she killed him, remember?"

"No," he said. "I don't."

"Think. She had this little Yorkie dog that you thought was the cutest thing. Now do you . . . ?"

I listened to Kranak slurp his tea, and I could picture him so clearly in the bunk on his beautiful sailing boat, aka home, that was docked in Boston's harbor. His eyes would be red, his hair in disarray, his jowls sagging, just a bit, and his mind crackling sharp.

"Got it," he said. "Yeah—that was some cute dog. The old guy had a disease. A death sentence. It was bad. Really bad. Which is why she whacked him."

"Yes. It was terminal and like Alzheimer's, and caused him to shake and slur his words and have fugue—"

"Wasn't Parkinson's, huh?"

"No." I paced the room. "No. See, it was different. It was—"

"Huntington's chorea," he said. "Yup, that was the name."

"Darlin' Rob. You are so horribly, terribly right."

"Somebody up there have it?"

"Maybe. Yes, I think so . . . Yes, he does."

Chapter Twenty-five
Deceptive Appearances

I walked to the couch where Carmen was sleeping, dithering whether I should nudge her awake. Huntington's disease. I needed to know the truth about Drew, and so I started framing words. When I felt ready, I placed a hand on Carmen's shoulder. "Carm?"

She levitated off the bed. "*Mierda!*"

"Sorry, Carm. I've got to talk to you."

"You scared the hell out of me!"

"Big apologies. I need to understand about Drew. I can see him so clearly, the way he used to be."

She propped herself up on an elbow. "Hank said you met him. That he was filled with a lot of wild ideas about Steve."

"Wild? I'm not so sure."

Carmen shook her head and moonlight splintered her face. "With those two, it's tit for tat. I can't believe any of it. Not Laura's death. Not Gary's. Not this here tonight. How could anyone I know do such awful things? I grew up with both of them, Tal."

"That's how it sometimes works."

"I guess."

"Tell me about Drew."

She sighed. "You never did give up."

I didn't respond, aware of how often my dog-with-a-bone trait had led to disaster. "Drew," I said. "I have such sweet memories of him."

"We all have," she said.

"It's not drugs."

Carmen shook her head. "He's not the addict type, Tally. I should know."

Her face was in shadow, but I could feel her sorrow. "You?"

"I was into cocaine in a big way," she said. "Yeah. I had some bad times. It started at college. Way before my husband and Town Farm. Bob saved me. Bob and Drew. They put it on the line to get me straight, and later helped me create the restaurant."

"And you've come through. It's a terrific eatery. A great place to hang out."

"Thanks. No, you're right. Drew's no addict."

My heart squeezed tighter. I was sure about the Huntington's, but . . . "AIDS could also induce his dementia. So could advanced STDs. My gut says his symptoms are the result of some physical precipitator."

Carmen bit her lip. "Others have thought that, about AIDS, I mean."

"Identical symptoms, right? Full-blown AIDS sufferers can experience dementia. The shakes. Short-term memory loss. The slurred speech can even be similar."

"Yes." She turned away from me.

"But the needle tracks aren't for his AIDS meds and the

scabs on his arms aren't from Kaposi's sarcoma. He's on intravenous antibiotics, and sometimes when he's in a state, I'm guessing he'll scratch himself raw. That's where the scabs come from. It breaks my heart to say it, but I believe Drew has Huntington's disease. Some call it Huntington's chorea. It's a sentence without a reprieve. That was Woody Guthrie's illness. It's genetically transmitted. Inherited. Am I right?"

She nodded. "How did you know?"

"Someone I counseled killed her husband at his behest. It was a terribly sad case. She was very elderly, frail. They loved each other very much. So I read up on it a bit. Long time ago."

"Daniel passed it on to him."

"His father is asymptomatic."

"All Daniel needs is a cane," she said. "Huntington's is a nightmare crapshoot. If you inherit the gene—which not every child does—for a long time everything's perfectly normal. If it wasn't diagnosed in your 'senile' grandfather or mother or aunt, you usually have no idea you carry the horrible gene. They weren't even able to test for it until about twenty years ago. And as with many genetically transmitted diseases, one sibling might get the bad gene, yet another sib could be free of it."

I smoothed my hand across Penny's soft fur. "I can imagine how Patsy Lee reacted to the news. First off, I can't believe Drew married her. She must have been horrified when she found out."

A tear lit by moonlight slid down her cheek. "That isn't the half of it. She's *una puta*, a bitch. She was supposed to love him. When Drew found out he had Huntington's, she blamed him, as if he had some control over it."

I was filled with an intolerable sadness. "I'm going to get some water. Want something?"

"Naw."

When I returned, I found the window open, salty air and a deep chill filling the room. Carmen was hunkered beneath the down comforter. I dragged the afghan over and crawled into the wing chair. Penny lay on my feet, a snuggly lump of warmth.

"I'd never heard of it until Drew got it," Carmen said. "And the stuff I read about it at first said it was an old person's disease."

"It's not," I said. "Although some victims don't start showing symptoms until they're well into their forties. What about Drew's brother?"

"Mitch? He escaped the gene. Only the good die young, remember?"

"So how did Drew find out he had it? I assume Daniel didn't know."

"About three years ago, Drew started having occasional short-term memory loss. We joked about it, calling them Alzheimer's moments. Everyone has them. But it got worse. And the tremors started. Sometimes he'd lose his balance. Just keel over. The doctors still didn't get it. Not until Drew found a cache of letters in the attic of Daniel's place. His grandmother, who was fiftyish at the time she wrote the letters, talked about identical symptoms, although the old gal had no idea what was wrong with her. Never did, in fact. Drew did some research. He lit on Huntington's. They tested for the gene, and there it was."

Drew was young for Huntington's symptoms, at thirty-eight only four years older than I. Imagine starting to forget things. To stand before your class or coworkers or, in Drew's case, Congress, and no longer recognizing the people. Talking to a parent, a lover, a friend and suddenly beginning to shake. Or making love and forgetting who you were making love to.

And fighting against it, beating at it, fending it off, yet *knowing* you could never, ever win.

Daniel had to be devastated, doubly so because he'd given it to Drew. And what of Annie and the others who loved him? "There is no cure," I whispered.

Carmen shook her head. "None. That's why we protect him. He was Winsworth's shining light. A great man, really. When you first wanted to know about Drew, and you never said you were Emma, I thought . . . Well, maybe you were one of those creepy reporters, digging up dirt on a former congressman. Or something worse, even."

"I understand. Drew's condition explains so much."

"But not why Laura was murdered."

"No. There's some component to Laura's death we're not seeing, Carmen. It's conceivable that Drew killed her, then killed Gary."

"It's not in his nature, Tally."

I sighed. "You mean it *wasn't* in his nature before the disease affected his brain."

Carmen flicked off the light. In the darkness, she whispered, "I've thought the same."

Dawn's cool fingers poked me awake. After my talk with Carmen, I'd slept fitfully and awakened with cotton brain.

I unfolded myself from the chair. Boy, was I stiff. I opened the mudroom door to let Penny out for her morning amble. I did a few yoga postures but wasn't able to focus. Two jays squabbled outside the kitchen window, their squawks sounding almost human.

Six A.M. was never my favorite hour. Today it was even less so.

Time for a crisp outdoor shower to clear out my cotton brain. I grabbed a fresh towel, walked around the path through the bracing air, and opened the outdoor shower door.

"Yikes!" I jumped as the neighbor's sleek black cat exploded past me. Except he'd looked mangy and ruffled and very pissed. Made no sense.

Ouch. When I'd showered outdoors last night, I must have locked him inside. That would tick him off, for sure. I took a swift shower and felt no better off than before. The sun was gradually warming the day, so I lay on the chaise and watched Penny.

I dozed. When I awakened, the smell of a rich Colombian brew drifted through the cottage window. I pushed myself up and went to get a mug. Carmen's note sat propped against the coffee machine. She'd returned to town, and I was to call her.

Later that day, I still lacked any enthusiasm for cleaning up the office. But it had to be done. I needed some extra cleaning stuff, so off I went to the Surry Store.

As I approached my truck, I spotted one of Lewis Draper's infamous Post-its beneath my windshield wiper. Just what I didn't need. I pulled it off, frustrated that creepy people kept invading my space.

He was wedged between two rocks. He would have died with the tide. I put him in the shower. UL.

He? Who was . . . The cat! Sure. That's how the black cat had gotten in the outdoor shower stall. No wonder he looked so crummy this morning. Draper had placed him there to keep him safe. Made an odd sort of sense.

Who the hell would try to drown a cat like that? Sick.

I slung my backpack into the truck and took off. The truck bumped and lumped up the driveway and onto the Surry Road.

I'd sensed the intruder's anger as he'd trashed my office. But the cat between the rocks, that was cruel. I now saw the invasion of my home as more than a bid for attention.

It could have been Draper, of course. The Loony Louie I remembered might do something like pretending to rescue a cat from faked danger. But I wasn't seeing it. No, the cat must have been fussing about something or gotten into the camp, and so the intruder had given him a death sentence to get him out of the way. But why bother? Why not just let him go? Then again, trapping and torturing a cat with drowning was a scenario that uncomfortably echoed Peanut being caught in the leg-hold trap.

If the guy who'd trashed my office had tried to kill the cat, then I would bet the same person had killed Laura Beal. Same unhealthy scenario as with Peanut. Similar fury and passion.

I didn't like that one bit. Nor did I much like Draper following my every move. Things were getting complicated. I expected they'd get even uglier.

I did a speed clean of the office. The cops had taken the feces, and I got some pet cleaner to take care of the urine. The place no longer stank, a huge relief. I suspected I'd end up paying the landlord for damages.

I left the Fantastik piled with the rest of the cleaning stuff by the office door and called Ethel Gropner, the receptionist at Laura's radio station.

"WWTH," said a chirpy voice I didn't recognize.

"Hi. This is Tally Whyte. Is Ethel around?"

"Hold a moment, please."

While the station played ads, I rehearsed what I'd say to Ethel. A click interrupted a jingle for the Trenton Lobster Pound. "Ms. Whyte, it's Foster."

"Hi. I was looking for Ethel."

"That bitch."

"Pardon?"

A sigh. "Oh, I shouldn't be so irritable, but she's left the whole transition to the new owner thing right in my lap."

"In other words, Ethel quit?"

"So it appears. And without a minute's notice, either. She didn't come in this morning, and when I called her place, I got one of those disconnect messages."

"Was there a number where—"

"Not on the recording. And there's no forwarding anything on her employee card, either. I drove out there. The place was empty. I ask you, how could she do this to me? She hated the idea of Mr. Beal selling Laura's station, but . . . Can I help you?"

"Um, no. I was calling to make a date for lunch. Hmm. She didn't mention anything about leaving to me."

"Ever since Laura . . . Well, Ethel's been pretty unhappy here. Did she tell you Mr. Beal wasn't planning on keeping her on?"

"I'm not surprised there was no love lost between the two. I'd like to come over and—"

"Impossible. Mr. Beal has left strict instructions that no outsiders be permitted to visit until the station's sold."

"But—"

"I'm sorry, but no."

"Sure. Okay. Thanks anyway, Foster."

I felt a niggle of concern about Ethel as I put the phone on its cradle.

It rang. "How goes it?" Carmen asked.

"Fine, I guess." I told her about Ethel's departure.

"Not to worry," Carmen said. "I saw her this morning in that clunker Bob's Limo uses to take people to the airport."

Relieved, I described Laura's mural and Foster's inflexibility about letting me back into the office. "There might be something important up there."

"You could always ask Noah," she said.

"Not funny," I said.

"We can break in."

"Another lame joke, Carm."

"No, I mean it," she said. "Um, well, it's not something I'm proud of, but during my druggie years, I got pretty good at it. I never got caught."

"There's always a first time. I'm not eager for publicity, let me tell you."

"Didn't you just say something important might be there?"

"Don't remind me," I said. "Let's forget it."

"I'll do it myself."

"My ass, you will."

"Just tell me what you need," she said. "And I'll find it."

"It's not the same as cooking eggs, dammit."

"Aren't we the superior psychologist."

"Come off it."

"No, you. Are you in or not?"

I pictured a funeral home I'd once entered unheralded. That had been another life. "Yeah, I'm in."

We decided to wait until dark, Carmen's one sensible idea. Hank phoned at two and reported that so far the prints lifted from the office didn't belong to anyone identifiable. He wanted to see me that evening, and I put him off with a fabricated sore throat. That started the guilt thing going.

A knock at my door around three increased my angst. I'd

been trying on my B & E costume and hadn't heard anyone in the driveway.

I stripped, pulled on shorts and a T-shirt, and opened the door to Annie and Steve Sargent. Annie held a cookie tin and wore a smile.

"Hi," she said. "We thought we'd drop by."

"Hope you don't mind." Steve doffed his bill cap and they came inside.

"I made these for you." Annie handed me the cookie tin. "Do you still like them with walnuts? Like you used to? Oops."

"You betcha." I opened the tin. Fat, luscious chocolate-chip cookies were piled high. I got out the milk and glasses. Steve leaned on the island counter, while Annie took a stool. "And it's cool if Steve knows, Annie. Just about everyone does at this point."

"Knows what?" Steve said.

Annie smiled her pixie smile as she told him about me. His surprised expression looked genuine and blissfully free of guilt. Soon, we were reminiscing about our youth.

I bit down on a cookie, crunched a savory walnut-chip combination. "Divine. From scratch, right?"

Annie blushed. "It's easy. Carmen told me about last night. I thought you might need some comfort food."

"That's for sure," I said between mouthfuls.

"I'm sorry about your stuff that got trashed," Steve said. "If I can help . . ."

"Thanks. It could be worse. No one was hurt, thank heavens."

Annie laughed, a wind chime sound that I hadn't heard since we were kids. She was healing.

Steve frowned. "Have, um, have you made any progress with Laura's murder?"

"You still don't think Gary Pinkham did it."

"I don't," said Steve. "And neither does Annie."

Annie flushed. "All I said was I wasn't sure."

Steve laid his hand over Annie's. "I know your feelings, hon."

His possessiveness disturbed me. Annie was such a pleaser. I wished I knew where her true feelings lay. "I met Drew yesterday," I said.

Steve reddened. "Annie and I hoped to talk to you about, well, our relationship."

Annie folded the napkin, running her hands along the creases.

"How about Annie speaks for herself, eh?" I said.

"We, uh, well, Steven and Drew and I—"

The rumble of a car interrupted.

"That sounds like Daddy."

"Shit," Steve said.

Chapter Twenty-six
To Catch a Thief

Annie wouldn't meet Steve's eyes. "He had to drop some papers off down on the Island. I didn't think he'd be so fast."

"In other words," Steve said, "you told him you were coming out here."

"I had to. You know how he gets."

Steve sighed, kissed Annie on the lips, and gave me a waved salute. "I meant that offer about helping out."

When I answered Noah's knock, he and Steve breezed by each other exchanging crisp nods.

Once Steve was out of the way, a beaming Noah strode into the living room, arms spread wide. The curmudgeon had vanished. I'd seen it a thousand times, knew it was temporary, and wondered if he was just trailing Annie or if he wanted something from me.

Worried that Annie would pay later, I said, "Gee, Noah, good to see you. Annie said you might stop by. I asked Steve to give her a lift out."

He put his pipe to his mouth, about to light it.

"Since this is a rental, Noah," I said, "maybe you should do that outside. Do you mind?"

He smiled around the pipe stem. "Not in the least. The place looks good. If Harm ever wants to sell, he'd better give me a jingle."

More beaming. Noah's affable-realtor mode was scary as hell.

I held out Annie's cookie tin. "Have one."

"Don't mind if I do." He plucked the largest one from the container. "Annie's the best cook I know. I've been meaning to thank you for all your help during our time of trial."

"What little help I gave, I was glad to do it."

"More than little, m'dear. I apologize if I seemed . . . out of sorts at times."

Hell. An apology from Noah meant he wanted something. "No need for an apology."

"At least Laura's killer is dead."

I cut my eyes to Annie, who was studying the floorboards. "Do you really think it was Gary Pinkham?" I said.

His brows beetled. "Of course it was. No doubt about it."

Annie's eyes, wide with fear and pleading, cut to mine.

Would that I understood the relationship better. I didn't like Annie's fear. She adored her father, but their relationship was more complex than most. Her affect bothered me.

"Terrible about your home invasion," Noah said.

Why Winsworth bothered printing a newspaper eluded me. "It's already cleaned up."

"And you on vacation, too."

His eyes, keen and jabbing, probed mine. Looking for weakness. I didn't want to accommodate. "Yes."

"I'll send Will around to help out. How'd that be?"

"Will Sacco?"

Noah chewed on his pipe. "Does some handyman work for me."

"You don't mind that he was Gary Pinkham's father-in-law."

"Can't blame him for the boy's behavior, now can we?"

"Well, thanks for the offer, but—"

"I insist. It's the least we can do."

"Thanks, but no." Our eyes locked. It was a test. Ahhhh. Of course. Noah knew I was Emma. He also knew I was here to learn about my father. I'd swear he was telling me swords were drawn. The man understood the art of power.

Then again, I was no pushover.

What should I be hearing? That he'd been the one to spread the rumors about my father. That he would continue to stain my father and myself with arson and theft. That he owned Annie and would never release her. His eyes, cold and fathomless like the sea they resembled, dared me to see the truth. He was a masterful deceiver, yet not totally adept. After all, a true ruler doesn't have to hide much.

His desire—Trenton-by-the-Sea—attained. Oh, he'd vilified my father, all right. Had he gone the next step?

The fury grabbed me. I wished to spit accusations, demand answers. Noah's smile widened.

Too soon to smile, Noah. Way too soon. He thought he had me. And for a moment, he did. But I wasn't my dad.

I nodded, grinned. "Of course, Noah. Send Will along. I can't thank you enough. I'm sure I'll enjoy his company, having met him out at his place just yesterday."

Noah frowned, but recovered fast. "I'll see what his schedule is. Let's go, Annie."

Annie and I hugged, and as she did, she whispered, "I'm marrying Drew next week. I wanted you to know."

I tightened my arms. "Annie, don't. No. Drew's illness. You and Steve. Let's talk."

She softly pushed me away. Her eyes were dead. "It is what it is."

"Daughter!" barked Noah.

"Coming, Daddy."

"Wait, Annie. You—"

"We're going to Portland for a few days to buy my trousseau."

I closed the door as Noah's Jeep vanished up the drive. Annie marrying Drew, a disaster.

Something was very wrong. I felt it in Annie's tremble and Noah's triumph. Annie *must* know about Drew's illness. But what if she didn't? I checked my watch. I barely had enough time to change clothes again before I met Carmen downtown.

Black leggings, black turtleneck, black hat. Even black sneakers. I looked like something out of *The Matrix*. Although I felt foolish, the outfit made sense. I carried my fanny pack, which held my digicam, gloves, a Mini Mag lite, and my lucky faux rabbit's foot. The last thing I wanted was to get caught, especially by Noah.

I wished I could bring Penny, but that wasn't a smart idea.

I was doing this to cement my relationship with Carmen as much as to find Laura's killer. Noah had to have cleaned out her office.

As planned, Carmen stood waiting in the library parking lot at nine. Not as planned, she wore a Hawaiian print shirt over jeans.

"Geesh, Carm." I strapped on my fanny pack. "What happed to the 'we'll wear black' routine?"

"My hubby happened. I couldn't. Not to worry."

"You say that way too often." I pulled on my gloves. "Annie stopped by today. She told me she's marrying Drew."

"No way," Carmen said.

"Seems like, according to Annie."

"*Imbécil!* It's all Noah's doing, I bet."

"Why am I not surprised? What's the deal?"

"Emerald Shores. Tell ya later. We'd better go."

We trotted around behind the library, moving from tree to tree, then we sprinted across the treeless grounds behind WWTH. Carmen waved me over to the lone maple about sixty feet from the rear of the building.

She pointed to the light shining from the old Victorian's second story. "That's the studio area. The light on the first floor is for the downstairs hall. That's it. Noah's so cheap."

We made a dash to a padlocked bulkhead and crouched beside it.

"I checked it out this afternoon," she said. "Piece of cake. I got a lot of practice at Cornell."

"Cornell?"

"My alma mater."

Mine, too. Twilight Zone time. Carmen and I had a lot to talk about, including Annie's marriage and Gary Pinkham's Popsicle-stained shirt. But not at that moment, since she'd already picked the lock. She squirted some WD-40 on the hinges, then opened one of the wooden doors.

It creaked.

"Swell," I said.

"Oil doesn't always work," she hissed.

We listened. Heard nothing.

Carmen let out a breath. "Go down the bulkhead steps, then turn on your light. There are two staircases. Take the one on your left. It leads to the third floor and Laura's office. As you insist, I'll stand lookout. I don't see why—"

"Forget it, Carm," I hissed. "You've got kids now. If you got caught . . ."

Carmen squeezed my shoulder, whispered "Good luck,"

and I descended the old fieldstone steps to the dirt-floored cellar. I flicked on the flashlight and it caught a rat scurrying across the floor.

I turned to run, but Laura's face, the one in her painting where the mother cradled her babe in her belly, begged me to climb the staircase.

I climbed.

It was close and confining, and each step was steep and narrow. A servant's staircase. By the time I hit the landing on the third floor, I was breathing hard.

I paused. My Mini Mag showed me the doorknob. I flicked off the light, turned the knob, and held my breath.

Pale light leaked up from the stairwell fixture on the landing below. The place was silent. I squeezed out the door, closed it, then tiptoed across the carpeted hall to Laura's office, turned the knob.

The door was locked.

Crap.

I assessed my options. I could kick in the door. Go get the DJ to let me in. Try the credit card trick. I scratched my head, which itched from all the sweat accumulating beneath my wool hat.

My watched read 9:30. In and out in one half hour was what I'd told Carmen. Even the best-laid plans . . .

I went and got her.

Carmen was obviously in shape, for she was barely panting when we arrived at Laura's office door. She used her same set of lock picks, and in seconds swung the door wide.

"I can't believe you have those things," I whispered.

"Always do when breaking and entering. I'll keep lookout. You'd better hurry up, Tal."

I caught her smile as she turned to go back downstairs.

* * *

I closed the door, locked it, and allowed my eyes to adjust to the room's light. The window shade was up, so I sprinted across the room, closed it and the drapes, then flicked on my flashlight. I did a quick sweep of the room.

I felt sick. Noah had covered Laura's stunning murals with coats of puke-green paint. Trite seascapes of Maine's rocky coast hung in their place. Laura Beal would have hated the mediocrity of those paintings.

I sighed, checked behind the "art" for a wall safe, then started in on Laura's desk. A few papers remained—bills and articles and notes, I presumed. I skimmed them, spread the papers out on the desk, and photographed them.

After each set, I replaced the papers, then went on to the next. My belly growled. Stomach cramps. I was not meant to be a burglar, no sirree.

When I finished with the desk, I moved to the filing cabinet. I ran the light down the names on the tabs. More bills, Howard Stern, Ratings, Personnel. Everything seemed related to the station, and I hadn't time to photograph it all.

I opened the closet. It was jammed with clothes. I guessed she often changed at the station. I tried to put myself into Laura's head. If I had something to hide, where would I put it? I ran my hand beneath the sweaters piled on the closet shelf. Nada.

I closed the door, then explored the bathroom. I flipped through the magazines on the floor, unzipped the makeup bag, looked inside generic medicine bottles, and spotted the diaphragm case in the medicine cabinet. It looked awfully unused, and I couldn't picture it being the birth control of choice for Laura. Hmmm. Of course, no guy would touch the thing. I opened the case and lifted the diaphragm from its plastic house.

Ha! She'd stashed a pair of moonstone earrings beneath the diaphragm. Pretty clever. Did the earrings mean something special or was she simply keeping them safe from theft?

I leaned against the sink, panned the room with my eyes. Perfumes, a dried-flower arrangement, a basket with a lid. I searched them, found nothing. The tiny linen closet held towels, more potions and lotions, and a box of Tampax. The box looked awfully old and well-worn, like she'd opened and closed it a lot. Another oddity. We girls need a new box each month.

I lifted the lid. Bingo.

I dumped the box's contents on the desk blotter, spread them out. A dried rose. A moonstone necklace that matched the earrings. Two Howard Stern hate letters. Whoa. One was written by Will Sacco. Papers on Emerald Shores. And a Dear John letter signed by . . . I was having trouble reading it.

Footsteps on the stairs.

Shit! I scooped everything back into the Tampax box except the Emerald Shores papers, which I slid into my fanny pack.

A key grated in the door. I grabbed the box and ducked into the desk's keyhole.

I finally knew the meaning of a cold sweat, except I was hot as hell.

The door whooshed open. The lights flashed on.

I bit my lip until it hurt.

"Hey, man, I told you no one was here."

I didn't recognize the voice. Then footsteps, a door inside the office opening, then another. The closet and bathroom.

"Hey, old man Beal got me out of a warm bed because of some light he thought he saw when he drove past?"

Foster.

"You're such a suck-up," said the other man. "Maybe it's Laura's ghost."

"Not funny, man." A ripping paper sound. "Here's the lock I bought. Do it now."

"Fuck you, man. You forget I'm Winsworth's number-one DJ? Just because you're gonna own this junk heap doesn't mean—"

"It means you'll be out of a job if you don't play handyman. I'll take care of the booth. And make sure you don't lose the combination."

The door closed, and then the screech of a drill.

A combination lock on the door. The *outside* of the door. Swell.

I sat there, scrunched in the keyhole, listening to the DJ change the door lock. So Foster was buying the station. He'd lied about that. He could have lied about Ethel and fired her. What other horse hockey had he slung at me?

The drilling stopped, and then footsteps, heavy ones, going downstairs. I sat for another endless ten minutes. Sweat drenched me when I emerged from the keyhole. My legs weren't too happy, either, and something in my left knee went crunch—an old ski injury.

I shined the Mag on my watch. Ten-thirty. Time sure flew when I was having such a ball.

I was screwed, literally, by the new lock. I fought the urge to scream for Carmen. Ms. Magic Fingers could get me out, I was sure. I sighed. At least I could do something productive while I figured out the mess I was in. I undid the Tampax box and photographed everything. I replaced it in the linen closet. Bet that was one item Foster knew nothing about.

257

I double-checked that I'd returned everything to its place, which I had, then probed for secret passages, of which I found zip.

I slumped on Laura's couch.

How the hell was I going to get out?

I ran a finger beneath my wool cap. Yuck. I wiped it on my black jeans. What to do? No secret passage. No Carmen. No clue. Well, maybe one, which had about as much appeal as skydiving. Nonetheless . . .

I peered out the bathroom window into the blackness. Lights shined from the hill, cozy people in the comfort of their homes. I could probably squeeze through the bathroom window. Then what?

The old Victorian had lots of roof projections and plenty of angles where my sneakered feet could find footholds.

Except I was on the third story. It was a hell of a long way down.

If Foster discovered me, I'd have to explain what I was doing there and why. He'd call the cops. Hank would appear. Cripes. I might spend the night in lockup, and for sure, Noah would find out. Annie, too.

The scenarios were worse if Foster was Laura's murderer.

There was always the roof. I shoved up the bathroom window. It opened easily. Chill Maine air cooled my face. The outdoors was right there.

I peered down, into the blackness. No way could I do that.

Then again, Foster had emphasized his warm bed. Perhaps he was back there and off the premises. That left just the DJ. The number-one DJ in Winsworth, as he'd pointed out. Oh, yes.

* * *

I pounded on Laura's office door and yelled, "Help! Help!" Soon, footsteps thundered up the staircase.

"Who is it?" came a voice through the door. He sounded nervous. Fearful, even.

"A friend of Ethel's," I called. "Please get me out of here."

A pause, then the lock rattled and the door swung open, presenting a scraggly-bearded doughy-faced guy about my height.

"Hi!" I said, thrusting out a hip. I'd stashed my cap and gloves in my fanny pack, dabbed on some of Laura's makeup, and shimmied into a red miniskirt from her closet.

"How the fuck did you get in?"

I smiled, wide-eyed. "The front door. It was unlocked."

"What were you doing in there?"

I flicked my hair, went with a chagrined look. "Hey, I know this is sort of uncool, but Ethel promised I could shoot Laura's murals for a project I'm working on. I, um, Foster put the kibosh on that, and they were so cool-looking that . . ."

He crossed his arms. "Yeah, and . . . ?"

I licked my lips. "I sort of snuck in to do it. I didn't know the paintings were gone. I heard you guys, and I hid."

He smirked. "What did you think when we put on the lock?"

"Um, I was scared."

"Yeah?" He grinned.

I lowered my lids, rested a hand on his arm, deepened my already husky voice. "I was really scared. I'm glad you showed up."

"Yeah?" He moved his hand to my hip, wiggled his eyebrows. "There's a couch in there."

Gross. I stuttered, just a little. "Wha . . . What about Foster?"

"Gone."

Yes! "Aren't you supposed to be doing your DJ thing?"

"No problem. I've got a block of tunes going. Hey, I can be quick."

I just bet. I smiled. "Um, sure." I took his hand, led him inside the room.

"No lights!" he said.

"No way." I turned, laid my arms on his shoulders, kissed him, tongue and all, which was extremely unpleasant.

"Nice," he said.

I lowered my voice to soft and smoky. "I'm so glad you're, um, interested." I had *no idea* how I was going to get out of this mess. But maybe . . .

"Been a while, has it?" he said.

"Well, yeah. Some guys get . . . paranoid."

"Paranoid?"

"The dumb HIV thing."

He jerked back, swiped a hand across his lips. "You bitch. Get out. Get the fuck outta here."

I fled down the front staircase. I heard swearing and the water running at Laura's sink.

Maybe my timing wasn't so bad, after all.

Chapter Twenty-seven
Smiley Face

I filled Carmen in on my "capture" as we raced back to my truck.

"I'll drop you at Town Farm," I said, tossing my gear into the 4-Runner. In the restaurant parking lot, I pulled beside her electric/gas car. We sat for a minute, catching our breath and our sense of where we were and what we'd just done. It was late. The lights on Main glowed on empty streets. Even the tourists had called it a night.

"Please explain about Annie marrying Drew," I said.

"Noah wants Drew's property for his Emerald Shores subdivision. And Drew's determined to make things right with Annie before he loses it completely."

"I thought Noah was hurting for money."

"Money?" She snorted. "The deal involves money, but this is more like a slave trade, if you ask me."

"Nasty way to put it," I said. "But I see what you mean. Annie for Drew's property."

"That's how it works for Noah. It sucks." She started to get out.

"Wait." I laid a hand on her shoulder. "How come you knew about Gary's Popsicle stain?"

"Huh?"

"The purple Popsicle stain. He got it the night he paid me a visit. The Popsicle was from my freezer. If you saw the stain, that means you saw him afterwards."

She ran her hands through her auburn hair. "I did. Briefly. He blew into the restaurant looking for Drew, then blew out again. I told Hank. He didn't think it meant much."

"I—"

"It's okay." She hugged me, and we promised to connect tomorrow.

The ride home seemed to take forever. I opened the windows and let the cool summer night dry the sweat on my face. My scalp itched. Tonight was one of the lamer things I'd done. I'd just committed my first burglary. Annie was being sold for Drew's land. And Gary had been looking for Drew the night he died. Which ones were connected to Laura's murder remained up in the air. I knew which linked to Noah's greed.

A car followed me into my dooryard. No lights. Damn. I wasn't in the mood for any of "Uncle" Lewis's games.

The cottage's sensor floodlight beamed on. Oops. It was Hank, out of uniform and driving a pickup. And he was looking none too happy.

"Hey!" I slipped out of the car. "What's with the lights off?"

His scowl deepened. He walked over to me. I spotted Penny at the window, watching. Hank whooshed out a breath. "Hot red skirt and lipstick, which is smeared, by the way. Is this how come you couldn't have dinner with me?"

"You bet . . ." I caught the hurt in his eyes. The big lummox. I caressed his cheek. "I haven't eaten. Come on inside, and I'll let you cook while I tell you all about it."

Hank cooked while I told him of the night's adventure. He didn't blink when I described burglarizing Laura's radio station and kept right on sautéing mushrooms for the omelet he was concocting. His only "tell" was a tightening of the lips, a sure sign of his displeasure.

"I should frigging arrest you," Hank finally said.

"I don't blame you." I poured the cabernet I hoped would soothe his ruffled feathers. "Since you're the county sheriff, technically it's not your jurisdiction."

"Fuck my jurisdiction."

"That's exactly what you've been doing, investigating Laura's death."

"Stop trying to sidetrack me. I'm not amused, *Emma*."

I snorted. "I didn't break into the station to amuse you."

"It was wrong."

"It's done. It's over. Fageddaboutit."

Hank didn't smile, and his hand whitened as he squeezed the stem of his glass. "It was illegal. Plus, you could have been hurt."

"That's why I didn't climb out that window."

"Christ Almighty!"

I put plates mounded with fluffy omelet on the table, then sat. "I was scared. Okay? I didn't like it, and I won't do it again. Can we lighten up here?"

"So who helped you?" Hank asked.

I stopped midforkful. "No one."

"Tally." He drew it out like a three-syllable word.

"What? You don't think I could do it myself? That hurts, Hank. This omelet's terrific, by the way."

"Don't change the subject. And, no, I don't think you could get inside the station by yourself."

"Well, I did."

"Liar."

"Prove it."

"I plan to." He took a pull on the cabernet. "So, what exactly did you accomplish on this misguided adventure? Other than scaring the hell out of Mark 'Cruise Machine' Smith?"

"First off, I saw Will Sacco's hate letter."

He nodded. "Good, but not great, since it was about the station playing the Howard Stern show."

"Yeah, but Ethel told me she and Laura joked about those letters. So why hide Will's in her Tampax box?"

He nodded. "Valid question." He polished off his omelet.

"Second," I said. "Foster's about to become the new station owner. Did he fire Ethel because she knew something, or did she leave of her own accord?"

"Go on."

"Also, were Foster's feelings about Laura genuine, or were they an act to cover her murder and his subsequent purchase of the station?"

"A stretch, especially since according to your theory, the killer did Gary, too."

I cleared our plates. "Yeah, but I thought we agreed Gary was killed because he knew something."

"We didn't agree at all, dammit. But what you're saying means that the killer had to know Gary pretty well. I doubt he and Foster ever met, but I can find out."

"Next up. Emerald Shores. I found some papers."

"And . . . ?"

I stopped rinsing the dish. I wasn't about to tell Hank that

I'd taken them with me. "I have to wait until I see the photos of the documents, since I didn't read them there."

"Why not? You did everything else."

"Very funny."

Hank walked over to the sink. "Drew was considering going in with Noah on Emerald Shores. At the last minute, he opted out."

"Because of his Huntington's?"

Hank paused. His eyes were the bluest I'd ever seen them. I was shocked by the grief he allowed me to see.

"Carmen told you," Hank said.

"Yes."

"Drew has no use for any long-term investments."

"No, I guess not. It's terribly sad."

Hank took the plate from my hand, finished rinsing it, and put it in the dishwasher. "I'll admit, Emerald Shores has piqued my interest, too."

"I saw the sign out there. What happened between Noah and Steve?"

He rubbed his thumb against his fingers. "Bucks. Noah was underfinanced. At least that's how I heard it. Steve has pulled his crew until he gets more money. I see Steve's point, him having to cover payroll and all. But it put Noah in a tizzy."

"So how does Laura figure into all of this? Why did she have Gary buy an Emerald Shores condo? For a lark? To get money for Noah? I wonder. And last, but not least, there's the Dear John letter."

"From . . . ?"

"I'm not sure. That was when Foster arrived at the door. But I read it later. The signature was smeared. I think it read 'Striker'."

"Striker? Are you sure? Only one I know by that name is Helen Striker, out to Winter Harbor. She's got seven kids, a bunch of grandkids, none around here, and is about seventy-five. What did the note say?"

"It wasn't very clear. The whole page was written with a felt-tip or something. Laura must have cried all over it. From what I could tell, it was the usual 'I'm sorry to hurt you like this, but it's good-bye' kiss-off from some man she was seeing. It was hard because of the smudging and the lousy light."

"Maybe the photos you took will help."

I sighed. "That's a problem. I thought I was so smart, using my digicam so I could see them on the computer. But my home invader trashed my computer. I'm stuck. Is there an Internet café in town?"

"Nope." He flipped open his notepad, wrote, then handed me the page. "Here's Everett Arnold's number. Use my name. He's got a state-of-the-art Mac."

"Super." I reached for the phone.

Hank rested his hand on mine. "You've been away too long, Tal. Everett probably went to bed around eight."

"Oh. Right. I'll call in the morning. Hank, why didn't you tell me that Gary Pinkham was looking for Drew the night he died?"

"Because he never found him."

"According to Drew?"

"Who else?"

I let it lie. "I've got an itch."

"Huh?" Hank said.

"I don't know. There's something . . ." I leaned my hip against the counter. "Bugging me. Yeah. But . . . I'm not getting it. I'm beat. Time to call it a night."

He pulled me close, kissed me, then walked off.

"What are you doing?"

"Forgiving you." He returned wearing nothing but a smile, as the saying goes, and carrying some bath towels. "Thought a shared outdoor shower might revive you long enough to . . ."

"Yum."

Wednesday morning around eight I awakened to the trilling of some bird I couldn't identify. I'd left my bird books in Boston, along with my feeders. A shame.

Hours earlier, I'd felt Hank's lips on mine, then heard him descend the staircase. Sigh. Last night had been spectacular. It wouldn't be hard to become addicted to the Winsworth sheriff's loving.

During my shower I pondered why certain men got under my skin and others didn't. No flash of insight hit me. I fed Penny, then poured a mugful of coffee. I dialed Everett Arnold and was told by his wife that he'd gone to Bucksport and should be back by three.

I could always use a PC, yet I'd feel more comfortable on a Mac. I'd wait for Arnold.

The Emerald Shores contract was burning a hole in my virtual pocket. I plucked it from my fanny pack and retired to the deck with my bowl of Cheerios, more coffee, and a glass of juice.

Ugly clouds dueled the sun. I hoped the sun won.

Penny curled up on the deck beside me as I began to read.

Lawyer-speak is my least favorite form of literature. I laid the contract on the table, pressed two fingers to my eyes. They hurt from the ten pages of gobbledygook I'd just read.

I scratched the top of Penny's head. "Pretty informative, eh?"

She sighed.

Noah Beal. Laura Beal. Steve Sargent. Patsy Lee Jones. Chip Vandermere. And Daniel Jones. All had invested in Emerald Shores. Quite a crew. Shareholder meetings must have been a scream.

The big surprise was Drew's name and signature. Carmen and Hank had been wrong. He *had* invested heavily in Noah's debacle.

For a moment, I wondered where all the contracts had gone for my dad's Trenton-by-the-Sea. They'd offer a lot of information about who stood to gain from my father being out of the picture.

But like Dad, they'd disappeared.

Back to Emerald Shores and Laura's murder. If Gary's homicide was a result of Laura's, and if Laura's murder was only meant to look like a murder of passion, then her killing very well might have to do with the Emerald Shores subdivision.

Stapled to the Emerald Shores contract were plot plans— at least that's what I thought they were called. One showed the land's topography, another the layout of the condos and recreation buildings, and a third the wells, septic system, and leach field.

It was the topographic page that set off my alarm bells. I lifted the page, twisted and turned it. Along with a bunch of numbers, the draftsman had used landmarks like streams and roads to indicate property lines and the undulation of the land. Sort of like pointers for amateur map-readers like me. Maybe they always did that.

I conceded how in Maine's notoriously rocky soil there could be more than one Godzilla-sized rock. Maybe a few even sat beside roads that paralleled brooks.

But this whimsical topographer couldn't resist sketching a

smiley face on the rock he'd drawn. Just like the real smiley face was painted on the real boulder that sat on Drew's camp property.

Except on the map, the property didn't belong to Drew but to Emerald Shores.

I reviewed the players—Chip Vandermere, Patsy Lee Jones, Daniel Jones, Drew, Noah. Of all, Vandermere was my best bet. I called, and he not only agreed to see me, he was eager, in fact, once I dangled the lure of my investing in Emerald Shores before his greedy eyes.

I dressed, tucked the contract into my bag, then set my course for the Vandermere Funeral Home.

Chapter Twenty-eight
The Taste of Blood Sucks

A smiling Chip Vandermere opened the back door to his funeral home and led me upstairs to his living quarters. Gave me the heebie-jeebies for no comprehensible reason. Someone had spent a fortune on mahogany paneling and silk wallpaper. The furnishings were no less plush, with the accent on leather and brocade.

I followed Chip into the farmhouse-style kitchen. He seated me at a massive oak table while he fussed with a gleaming espresso machine. After he piled a plate with shortbread, he brought it and our espressos over.

His nervous excitement rippled across me like a psychedelic blanket. Whew—intense and odd.

He pulled up a chair beside me—way too close—and rested his chin on his hands. He offered major teeth. "So, Ms. Whyte, you're thinking of investing in Emerald Shores."

"Tally, please." I took a sip of espresso. "I know there

have been problems, but I've got some extra dollars, so I thought I'd invest in Winsworth's future."

"Good. Good." He nodded. "Well, how can I help?"

"As I mentioned on the phone, I'd like to review a copy of the contract."

Much head-shaking. "No point to it."

"Because . . . ?"

"It's being restructured."

"In what way?"

More teeth. "I've got some great reasons for you to come aboard. First—"

"Mr. Vandermere . . . Chip. I can't begin to consider investing until I see the contract."

"Like I said, there's no point to it."

I pushed myself to my feet. "I'd better be going."

Chip sprang up. "Don't go, Tally."

"Why not? I want to see something. You're not showing it to me. There's no point in my staying."

Chip scowled, then, struggling, turned it into a smile. "Sure, sure. Be right back. Look around, why don't you."

I wandered into the living room. Waterford crystal and other costly pieces were scattered around the traditional-style room. I stopped in front of a mahogany bookshelf filled with what looked like funeral urns. A brass nameplate gleamed from the bottom of each.

"Champion Duster." "Chip's Darling." "Rambling Rose." "Champion Van's Crimson."

"Our treasures," Chip said, joining me.

"Treasures?" I said.

Chip ran his fingers across an urn. "Our babies. Dobermans. My wife and I, um, we can't have kids, so . . ." He shrugged.

It was the first hint of humanness I'd seen peek from beneath the man's plastic veneer. I found it both sad and touching. "Do you have any here? Live dogs, I mean."

"Madeline's off showing two of them today."

"She must enjoy that."

"We both do. I go whenever I can."

We returned to the kitchen, and Chip refreshed our espressos. He reseated himself, moving his chair so close to mine I could smell his Listerine.

He slid a folded sheaf of paper in front of me. "Here you go."

I unfolded the contract and read. His eyes tickled my neck.

Ahhh. There it was. Chip's contract definitely differed from Laura's. He'd made pencil notes along the margins, and the dates were different, too. Laura's contract predated Chip's by a week.

I skimmed the text, but with all the legalese, I gave up after page one. I offered Chip a reassuring smile, then flipped to the signature page. Drew had signed Laura's contract, but only his typed name appeared on Chip's. No signature.

I moved on to the maps.

Chip's topographic map clearly had a different shape for Emerald Shores than Laura's did. Hers encompassed Drew's land. Chip's did not.

The kicker was the leach field. On Laura's contract, the Emerald Shores leach field was on Drew's property. Chip's contract, minus Drew's property, put the leach field in a different spot. Chip's note, with many exclamation marks, read: *Not Approved. Doesn't perc!*

Wowsa.

When I looked up, Chip's face was a classic study in anxiety—tight mouth, thinned lips, eyes squinted and full of fear. He tried on a garrulous smile. "Looks pretty good, doesn't it?

Those condos'll be spectacular. Noah got a top-notch designer. People will be banging down the doors to buy."

"Not if the property doesn't perc."

"But it will. It will."

"What happened, Chip?"

"Um . . ." His eyes shifted to the window. "We had to move the leach field at the last minute."

"Because one of your investors pulled out? Drew Jones maybe? I see his typed name, but no signature."

"Yeah, Drew withdrew." He chuckled. "Not a big deal."

"No? But he took his land with him, right? That's where the leach field was, I bet."

"Okay. Yeah." Chip rotated his wedding ring around and around. "And I'll be honest, it's caused some delays."

"It doesn't look good for the project."

"Not really. Noah's clearing things up."

"Is he? Perhaps the same way he cleared up Laura's interference?"

"Interference? Laura was the . . ." His lips compressed.

"The what, Chip?" I said, going with a bland smile.

Chip narrowed his eyes, then snatched back the contract. "This isn't about investing. You're snooping. There's nothing illegal here. So what's your deal, huh?"

"Laura Beal's death."

"*What?*"

He seemed genuinely surprised by my answer.

A sudden howling of dogs startled both of us. The sounds turned to barking. Chip leapt up from the table. "Madeline's home with the dogs. You'd better go."

"What? And not see Madeline and the dogs? How come?"

"She'll be tired. And messy from working the dogs this morning. That's all."

I peeked out the window. Madeline was leading a red and

a black Doberman around back. "What if Laura Beal died because of Emerald Shores? What if some investor was furious because the deal fell apart?"

"That's stupid. How dare you come to me with this?"

"Because there's something hinky going on here, Chip."

"Then go ask Daniel Jones or Patsy Lee."

More ring turning. Made me wonder . . . "I've been told Laura was very active sexually. Did you sleep with Laura Beal, Chip?"

"Oh, come on."

"You seem terribly nervous. Why?"

"You're being ridiculous."

"I don't think I am."

Chip's chest expanded. "Don't you dare tell Madeline about Laura."

"I never intended to. But I'm questioning your motives. A woman was brutally killed, Chip. And no one seems to want to help me very much in finding out who and why."

A knock on the door, then Chip's assistant poked in his head. "Chip? Madeline says she needs you downstairs."

Chip offered his patented grin. "Tell her I'll be there in five."

"Sure."

Once the door closed, Chip's grin faded. "See, I've got to go."

"In a minute. Who do you think killed Laura?"

"Gary Pinkham, of course."

"It doesn't fly. At least not with me. I think Gary died because he *knew* who killed her. Someone trashed my office, wrecked my computer." I rested my chin on my tented hands. "If I'd been home, would they have killed me, too?"

"How can you—"

"The murderer killed twice. Am I next? Are you?"

His eyes widened. "Of course not. I . . ." He cradled his face in his hands. "It's been a mess from the beginning."

"What has?"

"Emerald Shores." He wouldn't look at me, but rearranged the remains of the shortbread.

"Time's running out. Madeline. Remember?"

"I *know*," he snapped. "Laura was blackmailing us."

" 'Us' who?"

"All the investors, except for Noah, of course. She did it for him. To get back into his good graces. She blackmailed us into investing in that loser development."

"You'd slept with her, right?"

"I . . . Yeah." He deflated and slumped in a chair. "She said we'd have a kid together. Madeline's the one who . . . I don't mind about Madeline. Not really. But Laura got to me with that business about a baby. Then she started holding our relationship over my head."

"What did she have on the others?"

"I don't know."

"Chip?"

His head bobbed up. "I swear I don't. But I do know this. She had fits when Drew pulled out."

"So she wasn't blackmailing him."

"She *was*. He finally told her to go scratch when she demanded another twenty thousand dollars. They had a big fight. Boy, was she ripped."

"What made him pull out?"

"I said I have no idea. But he took us all down with him when he did that."

"The leach field."

"Yeah. On his property it perced."

275

"So Emerald Shores is done."

"No. Noah has a plan for us to recoup our investment." He grinned. "And to make a bundle on it."

Annie as trade goods for the leach field. Sickening. "One more question, Chip."

He laughed. "You sound like frigging Columbo."

"Gee, thanks. What kept you occupied the night Laura died?"

He slapped the table. "Oh, come on."

"Chip?"

"Madeline and I rented three James Bond videos and had a Bond marathon."

Not hard to figure whose idea that was. "Anything else?"

Another knock at the door. Chip sprang to his feet. "If I don't go downstairs and help Madeline, she'll think something strange is going on. I don't want her to even see you. Not today."

"I'll let you off the hook for now. I'm sure Madeline's a nice lady."

"She is. I really do love her, but . . . By the end, I hated Laura."

I had a feeling he wasn't the only one.

Chip followed me downstairs, then scooted around the back of the building. I heard the dogs yipping with glee.

I got into the truck and pointed it toward the county courthouse. Hank would have some insight I could use.

The shocking thought of Chip murdering Laura and Gary occurred to me. I tossed it away.

Chip appeared to be an excellent covert manipulator, but he was basically a coward. His eyes had sparked with fear when I'd mentioned the killer. He wasn't that accomplished an actor. At least, I didn't believe so.

Chip's wife, Madeline? He'd described her as sweet, patient, and I suspected she was somewhat dull, yet . . .

But a woman who couldn't have children, one who discovered her husband's affair with a beautiful and younger woman. Maybe then learning that it was all about him wanting a baby. Maybe Laura laughing at her.

Put that way, Chip's wife killing Laura Beal didn't seem far-fetched.

I'd been sure that the mind that had committed the murders was working on its own internal logic. Laura's butchery, Gary's suffocation, Peanut caught in the trap, the neighbor's cat wedged between two rocks—I kept returning to the killer as a deeply disturbed individual.

Perhaps it wasn't like that at all. Could both murders have pivoted on Emerald Shores and greed?

Except they didn't *feel* like that.

Christmas.

Scenarios were all well and good, but not one felt right. Even the land motive seemed out of whack. What a mess. Laura had been dead eleven days, Gary Pinkham, four. And this contract thing made me feel more tangled than ever about their deaths.

As I turned into the courthouse parking lot, I kept my foot on the gas. Hank would blister my butt for stealing Laura's contract. I wasn't in the mood. I could visit Drew, except I was furious about his impending marriage to Annie. When I *did* talk to Drew again, I wanted to be wearing my "rational" armor.

I'd been warned by the killer or his accomplice. I'd been followed. My home invaded. I had to be getting close.

Hell, why wait around for the killer's next performance? Time to stir the pot.

It was nearing noon when I drove down Grand Street toward Patsy Lee's Perceptions.

Patsy stood behind the counter fawning over a woman dripping in diamonds and silk. How did people not see the insincerity of that smile? Life was full of conundrums such as that one. I meandered over to the sale rack. Several $600 sweaters had been reduced to $550. Such a deal.

The diamond lady finally departed in a flurry of shopping bags and a billow of Chanel No. 5. Patsy winked at me, then smiled—one of her slow, meandering ones that spelled trouble.

"Why, if it isn't little ol' Tally Whyte. Or should I say Emma Blake."

I walked toward Patsy. Damn if I didn't want to flip her the bird. "Call me Tally. Everyone does nowadays."

Patsy sat on the arm of the sofa. "Cute act the other day, *Tally*, pretending you were looking for Drew."

"I was."

"And did you find him?" Her grin was mean.

"In a manner of speaking."

"So what ever became of your no-good father?"

"Give it a rest, Patsy. Daddy died a long time ago. I'm here to talk about the present."

She compressed her lips, turned her head away. "You've improved since your skinny-kid days. You were a mess."

"Thanks for the compliment."

She leaned forward. "Is it true, what I heard? That you're a national figure or something?"

I wondered who beat that tom-tom. "Not really. I'm known in certain professional circles for what I do."

"Something with corpses, right?"

"Gracefully put, as always. I'm a psychologist. My specialty is counseling the families of homicide victims."

"How disgusting. Too bad you couldn't get something more, er, normal."

I laughed. "How could you be so far off the mark? Amazing. Look, I want to talk about you and Drew."

She waved her red nails. "Like your father, old news."

"Is it? Why did I think you weren't divorced yet?"

Her magnolia skin mottled. "We're not, and don't let anyone tell you different. Hear?"

"What I hear is that he's planning to remarry."

She inhaled, deeply, then smiled. "Not until I sign those damned divorce papers, he's not."

"I see. By the way, what's your involvement in Emerald Shores?"

"You bitch!"

I smiled. "Upset you, the mention of Emerald Shores? Maybe because it has to do with Laura Beal's death?"

"Get out," she screeched. "And never darken this door again."

As the plate-glass door closed behind me, it caught the shoe aimed at my head. I turned and waved. Patsy screamed something I couldn't hear.

When it came to Patsy Lee Jones, life did hold some small satisfactions, after all.

Ella Fitzgerald wailed from the speakers as I crossed town, headed for Daniel Jones's home on Park Street.

For all I knew, Laura could have slept with him, too. And Steve. Drew? Maybe. What could she have used to blackmail Patsy? Only a million things, given Patsy's long career of dirty tricks.

Did Joy know about Laura's blackmailing? My gut said yes, my head, no.

I drove down an oak-lined street off Main and pulled up in front of a blue Cape surrounded by equally traditional and modest homes. Two massive oaks shaded the house, and it was bordered by a sea of pachysandra. A painted "Welcome to the Joneses" sign hung beside the mudroom door. I wondered when Mrs. Jones had died.

The house had a long-lived-in look, and if I were guessing, I'd say Daniel had brought his bride here after their marriage and stayed, which told me the former governor didn't need any fancy digs to proclaim his importance.

I rang the mudroom doorbell and a dog yipped inside, but no one answered, so I headed over to the Jones Jeep/Chrysler dealership on Grand Street.

If anything, the mystery of Laura Beal had deepened for me. Who was she? An artist, a mover and shaker, a nonconformist, the doer of good works, the lover of Hank. And a keeper of secrets and blackmailer. A woman of many parts, as are we all. The question was which one had caused her demise.

It was almost two. I had time for a drive-through burrito at Taco Bell and a talk with Daniel before I called Everett Arnold at three about using his Mac to upload my photos.

I drove onto the lot of the Jones Jeep/Chrysler dealership and parked under a metal canopy by the service entrance. I sat for a moment marshaling my thoughts.

If Daniel had slept with Laura, that would give her leverage, especially since Daniel and Dr. Cambal-Hayward were an item.

Daniel had seemed warm, friendly, and sincere. Not so different from the sixty-five-year-old teacher who'd murdered his twenty-something lover. I'd counseled that girl's family, and too many other bereaved souls to take people at face value anymore. A part of the business.

But it was also doubtful a man of Daniel Jones's age, physical infirmities, and temperament would have had the strength and intensity to stab Laura Beal again and again.

The truck door flew open.

"What the—"

I was roughly dragged from my seat by a guy wearing a party mask. He shoved me against a wall, and the world dimmed. Bright lights exploded in my head.

I reached for him, but he'd trapped my hands at my sides. He again slammed me against the stone wall. Bile surged to my throat, and my stomach heaved, urged on by the guy's halo of alcoholic fumes.

"Leav' her alone," he slurred. "Or I'll get you good."

I heard Kranak's voice, jerked my knee up and scored.

"Aargh!"

My attacker's grip loosened, and I shoved hard with my body, trying to get my hands lose, but I couldn't free them, dammit, and his hand wrapped around my throat and he squeezed.

I gasped for breath. I tried to knee him again, failed, kept squirming, my lungs burning.

"You shouldn'a done tha'," he said. "You'll be sorry."

I made myself relax, slumped forward, found an ear with my tongue.

I bit down, hard, kept it up, kept it up, tasted blood, even though he howled and jiggled, and I started fading, gasping.

"Hey!" someone shouted.

And then I was free.

Chapter Twenty-nine
Familiar Faces

Hank leaned against his office desk. "You bit him." It was said quietly, but a banked fury boiled beneath the words.

"I did." I sipped the ginger ale he'd supplied, which washed away the foul taste of the Maalox, also provided by Hank. His office had stopped spinning, and I no longer felt the urge to lose my lunch.

Hank had abandoned his concerned phase—where he'd gently wiped my face, tenderly checked for serious injury, and coddled me on the drive to his office—and moved onto a barely controlled anger, whether with my attacker or with me I wasn't sure. He'd left two Winsworth police officers to gather the details of my attack from the service manager. Although he'd been the one to interrupt my attacker, I suspected he'd seen nothing.

Hank folded his arms. "We're lucky we didn't have to hospitalize the service manager."

"Sorry about that. Must've been all the blood on my face from when I chomped on the guy's ear."

He scraped a hand through his hair. "Why the hell didn't you scream?"

"I . . . I guess I didn't think of it."

"Christ Almighty, what have you been doing to piss someone off so bad they'd assault you like that?"

"Lousy breath?"

Hank's face turned scarlet.

"My winning personality?" I said.

His fist crashed onto the desk. "Dammit, Tally!"

The dispatcher poked in his head. "Everything okay here, Sheriff?"

Hank growled and the guy scooted. "I'm going to wait you out, Tal."

"Everett Arnold—"

"Isn't going anywhere. Let's get real here, Tally. Are your investigations really about Laura and Annie, or is this all about your father?"

I leapt to my feet. "That's absurd. I . . ."

The room twirled.

I see Daddy and a man, a tall man. They're talking in the parlor of our home. What a pain! Daddy's supposed to take me fishing, and he said if we don't go soon, we'll miss the light.

He's promised to finally teach me to fly fish, and I can't wait. At eleven, he thinks I'm grown up enough. Way cool.

I creep closer to the parlor. Who's that guy? Huh. It's Mr. Beal, Annie's dad. If I could only hear them, I'd know how long Daddy would be. I move even closer, and Mr. Beal is talking about something called Trenton-by-the-Sea. I wonder what that is.

"It would be a mighty fine investment, John," Mr. Beal says to Daddy. "Mighty fine."

"I don't think so, Noah. I don't think so t'all. But thanks for the offer."

Daddy and Mr. Beal start walking to the door. Daddy sees me, and he raises one of his furry eyebrows in a way that tells me to scoot.

I don't want to, but . . .

He does it again, and the second time means we won't go fishing if I don't do as I'm told. I step back and silently close the parlor door.

A little while later, Daddy leaves our home with Mr. Beal. He says he's sorry, but we'll have to go fishing another day.

Another day. . . .

A cool cloth on my forehead. I blinked over and over, until the room swam into focus.

"Whew," I said. "Never did that before."

"Are you all right, Tal?" Hank asked.

"Yes. Fine. Sorry."

I rubbed my temples. What a strange memory. That scenario said Noah Beal had initiated the land deal with my dad, not vice versa. If it was true, it changed everything. Noah used my dad as the front man, while he was the one who made the investors' money disappear. He then used that same money to bankroll his own Trenton Shores. Noah had much to answer for.

Would I ever find the real truth of it?

I folded myself back into the chair and curled my legs beneath me. For all that he was unreliable and a spendthrift, my dad was warm and loving and a teacher, too. That following day, he'd given me my first casting lesson with a fly rod. I smiled. He was a hard teacher, but a fair one, and lavish with praise.

"Tally?" Hank said softly.

"Oh. Sorry. I've been woolgathering. It's possible that if I wasn't on the hunt about my dad, I wouldn't have jumped into Laura's homicide. I honestly don't know, Hank. But for now, no more yelling, or I'll barf all over your desk. Nasty thing to clean up."

He raised a single eyebrow. "I'll try."

"You'd best keep your word," I said, then I spilled the beans about taking Laura's Emerald Shores contract from her office.

Hank loaded me into his Pontiac. He hadn't locked me up for theft. Given his stupendous silence during my narration, I guessed I was lucky.

"I'd rather go out to Everett Arnold's on my own," I said.

"Not a chance. I don't trust you or your assailant."

"I don't think the guy'll follow me or—"

"You don't think. Period."

"Nice. You're acting like I'm some sort of criminal. All I did was—"

He slapped the steering wheel. "All you did . . . You broke into the radio station, stole a document, and confronted some people, one of whom you obviously pissed off royally."

I bit my lip. "You're afraid for me."

His hands tightened on the wheel. "Let's bag the cat-and-mouse shit, all right? I'm pretty sure I know who went after you."

I snapped my head around. "Who?"

"Mitch. Mitch Jones."

Not what I'd been expecting. Hank filled me in as we drove up the Bucksport Road at his usual snail's pace.

"Drew's brother? You're saying Mitch Jones is a wet noodle," I said. "That's not what the bump on the back of my head is shouting."

"Knowing Mitch, that was all about courage from a bottle."

"Well, that 'courage' hurt like hell. He slammed me into that wall, tried to strangle me, for God's sake. Was the choking an accident?" I could still feel those long fingers tightening around my throat, so I couldn't breathe, begged for breath. I looked away. Hank shouldn't see how frightened I'd been. "If I hadn't bitten him . . ."

"I haven't forgotten. But basically, Mitch is a limp dick whose bottled balls have him do stupid things. He must be more nuts about Patsy than I thought."

"How could Drew marry that woman? Remember the way she'd go after Annie in junior high?"

"Yup." He rubbed the back of his neck. "She kept at it all through high school, then turned sweet during college."

"Which is how she landed Drew, I presume."

"That. And her other, ahem, attributes."

"Right," I said, momentarily amazed at the cluelessness of men. "Geesh, can't you go any faster?"

If possible, Hank relaxed even more. "We'll get there. Always do."

"Yeah, but in what decade?"

He smirked. "I'd be surprised if Patsy wasn't in on your little fracas. The guiding light, so to speak. It won't happen again."

The man was *smiling*. "Look, don't do anything dumb."

"I don't do dumb, Tally. But I guarantee that if Mitch is wearing a gnawed ear, he'll stay away from you. Permanently." His smile widened.

Good heavens—Rambo. "What if he was Laura's killer?"

"Gary killed Laura."

"You're still singing that song?"

His reply was a snort, an annoying one.

I slumped in my seat, frustrated and grouchy.

We passed a huge former cow barn turned used-book store. The washed-out paint was gray in places, and the roof looked like a swaybacked horse, yet the thought of all those books was hugely alluring.

Hank hooked a left onto a peastone road. "What about Vandermere?" he said. "From what you've told me, he's got to be at the head of your murder-suspect list."

"I can't see it. Sure, he's a manipulator, but also a fussbudget who'd hate such a messy crime. Of course, he does work with corpses. But he was *scared* when I mentioned the killer. He couldn't overpower a guy like Gary, either. How about Daniel?"

"Drew's dad? That's the dumbest thing to come out of your mouth yet."

"Gee, Hank, time to cut the flattery. Daniel seems kind, the genuine article. Yet I bet in his day he was one hell of a roughneck. Maybe he's weakened physically, but he's still got the power. I saw it at Laura's wake, that magnetism. Drew's got it, too. The thing is, Daniel has an alibi for the night Laura died. Ditto Noah. They were playing poker with Dr. Cambal-Hayward until five in the morning."

"You got that wrong," he said. "The doc was over to the hospital until well after three A.M. Saw her there myself. Maybe Noah meant Seth Spinner. They play over his place at least once a week."

"Why not call him and see?"

Hank gave me the rolled-eyeball routine, but he pulled out his cell phone, got the number, and dialed. He left a message when he got no answer. "Happy? Not that I can see either Daniel or Noah as conspirators."

"Maybe, but I wonder what blackmail item Laura had on Daniel."

The road snaked to the right and Hank hit a pothole,

which bounced my head into the car roof. "Ouch, dammit. Have you gotten any forensics back on Gary?"

"Gary took some Valium. We found a newly filled prescription bottle under the front seat of his Bronco. Valium's a pretty common suicide facilitator."

"I know," I said. "Except it wasn't in this case, since he was murdered. What about Will Sacco? He was furious with Gary. He wouldn't even bury him. Was he connected to Laura in any way?"

"Only the dumb Howard Stern letter you told me about, and Joy."

"She's taken to wearing Laura's clothes. She's desperately trying to cling to her friend. Perhaps Will was jealous over their relationship and . . . ?"

"Killed Laura? Hell, who knows. But I doubt it. They were tight long before Will Sacco entered the picture. Since grade school they were close as sisters. Let's just bag the questions, okay?"

"Not okay. What about your friend in the Army? Has he gotten back to you about Gary's Army connection? His medical record?"

"We're almost there," he said.

"That's not what I asked."

"Time for you to bow out, babe."

"You're kidding me, right? What did you find out, Hank?"

"You are like a friggin' pit bull. It *appears* there may be some validity to what Gary said about being sterile. According to my friend at Fort Dix, he did have a bad accident when he was there. He lost one testicle and damaged the other one."

I slapped the dashboard. "There you go!"

"We don't go anywhere. All I said was, it's possible. We have nothing concrete on whether Gary was sterile or not."

"Well, your friend's report is a damned good indicator. And if he wasn't the father of Laura's baby . . ."

"I'll give you a maybe. If it's any comfort, Sergeant Thibideaux, one of the state homicide detectives, is continuing her investigation. So just let it be."

I kept my mouth shut, but I couldn't turn off my mental hamster. Laura was pregnant. Most likely, she didn't know it was an ectopic pregnancy. So she really believed she was having someone's child. Laura Beal wanted a baby. And she was a control freak. "I don't think it was any accident that Laura got pregnant. I bet she engineered it. I think she cherry-picked the father. Who would she have chosen, Hank?"

"Dammit, I don't know. But it wasn't me!"

"Do you wish it was?"

"No," he growled.

"Are you sure?"

His jaw muscles bunched. "No, dammit, I'm not."

I let the words sit there for a minute, then softened my voice. "Why *did* you break up, Hank?"

He sighed, rolled his shoulders as if trying to ease a familiar ache. "We'd planned a life together—having kids, building a house. It was raining that night. I'd intended to work late. Paperwork. Then I said screw it, and drove over to her place. I walked in on her and Steve fucking their brains out. She begged me to stay, tears, hysteria. She said she couldn't help herself. That it was just a one-night stand."

I laid a hand over his. "That's rotten."

He smiled in that ironic, endearing way of his. "Yeah, I thought so, too. Funny thing, I believed her. Didn't stop me from leaving, though."

We neared what looked like the end of the road. Long grasses and alders and a sprinkling of pine trees faced us.

Hank hooked a left and we jounced along on a hard dirt track flanked by the long grass.

"Everett Arnold must like his privacy," I said.

"That he does.

"Did you confront Steve?"

"Nope. Steve came to me the next day. Apologized, disgusted with himself. Didn't make excuses. I knew Laura had somehow lured him into it. Steve was ashamed, especially since his heart belongs to Annie. Has for years."

"Where was Steve the night I picked up Drew on the road, the night of Laura's murder?"

"I asked around. According to Steve, he worked late on a job in Calais, then stayed in his camper for the night. I've gotten verification for that up until seven that night."

"So he could've driven back in time to kill Laura."

"I can't see him killing Annie's sister over a one-night stand."

"What if he was her baby's father?"

Hank didn't answer.

"From what I saw yesterday," I continued. "Steve doesn't know that Annie's marrying Drew."

"Not if he didn't throttle Noah when he walked through your door."

"Steve will try to stop it. So will I. I don't believe she wants to marry Drew. It's all about Noah and land and guilt."

"Stay out of it, Tally. Annie's feelings for Drew go way back."

"I know that. But she's my friend. Plus my training as a psychologist says it's Drew's illness that's pulling at her emotions. Not love. That's not a reason to marry someone."

"Christ, Tally. How many things can you poke your nose into before it gets burned off? Huh?"

THE DEAD STONE

He cut a left and an old whitewashed cape came into view. It perched low on a bluff above a narrow bay. Laundry flapped on the washline and whitecaps danced and pink rosa rugosas bobbed in the breeze. When we pulled into the dooryard, the lanky brown dog curled on the stoop stood and began to bark.

Hank stretched his arm across my seat back. "All we've got are a bunch of fragments. Confusing ones. Maybe your photos will pull it all together."

"Except for Chip, you've got a reason for why everyone we've mentioned couldn't have killed Laura."

He swiped a hand across his face. "This thing's got me crazy as hell. And you're giving them all excuses, *including* Vandermere. You don't want to know this killer, either."

"That's true."

"New York was ugly and vicious, but at least there killers didn't wear faces I've known most of my life."

A fiftyish, African American man in chinos and a denim shirt opened the screen door of the Cape and waved.

"Come on," I said. "Let's go upload some photos."

Chapter Thirty
Strider

Mrs. Arnold, a beaming woman in an apron with hands even sturdier than mine, plied us with homemade biscuits, her own "put up" blueberry preserves, and the strongest coffee I'd ever tasted. Then Mr. Arnold led me with pride to his bank of Macintosh computers. He had a powerful setup, and he pointed to an Epson where I could print out whatever I liked.

He was kind enough to leave me alone with my work, perhaps reading something in my eyes that said I needed privacy, and I took out the two compact flash cards I'd brought and set to it.

The viewing took a while, even using the Mac's dedicated photo program, as the images were large ones. I made mistakes, too, doing what was usually second nature.

The photos were decent but not great, and I ended up having to tweak most in Photoshop so they could be easily read. That took more time, and for some reason, my hands started shaking so badly that I stopped working for a moment and took a deep breath.

The assault was finally sinking in.

I took a break, stretched, and peered out the bow window at the bay below. On that crystalline day, it was a magnificent sight, the navy-blue water crowned by whitecapped waves, the sea stretching for endless miles.

At first, I'd felt so strange in Winsworth. The country, the quiet, the connectedness of life. All that I'd dreamed about, yet a frightening prospect in reality. Now I felt a part of it, liking it more and more, stroked by the ease and naturalness of lives well lived.

I felt between, in a space I remembered from childhood when my dad had tugged me from Winsworth to Boston to Lexington.

Oh, but that ocean was the same in Boston. I loved its infinity.

"Going okay in there, Tal?" Hank hollered.

I sat back at the computer. "Just fine. Almost done."

I held my bundle of prints. "Is there any place we can spread these out, Mr. Arnold?"

He led us to a dining room filled with oak furniture. "Be my guest."

Mr. Arnold retreated, and I spread the photos on the dining table's lace cloth.

"Let's see what we've got," Hank said.

"I put them in the order I took them."

Hank picked one up. "These came out pretty good."

"Yeah." I scanned the first series, the ones of the bills, articles, notes, and papers I'd found around Laura's office. "You see anything?"

"Nope," he said. "Just the usual stuff."

"These next are from the Tampax box."

Hank whistled. "That's Mr. Smiley-Face."

"The rock."

"Yup. Drew and I painted that some ten years ago."

"That rock is the tip-off that Emerald Shores's leach field was originally on Drew's property."

"Noah sure has brass ones," he said.

"Do you think Laura's blackmail is why Drew signed the original contract? If she had something on him, how come he pulled out at the midnight hour?"

"I'll just ask him, Tal. It's not that hard."

A lick of breeze ruffled the sheer curtains.

"No? What if Steve's right in accusing Drew?" I said. "Maybe Drew wanted Laura dead for something she'd seen, something she knew. How can you be sure that the night before Gary died, when he was looking for Drew, that Drew wasn't around?"

Hank ignored me and continued reviewing the photos. He flapped the print of the moonstones.

"Pretty, aren't they?" I said.

"Yeah. They were bought downtown at Hobbs Jewelers." He slid his hands into his pockets. "She was dying to have them. I, um, they're set in eighteen-carat gold. Serious bucks I didn't have at the time. I wonder who bought them for her."

I rested my hand on Hank's arm. "Maybe she bought them for herself."

"Not Laura. She had a way of getting things she wanted from others."

"Gary could've—"

"Are you kidding? Oh, the boy had money. But the last thing Gary Pinkham would buy for a woman was that necklace."

"You can't be sure."

"No, I can't. Bet Joy would know. Women talk about stuff like that."

"Sometimes." I would ask Joy about the moonstones.

We continued around the table. "There's the letter from Will." Hank lifted the first of two photographs, read it, went on to the second. I read the first page, which began with *Hell's waiting for Howard Stern. I'm disgusted your having a man like him on your radio station.*

"It's computer printed. I guess Joy typed this for him on her machine. I wonder what she thought of it."

Hank shook his head as he handed me the final page. "The stupidity of man never ceases to amaze me."

Hank went on to the next photo, while I read the rest of Will Sacco's diatribe and wondered if Howard Stern was enough motive for him to butcher Laura. Scary thought. "Will has a real thing about what he calls loose sex, doesn't he?"

"There were rumors going around that his daughter, Tish, didn't get AIDS from working at the hospital, but . . . You get the drift."

"Joy said that Tish had a miscarriage. That's why Gary couldn't be sterile. But if Tish was messing around, that could explain her pregnancy."

"You notice you got the signature wrong?"

I popped my head up. "On what?"

"The Dear John letter to Laura. It's not Striker, but Strider. I don't know a single person in the county with that name."

I bent close to the photograph. Strider. Of course. Transparent to me, but a mystery to anyone who hadn't read or seen Tolkien's *Lord of the Rings*. Strider was another name for Aragorn, the future king and Arwen's love.

The mural of Arwen and Aragorn showed Laura's face as Arwen. Did it also depict the face of the man who'd impregnated her? I tried conjuring Aragorn's face in the mural, but it was a no-go. I hadn't reacted when I'd seen it. I wondered if my intruder had been looking for those images.

I didn't have them anymore. I'd uploaded them to a commercial photo site, ordered a bunch of prints, then deleted the images so I could reuse the disks.

Maybe Laura *hadn't* given Aragorn her lover's face.

But I'd bet money she had. After all, she imagined herself a romantic.

While Hank and Mr. Arnold schmoozed about hot fishing spots, something I hated missing, I checked the shipping date online. I should have the prints tomorrow.

I didn't mention the prints to Hank. A stupid move if there ever was one.

Hank dropped me off back at my truck, which was still parked on the Jones Jeep/Chrysler lot. He insisted I wait, then quickly returned with the news that neither Daniel nor Mitch was around.

He left me there without so much as a promised phone call, and I suspected he was about to pay Mitch Jones a visit at home. I would *not* like Hank Cunningham as my enemy.

I backed out, changed my mind, and reparked around front. Even if I did feel like hell, this was a perfect time to chat up some workers about the Jones family.

When I swung open the double-wide glass door, the woman sitting behind a side desk popped up. Grin fixed in place, she crossed the showroom floor in record time.

"What can I do for you today, Ms . . ."

"Whyte. I was admiring that car." I pointed to the old black LeBaron parked front and center in the showroom. It sparkled like new, its chrome gleaming in the afternoon sun that poured through the glass.

She patted the car's fender. "It's our signature car. The governor drives one just like it."

"Daniel Jones?"

"Ayuh. To show how great and long-lasting Chryslers are."

"We had one a lot like it, except I think ours was even older. From the early sixties. An Imperial LeBaron."

"Really. Be worth quite a bit to the governor if you still had it." She looked longingly at a young couple toting an infant who entered the showroom. Another salesman headed in their direction.

She winked, leaned close. "Though the governor loves the old ones, the new ones are even better." She pointed to the sculpted car that sat beside the LeBaron.

I ambled over to the glossy red sedan. "Pretty. I can see Mitch Jones driving something like this."

"Absolutely, although he loves our Jeeps, too."

"I wonder," I said. "Didn't I see him here this afternoon?"

"Why, yes, he . . ." She compressed her lips. "No. Now, this sweetheart gets great gas mileage." She opened the door, exposing black leather seats. "Would you like to test-drive it?"

"Maybe. Are you sure Mitch wasn't here then?"

"I had the days confused. Isn't it awful when that happens?"

"Sure is. Do you know Drew Jones?"

She sucked in her cheeks. "Not well. Why are you asking?"

"Well, I'm . . ." I groped for a specific, one not related to Winsworth. "I went to college with him."

That earned me a lemony smile. "So you went to Harvard, too?"

A man in a leather bomber jacket opened the showroom

door, and my saleswoman offered an "excuse me" and walked over to him.

So much for my clumsy sleuthing. My rhythm was definitely off. Nonetheless, I chatted up several other salespeople, all of whose gift of gab evaporated whenever I dropped Mitch or Drew or Daniel's name in reference to anything but cars. The office and service employees gave me, if possible, even shorter shrift.

I drove home with the taste of failure on my lips and a Tyrannosaurus-sized headache.

I needed a little R & R, so I gathered my fishing gear and Penny, and walked to the pond across the street. Although dry fly-casting relieved my headache, it failed to calm me like usual. I spent the evening playing rope with Penny.

When I slid beneath the covers, I still felt restless and edgy. So much had happened . . . and not enough. I wished Laura's mural photos were here now.

I picked up the latest Brady Coyne mystery. Six chapters later, I was sure Hank wasn't going to call, which meant that no grumpy cop would be stealing my covers and snoring beside me tonight. I laid the book on my lap. Not only did we have great sex, but I sort of liked it when he shared my bed.

Whoa. Lose that thought.

I returned to Brady. He was up to his ears in homicide when the phone rang.

"Ach," said the dear, familiar voice. "So you *haven't* joined a cult."

"Hi, Vede. I miss you, too."

"I could tell, what with all the phone calls and e-mails."

"My computer's out of commission." Many "tsk, tsk"s accompanied my Tales of Tally, as we liked to call them.

"So that's the whole scoop, as of five P.M. today."

"The whole scoop, is it? My dearest Tally, open your eyes. It sounds as if you're doing penance on this Laura Beal thing for your father."

"Pardon?"

"Are you trying to get yourself killed?"

"You're being ridiculous, Vede. Laura's homicide has nothing to do with my dad."

A laugh. "Of course not, my dear. And the moon is made of green cheese."

"Veda, stop. I've put Dad's stuff on hold while I work on this thing."

Her sigh was long and loud. "Oh, I hear you, my dearest Tally. *Ach.* Why do you think this poor old woman's hair is gray?"

"It's black, you dye it. And cut the old lady act. You're anything but."

"You're not thinking of staying up there, are you?"

"I'll be home in a week."

"Lord willing."

"Stop it!" Of course. Veda's real fear was that I'd move to Winsworth. I'd been oblivious.

"In a week," I repeated.

But it wasn't a lock, and we both knew it.

The next morning, I woke up logy from surreal dreams that put me in a crabby mood. For painfully obvious reasons, I'd filled my sleep with Annie eating pie using Gary Pinkham as the table, Steve Sargent swing-dancing with Joy Sacco, and Hank romping with my old secretary, who in reality had run off with my former husband. Small wonder Mr. FedEx gave me a worried look as he handed me the cardboard envelope from my photo club.

I ripped off the envelope's tab and spread the photos of

Laura's murals on the coffee table. I'd had two shots printed of "Aragorn" and "Arwen."

I held my breath as I carried the two into a puddle of early-morning light.

Oh, my. Aragorn wore Drew Jones's face. No, not his current, ravaged one, but the handsome, confident face of a man in his prime, before Huntington's had laid waste to it.

Drew and Laura.

I peered out to the ocean, felt the soothing rhythm of its waves. I had to think, to rearrange my perceptions of what I knew and what I thought I knew and what was real.

Drew Jones was Strider—Laura Beal's lover and the father of her baby. Of course. Laura wouldn't pick Gary Pinkham, but someone bright and handsome and commanding like Drew. Someone with presence.

I rested my forehead against the cool glass. But a man with a genetic disease? An illness that had a fifty percent chance of being transmitted to her child?

Maybe she didn't know about the Huntington's. But she *had* to have known.

Why would she do it? Laura was smart, gutsy, confident . . . and willful, a control freak, desperate. Self-delusional? Sure. Jealous of her sister? Absolutely.

What nerve. She'd gone for the odds. Done it anyway. Or maybe she'd planned to abort the baby if it carried the Huntington's. Amniocentesis might reveal the gene. Or Laura had convinced herself that it would.

Penny whined. I realized I hadn't let her out or gotten her breakfast. I did both, my brain whirring in overdrive.

Had Laura tricked Drew into getting her pregnant? Or had Drew initiated their affair? It didn't matter. In the Emerald Shores blackmail, Laura's tool was simple: Annie. She'd threatened Drew that she'd tell Annie that he was her baby's father. So he went in on the land deal. Then Laura pushed too hard. Easy to picture her doing that. And Drew, fed up with her schemes, pulled out of Emerald Shores. But maybe she'd twisted his arm one last time, one time too many. And he'd killed her.

That last . . . I still couldn't see it. Could not.

But I knew who had the answers.

Penny appeared at the sliders, and I let her in. "Here's your breakfast. Then we're going for a ride, girl." I ruffled behind her ears.

I grabbed my purse and headed for Drew's.

Chapter Thirty-one
Anyone for S'mores?

I loaded Penny into the truck, then started it up. Except it wouldn't start. *Dammit!* I tried again, heard the battery crank down, slower and slower. Got out, prowled around.

I'd left the frigging lights on.

I leaned my fanny against a fender. No. I had not left my lights on. Even with last night's monster headache and gloomy mood, I would have heard the annoying bell that dinged whenever I did that.

I wasn't sure I could even leave the lights on if the truck was turned off. They'd have to be rigged.

Covering my hand with my shirt—fingerprints, after all, or paranoia—I turned off the lights, then walked around the truck in search of clues. No cigarette butts or candy wrappers or matchbooks with trucker-school ads. But fluttering in the bushes was yet another damned neon-orange Post-it note.

I don't want you hurt. UL.

Uncle Lewis.

Geesh. He was obviously sneaking around me all the time. Gave me the creeps *and* pissed me off. Talk about paternalistic.

Fuming, I tried reaching Hank, failed, then learned that Triple A would take at least forty-five minutes. I called the gas station in Winsworth for a jump.

It still didn't start, so the guy from the gas station played detective and found the distributor cap missing. Cute. He insisted on not only replacing the cap but checking out the whole truck to make sure no more mischief had been done. I accepted his offer of a tow, left Penny at the camp and told her to guard, then hitched a ride with the tow truck driver.

"Won't have that cap until tomorra morning," the attendant said as we sped down the Surry Road in his tow truck, dragging my 4-Runner behind us.

"Someone fixed me but good, didn't they?"

"Ayuh."

"Any chance you could give me a lift out to the Penasquam Road?"

"Happy to."

"That's swell." Loony Louie was not going to stop me from talking to Drew.

The attendant dropped me off at Drew's camp road. I trotted down the lane beneath a blazing blue sky, past the smiley rock and the stream, and by the time I made it to the dooryard, I was sweating.

Drew's van wasn't there, but I wasn't about to fold my cards yet.

I jogged down the steps and lifted my fist to knock.

A whine came from behind the closed door. Peanut.

I reached for the doorknob.

* * *

Drew was asleep on the couch, bundled in quilts so only his nose poked out, just like the last time. He wore an oversized Red Sox cap, something I found terribly poignant, and his right arm dangled down to the floor.

I wanted to tuck his arm beneath the covers, but I didn't dare for fear of waking him. He looked frail and small, so finite in his illness. He couldn't be a murderer, could he?

I didn't have the heart to wake him, at least for a little while.

The place had a medicinal smell that wrinkled my nose. At least the air conditioner was on. The drapes were closed, but a lamp beside the wing chair gave me enough light to read *The Winsworth Journal*. A furry head weighing a ton settled on my lap.

"Peanut," I said in a whisper. "How long has your master been asleep?"

Peanut woofled a sigh, which didn't exactly answer the question. I scratched behind her ears and began to read. When I finished the article on Trenton clamming, I sampled one of the chocolate-chip cookies sitting on the table beside the glass of milk. Fabulous. Just like the ones Annie had brought.

I hadn't had breakfast, and since the plate held at least a dozen homemade cookies, I figured Drew wouldn't mind if I stole one. Or maybe two.

Peanut whined, I scratched her head some more, and she woofled another contented sigh. In the middle of an article on the blueberry crop, my eyes grew intolerably heavy. My nightmares had caught up with me. Exhaustion seeped into my bones.

I put the paper aside, intending to get up and awaken Drew, but he was resting so comfortably. And I was so tired. Chilly, too, so I tugged the crocheted throw around me.

I'd close my eyes for just a minute, then have that heart-to-heart with Drew about Laura's pregnancy.

THE DEAD STONE

* * *

The growling awakened me. I pressed fingers to my lids, rubbed them, pried open my eyes.

Peanut's bared teeth greeted me.

She stood beside the couch, snarling at the porch door.

I tried to swallow away my cotton mouth, slapped my cheeks to banish the woozies. I felt like crap.

"What is it, girl?"

She kept growling. The sound was bad, the vibes, worse. I trusted dogs more than most humans.

I'd better wake Drew up. I stood and gently shook his shoulder.

I recoiled. His flesh was hard, granite hard, rigor mortis hard.

Dear God.

I knelt beside him and inched the quilts back from his face. *No. Oh, no. Please.*

Drew's mouth was frozen open, his eyelids at half mast. I lifted the blankets, saw no wounds, nothing.

The movement jarred his bill cap. A small blackened hole marred his right temple. I pulled off the cap. The left half of Drew's skull was gone, along with the left side of the baseball cap.

I slid back on my heels. Tears battled for release. Drew was dead. *Dead.* Long before I'd ever gotten there.

But that couldn't be. How . . . ?

Where was the gun?

I took a breath and carefully ran my hand along Drew's body, then the floor. A large revolver lay on the pine boards. I made a point of not touching it again.

I wrapped my hands around Drew's stiffened one and rocked back and forth. *I'm sorry, dear Drew. So sorry.*

Again I saw the boy who'd rescued my candy and me from

the bullies, the boy with the sweet smile and gentle ways who'd made me feel special and unafraid. And I cried big, gobby tears and rocked in sorrow. After a time, I felt the warmth and wetness of a tongue. Sweet Peanut was licking my face, patiently trying to soothe my sorrow.

"I'm sorry, girl," I said, resting my head against hers. I stuttered in a breath and exhaled a smooth one. Time to go to work.

I wiped my face with a corner of the quilt. I added Drew to my mental photo album of the dead, tucked him beside Laura and Gary and many others.

Now speak to me, Drew.

I examined him with my eyes.

A large-caliber bullet had made the hole in his right temple. It had bled little. The baseball cap appeared old and worn. He'd recently spilled something on his otherwise clean chamois shirt. His belt was notched on the very last hole. From his weight loss, I supposed. He wore jeans.

I bit my lip, finding it hard going.

Through the blanket, I touched his foot, then rocked his leg back and forth. I squeezed his thigh. No rigor there, either.

Rigor mortis moves from the head down to the extremities, then releases its grip in the opposite direction. So Drew had already been fully rigored and now the relaxation process was moving upward. Only his shoulders, neck, and face were still stiff. He'd been dead for quite a while. My guess was that he'd died somewhere between eleven last night and five this morning. But I was no expert, and I knew the room's warmth was a factor.

I hadn't smelled him or the cordite from the gun because of the medicinal odor in the house.

Peanut whined again.

What was I thinking? I had to call the police, Hank. Poor Annie. Hank would take it hard, too. Very hard.

I reached behind me for the portable phone resting on the coffee table. My hand knocked something, and I felt a wet warmth seep through my shirt.

I'd spilled the milk, dammit, which was soaking everything. I scrambled to gather the newspaper. I shook myself. Spilled milk mattered very little at that point. I picked up a white vellum sheet, one with typing on it.

Dearest Family and Annie,
At the moment, I am of sound mind, but I know it will not last. I . . .

Peanut let out a deep-throated bark. She stood, her body bowstring tight, then growled, teeth bared, and stalked slowly over to the library alcove.

The hair on my scalp prickled. Not good. Not good at all.

I tucked Drew's suicide note into my purse and followed Peanut. I tried to be casual as I peered out the library's half-open window. I saw nothing.

But I heard something. Outside. Whistling. Someone was outside, whistling a song. Poorly. It was a song I knew, but . . .

Gasoline stung my nose. I leaned closer to the window, inhaled deeply. Shit. It was gas, all right.

Just peachy.

I raced to the phone, lifted the receiver, heard dead silence. My cell!

I snapped it open. No signal. None. Nada.

Now what? No way could I use the porch door, since it was too close to where Gasoline Man was busy doing things I didn't want to think about. I leashed Peanut up and crossed to the sliders beside the couch.

I stroked Drew's face one last time, then pulled the slider's handle.

The slider didn't budge.

I made sure it was unlocked, that the track was free, and tried the door again and again. Wouldn't move.

Swell. Peanut and I would *have* to go out the porch door.

Leading Peanut, I headed for the door. An enormous whooshing sound, like a tornado or . . .

Flames! I cut my eyes to the windows. Flames everywhere. Fire ringed the house and smoke billowed.

I grabbed the porch doorknob, turned it. It was stuck, locked, whatever. It wouldn't move at all.

A window. I could smash one. And get shot. The porch was a bad idea.

"Stay, girl. I'll be right back."

I raced to the bathroom. The window looked just big enough. If I stood on the toilet, I could lift Peanut up and out, then crawl out myself.

I ran back into the great room.

Peanut was gone.

Chapter Thirty-two
Who's Got a Hammer?

Eels of smoke curled into Drew's home. I ran around slamming windows closed, then zoomed upstairs, calling Peanut, checking every room. No dog.

She had to be somewhere.

"Peanut!"

Back downstairs. More smoke. I had trouble seeing. My eyes burned. More tears, this time not from sorrow.

I got on my hands and knees and started scuttling around. Much less smoke down here, but the perspective was bizarre. "Peanut!"

A bark. Somewhere far away. Coming from . . . I couldn't tell. *"Peanut!"*

Another bark. The cellar? Maybe. So where was the door?

I ducked beneath the second-floor balcony overhang, reached for the door. A closet. Peanut couldn't open a door, anyhow. What was I thinking? I gnawed knuckle skin. Think. *Think.*

I scuttled along the floor, coughing. More smoke, lower down. *Bam.* Dammit! My head. Wait a minute. A door, half open. Yes.

I stood in a crouch, then edged forward, flapping my hand on the floor, careful not to topple down empty space, the other hand groping for a railing, a light switch, anything. Coughing more. Smoke everywhere. A flame, licking up the far wall. Groped for a light switch. Found it. Switched it on.

No light.

Screw it. What the hell. Maybe the fire consuming the house wouldn't eat those in the cellar alive. Right.

"Peanut, dammit!"

An answering bark, closer, but still not close enough.

My foot felt for a step, then the next, and I scooted downstairs on my bum until I stood on a hard floor.

No windows at all, which I guessed was a plus, fire-wise, except I couldn't see squat.

Something icy and damp nudged my hand. Yuck! Then a large body pressed against my leg. "Peanut." I sighed.

I hunkered down and hugged her hard. She was shivering like mad. So was I. Even my teeth were chattering.

"Any ideas, girl?"

Guess who didn't answer. I stood, dithering.

There was something odd about the cellar. Drew's was a new house, but something . . . I tapped my fingers to my lips. The feel? The smell? The . . .

Fresh air.

Fresh moving air was coming from someplace. I pictured the smoke and flame curling beneath the upstairs cellar door. Geesh. I found Peanut's leash and followed my nose.

We moved slowly, my hand held at arm's length in front of me, hoping to avoid leaping objects that might trip us.

The fire was loud now—booming and crackling and hungry with purpose.

Shit.

Odd how I could hear the click clack of Peanut's nails and the thump, thump of her cast on the cement floor.

I sniffed the air and caught a whiff of the fresh air, although I had no clue if we were moving toward it.

Peanut pushed passed me.

I followed the tug on the leash. Hell, why not?

I sensed, rather than saw, when we entered a passageway. Narrow, confined, moist. The fire's noise muffled. The floor softer, maybe dirt or wood.

We walked and walked, and I felt as if I were burrowing deeper into my own grave.

I chewed my lip, forced away the image of Drew's body consumed by the flames. "So, girl, where are we headed?"

I pressed my hand to where I imagined a wall. Stones. Not mortared. Small drafts of air tickled my fingers. Or was I imagining that?

I rammed into Peanut's butt. Why had she stopped?

With one hand sliding along her back, I moved down her side, then in front of her. I held out my hands for the wall of stone, toppled forward.

An elbow banged hard, but I caught myself before my face smashed, too.

Tears squeezed from my closed eyes. I saw Daddy standing in the doorway of my bedroom, then he shook me awake. *It's hot in the house, too hot.* Was this what little Emma Blake felt? Dear God, I was remembering the night we fled. Not now. Not. . . .

A tongue slurping my cheek.

I buried my face in Peanut's fur as I shook off the horror

of nearly burning to death in our Winsworth home. I gulped some deep breaths, cooling ones, not burning with fire. I held my hands in front of me and let them be my eyes.

I'd fallen on a staircase. A crude one. I crawled, hands first, up it.

The roof slanted. Wooden boards, narrow, tongue-and-grooved together.

A bulkhead door. What if it was locked from outside? I sat down. I was frightened. I didn't want to try. It might be locked. That would be the end.

Peanut nudged my butt.

I crouched on the stairs, hands above my head, and held my breath as I stood. I thrust all my weight against the bulkhead door.

It flopped open with a crash. Light streamed in. I stumbled forward, tugging on Peanut's leash, and suddenly we were outside, surrounded by woods, breathing fresh air.

I wept.

Minutes later, I looked around, saw what was what. A wind beat toward the east, thank heavens. I peered downward, to the stairs I'd just climbed. The passageway was an old cellar hole that Drew had kept in repair. Thank you, Drew. Thank you once again.

I looked behind me. There, maybe thirty feet from the bulkhead entrance, was Drew's cabin, engulfed in flames.

Flame shot to the second story, and I felt the inferno's broiling heat, saw the trim paint peeling, heard the fire's bellow.

It was horrible and beautiful, the dancing colors—red, yellow, orange, even blue in places.

Peanut whined, and I remembered someone had set this. Whoever it was might still be prowling around.

I led Peanut deeper into the woods, away from the small,

lovely cottage wrapped in a coat of flame and smoke. I came to a large rock beside a spring-fed stream. We drank greedily, and then I sat and confronted my demon, the one I'd seen in the cellar.

My eyes dart around my bedroom. I smell smoke and hear noise, like a roar. "Daddy!"

"It's all right, daughter. I'm here."

"But what . . ."

"Get dressed."

I run to the window. My tree fort! We can get out that way.

And I see two men. Outside. One's face is splashed by the light from our living room. He's wearing a wool hat and a peacoat and a funny beard, all just like my dad's. And he's tall, like Daddy, but thinner.

"Come, daughter. We must go. Now!"

"Wait!" I press my hands to the glass. My nightgown billows about me. And the man turns and looks up, straight at me.

Daddy scoops me up, and I reach for my doll, Gladdy, and Daddy carries me from the room. He bundles me in my jacket and hat and boots and picks me up again. He's carrying a suitcase, too, and it's heavy.

We run from the house, down the dirt lane. And I hear a crack, and we fall, tumbling over and over until we stop near the river. I'm dirty and bruised. And Daddy has a cut over his eyes. It's red, bleeding. He takes my hand and we walk to our boat, moored at the river's marina.

I shiver, and he seats me at the bow of our small sailboat and bundles a scratchy blanket around my shoulders. He doesn't hoist the sails, but fastens the oarlocks and oars and begins to row.

His shirt is all black and stained, and it scares me more.

It's night, and I can't see the stars and moon because the sky is red and orange and smoky.

Daddy rows, and I watch as the fire from our house grows more and more distant.

"All will be well, daughter. You'll see."

It never was again, of course. I hugged Peanut. My dad saved us that night. And if Peanut hadn't been there to save me, we would be burning right now in Drew's cellar.

The memory of the night we'd fled Winsworth wasn't a new one. I'd seen it time and again over the years. I'd been so afraid!

This time, for the first time, I saw some details more clearly than ever.

I recognized one of the men watching us, even though he'd dressed up to look just like my dad, including a fake beard. It was Noah Beal, and he'd been carrying a container. A red gas can.

Daddy hadn't set the fire. Noah had.

I swiped a hand across my forehead. It felt good knowing the truth. There was really only one decision to make. My dad was dead, and I couldn't take Annie's dad from her. Sometimes even bad things are better left to sleep.

Drew's death and the fire at his camp was now. At the very least, payment would be made for that.

In the distance, through the woods, came the revving of a car. I'd find the arsonist, that I would, but first I'd get us a lift.

I steered Peanut deeper into the woods, in the direction of the car I'd heard. I guessed there was another camp road, close by, that ran parallel to Drew's.

The day had turned gray and blustery, a fitting reflection of my mood. I smelled the flames, the burning of cloth and wood and flesh. Someone must have called the fire department by now.

We hiked up a wooded hill and down a dale, and even passed a crumbling tree fort built who knew when. I looked back once, as we paused on a small rise. Smoke from Drew's camp curled skyward.

A little farther on, I heard the bam of a car backfire. I tried to anchor the sound.

"Come on, girl. It can't be that far."

We walked down a slope, through a mucky skunk cabbage patch, then climbed to a large maple atop a hill.

Down below, a pea gravel road ran parallel to where I stood.

"We made it, girl." Peanut sat on her haunches, sniffing the air.

Across from us was a large barn surrounded by wire mesh paddocks, and just up the road sat the Saccos' cheerful yellow house.

Like Rubik's Cube, it all clicked into place. The song I'd heard whistled by the arsonist was "If I Had a Hammer," the same one hummed by Will when I'd visited his house after Gary had died.

I'd walked here without too much trouble, just as I suspected Will had walked from his house to Drew's place.

Will was the firebug. My bones said it was so. Done in by a song, you stupid schmuck.

Had he also killed Laura and Gary? That was the billion-dollar question.

I didn't see why not, since he'd almost killed me and Peanut.

I half slid down the hill, Peanut beside me. Scooter was playing in the yard. The poor kid. Poor Joy, too. Except it gave me an opening. And some safety. I doubted Will would harm me in front of his wife and child.

I walked toward the house.

* * *

"Hi, Scooter." I squatted down next to his Big Wheel. He'd been riding it around the old LeBaron. The screen door slapped, and I looked over my shoulder.

Joy stared at me, her eyes wide with surprise. "Tally! What the heck happened to you?"

"A fire happened," I said. "Peanut and I barely made it out alive. I've got to call the fire department and the police."

"Uh, sure. Come on in and clean up."

I looped Peanut's leash around a skinny beech, and Scooter instantly toddled over to the dog.

"What are you saying?" she asked as she lifted Scooter onto her hip.

"Doggie, Mama! Noooo!"

"Doggie has germs, baby," Joy said as she drew me into the living room. She handed me the phone. I dialed the fire department, then paced as I told my story to the dispatcher, adding that they should inform Sheriff Cunningham. Then I collapsed onto a kitchen chair. I suddenly realized how crummy I felt.

Joy sat Scooter on the sofa with a book and pulled up a chair beside me. She wrapped her arm around my shoulder. "Are you sure you're okay? What happened? I couldn't hear over Scooter's wails."

"Is Will around?"

"Um, no. He was out puttering in the garden all morning, but I heard him take off in his pickup a little while ago. How come?"

"Mama!"

Joy bounced up and gave Scooter more books.

"Someone burned down Drew's camp," I said when she returned.

"Oh, no! And you saw it?"

"I was inside it."

"Lord have mercy."

"Yeah. I don't know if the arsonist knew I was there. I'd gotten a lift out to Drew's since my truck's temporarily out of commission."

"Tally, how awful."

"You didn't ask about Drew."

"Well, no. I assumed he wasn't there."

"He was there. Dead. It appears he killed himself."

She pressed her hand to her cheek. "I was afraid of something like this. Oh, not the fire, but Drew. Him being so sick and all. Then with Laura and Gary's deaths. I guess they tipped the scales. You don't think he could've killed . . . ?"

"I don't know. His actions make little sense. He was about to marry Annie."

Joy rolled her eyes. "That rumor's been chasing around town for years, ever since word of his sour marriage got out."

"It's not a rumor. Annie told me."

"That's plain nuts, what with his disease."

"I thought you didn't know about the Huntington's?"

"What's that?" she said.

I saw the lie in her eyes but let it pass. Still protecting Drew. And now there was no point. "I'm not feeling so hot."

Joy bent over me. "What can I get you. Juice? Aspirin? A shot of whiskey?"

"Thanks. I'd better stick with the juice."

While she poured, I said, "I could use some truth, too."

Over her shoulder: "What?"

"The truth about Will."

She handed me the juice. "What are you talking about?"

I drank half the glass, then set it on the table. Joy's eyes were wide. I hated doing this. "I think Will set the fire today."

"Oh, come on. Don't be silly."

"I'm not, Joy. And I'm worried for you and Scooter. Arson is serious. Jail serious."

"Well, my Will won't be going to jail. He wouldn't set any fire."

"Are you sure?"

She slapped a hand to her hip. "I'm damned sure, is what I am. How dare you come into this house and suggest it?"

Maybe I was wrong. But that song I'd heard . . . "I have no proof. Yet. But I believe it's true."

She pulled up a chair. "It's because of the fire. And finding Drew. You're all shaken up. Will is the dearest man."

"What about his fire-and-brimstone feelings for Gary? About sex?"

She waved a hand. "I'm telling you, he wouldn't do it. There's no reason."

I leaned close, laid my hands over hers. "Noah Beal is a reason."

She jumped to her feet. "There you go again. Not listening."

Sirens whined in the distance.

"Noah wants Drew's property," I said. "More than almost anything. Doesn't Will work for Noah?"

"Only part-time. It's no big deal."

"What do you know, Joy? You're not hiding it very well."

Her eyes bubbled with heat. "Are you planning on telling the police your lamebrained theory?"

"I have to. I could have died in that fire. Drew, too."

"You said he was dead already and . . ."

Cars with blaring sirens careened into the yard. Scooter yelled, "Mommy!"

"And what, Joy?"

Her eyes grew wide, her hands, frantic. "Don't you understand? If Will finds out you've told this to the police, I don't know what he'd do to you."

Chapter Thirty-three
Cookies and Milk

Hank barreled through the door, followed by two Winsworth cops. He grabbed me tight and smooshed me into his chest. I wasn't quite sure if he was going to choke me or love me. Fortunately, it was the latter, but I suspected it was a close thing, given his subsequent lecture at my latest brush with disaster.

Another hug, this time from me. I drank in his strength and solid presence, and felt a breathless urge to make love on Joy Sacco's couch. Then everything began spewing out of me, except for my thoughts about Sacco. Those I saved for Hank and privacy, not because I feared Will Sacco, which I did, but because there was no proof. Joy and Scooter deserved a break.

Joy stood in the background holding Scooter and listening. She watched with wary eyes as I told how I found Drew dead and the fire. Before I'd finished, she'd slumped on the sofa rocking her child.

She'd taken it all to heart, and I felt sorry for her.

I felt more sorry for Hank. He'd just lost his closest friend.

"I'm so sorry, Hank. About Drew."

Hank looked away, lips compressed and wobbly. The two Winsworth officers stood silent, their hands folded in front of them.

"It happens, Tally," Hank said. "You know all about that."

"I do. But it doesn't make the hurt any less."

"You've got the note?"

"Here." I handed it to him. "It started off like a suicide note, but I didn't get a chance to read much of it. That's when all hell broke loose. You will . . ."

"Show it to you?" Hank said. "Yeah." He slipped it into a plastic bag, then tucked it into his shirt. "Come on. We'd better get over to Drew's."

"Peanut and I will ride with you," I said.

"Damned straight you will." He massaged the back of his neck. "I'm glad you could save Peanut."

"Are you kidding? She saved me. I thought I might keep her. Penny would love a pal."

That earned a lip twitch from Hank as he opened the screen door. "Take care, Joy. Thanks for helping Tally."

I cut my eyes to Joy. She was bent over Scooter and wouldn't look at me.

"Are you going to be okay?" I asked her.

She nodded.

"Joy?"

She waved me off without looking up.

On the short drive to Drew's camp, I told Hank my thoughts on Will Sacco being the arsonist. He nodded but didn't say much. When we arrived, I first noticed the noise.

THE DEAD STONE

It was deafening. Drew's home still burned, although the firemen, their hoses fed by a fire pond in the meadow, covered it with streams of water. Remarkably, two of the outer walls remained standing. The acrid smoke burned my nose and sparks shot toward the pewter-colored sky.

Hank walked over to the man with "Chief" taped to his yellow slicker. I stayed in the car with Peanut. It gave me too much time to think.

Again I saw Daddy carrying me from our burning house, tugging me across the field and down the slope, our lone suitcase banging against his thigh, our fall and roll down the hill.

I rested my head in my hands, closed my eyes, but the images only became brighter and fiercer. Fire danced behind my lids, and I felt eyes watching me as I tripped and stumbled in my nightie.

My eyes flew open and locked on a man in a yellow slicker standing off to the side of the drive. He was staring at me, his face in shadow from the fireman's helmet he wore. His arms dangled at his sides while the fire raged below. Will Sacco.

I scrambled from the truck and tore after him.

I was closing on him when a tree root snared my foot. I slammed into the soft, mulchy ground, and by the time I pushed myself to my feet, he was gone.

A few yards from where I'd fallen, a Winsworth fireman's slicker and helmet lay abandoned behind some fallen trees.

I went and got Hank.

"I felt him staring at me, I swear it."

"You've had a hard day, babe," Hank said as he pulled on a pair of latex gloves.

"Then why did he run?"

"Check out the mirror."

"Not funny."

His hand cupped my chin. "Just trying to make you smile, Tal."

"Oh."

He lifted the fireman's hat first, turned it in his hand, then picked up the slicker.

"It was Sacco," I said. "I know it."

Hank peered at me over the rims of his Ray-Bans, then began examining the coat. He paused, his hand deep in one of the huge outer pockets, then pulled something out.

A pad of orange Post-it notes.

We walked toward the remains of Drew's camp. Somewhere inside, his body lay on the sofa, charred beyond recognition. Hank passed off the fireman's gear to one of the Winsworth officers, then slipped his hand into mine.

"Won't be long now," Hank said.

"What do you—"

A thunderous explosion made the firefighters jump back in unison. Flames shot skyward, then, in what looked like slow motion, the remnants of the camp crumbled inward with a snap, crack, and then a whoosh as the structure folded in on itself before collapsing into the cellar.

Cinders and soot billowed outward, and the firefighters kept shooting arcs of water onto the smoldering remains.

Hank turned away.

"You're a mess." Hank smiled just before he handed me off to an Officer Gray.

"So are you." I pressed my hand to his cheek.

Hank's eyes held Gray's. "Take care of her, Reba. And this

old mutt." He ruffled Peanut's head. "My Charm was her daddy."

"Don't forget about the gun," I said.

"I expect that chore'll be for tomorrow," Hank said. "When stuff cools off."

"Come by the cottage later?" I asked.

"I'll try."

I gave my statement to Rebecca Gray, who first plied me with a burger and soda because "you look to be fainting, ma'am." She supplied Peanut with the same fare, substituting water for the soda, and the exhausted dog now slept in a corner of the Winsworth police station.

I went into detail about the condition of Drew's body, since the medical examiner wouldn't have much to work with.

"Coffee?" Gray asked.

"No," I said. "We'd better go on. I'm sort of falling apart."

She nodded, her eyes sympathetic. "Let's review when you first entered the camp. What about the smell?"

Again, I tunneled back to hours earlier. "There was a strong medicinal odor in the air."

"No smell of excrement? Urine?"

I shook my head. "If there was, it was mingled with the medicine-y smell. The air-conditioning was on, too."

"And you could only see Drew Jones's nose."

"Yes. In retrospect, I guess I should have checked. But I thought he was asleep. I knew about his illness, and even though I wanted to talk to him . . . Well, I just didn't want to wake him up."

"I understand. But you didn't see the bullet hole in his temple when you looked down at him the first time."

"No." I ran a finger across my lips. "No, only his nose and right arm. I'm guessing the force from the shot knocked the hat forward, covering the bullet hole."

"Why again did you visit Drew Jones?"

"Because I wanted to talk."

"About . . . ?"

"Just like I said earlier, I wanted to see how Peanut was doing."

Gray sucked in her cheeks, then scribbled on a pad. She looked up at me. "You're sure that's it?"

"That's it."

She loaded Peanut and me into her cruiser and drove us home. At the cottage, I said good-bye, but Gray insisted on checking the place out. I explained about Penny, whom she asked to meet.

It was awkward saying good-bye. Even with Penny and Peanut there, I felt oddly frightened and ridiculously alone. She rubbed her palms together. "All set. You think you'll be all right, alone out here?"

"Sure. I've got Peanut and Penny."

A smile. "You're positive I shouldn't call somebody human?"

"Hank's coming over later. He's almost human."

We laughed, but her brown eyes asked questions about today that I refused to answer.

"Lock up," she said on her way out.

"I intend to."

Hank arrived around ten, after I'd showered and slept and dreamt of things I'd rather not have.

We hugged for a long time. I kissed his sooty face. In turn, he embraced me so tight I momentarily forgot the sound and fury and fear of nearly being burned alive.

When I lifted my head, Hank held me at arm's length. "You're still afraid."

"Yeah. Not from the fire, although I think I'll dream about it for a while. Hank, at first, I was sure Drew was a suicide. But the more I think about it, the more I believe he was murdered. I believe the killer is tying up loose ends. There are still some dangling ones."

He chewed his mustache, then said, "I think you're right on both counts."

"Why? Why do you believe now?"

"Because it's too much. Laura. Gary. Drew. Three people dead, homicides. That's way too much. Now listen up. You're a pushy woman. Stop pushing our boy."

"Will do."

"Dammit all, Tally. Stop placating me. Aren't you the least bit scared?"

"Very much so." I chuckled—a hollow, empty sound. "But I was never good at playing passive."

Hank's eyes turned ironic. "Don't I know it." He tossed his sooty hat on the kitchen counter, then dug in the cabinets until he produced my Old Granddad. "Reba Gray said you held things back."

I slid onto a counter stool. "She's a nice lady, but, yes, I did."

He started unbuttoning his filthy shirt. "Pour me a double while I shower."

"I'll pour one for me, too."

Fifteen minutes later, he returned barefoot, wearing fresh jeans and a blue button-down shirt. I handed him the double I'd splashed with water, the way he liked it. Mine was straight, on the rocks. I ran my finger across his mustache. "You singed your mustache."

"Got too close to a burning limb. I'm deciding whether to trim it or cut it off." He glanced over to the fireplace, where

Peanut lay curled near the crackling flames. Penny lay beside her. "Okay, let's get down to it."

I lifted the drink I'd built for myself and we moved to the couch. We each took an end, stretched out our legs, and touched toes.

"Why'd you keep stuff from Reba?"

"I needed time. To think. Piece some things together. It was Drew who got Laura pregnant."

He sipped his bourbon while he absorbed that leveler. "Go on."

I showed him the photo of Arwen and Aragorn, alias Strider. "In her painting, Laura was Arwen and Drew was Aragorn/Strider."

"I can't see Drew doing that, but Laura was a powerful persuader. What else?"

"My truck was sabotaged." I described how I found it.

"Looks like Loony Louie had the right of it. You *do* need taking care of."

I rolled my eyes. "Sure, Hank, like he knew."

"Maybe he did."

"But he couldn't."

Hank shivered and pulled the faux tiger throw over both of our legs. "I'm coming down with something. Louie could be involved. I don't like that he's made you his pet project. But I think you're dead on about Sacco setting the fire. We found some footprints in the woods. Small ones, but they were real wide, like a man's."

I sipped my drink. I didn't want to tell Hank about the memories I'd recaptured from the night of my fire. But I was hungry for facts. "I'm curious. Sacco does some work for Noah. Did he work for Noah years ago, when we were kids?"

"I see where you're going, Tal. Will Sacco did work for Noah full-time back then. But you're painting Noah as the villain back then and in all this."

"If Noah solved one land deal with fire, there's no reason he wouldn't keep at it. But I don't see him murdering his own daughter."

"According to Seth Spinner, he couldn't have. Seth confirmed that Noah and Daniel were playing poker at his house until five that morning."

"Could one or both of them have left at any point?"

"Seth says no."

"Do you believe him?"

Hank shrugged. "They're thick as thieves, those three."

"Maybe Will killed Laura on his own."

"Motive?"

"Her pregnancy offended him? I don't know. She could've been blackmailing him, too."

He pulled a folded piece of paper from his pocket and handed it to me.

Dearest Family and Annie,
At the moment, I am of sound mind, but I know it will not last. I must tell the truth, on this, the final day of my life. I am the man who killed Laura. She was having my baby. In a fit of madness, we made love on that big, black stone in the quarry. She got pregnant, and as I wanted to marry Annie, I could not let Laura blackmail me with telling Annie.

Gary Pinkham found out, and I killed him, too. He would have ruined everything.

But I am sick with guilt, so even though Annie and I are soon to be joyfully joined in wedlock, I am ending it.

Forgive me.

It was signed "Drew Jones."

I sighed, read it again. "Since it's a xerox, can I keep it?"

"I don't see the point."

"I want to study it, to read it when I'm calmer. I need to hear the letter writer's voice more clearly."

"Sure, you can keep it. Doesn't matter. I don't know who wrote it, but Drew sure as hell didn't."

"Explain," I said.

Sweat beaded his forehead. He shivered.

"One sec." I returned bearing three ibuprofen and a glass of water.

He downed them with Old Granddad instead. "Drew was a down-home boy. A man of the people, as the political wags call it. It wasn't bullshit. Not only would he not kill Laura or Gary, he sure as hell wouldn't write a stilted letter like that."

"Hank, people do things and say things when they're desperate that can seem unlike their normal selves."

"Doesn't matter. Those aren't Drew's words."

"Then whose? Noah's? Will's? Who?"

"Sure sounds like ol' Noah."

"Except Noah and Annie are in Portland, hunting up a marriage trousseau. Noah has what he wants, Annie marrying Drew. Why kill the groom?"

"Complicated, isn't it? Take Drew as the killer out of the equation, then what's motivating our murderer? What else didn't you tell Reba?"

"The cookies."

"Huh?"

"I'm now sure someone doctored them." I told him about eating Drew's cookies. "When I woke up, I felt lousy, like I'd been on a bender. If the cookies were doped, he'd fall asleep, like I did. The shooter could get Drew up close and make it look like suicide. No struggle. It had to be someone who

Drew knew. A careful planner, just like with Gary and Laura."

Hank rubbed his face with his hands. "Don't think we'll ever know now."

"No. There's nothing much left out at Drew's, is there?"

"Nope," he said. "See, the gun most likely belonged to Drew. Even so, it won't tell much of anything."

"Drew's death is a neatly wrapped package that explains everything, just like Gary's was. Even if there hadn't been a fire, what with the note and all, if drugs *were* found in Drew's system, they'd be chalked up to easing the way, again like Gary. All three homicides are messy crimes—a fire, a knifing, an asthma attack. Yet they're neat and tidy, really. All pretty."

"Too pretty," he said. "Which leads me to that damned Dead Stone out to the quarry. Why take Laura out there in the first place? Makes sense about Gary. A nice follow-up. But Laura, that's curious."

"I take it you've bagged the Satanism stuff?"

He snorted. "Yup-suh, sure have. I bet it ticked off our killer but good that he couldn't do Drew on the stone."

"You keep saying 'he.' Maybe it was a duo, maybe Patsy and Mitch?"

Hank chuckled, which turned into a cough. He waved a hand when I reached for the water.

"Speaking of which," he said. "Patsy's divorce papers, giving her only half of Drew's assets, were at the camp. Signed by Drew. I was to head over there this afternoon to mail them for him."

"Divorce or no, Patsy Lee still saw Drew as her property. I doubt she liked Laura horning in on her territory. She told me she was at a movie in Bangor the night Laura died. Easy enough to lie about. With Drew dead, Patsy gets it all?"

"Almost. The camp property goes to Annie."

I whistled. "Wow."

"Always has been meant for Annie," he said. "I knew. I'm betting other people knew, too."

Noah would get the land he needed for Emerald Shores. Just like he'd planned. Just like with Trenton Shores. "So either way, through Annie's marriage or Drew's death, Noah's got his leach field."

Hank's answer was a snore. He'd crashed. I dragged the afghan up to cover him.

Noah might think he had control, but he had me to contend with first. I scooched closer beside Hank and slept, too.

Chapter Thirty-four
An Artful Dodger

The sound of a truck rumbling in the dooryard awakened me the next morning. I peered out the mudroom window, anxious, wondering what the heck could happen next. My fears were unnecessary. My 4-Runner sat beside Hank's car, as the tail end of a tow truck retreated around the bend.

The phone bleeped, and I raced to the kitchen and yanked it off the cradle before it woke Hank, who was snoring on the sofa.

"It's Carmen. Are you all right?"

"Pretty much. Um, you've heard about Drew, then."

"Yeah," she said in a voice thick with tears. "If you're up to it, come on over to the house. Annie's here. She's hysterical. She's saying she's the one who killed Drew."

I left a note for Hank and flew.

Two mailboxes beyond Laura's cottage, I turned right and barreled down Carmen's drive. I spotted a man, I presumed her husband, working on a classic forties pickup. A curly-headed boy about seven was handing him tools. Three cats sprawled on outcroppings of ledge, watching. One was Tigger, Laura's cat. By the time I parked behind Carmen's old VW bus, she'd come onto the front stoop of the old farmhouse and was waving me inside. A little brown-haired girl about four clung to one leg of her overalls.

I ran up the path, Penny by my side. "What's happened?"

Carmen poked her granny glasses to the bridge of her nose. "Ei, yi, yi. Annie practically drove into Bob's pickup over there. She was all *loco* about Drew. Bawling her head off."

"Mommy?" The little girl raised her arms and Carmen scooped her up.

"What exactly did she say?" I asked.

"That she'd killed Drew." Carmen sighed. "And that's all I can get out of her. Wait'll you see her."

"I'll try and calm her down."

"Trust me," Carmen said as she led me through the parlor and dining room and into the kitchen. "That's not the problem."

Annie sat on a chair, hugging herself. Even though she wore a sweater and jeans, she was shivering in front of a small woodstove Carmen had going at a slow burn.

"She was freezing," Carmen said, jerking her head toward the stove. "Now it's roasting in here, but I didn't know what else to do. It doesn't seem to have helped."

I pulled over one of the kitchen chairs and sat facing Annie. Her cheeks were blotchy, her hair disheveled. Penny rested her chin on Annie's lap. Annie remained unaware. "Annie?"

She rocked in the chair. Her eyes were empty.

"Sweetie." I took one of her icy hands in mine. "How are you feeling?"

She kept rocking. No eye contact.

Not good. Not good at all. I squeezed Annie's hand and turned to Carmen, who sat at the harvest table with her daughter on her lap.

"Hey, Carm, remember when one of us fell out of the apple tree at Annie's and broke an arm?"

"Sure," Carmen said, giving me an *are you nuts?* look.

"Who was it?"

"Me. *Dios!* I remember it hurt like hell. You guys all laughed."

"We did not," I said.

"Did so," Carmen said.

I peeked at Annie, who was still rocking. I wrapped an arm around her, trying to give the comfort Annie so desperately needed. I nodded at Carmen, who winked back at me.

"Hey, Tal. Or is it Emma?" Carmen grinned. "Remember when Henry Cunningham stole that kiss from you?"

"Do I ever. At the time, I thought it was yucky."

Carmen chuckled. "Shows you what you knew."

"You've got that right." Penny had begun licking Annie's hand. "His kisses have definitely improved."

Annie had stopped rocking. Progress.

"I thought I'd die when Annie showed up with that hickey on her neck," I said.

"Me, too." Carmen pressed her cheek to her daughter's head.

"It wasn't me," Annie said in a soft voice. She rested her hand on Penny's head.

Hooray. "Sure it was you. You tried to wear that awful pink scarf to cover it up."

Annie shook her head slowly back and forth. "No, it was a blue scarf. And it was Carmen. Admit it, Carm."

"Annie's right," Carmen said, beaming. "It was me who had the hickey."

"Gosh, my memory stinks," I said. "Who gave it to you?"

"Caleb Farley," Carmen said. "And he tried to cop a feel, too."

"Carmen!" Annie said.

"Well, it was true, Annie. He did."

"You should cover Sadie's ears, talking like that."

I giggled. "Was it gross, Carm?"

"I sort of liked it." Carmen set her daughter Sadie on the floor. "I'm going to put on some tea. Annie, you want some?"

Annie inhaled a sob. "Ohh . . . okay."

"Would coffee be better?" I kept eye contact with Annie.

"Yes," Annie whispered. "I'd rather."

"Always causing problems," Carmen said with a chuckle. "I'll have some, too." She bustled over to the stove and reached for the teakettle.

I touched Annie's cheek. "Hon? You think we might talk a bit now?"

Her eyes slid from mine and she ran nervous fingers across her belt buckle. She hugged Penny. Finally, she whispered, "Yes."

"Remember you came to my cottage before you left for Portland with your dad?"

Another "yes" stumbled out.

"And didn't you have a good time in Portland?"

She shook her head. "I told Daddy I felt sick, so we came home the next day. I, um, I lied to Daddy about that. When he went to have coffee with his pals, I drove out to Dr. . . . Drew's camp."

"When was this, Annie?"

"Right after dinner."

"And was Drew all right when you got there?"

"No." She pressed her hands to her face. "He was mean and belligerent. He yelled at me when I told him I wouldn't have his baby."

Whoa. "He suggested you have a child with him?"

"*¡Qué lío!*" Carmen said.

Annie nodded. More tears.

"And then what happened, sweetie?"

"Drew said he wouldn't marry me unless we had a baby. I said we couldn't. Then he said he was still a man. I keep seeing him, Tally, yelling at me. Screeching about this baby. He was crazy. Out of his head. I tried to explain to him. That his Huntington's made him sick. That the baby might get his sickness."

Carmen handed Annie a mug of coffee. Annie wrapped her hands around it, her head shaking back and forth. "Drew said no baby of his would get the disease."

"But you knew that a child might, didn't you?"

"Of course." She closed her eyes. "And I couldn't do that. I couldn't do that to a baby. Not even for Drew. Although we'd talked about it for years, and I'd wanted that so badly forever and ever. But now, I couldn't do it. And I felt ashamed when I told him I wouldn't marry him. I felt so bad. But I wouldn't change my mind."

"I see. And you think he killed himself because of it."

"There's more. Daddy arrived. He was so mad. He started yelling at me, too, after I told him I wasn't marrying Drew. Then they were both yelling at me."

Her eyes grew huge. "Daddy wanted me to lie to Drew. To pretend I would have his child. They both kept it up, ranting and hollering, like they were crazy, but for different reasons. So I locked myself in the bathroom and ran the water."

I smiled. "Not a bad move, hon."

"I've always been such a chicken. Not like you or Carmen."

"You're wrong. Courage comes in all different shapes and sizes."

She shook her heard. "I sat down on the toilet seat and thought a lot about stuff. You see, I couldn't lie to Drew. We've meant so much to each other over the years. All those long-ago times. I kept thinking about them. What we'd been, what he'd been—so tall and strong and bright. I've loved him for what seemed like forever. I still do . . . did, but not in that special way. I realized I love Steven that way now. You know what I mean?"

"I know," I said, thinking about Hank and how life was seldom simple.

"While I was sitting there, I finally accepted how sick Drew was. That it wasn't my fault, not any of it, and that I still could help him. I would do it gladly. But no matter what, I couldn't marry him."

"All of that makes sense, Annie." I hugged her tight. "These are good things you've discovered, not bad."

Little Sadie pushed herself off the floor and walked over to Annie. She held out her arms and Annie pulled her onto her lap.

"I do want babies." Annie sighed. "So much. While I was in there, I could hear Daddy and Drew screaming at each other, so I came out and interrupted them. Daddy started yelling at me again, but this time Drew told him to shut up."

"That sounds more like the old Drew," I said.

"It was. Then I promised Drew I'd stay with him and nurse him. For as long as it took. But I wouldn't marry him. Drew held me and said that it was okay. Then he got up, because he said he was supposed to go to town that night. Daddy went nuts again, just shouting at me that I had to get married to Drew. Drew shouted him down and said I didn't have to do anything I didn't want to do."

"What did Noah say after that?"

She stroked Sadie's curls. "That I wasn't a daughter of his anymore. He left then. How could Daddy say that to me?"

"I don't know, hon. But I'm sure he didn't mean it." I silently asked for forgiveness for lying to Annie.

She shook her head. "I love Daddy, but . . ."

"So you stayed at Drew's for a while."

She nodded. "We talked, oh, about all sorts of things. It was wonderful. He didn't seem sick at all then. He said he loved me but that we shouldn't get married. Or have babies. That he was too sick. And he started to cry, because he'd always wanted children. He looked so worn, Tally. Like he knew he was losing the fight. I offered to drive him into town, but he said no. He was too exhausted. He lay down on the couch, and just before he fell asleep, he gave me the sweetest smile."

"So that's when you left."

"Yes," she said, sobbing. "I felt so bad for Drew, but good for myself. Stronger. But if I had stayed, he would be alive. If I had said I'd marry him, none of this would have happened. I know it."

"That isn't true. Believe me."

I suspected it was just the opposite. That because someone thought she *was* marrying Drew, they'd killed him. I could never tell her that.

Carmen sat beside us and poured Annie more coffee. Annie smiled a thank-you.

"I'll explain everything soon," I said. "I promise. Just trust me."

"I do," Annie said. "Penny's a wonderful dog."

"She is," I said. "One more question? Did you bring Drew some cookies that night?"

Annie scrunched her forehead. "No. How come?"

"When I was there the next morning, there were some chocolate-chip cookies on the table, just like the kind you make."

"They weren't there when I left around midnight."

Carmen accompanied me to the truck. The cats watched our progress, their eyes following Penny, while the boy and man ignored us, engrossed as they were in their truck tinkering.

"I needed to talk to you," Carmen said. "Alone."

"I sense Annie will be all right. Stronger, you know."

Carmen rested a hand on my arm. "Yup. I, um, keep thinking about Patsy in not-so-nice ways."

"What made her come to mind?" I asked.

"Don't know. But I don't trust her, not where Drew's concerned. She's easy to dislike."

"So's Noah."

"Yeah." She pushed the bridge of her glasses. "Truth be told, I'm more disturbed about Steve. I . . . I, ah, when Annie and Noah were in Portland, I blurted out to him that Annie was marrying Drew."

"Geesh, Carm."

"Well, I'm sorry, dammit! But Steve kept badgering me about where they went."

"Did you know that Hank walked in on him and Laura in bed?"

"That was *Steve*? *El idiota!* I never figured it out. Did *you* know that Laura pretended she was pregnant with Hank's kid?"

I hadn't, and it disturbed me. "So maybe Laura blamed Steve for losing Hank."

"Either that, or Steve fathered her baby, and . . ." She turned away from me.

"You don't want to think about the 'and,' do you?"

"Not much. It could mean Steve killed all three. Damn Laura and her crazy ways."

I rested an arm on her shoulder. "You don't really mean that."

"No. Well, sort of. Her life . . ." She threw up her hands. "It was a series of scrapes and escapes. What if Steve was the father of her baby?"

"I'm pretty sure it was Drew. Something to ponder. I've got to go."

I hugged her, Penny jumped into the front passenger seat, and I slid behind the wheel of the truck.

Carmen leaned on the open window. "There might have been someone over at Laura's last night."

"Really. Because . . . ?"

"Around nine I thought I saw a light, but . . . Bob was gone. I couldn't leave the kids."

"You wouldn't go over yourself at night, right?"

"Damned straight, I would. Me and my .45. And don't tell Bob I said that."

"Remind me to take you into battle with me," I said. "It could have been the killer. He's murdered three people. I doubt he'd mind adding one more to his list."

"Not if I could help it. I did go over there this morning. Everything looked fine to me."

"Whoever is committing these homicides is a very ill person. Do you realize that?"

She dug her hands deep into the bib of her overalls. "In other words, whether it's Patsy or Steve or whoever, the killer is one large fruit loop."

"Unfortunately, yes, which makes him especially dangerous. Look, um, do me a favor. Sort of spread the word that I've gone over to Laura's. That maybe I've found something."

"Talk about dumb! No way, *senorita*."

"What if he's got someone else in his sights, Carm? Someone who has no idea. At least I'm sort of prepared."

"Forget it. I'm not saying squat."

I sighed. "I'll stay around Hank, I've got Penny. We've got to push him, Carmen, or someone else will die."

I drove to Laura's house with Carmen's promise that she'd think about my suggestion. Which meant she wouldn't do it.

Carmen was right. It was a dumb idea.

Laura's door was still unlocked, and I'd swear ghosts followed me as I walked through her home again. Laura had been a secret keeper. I was sure I'd missed some secrets the first time. A "something" that the killer might have retrieved last night? I should have returned sooner.

I brushed my fingers across her art, her books. I enjoyed her love of whimsy. Again I straightened the Far Side cartoon, which insisted on tilting. I'd forgotten Laura was more than a deceiver and blackmailer.

I opened and closed kitchen cabinets and pored through trunks of old clothes in the cellar. Same ol', same ol'. In her bathroom, I lifted her hairbrush and stared at the long strands of black hair caught by the bristles.

Everything looked the same in the bedroom, too. I pulled a book on genetics from the bookcase, wondering if Laura had engineered her pregnancy or if she'd been horrified that her child might carry Huntington's disease.

Unanswerable questions.

I closed the book, pushed it back in.

If Laura's baby was Drew's, what if Annie had known? Could she be the killer?

Absurd thought, but . . . No, Annie could not do that. That I knew in my soul.

I walked over to the painting of Annie and Laura on the easel. It was even lovelier than I remembered, with many layers of oil enriching its luminescent quality.

My eye snagged on something. Was I imagining it?

The girls were seated on a couch. They wore straw hats and peasant dresses. Laura's left arm was draped over Annie's shoulder, and Annie's right was wrapped around Laura's waist. Their other hands lay in their laps. But where were the belts, the ones with flowered art nouveau buckles that I'd seen on Joy and on Annie earlier today? I was sure they'd been in the painting. Now, just above their resting hands, each girl's belly was faintly swollen and hidden within was a crescent-shaped . . . fetus. It could be, although they were much smaller and not as cleverly done as the baby in Laura's office.

Was this one of Laura's camouflage paintings, and I'd missed the fetuses the first time? Maybe because of the light or the angle. Had I imagined the belts or . . . ? No. The painting *was* different.

I pressed a finger to Laura's belly, then moved in close. I'd just made a faint but discernible fingerprint. The oil wasn't completely dry. I rubbed my fingers together.

This was what the intruder had done last night—painted fetuses on Laura and Annie.

Maybe Annie was pregnant, too. Or maybe she'd once been. I didn't know if Annie painted, but . . .

Steve did. Carmen had said that was one reason Laura had found him attractive.

Altering the painting was too weird.

I gave the canvas a final look. The green-handled paint-brush, the stiff one that had rested on the easel, now poked from the jar of turpentine.

I left Laura's house more disturbed than ever.

Chapter Thirty-five
The Gang's All Here

During the drive home from Laura's place, I felt increasingly disturbed by the painter's behavior. If the previous night's artist and the killer were one and the same, the person's psychosis could have sprung from a variety of factors. His or her relationship to the world might be a product of a dissociative disorder or a bipolar personality or some adjustment disorder that was increasingly manifest. The killer might also have a depersonalization disorder. Hard to know, harder to understand. But whichever the diagnosis, I felt the killer's condition was deteriorating.

Something had radically changed for the killer to murder Drew. But what? Only Annie's impending marriage to him was new. Except she'd reversed that. Of course, the killer might not have known that Annie had canceled the wedding.

I drove into the dooryard way too fast. I was overthinking all of it.

Drew and Laura—connected. *Focus on that*, I told myself.

Penny jumped from the seat, and she was greeted by Peanut, her tail thumping away. She and Penny touched noses and took off. Inside, I found Hank still asleep on the couch, his head hot with fever. I draped a cool cloth across his forehead, got more ibuprofen into him and some apple juice down him, which he promptly threw up.

I cleaned the mess and renewed the cool cloth.

"I'll call the doctor," I said.

"Don't even think it," he growled.

A good sign he'd live. "If you're not better tomorrow, I'm hauling your butt to the doctor."

A grunt was my answer. I didn't want to leave Hank again while he was feverish. I gobbled a fistful of vitamins and slipped outside. The breeze cleaned out my cobwebs. I was going to miss this place. I hunkered into the aluminum chair and crossed my legs on the deck rail. I watched Penny and Peanut romping on the beach.

I felt as if I were on a precipice and the world was teetering toward an explosion. I'd been in this place before, where the skin on my body tingled. It wasn't a good place.

The day passed with little activity and much worrying—about Hank and Annie and Joy and Steve and Daniel. Even about Will Sacco. I managed to tie myself into intellectual knots as to who could have done what, when, and to whom.

Every few hours, I dosed Hank with ibuprofen and cool cloths. I also cleaned up two more messes, the results of futile apple juice attempts.

By nine that night, Hank finally kept down some Coke, then a cup of chicken broth. I received no strange phone calls, no one invaded my home, and the note I'd hoped for from Uncle Lewis—naming the killer—failed to arrive.

My computer remained out of commission, but I started a handwritten list of who was where the night Laura was killed. I decided to make some calls. I called Chip Vandermere's place, got his wife, and listened to an echo of the Bond marathon Chip claimed they'd watched that evening. Mitch Jones started coughing when I said my name. But he, too, said that he and Patsy had been at the movies the night Laura died. Both alibis could be fake, but it would be difficult discrediting them.

I dialed the only Seth Spinner in the book. Mr. Spinner slammed the phone down on my ear when I mentioned his poker game with Daniel and Noah. I called back, got out a few more words, then down went the phone again.

My, what a prickly fellow, and all over a poker game.

I ran my finger down my list. Will Sacco had picked up Scooter's prescription that night. To check, I called LaVerdier's Pharmacy. The pharmacist named Crowley said Joy, not Will, had retrieved Scooter's prescription the night Laura died. He remembered because they'd talked about Will's vegetables and his chances at the fair. Mr. Crowley competed, too. Joy was protecting Will. From what, I could only speculate.

I got out my Calais phone book and called around about Steve. No luck at the diner or the convenience store. But bingo at the gas station on Main Street. Sure, they knew Mr. Sargent. Came in whenever he was in town. In fact, they were so helpful, they pulled out Steve's running tab, the one he paid monthly. Ayuh—Steve had bought gas there the night Laura Beal died. Purchased it at 9:05 P.M.

That was two hours after Hank had pinned Steve in Calais. But not late enough. He still could have made a run back to Winsworth that night and murdered Laura.

Hank woke up again, so I stopped my sleuthing and took his temperature. For the first time all day, it read less than a hundred. He was also grumpy, a sure sign of recovery.

After I kissed him goodnight, I made plans for the following day. I would talk to Noah, then go back out to the Saccos'. Time for Joy to tell me the truth about Will's activities the night Laura died.

I fell asleep wondering if a man could stab his own daughter a couple dozen times.

That answer I knew.

I awakened with the shivers around nine the next morning. Not with the virus, but from the nightmare. Hank was still asleep, surrounded by Peanut and Penny, so I dressed, tiptoed downstairs, and dialed Annie at home.

While it rang, I saw my dream again. A shadowy killer was plunging a butcher knife into Annie's belly.

What if the person who'd "completed" Laura's painting intended to murder Annie? Why hadn't I thought of that? Whether she was really pregnant or not, could the fetus painted on Annie's teenaged self be an arrow to the next killing?

Noah's machine clicked on, and I left a message for Annie to call me. I did the same when I got a no answer at Beals Realty.

Now I was really worried. I guessed Annie could be out and about, but she'd been so shaken the day before that I pictured her cocooned at home.

I paced the floor cradling the portable phone. I poured myself a glass of orange juice, ate a granola bar, and downed more vitamins. Think, think.

What had Annie said yesterday about Noah? That he'd shouted that Annie wasn't a daughter of his anymore.

I called Carmen, who wasn't at home, either. I dialed the restaurant. Carmen came on, said Annie was there and that she'd spent the night at Carmen's house. I whooshed out a sigh of relief. Annie was safe.

"Annie!" I said when she came on the line.

"Tally?" Annie said. "You sound funny."

"Uh, do I? Gee, I don't mean to. I was looking for you. Everything okay?"

"I guess. Well, yes, I'm pretty good. Daddy, um, he wouldn't let me in the house last night, so I stayed with Carmen."

That shit, I thought. "Oh, he's probably just upset. You know how he gets."

"I do. And I kind of realize how it's him and not me."

"You're right about that, sweetie. I, um, are you wearing that belt I saw yesterday? The pretty one with flowers?"

"Yes," she said. "I love it. How come?"

"I was wondering. Isn't that the same belt you were wearing in that painting of you and Laura?"

"You mean the one set up in her studio?"

"Yes."

"Sure. That was what she was working on when she, um, when she died."

"Exactly," I said. "And that's the belt from the painting, right?"

"Yes. Laura was wearing it. It's hers."

"What happened to yours?"

"I never had one."

"But you and Laura were wearing identical belts in the painting."

Annie laughed. "Oh, now I get it. That's not me in the painting. It's Joy."

347

"Joy Sacco?"

"Yes. In fact, Joy made the belts. It was one of the first art things she ever did."

The world shifted. If Joy was the other girl in the painting, then Joy had the fetus now painted on her belly. And it was Joy who could be the killer's next target.

"Tally?" Annie said.

"Oh, um, sorry. Thanks so much. Gotta run. I'll talk to you later. Stay with Carmen today, huh?"

"I planned on it."

"Great."

As soon as we clicked off, I called Joy.

Will answered the phone and said Joy couldn't be disturbed.

"I'm coming out there, Will," I said.

"That's what Joy said. That you'd hightail it out here today."

"I expect to see her when I get there."

He chuckled. "Sure you will. She's looking forward to seeing you, too. In fact, she was gonna call you to come out for a visit today."

Maybe I'd misinterpreted the whole painting thing. And the whole Will thing with the fire. Naw. "We've got to talk about some stuff."

"Don't I know it," said Mr. Sincerity. "Clear up some of these misunderstandings we've been having."

Misunderstandings? Not. Will's jolly affect was at odds with the dreadful deeds he'd committed of late. Made no sense, and I didn't like it one bit. When we hung up, I headed for the Saccos' place at Mach speed.

I didn't park in the Saccos' dooryard like usual, but down below the barn, making sure my truck was hidden from sight. I preferred the advantage of surprise, if at all possible. Probably a delusion, but what the hell.

I headed up the road. Could Will have changed the painting? Or Steve? For all I knew, Noah painted. Or even Patsy.

I hoped to hell Joy was okay.

The Saccos' place looked the same. The large oak, the derelict car, even Scooter's Big Wheel. A butterfly perched on the curve of the old car's tire, then fluttered off, alighting on the tricycle.

I walked down the path toward the front door. As I got closer to the house, I heard whistling coming from the backyard. Same song, same whistle: "If I Had a Hammer." Dammit, I used to love that song.

The day was warm, but I felt cold and rubbed my hands up and down my arms. I'd been so sure I was ready to face Will Sacco. Now I wasn't all that confident. For insurance, I moved my bag to my shoulder and tucked my hand inside. I gripped the pepper spray. I should have brought Penny.

I walked around back. Will was pruning a weeping cherry tree. He caught sight of me and laid down the shears. Big grin.

"Hey." He lifted his bill cap and ran a hand through his hair. "You're a speedy one."

"Sure am." I started across the lawn.

He wagged a finger. "Just stop right there. See all that dug-up earth and brush? Came out this morning and we got us a damned woodchuck tearing up the place. Joy says someone could twist an ankle bad in one of these holes, and she's right."

He might be smiling, but his nerves were all on the surface, jittery as anything. I backtracked and waited while he walked along a meandering dirt path to meet me. He notched his head, and I followed him around to the front of the house. Grim thoughts about what he might have buried in those "woodchuck holes" flitted through my brain.

"Where are Joy and Scooter?" I asked.

"In the house," he said, leading me over to the oak.

"Did you change the painting, Will?"

"Huh?"

"The painting of Laura and Joy."

"All I ever painted was this house, and that's God's truth."

"But you know what I'm talking about."

"No," he said. "Can't say I do." But his eyes showed the lie.

"I'm going in to see them." I started for the front door.

He held up a hand. "Now, hold on. Scooter's napping. Joy might be, too."

"I thought you said that she was expecting me."

"I did. I did. But I figured we'd clear up a couple things first."

Joy poked her head out the screen door, waved, then vanished again.

She was safe, and I relaxed, even though I didn't trust Sacco at all. "The only thing I'd like cleared up, Will, is why you set the fire."

He jammed his hands into his back pockets. "Didn't."

"Look, I was inside that camp when it burned, as you know. It wasn't fun."

"Musta been terrible. But I had nothing to do with it. I was out working my garden. First I knew about it was when Joy told me all of your crazy ideas."

"I heard you whistling, Will."

"Everybody whistles."

"Not 'If I Had a Hammer.'" I rested my hand on his arm.

Will jumped back, eyes wide with terror. "Don't you touch me, hear? Don't you come anywhere near me."

I moved closer, stealing his space. "Why, Will? What's bothering you?"

He took a step back. "You could have the AIDS."

"What are you taking about?"

"The AIDS, the AIDS. You're not a stupid woman. You touched his blood, I bet. You could have it."

"This is ridiculous."

"Call it what you will, but don't you come near me."

I touched his blood? "You mean Drew?"

Will wagged a hand. "That's right. I heard you were inside with his body and there was blood everywhere. I bet you touched it."

I studied him. There was fear in his eyes, and sweat beaded his forehead. Someone had fed him this cockamamie story. "Will, Drew didn't have AIDS."

Will rolled his eyes. "Of course he did. I should know. My Tish died of it."

"But . . ." Could Drew have had AIDS and not Huntington's? No. Hank had confirmed the genetic disease. "Drew didn't have AIDS."

A car bounced up the dirt road, its muffler loud, drowning out my words.

Noah was driving the car.

Chapter Thirty-six
Jaws

When I turned around, Will was scooting into the house.

"Dammit," I said.

I walked after him, pounded on the door, and heard yelling. Joy and Will, then Scooter started to wail.

In a billow of dust and squeal of brakes, Noah halted in front of the Saccos' house.

I dogtrotted over to where Noah had parked.

"Noah," I said.

He peered at me out the window, his eyes narrowed. He pressed a button and the window slid down. "Stirring things up, eh?"

"I'd say it was the reverse. You have a lot to account for, Noah Beal."

A metal door slammed. Will and Joy stood on the stoop, Scooter riding Joy's hip.

"I called Noah." Joy nudged Will forward.

Noah left the car, slamming the door behind him. "That you did, although I'm not clear why you need my help, Joy."

"Because it's time you straightened things out," she said. "You've always had Will to do your dirty work, and we're finished with it. Tell Tally how you had him set fire to Drew's camp."

Noah folded his arms. "Insanity."

Joy closed the distance between us, Will following behind. "Tally thinks Will could've killed Drew," she said. "Then burned the house to cover it up. But it's not true. Is it, Noah?"

"How should I know?" Noah said.

"Because you were the one that got him to light the torch," Joy said. "All because of that stupid story of yours."

"Don't, Joy," Will said.

They made quite a tableau. Will, poking his feet in the dirt. Joy, red-faced, glaring at Noah. And Noah, shaking his head, disdain written across every inch of his tanned face.

Noah turned to leave.

"Wait a minute, Noah." I stepped between him and the car door. "Was it you who planted the AIDS story in Will's head? Will just said he was afraid of me because I'd touched Drew's blood. And that Drew had AIDS. Drew didn't have AIDS, did he, Noah?"

"How should I know?"

"Of course you know. Until yesterday, Annie was planning on marrying him."

Noah shrugged. "Who's to say he didn't have AIDS?"

"Oh, come on," I said. "Drew had a genetic illness. Huntington's disease."

Will looked from Noah to me. "You're saying it was some inherited thing that made him shake? And what about those track marks and scabs on his arms? And he was crazy half the time. Boy, do you have it wrong, Tally."

"Do I?" I said, cutting my eyes to Noah's.

"But . . ." Will sputtered. "But there's no disease like that. Is there, Noah?"

Noah's jaw tightened.

"Will," I said. "It's easy enough to prove. There are records at the hospital. He was a patient of Dr. Cambal-Hayward's. I'm sure now that Drew's dead, she'd tell you all about it."

Will's gray eyes filled with confusion. "I . . ."

"It's true, Will," Joy said. "Tally's right."

"But, Noah," Will said. "You told me to burn that house because of the infection."

"And so Noah could get the property," I said. "Right?"

Will shuffled his feet.

"Tell her, Noah," Joy said.

Noah puffed his pipe. "How can I possibly admit what is patently false?"

Joy shifted Scooter to her other hip. "But it *is* true. Will told me last night. You scared the hell out of him, saying how Drew was infected just like Tish. You made him afraid for Scooter. You fed his fears, Noah. You know you did."

Noah smirked, as if he were dealing with a lower life-form. "All a fantastic fiction concocted by your husband." He made to move me away from his car.

"Did you urge Will to kill Drew because of his supposed AIDS?" I asked.

Will wagged a finger at Noah. "He knows I didn't kill Drew. Because he knows who did. It was all supposed to happen two nights ago."

I locked eyes with Noah and saw the knowledge there. And the fury. Will wasn't lying.

"What did Will see that night when he went over there to burn the place down? Eh, Noah? Who are you shielding?"

"Tell her," Joy said.

Noah produced one of his sage nods. "When you called, Joy, I came to help. Impossible." He reached for the Jeep's door handle.

Will grabbed his arm. "Swear to God, Noah, I'll tell her the truth of what I saw that night."

"Shut up," Noah said.

Will grabbed Noah's shirt. "I saw a car that night, didn't I, Noah? And that's how come I didn't fire the camp then. It was a big old black car barreling down the camp road. I never saw who was in it, but I know Drew answered the door. I waited to see what was up, and maybe fifteen minutes later, the car left. No passenger, so I walked back home and called you. You said I should do the camp the next morning, when Drew had an appointment with you. And then he didn't show up and you heard he was dead. We both know who killed 'em, don't we, Noah?"

Noah towered over the diminutive Will. "Don't say another word."

"Who was there that night, Noah?" I said. "Who was the 'someone' that was the last person to see Drew alive? Someone who drove a big, black car. An old one. You're protecting a killer."

Noah puffed out his chest, glanced at Will and Joy, then got into his Jeep. He fired it up.

I ran around the front and got in beside him. "You're shielding Daniel, aren't you?"

Noah lifted the pipe from his mouth. "Well, well. Such a smart woman, Ms. Tally Whyte. Grown from that little pain-in-the-ass Emma, into a big pain in the ass. What's the point of this? What's it all for?"

"Daniel murdered his son, Noah."

Noah shook his head. "He put the poor boy out of his misery, is how I see it. You can't imagine the agonies Daniel's gone through with that disease. Knowing he was the cause of Drew's illness. Yet for some reason, Daniel hasn't shown most of the symptoms. The dementia. The temper. The memory loss. It's made for an almost intolerable burden."

"I'm sure it has. But that's not a reason to murder three people."

He swiveled in his seat. "*Three?* Whatever are you talking about?"

Noah's smoke-gray eyes widened with curiosity. He honestly hadn't connected Drew's death to the others. "Whoever killed Drew murdered Gary and Laura, too."

He jerked. "Don't be absurd. Daniel didn't kill my Laura."

For all that he was a greedy, manipulative arsonist, I pitied him. "Couldn't he have? Not if the child in her belly carried the dreaded Huntington's?"

Noah's condescending smile grated. "You're wrong. Completely wrong. I've known Daniel for fifty years. He was with me the day I learned Laura was pregnant. This was *after* she was dead. He couldn't have feigned the shock I saw on his face."

"People do, Noah. Fake it, I mean."

"They don't fake being someplace else, God dammit!"

"I spoke to Seth Spinner last night. He hung up on me. Twice. It made me wonder if you and Daniel weren't playing poker there the night Laura died. Do you *really* have any idea where Daniel was?"

"Of course I do. He was with me, down to Portland."

"Then why didn't you tell this to the police? What's with the poker story?"

He shifted in his seat. "Because our activities aren't something either of us wants bandied about. We may not be twenty, but we still have needs."

"You were visiting a prostitute?"

Noah cleared his throat. "Just two woman friends. That's all. The gas receipts will show up on Daniel's MasterCard, for God's sake. We were there until two in the morning, then drove back."

"So you got Seth Spinner to lie to Hank."

"Seth visits that place, too. He understands." He ran a hand over his silver hair. "Don't you see? We couldn't explain that night."

I saw. But it only complicated things. Could there possibly be two killers in Winsworth?

"And you're sure it was Daniel's car the night Drew died?" I asked.

"Of course I'm sure. Will described Daniel's big old LeBaron. When I broached the subject with Daniel, he wouldn't even admit to me, his best friend, that he'd been there."

Someone must have arrived after Daniel had left, but *who*?

I looked toward the house. Joy and Will sat with Scooter on the stoop. They were holding hands and talking. Scooter was peering up at them, his blond head tilted back, his eyes squeezed almost shut as he laughed.

Eyes squeezed almost shut . . .

A shock wave rippled through me as I was pulled back to that long-ago Halloween with Drew. I had to look away, my vision blurred with tears.

Dear God, no.

The truth sat there for anyone to see. Hidden in plain sight. How clever. I would have smiled if it weren't so horrible.

It all came down to Scooter's laugh and a derelict car.

"Noah, I don't think Daniel killed Drew."

"What?" he said.

I stared at the car that crouched on the front lawn. It was big and black and old. An Imperial LeBaron. It still had one dented fender, a broken window, and some rust. But at night, from a distance, it would be hard to see those things. It was almost a twin of the one Daniel drove. But not exactly the same.

I walked closer to the car and pushed aside the tall grass. Today, all of its tires were inflated. I never would have noticed if it weren't for the butterfly that had perched there earlier that day.

Would I find the keys in the ignition and the gas tank half full?

"You screwed up bad, Noah, but you're not a killer. Neither is Daniel. You'd better go home. On your way, call the police on your cell phone, eh?"

As I walked slowly down the path, Noah began to back up, turning his Jeep in the dooryard.

My feet felt heavy. Dear Scooter—so loved and protected by Joy. Her little genius, she'd called him, and then she'd talked about his grand future, his going to Harvard. The obsession with germs, as if that would make a difference. I pictured him zooming around on his Big Wheel, playing with my keys, laughing. It was the laugh, the eyes almost closed shut with joy, that finally connected everything.

I jumped at the crack of a gunshot, jerked around, saw Noah slump against the wheel, the Jeep careening forward until it hit a maple on the other side of the road.

I dashed toward the Jeep.

"Tally, stop! Now turn around."

When I did, Joy stood on the path pointing a large-caliber

handgun straight at me. She still gripped Scooter firmly on her hip. He was crying, his hands wrapped around his ears.

Will gaped at his wife. "Joy, honey?"

"It was him," Joy said. "Noah. Tally was letting him get away."

Her face was stiff, her eyes distant. I snuck my hand into my purse, found the pepper spray. I carefully moved toward the family. "But it wasn't Noah, was it, Joy?"

She wiped her forehead with the back of her hand. The sun glinted off the gun's shiny barrel.

"Go inside, Will, and take Scooter."

"But . . ."

"Do it." She handed the boy over to Will, who gave me a long look as he took Scooter into his arms.

Scooter wailed "Mama" and a ripple of pain crossed Joy's face.

Now it was just Joy and me. For such a heavy gun, she held it surprisingly still.

"Is this how you got Gary out to the Dead Stone?" I tried to catch her eyes, but they darted everywhere. "Talk to me, Joy. Help me understand."

She waved the gun, indicating I should walk out back.

"You understand," she said.

Comprehending psychosis isn't all that easy. But I thought I understood Joy's, at least a part of it. "Your best friend was going to have Drew's baby. Another Huntington's baby."

She stopped. "What do you mean, 'another'?"

"Scooter." She still wouldn't look at me. Bad sign. "I know about Scooter. He's Drew's child, not Will's, isn't he? Did it happen when Drew's marriage collapsed?"

"We were so close from the YMCA board and he needed me and . . ."

"But Laura's child might not have had the disease."

"She had no right. She was my dear, trusted friend. My very best friend. The only one who knew about my love affair with Drew."

"Did she know who Scooter's father really was?"

"Of course. I told her. And she got really mad. She was jealous of my baby, of Drew. That's why she got pregnant, even when she knew her baby could inherit the disease. She said it didn't matter about Scooter. That the chances were good that *her* baby would be fine, even though my Scooter's going to die. And he is. I had him tested."

She wailed. A terrible sound. Tears splashed down her cheeks and the gun wobbled.

I reached out to her. "Joy, let me—"

"Get back," she said through gritted teeth. "Curse her! Laura was like my twin. We did everything together. Except she shouldn't've gotten pregnant. When she told me, I knew she had to have an abortion. *No more sick babies*."

I was finally getting it. Too late. Much, much too late. "So the night she died, you swung by the Giddyup after you got Scooter's prescription. Maybe you wanted to apologize to Laura and Gary for not meeting them like you said you would."

"How did you know that?" she asked.

"It's not hard, Joy, when it all makes sense. Everything connects. Except, Gary wasn't there. Only Laura, in the parking lot. Alone. Angry because Gary had left her. She asked you to take her home, not to her Jeep, didn't she?"

Joy nodded. "She'd had one too many, and she never drove like that."

"She started painting," I said. "Something she did when she was frustrated. You told me so yourself. She was working on the oil of the two girls. I'd thought it was of Laura and

Annie, but the other girl was you. That's when she told you about the baby, isn't it?"

Joy leaned her head against the side of the house. One hand rubbed the art nouveau belt buckle, as Annie had done. Was it only yesterday?

"Did you and Drew make love on the Dead Stone, Joy?"

"Yes. It was summer and hot, and I thought it was the most magical night of my life." Her lips trembled. "Some magic, huh."

"You were so careful, Joy. Wiping Laura's hard drive, using the Satan medal, forging the notes. You're good with details."

She straightened. "I sure am," she said with pride.

"Except you couldn't resist putting the stiffened brush back in the turpentine. So what made you go and put the babies in the girls' bellies?"

"She didn't finish it, don't you see? It needed to be complete, so that we were still twins."

Oh, boy. "You must be in a lot of pain."

"Pain?" She laughed. "You don't know pain. You don't have a child. You can't picture them growing tall and strong and bright, then withering, just like Drew did. My son will die before me. Picture that."

I could, and it saddened me, but my fear overruled it. Again she poked the gun toward the backyard and motioned me to move. A dog yipped in the distance. I shivered. Hank was too sick to even be looking for me. Noah? I hoped he wasn't dead.

"You figured out the car, didn't you?" Joy said.

"The LeBaron's inflated tires. You're a planner. And you're very clever, Joy. But you forgot to deflate the tires again. Why didn't you just walk over to Drew's?"

"I had to take Scooter with me, didn't I? You know, Drew never caught on that Scooter was his. Just as he was drifting off, I told him. You should have seen the look on his face. Damn those stupid tires."

"It wasn't only the car. When he laughs, Scooter looks just like Drew did as a child."

"I was afraid you'd finally see it. You were snooping around so much, talking to people. To Drew. That's why I messed up your studio. And I sent you the fake finger, to remind you of that Boston killer I read about. I thought that would get you to leave it alone."

"Those things wouldn't do it."

"I hoped the cat would." She shook her head. "Putting him between the rocks was sort of fun. He was helpless, like Drew and Laura and Gary. They all underestimated me. I told Will that you'd show up today. And then you called. If you hadn't, I would've called you. See, I had it all planned about the ruckus with Noah. I hoped you might be put off. Not see the whole picture." She pursed her lips. "Too bad it didn't work."

Too bad, indeed. "Why didn't you kill Drew in the beginning?"

"That wouldn't have been fair, not since Laura's pregnancy was all her fault. I was . . . mad at her. She was supposed to promise she'd get an abortion and say she was sorry that night. That was all. But whenever I'd ask about the abortion, she'd say no."

I wondered if that was before or after Joy was plunging the knife into Laura's belly. "Is that why you watched?"

"You *do* understand," Joy said with urgency. "If she'd said she'd have the abortion, and apologized, it would have been okay. But Laura was always so stubborn. So I gave her an abortion myself."

The image sickened me, and I stumbled. She caught me. It made me want to laugh. We rounded the corner and the cherry tree came into view. Maybe I could plead with Will. I cut my eyes to the kitchen window, hoping to catch his. He wasn't there.

I wondered where she was taking me. "Then Gary found out, yes?"

"Yeah. He found out I'd gone out that night. I said it was only to get Scooter's medicine, but he figured it out. I feel bad about Gary."

"Even with the hikers, you watched him die, didn't you?"

"I *had* to. They never saw me."

"But why kill Drew? He was dying, Joy."

"He was going to marry Annie and have a baby with her. He told me one day when I was over visiting him. I couldn't let that happen."

If I upset her, she might falter. She was cool, composed. I felt a desperate urge to run. I was certain she would shoot me. "You didn't know the truth about Laura's pregnancy, Joy."

"Of course I did."

"No, I'm afraid you didn't. She was pregnant, but with an ectopic pregnancy. The fetus would have spontaneously aborted."

She hit me on the head with the gun, and I staggered, saw bright lights exploding on a black canvas.

"You lie!" she screamed.

"No, Joy, I'm not lying. She never could have had that child."

A pause, then: "What's done is done. I don't care."

I rubbed sweaty palms down the sides of my jeans. Joy also didn't know that Annie had called off the wedding. I had to get the gun away from her. Take out the pepper spray. Do something. I started to sneak the pepper spray from my purse.

"Walk over there." She pointed to the cherry tree.

Pain spiked my head at the first step. I headed for the tree, careful to avoid the woodchuck holes. "How are you going to explain Noah's shooting?"

"They'll never find him," she said from behind me. "Will's driving the Jeep up to Aroostook. He'll dump it in some lake off a tote road."

"And me?"

"Oh, Tally. I'm really sorry."

A hand shoved me and I stumbled sideways, my foot catching on one of the woodchuck holes.

Pain seared up my leg, a rocket of it, and a snap, and then I screamed, falling, crumpling to the ground. I grabbed my injured leg. Felt the warmth of my own blood. Grew dizzy with it.

The world vanished.

Chapter Thirty-seven
To Stay or Not to Stay?
Ayuh, That's the Question

Pain woke me. It shrieked up my leg with knives for fingers. And there were voices, mumbling things I couldn't understand because of the hum in my ears.

I lay curled on the ground, my face pressed to the soft grass. I smelled the rich earth. The breeze licked my cheek. I remembered where I was. I bit my lip, then cranked open an eye.

The trap was the first thing I saw, its spiked metal jaws clamped just above my ankle. Horrible.

Two pair of legs—one set tanned and lithe, the other shorter and jean-clad—stood to my left. I raised my eyes.

Joy and Will stood not ten feet from me—arguing.

A shard of pain, and the world tilted.

If I passed out again, I feared the long sleep would take me, courtesy of Joy and Will.

"It's so easy," came the cinnamon-sweet voice. "Don't you get it, Will? I planted all those traps so I could push her into one."

"Well, what about the woodchucks?" Will said.

"There *were* no woodchucks. I made it up. All I have to do is wrap her in the blanket or something and bring her and the trap over to Drew's. I'll bury the trap deep in the woods and she'll die out there. It'll look like an accident. Like with Peanut. All natural. That's the beauty of it."

Joy. Cajoling Will to do her bidding.

"I don't see it, Joy," Will said. "And I wish you hadn't used my traps."

"Jeez-um. Just take Noah up to Aroostook and lose him."

"This is wrong, Joy."

They moved off. I couldn't see them any longer. I didn't *want* to hear them. Dear God, it hurt.

If I could get to my pepper spray.

I slithered an arm beside my body. My purse lay next to me. The pepper spray was gone. So was my cell phone.

Moving only my eyes, I panned the earth. I spotted it. Too far away.

Tears burned my eyes, and I fought them. I couldn't let go. Not now.

Bile spurted to my throat. I swallowed hard.

Wait. Something else. Wood. I tiptoed my hand toward the piece of wood lying half hidden in a clump of unmown grass. My fingers reached it and stroked the smoothness. I clenched them around the handle. I'd found Will's pruning shears.

I pulled them toward me, forcing myself to go slow. They smelled of sap when I hugged them close.

The slap of a screen door, then long moments when I battled pain and dizziness. A car rumbling to a start. Noah's Jeep, with its lousy·muffler. Joy was hollering good-bye as the sounds of the Jeep faded.

She would be coming for me soon.

* * *

I heard a noise close by, then Joy pushed up a wheelbarrow so it rested parallel to where I lay. She crouched in front of me, chewing gum. "I'm sorry about all of this, Tally."

"Then let it go, Joy." Pain throbbed in my leg and head. "Please."

"I can't." She smoothed a hand across my cheek. "This is going to hurt. I gave Gary the Valium and Drew the cookies with the Percocet. It made it easier for them, you know? But I can't do that for you. The cops would find out. I feel bad."

She took the gum from her mouth, rolled it between her fingers, and tossed it on the ground. She popped a new square out of its plastic shell and put it into her mouth.

"Let me guess," I said. "Nicotine gum. You're trying to quit, right?"

She sighed. "Yeah. Not that I ever smoked around the house or Scooter, but . . . Well, I sort of need to when I get all tense. I figured I'd better stop when one of my cop pals came into the post office and said that dumb dog of yours found those cigarette butts."

From cigarettes she smoked while watching Laura die. "What about Scooter and the traps?"

"Scooter's inside with the door latched. I gave him a big stack of books and a fruit bar."

"Think about your son," I said. "About how this will affect him."

"Not a bit. I planned it all out. The traps. Everything. I knew you'd end up out here. You're the last one."

"Did you say that about Laura, too? And Gary? And Drew? What about Noah?"

"He'll be dead before Will hits Aroostook."

"Joy," I said. "Think. I have hopes, dreams, friends. Just like you, people I love who love me. And the . . ."

She reached for me.

I started to thrust upward, my hands gripping the pointed shears.

A door slapped.

"Mama?"

"Scooter!" screamed Joy. "Stay there. Don't move, baby."

I swiveled my head around. Scooter was toddling down the back porch step, giggling as he headed for us.

"*No!*" Joy ran, jumping over the holes she'd made, flying toward Scooter. Then her foot snagged on a branch.

"Mama!"

She flew forward, stretched out, willing herself to land on the path, but . . .

Two rusted jaws leapt toward her face.

"Joy!"

She screamed, arms outthrust, reaching toward her son as the steel snapped shut.

I closed my eyes.

I lay dizzy on the grass, feeling little pain now, babbling as best I could to Scooter to stay there with his mommy, not to move. He sat on the ground, his small fingers wrapped in his mother's hair, talking baby talk to her.

How much time had passed I didn't know. When I looked at my watch, the numbers blurred.

Joy was long dead, the rusted jaws of the trap spiking into her neck and face. She'd shrieked for what felt like eons, yet in moments she was still. The trap had either broken her neck or hit the carotid artery. Her agony would live with me forever. Of course, "forever" was about to arrive. I was dying. I knew it. Though I'd struggled with the trap, I couldn't free myself, and my blood relentlessly trickled from my body.

I wondered how much longer I'd be able to talk to Scooter. I was terrified he'd get up and come over to me.

Oh, how much I wished Hank were here.

A car. Putt-putting up the road. Then the slam of a door and someone humming.

Thank heavens. Will would save Scooter, although he would no doubt finish me off.

"Didn't I tell you to take care? Good golly, Miss Tally."

I saw a pair of ratty sneakers, then Scooter swooped up by . . .

"Lewis Draper," I said.

He bounced the boy on his hip. "Uncle Lewis, remember?"

"Uncle Lewis," I mumbled, tears cascading from my eyes. "Right."

It took what felt like forever for Uncle Lewis to release me from the trap, not that I remember much of it, since I was soon buried by an avalanche of pain. I awakened in the hospital with a cast on my left leg and Hank hovering over me.

I hate hospitals, almost as much as I hate funeral homes, and so two long nights and days later I effected a daring escape back to my rented cottage. Just in time to be greeted by . . .

"Veda! Bertha!"

I was smothered in their embrace, which isn't easy since both foster mothers barely reach my chin.

"Oh, my dear, dear Tal." Much clucking took place, then Bertha summarily handed Hank two stuffed grocery bags and led me inside.

I snuck a peek at Hank. His expression could only be called combative. Veda and Bertha together can be quite intimidating.

*   *   *

A week later, I hobbled over to the loft balcony. The sound of pots and pans drifted up from downstairs. Since Veda and Bertha's departure two days earlier, Hank had the kitchen back.

"Hank?" I hollered downstairs. "You're sure you don't mind driving me back to Boston?"

"Not a problem, babe," Hank said. "I took the next couple days off."

"Swell. Are you sure you feel like cooking again tonight?"

Hank made a face. "*She* wouldn't let me make a single dinner."

"Bertha wouldn't let Julia Child cook a meal."

"Or empty the dishwasher."

"Poor Hank."

"The borscht was pretty good," he said. "For borscht."

"I love the stuff."

Hank sighed. "I thought they were moving in permanently."

"They've rented the cottage for a month."

Hank's look of fear made me laugh.

"Jeez," he said. "You sure know how to get a guy going."

I tossed some panties into my suitcase. Tomorrow morning, Hank was driving me home to Boston.

It had been a long week. What with all the hurly-burly, the hospital, the questions, the reporters, and the tears, I still felt out of kilter.

I spent the week berating myself that I should have seen the connection between Scooter and Drew earlier. That I could have saved lives. That Drew could have known about his child. All the while, Hank kept telling me I was being ridiculous.

I only half believed him, and I'd grow teary-eyed over Drew and the memory of a boy who'd once rescued a ballerina's Halloween candy.

Noah was okay, although I doubted he'd fare very well once he was released from the hospital and was charged with a variety of felonies. Then again, knowing Noah, he'd get them reduced to misdemeanors and receive only a wrist slap.

I gave him credit for guts. His shoulder wound had turned out to be minor, and he'd somehow wrestled the steering wheel from Will. They'd crashed halfway to Bangor and a state policeman had come to the rescue, much to a banged-up Will's displeasure.

The charges against Will were long and mean, including accessory to and intent to commit first-degree homicide. Hank said Will would enjoy a long stay in prison, but I wondered.

Will had been Joy's victim as much as anybody.

Poor tormented Joy. She'd been so clever. The irony hadn't escaped me—how I'd been casting lures for a killer while Joy had been setting all of those traps. Doubly ironic that those same traps had killed her while she was saving the son she so loved.

Annie had taken Scooter in and was talking adoption. Steve was all for it. Perhaps by the time Scooter was grown, some brilliant researcher would have found a way to stave off the effects of Huntington's disease. And perhaps Scooter would only manifest minor symptoms, like his grandfather, Daniel. Carmen had visited me several times. Like Veda and Bertha, she'd gotten mother hennish and had brought me a banquet from her natural-foods restaurant. My injury sure helped us dine in style.

She tried to talk me into staying in Winsworth, yet even as she said the words, she knew my life remained in Boston at The Grief Shop. I invited her down and knew she most likely wouldn't come, but she also knew I'd be back in

Winsworth. It pulled at my memories and at my heart.

Then there was Uncle Lewis, who'd scared me half to death at 2 A.M. my second night in the hospital. He snuck in, was proud of it, and told me he was "just checkin'." His Post-it notes continued unabated, always signed "*UL*."

The phone rang, and since I'd been plagued by reporters, I let Hank answer it.

He handed me the phone, his face grim and tight.

It was Kranak, calling about an upcoming court case, where I was to help the parents of a boy murdered by his uncle. A tough one. When I hung up, I wrapped my arms around Hank.

"We're just good pals, is all," I said.

"He calls all the friggin' time."

"I know. It's just business."

Hank said nothing, and I knew he was cogitating on us and our lives apart.

The phone rang again, and since Hank was outside with Peanut and Penny, I answered.

"Hello, Ms. Whyte. I'm Dr. Dexter Shelton, the chief medical examiner for the state of Maine, and I have a proposition for you."

We hung up fifteen minutes later. I sat down hard on the sofa, my cast bouncing and pain knifing up my leg. I hadn't known what to say to the chief, so I'd just listened. He'd made a pretty generous offer if I would become the homicide counselor for the state of Maine.

Hank banged back into the house, and after he gave the dogs their cookies, I caught his eye.

"Was the call from the ME your idea?" I said.

He sat beside me on the couch. "Sort of. I've been talking to some people. Up to Bangor. The state police. The ME's office in Augusta. We could use a, um, a homicide counselor up here. You'd have to travel. Go where the cases were. But you could be based out of Winsworth."

I sat beside him. "Whew."

Hank wasn't happy with our separation, and neither was I. Yet to leave MGAP and Boston and friends and family for a life in Maine seemed more wishful thinking than reality. And here I'd been offered a job. Poof. Just like that. Doing what I loved, what I needed to do.

I sighed. "I don't know, Hank."

"Think on it."

The following day, Hank began loading my 4-Runner for our drive back to Boston. He was keeping Peanut, and so she was joining Penny and me on the drive. I zipped my makeup bag closed and hobbled over to put it in the suitcase.

"You frown every time you walk," Hank said. "You're not ready for this."

"I'm ready," I said over my shoulder.

Two arms wrapped around my waist. "Are you?"

"You betcha." I twisted around so I was facing him. "I need to go back."

"Maybe."

I looked long into his eyes. Worried eyes. Caring eyes. Truthful eyes.

"I can tell you two things with confidence," I said. "I'll be back here. To visit at the very least. But I have to return to Boston and MGAP to sort out what being me means. Do I want to stay in Boston and counsel victims' families? Or do I want to live here and become Maine's homicide counselor? I don't know, Hank. But I do know I need to think it through."

He nodded, but I could see those weren't the words he wanted.

"I've learned a lot about my dad. Noah Beal cheated him. He vilified him with the town. He stole from him, and from me. I'm glad my dad's name is cleared, although no one will know the whole truth of it."

"I suspect they will."

"Sometimes people believe what they need to believe to be content. I've learned even more about myself these weeks. I need to sort out my past, what I really love and what is just a memory. I don't know the answer, Hank. But I very much hope you will be a part of it."

He wrapped an arm around my waist, pulled me close. "Lot pulling at you, Tal."

"I know. Drew's death. Joy's." I rubbed my forehead. "They hit me pretty hard."

"So what's new?"

I chuckled. "True."

"Counseling up here. Something to think about, Tally."

And it was.